GOBAITH

A STORÏAU ERAILL

KATE ROBERTS

GWASG GEE

Argraffiad cyntaf – 1972
Ail-argraffiad – 1982
Trydydd argraffiad – 1999

1999
Argraffwyd gan Wasg Gee, Dinbych

CYFLWYNEDIG

I'R

ATHRO J. E. CAERWYN WILLIAMS

CYDNABOD

STORÏAU wedi eu cymryd o wahanol gylchgronau a phapurau newydd sydd yn y gyfrol hon. Diolchaf yn gynnes iawn i berchenogion y papurau a'r cylchgronau a ganlyn am eu caniatâd i gyhoeddi'r straeon: *Y Faner, Y Cymro, Barn, Taliesin, Y Traethodydd,* ac i'r Brodyr Lewis, Gwasg Gomer, Llandysul.

Mae fy niolch yn gynnes iawn hefyd i Wasg Gee am eu gwaith glân a phrydlon.

Diolch arbennig hefyd i'r Athro Caerwyn Williams am ei garedigrwydd yn cywiro'r proflenni.

Oherwydd amgylchiadau dyrys methais ysgrifennu storïau newydd i'w rhoi yn y gyfrol.

KATE ROBERTS

C Y N N W Y S

CYFEILLGARWCH

'RWYF yn gwybod fy mod i'n ddiawl cas, ond mi wn fod y lleill yn gasach. Felly 'rwyf wedi teimlo erioed, ac wedi dwad i ddeall erbyn hyn pam mae pobl yn lladd, nid mewn rhyfel, nid oes teimlad ar gyfyl y lladd hwnnw, ond yn agosrwydd cymdeithas, ar bwyllgorau, mewn cyfarfodydd a phethau felly. Efallai mai dyna pam mae'r bobl ifanc yma'n codi twrw, efallai mai wedi magu casineb o'r tu mewn y maent, y casineb sydd i mi fel bywyd ym mol cyw 'deryn cyn iddo fagu plu, a minnau'n cael ei wared o ar fy mhen fy hun, heb fod yn un o dyrfa nac o nythiad. 'Dwn i ddim pa un ai casáu anghyfiawnder yr wyf, ai casáu awdur yr anghyfiawnder.

Ni allaf ddweud fod gennyf gyfaill yn y byd ond Jeff, a phrin y gellid galw hynny'n gyfeillgarwch, ffyddlondeb efallai, ffyddlondeb dyn fel finnau sydd heb gyfaill. Ond nid yw Jeff yn teimlo'n gas wrth neb, dyn anniddorol ydyw, heb lawer o synnwyr digrifwch, ac ni fedr dyn diflas, anniddorol binio'i lawes, hyd yn oed, wrth neb, heb sôn am ymgordeddu am bersonoliaeth neb arall. 'Rwyf wedi ei regi ganwaith oherwydd ei ddiniweidrwydd a'i ddiffyg ymateb. Yn y pen draw mae cael dyn cas yn erbyn dyn cas yn rhoi sbardun at fyw: dyna fy mwyd a'm diod i. Y nefoedd fawr, beth pe bawn i'n dweud hyn yn y seiat: mi ddôi cenfaint am fy mhen a'm bwrw allan. Pe baent yn onest fe fyddent yn dweud wrthyf fy mod yn dweud y gwir, ond rhyfedd fel y mae pobl yn medru eu twyllo eu hunain. Maent yn medru rhoi llen am eu teimladau a gweld yr anonest yn onest. Digon posibl mai dyna yr wyf i yn ei wneud. Mae geiriau yn swyno ac yn taflu hud dros feddyliau anonest, a gwneud inni eu credu. Efallai bod geiriau cas i mi yn fwy barddonol na rhai caredig, a bod geiriau caredig i bobl eraill yn feddal fwyn ac yn tywyllu eu meddwl rhag gweld beth sy'n iawn a pheth sy ddim. Fel y dywedodd yr hen athronydd, ni bydd uniawn barn lle bo cariad neu gas yn rheoli, a bod digasedd yn gweld bai lle ni bo, a chariad weithiau yn barnu'r bai yn rhinwedd.

Anwybodaeth pobl sy'n gwneud i mi eu casáu, anwybodaeth pobl sy'n agor eu cegau mewn cyfarfodydd yn lle bod yn ddistaw. Mae Jeff yn anwybodus, ond mae o'n gwybod pryd i dewi. Mi hoffais i o y tro cyntaf y gwelais o: mae ganddo wyneb mwyn, yn medru mynegi edmygedd, ac yn medru gwrando arnaf yn dweud fy nghwyn yn erbyn pobl. Mae o'n cydweld bob amser, ac yn ymddangos yn gynffongar, ond mae rhyw ddiniweidrwydd yn ei wyneb sy'n dileu argraff yna. Dyn wedi cael lwc heb ei cheisio ydyw. Ni fuaswn yn medru ei ddioddef am bum munud petawn i'n meddwl ei fod o'n cynffonna. Wrth gerdded efo fo hyd y stryd a phasio pobl y byddaf i'n gweld yn hollol beth mae o'n feddwl. Mi fydd yn edrych ar ei gydnabod y pryd hynny, cystal â dweud, 'Ylwch chi pwy ydi fy ffrind i. 'Rydach chi wedi troi'ch cefnau arna i pan fyddwn i'n siarad efo chi; fyddai gynnoch chi ddim amynedd i wrando arna'i.'

Gallaf ddallt y bobl yna: mae llais Jeff mor ddi-liw, a phob jôc yn disgyn i'r ddaear cyn ei geni. Ond efo mi, gwrando a nodio'i ben y bydd o. 'Rwyf yn cofio dweud wrtho ryw dro, petai Hwn-a-Hwn (ac enwi'r dyn casaf gennyf ar y Cyngor Sir) yn cael ei grogi yn gyhoeddus ar y sgwâr drannoeth, y buaswn i'n mynd yno i weld y crogi. A'r cwbl a ddywedodd o oedd, ' 'Fasech chi, Doctor?' Dim synnwyr digrifwch, a'm sylw innau yn disgyn i'r ddaear fel sgwigen wedi rhwygo. Y fi oedd yn teimlo'n ffŵl.

Mae Mari, fy ngwraig, yn wahanol. Mae hi wedi fy nioddef am dros ddeng mlynedd ar hugain heb dynnu'n groes imi, yn ddideimlad, yn ddiwrthwynebiad. Doethineb? 'Dwn i ddim. Petai hi wedi gwrthwynebu, buasai'r tŷ yma'n eirias fel gefail gof bob dydd. 'Rwyf innau'n casáu pobl ddoeth am eu bod nhw'n cael eu canmol am eu doethineb. Enw arall ar ddistawrwydd anwybodus ydyw doethineb yn aml. Y dyn doeth ydyw'r dyn sy'n gweld ei gamgymeriad cyn ei wneud. Ac eto, ni fuaswn i'n dweud fy mod i'n annoeth wrth ddweud fy meddwl am bobl. Pwy sy'n pennu ar y safon y cawn ni'n barnu wrtho, ac yn medru dweud fod bod yn ddistaw yn ddoethach na siarad? Mewn gair pwy ydyw'r barnwr?

Ond mae Mari yn gadael llonydd imi mewn dwy ffordd. Mae hi'n gadael llonydd imi yn y parlwr yma efo'm llyfrau: anaml y bydd hi'n twllu'r lle ond i'm galw at fy mwyd. Wedyn, mae hi'n gadael llonydd imi pan ddywedaf i rywbeth cas wrthi, neu pan fydd hi wedi fy nghlywed yn dweud pethau cas mewn cyfarfod cyhoeddus neu yn rhywle arall. Fy ngoddef i mae Mari, ond mae Jeff yn fy edmygu. 'Rwyf yn treio caru pobl yn ddall, ond yn methu am fy mod i'n dwad i'w nabod ac i weld pethau cas ynddynt. Mae'n rhaid nad wyf yn treiddio trwodd i nabod Mari na Jeff. Na'm plant chwaith o ran hynny. Dilyn cynllun eu mam y maent hwy, ac eithrio weithiau pan ddaw un ohonynt yma am sgwrs. Erbyn hyn maent i gyd wedi priodi, ac anaml y gallaf ddisgwyl i'r un ohonynt daro i mewn eto. A rŵan, 'rwyf yn difaru na buaswn i wedi bod yn gleniach efo nhw, neu'n hytrach wedi bod yn fwy o ddysgl i dderbyn eu cyfrinachau nhw.

Mae priodas Gwyneth heddiw wedi bod yn mynd ymlaen ers wythnosau, y siopa a'r cerdded ôl a blaen heibio i'r parlwr yma, y siaradach a'r chwerthin yn y parlwr cefn, a neb yn dwad yma i ddweud dim wrthyf i. Ond mi ddaeth Gwyneth neithiwr yn ei ffrog i'w dangos i mi, ac mi gofiais innau y byddai hi'n dwad i ddangos pob ffrog newydd imi pan oedd hi'n hogan bach. 'Roedd hi'n hynod o hardd, ac fe ddaeth lwmp i'm gwddf. Ond diolch byth, ni raid imi dalu am briodas yr un ohonynt eto. Wrth reswm, yr oedd yn rhaid imi siarad heddiw, ac yr oeddwn i wedi paratoi rhyw bwt o araith ymlaen llaw: wedi meddwl gwneud hwyl am ben y syniad o briodas fel priodas yr oeddwn i, a dweud y byddai'n well i bawb fyw tali efo'i gilydd, yn lle'r holl stŵr, ac y byddai pobl yn hapusach wrth wybod y medrent ymadael â'i gilydd bryd y mynnent. Mi gafodd y llwnc destunwyr gymeradwyaeth frwd, ond pan alwyd ar dad y briodferch, 'y dyn a roddai gymaint o enwogrwydd ar yr ardal,' mi gefais gymaint o glepian dwylo â sŵn iâr yn crafu mewn llwch.

Yna, mi ddigwyddodd rhywbeth rhyfedd. 'Roeddwn i wedi teimlo'n gas ers meitin, ac yn y dymer feddwl i ddweud pethau cas am briodas wrth weld y gŵr ifanc wedi meddiannu fy merch i'n barod. 'Roeddwn i wedi teimlo'n hapus wrth gerdded i lawr y llwybr rhwng y seti a Gwyneth ar fy mraich. Teimlo cynhesrwydd ei chorff hydwyth, helygaidd wrth fy ochr. Ond fe aeth hwnna wrth y bwrdd bwyd, a gweld y gŵr ifanc wedi ei meddiannu. Beth bynnag, cyn imi ddweud yr un gair o'r hyn y bwriadaswn ei ddweud, dyma rywbeth yn dwad imi, a 'fedrwn i gofio dim o'r hyn oeddwn i wedi'i baratoi. Dyma fi'n dechrau sôn am Gwyneth pan oedd hi'n hogan bach, fel y byddai hi'n prepian, mor dlws oedd hi, mor chwith fyddai gennyf ei cholli. Siarad hollol lipa, a sŵn dagrau yn fy llais erbyn hyn; mi dewais gan ddymuno'n dda i'r ddeuddyn a hynny yng nghanol banllef o gymeradwyaeth. Yr oedd llygaid Gwyneth a'i mam yn disgleirio. Ni fedraf egluro'r peth o gwbl. Mae'n anodd dweud beth sy'n dwad â pheth i bwy, a phwy i beth. Mae fel neges oddi uchod at y saint ers talwm. 'Roedd

Jeff yn crychu'i dalcen fel petai o'n methu dallt. Mi redais adre cyn gynted ag y medrwn i'r parlwr yma. Mae'r lleill heb ddwad eto. Y munud yma mi fuaswn yn licio gweld Jeff yn galw i edrych beth a feddyliodd o o'r peth. Mi fuasai clywed gair gan y dylaf ar wyneb y ddaear yn rhoi cysur imi, i *mi* ni faliodd erioed beth a ddywedai neb amdanaf. Mae'n amlwg bod siarad yn glên yn rhoi mwy o boen i mi na siarad yn gas. Heddiw, 'rwyf wedi bod yn rhagrithio. Toc mi ddaw pawb adre, ac mi allaf i ddychmygu Mari a'r plant eraill yn dweud, 'Tada, mi ddaru i chi siarad yn ardderchog.' O Dduw, ni fedraf ddal peth felly. Mi a'i allan am dro.

*   *   *   *

'Fedra i ddim credu fy nghlustiau. 'Does dim ond teirawr er pan oedd y Doctor a minnau allan am dro. Ymhen hanner awr wedi imi ddwad i'r tŷ dyma'r teleffôn yn canu a llais rhywun yn dweud bod y Doctor wedi cael strôc cyn gynted ag y daethai i'r tŷ. 'Roedd y meddyg wedi bod yno ac wedi dweud mai dyna ydoedd, ond nad oedd yn un drom iawn. Mi redais yno, ond wrth reswm, ni chefais ei weld. Yr oedd pawb oedd i lawr y grisiau yn siarad ar draws ei gilydd, a'r peth a glywn i amlaf drwy'r hwndrwd i gyd oedd, 'Ac 'roedd o wedi siarad mor dda y p'nawn yma.' Un oedd yn siarad yn wahanol, sef y brawd; 'roedd o mewn helynt yn treio cael gafael rywsut ar y pâr ifanc oedd ar eu ffordd i Lundain. Mae pethau rhyfedd yn digwydd.

Ar ôl imi fynd adre' o'r briodas, mi es draw i gyfeiriad tŷ'r Doctor. 'Roedd arna' i eisiau dweud wrtho mor dda oedd o wedi siarad yn y briodas, er efallai y buasai o yn cymryd bwyell at fy mhen. Nid dyna'i ddull o o siarad, ond yr oeddwn am fentro dweud wrtho fo, petasai o yn fy lladd i. 'Wyddwn i

15

ddim sut y buasai yn fy nerbyn, ac yn fy nghyfyng gyngor, penderfynais droi'n ôl adre'. Ond pwy ddaeth allan o'r tŷ ond y Doctor: dyma fo'n brysio i'm dal ac yn dweud, 'Mi awn ni allan am dro i'r wlad, 'rydw i wedi mygu yn y rhialtwch yna heddiw.' Diwrnod tawel mwyn oddi allan, a'r Doctor yn ymddangos i mi yr un mor fwyn. Mwg yn mynd i fyny'n syth o'r simneiau ac o'r coelcerthi chwyn yn y gerddi, a'r tywydd yn glaer. Dyma'r Doctor yn dweud, 'Mae p'nawn fel heddiw yn gwneud imi feddwl am gân Thomas Hardy, 'Yn amser dryllio'r Cenhedloedd,' a dyma fo'n dechrau'i hadrodd, â'r fath fwynder yn i lais, o gyfieithiad Cynan—

> 'Dim ond mwg ysgafn heb fflam
> O domen y chwyn;
>
> . . . . . .
>
> Acw dan sibrwd i'w dlos
> Daw llanc efo'i ferch . . .'

Mor wahanol i'r fel y byddai'n taranu yn erbyn cythreuliaid y capel. Adroddodd ddarnau o waith T. Gwynn Jones hefyd — Ynys Afallon. 'Roeddwn i wedi fy syfrdanu. A dyma fo'n mynd i sôn am lenyddiaeth, a dweud mor dda yr oedd y Beibl wedi'i gyfieithu, a dyfynnu o'r hen feirdd, pethau na wyddwn i ddim amdanyn' nhw. Minnau'n gwrando wedi fy nghyfareddu, ac wedi colli pob synnwyr o amser ac. o'r milltiroedd yr oeddym wedi'u troedio.

Yn sydyn, dyma fo'n troi'n ôl, a dweud, 'Waeth imi wynebu'r teulu yn fuan mwy nag yn hwyr, eu hwynebu nhw fydd raid. 'Rydw i'n gwybod y byddan nhw yn fy llyfu i am siarad fel y gwnes i y p'nawn yma.' 'Roeddwn i wedi penderfynu nad oeddwn i ddim am sôn am y briodas. Ond dyma'r Doctor yn troi ata' i ac yn gofyn, 'Beth oeddech chi'n feddwl o'r hyn ddwedais i?' 'Meddwl ych bod chi'n . . . (bu agos imi ddweud 'doeth') dda iawn.' 'Oeddech chi?' 'Wel oeddwn, mae'n rhaid inni weithiau fynd efo'r lli yn enwedig mewn priodas.' 'Rhaid, reit siŵr, ond i rywun beidio â dechrau rhyw hen arferiad gwirion. Trowch i mewn yr wythnos nesa' wedi i'r hwrli-bwrli yma fynd heibio.'

Ac wrth droi at ei lidiart meddai o, 'Nos dawch, Jeff' — y tro cynta 'rioed iddo fy ngalw wrth fy enw cynta'.

A rŵan dyma fo'n gorwedd yn ei wely ac yn methu siarad, a minnau'n gwneud dim ond meddwl — meddwl gan mwyaf am y deng mlynedd dwaetha' yma. 'Rydw i'n cofio'n iawn y tro cyntaf y siaradodd o efo mi — y stryd yn wag ryw noson y fo a minnau'n digwydd cyfarfod â'n gilydd. Dyma fo'n stopio i siarad efo mi, a minnau'n ddim ond rhyw fymryn o ddyn hel siwrin heb gamu fawr ymlaen. Cofio'r ias o bleser wrth iddo siarad; 'fedrwn i ddweud fawr ddim. Cofio'r wefr pan ddwedodd o, 'Cofiwch alw i 'ngweld i.' 'Roeddwn i'n rhy swil i alw, ond ryw noson mi es reit i wyneb y Doctor wrth ei dŷ, a dyma fo'n fy ngwadd i mewn. 'Fedrwn i ddweud dim call; yr oeddwn yn baglu ar draws fy ngeiriau, ond medrwn wrando mewn afiaith ar y Doctor yn bwrw drwyddi ac yn lladd ar y bobl. Medraf ddweud hyn, beth bynnag, fy mod yn cytuno â'i refru ar y bobl oedd o yn eu rhefru. 'Roedd *o* wedi dallt eu hamcanion nhw, 'doeddwn i ddim, ac felly y gwelais i bethau ar hyd yr amser, gweld ei ddealltwriaeth o sefyllfaoedd ac amcanion pobl. 'Roedd o'n agor drysau na wyddwn i ddim amdanyn 'nhw yng nghymeriadau pobl, a minnau'n dyfod i weld mor glir â haul trwy dwll.

'Fedra i ddim diodde eistedd yn y gegin yma. 'Rydw i am fynd i lawr i'r White Horse.

Dyma fi'n ôl ac yn difaru f'enaid imi fynd. Ni ches ddim byd ond un weipen ar ôl y llall. Y peth cynta ges i oedd, 'Dyma fo wedi dwad atom ni heno. 'Does ganddo fo ddim

Doctor i rwbio ynddo fo. 'Rydym ni'n ddigon da iddo fo heno.'

Y gwaetha' oedd bod hynny'n wir, ond beth oedd hynny o'u busnes nhw? 'Doeddyn' nhw byth yn gwrando arna' i pan awn i yno o'r blaen, ond yr oeddwn i yn gwrando ar y Doctor. 'Doeddyn nhw byth yn dweud dim byd gwerth gwrando arno fo hyd yn oed pan fydden' nhw yn rhefru ar bobl. Rhefru ar bobl well na nhw'u hunain y bydden nhw.

Meddai un arall, 'Doedd o'n gwneud dim ond lladd ar bobl y Cyngor Sir am dwyllo efo'u costau.' 'Mi'r oedd hynny'n wir,' meddwn i. 'Cwestiwn,' meddai rhyw athro oedd yn disgwyl cael ei wneud yn brifathro.

'A 'roedd o'n lladd byth a beunydd ar bobl grintachlyd,' meddai rhyw gybydd o ffarmwr, 'a 'doedd o byth yn talu am rownd pan ddôi o yma.' 'Nac oedd,' meddwn i, 'doedd o ddim yn hael wrth bobl nad oedd o ddim yn eu licio.' 'Pam 'roedd o'n dwad yma ynte?' gofynnodd un arall. 'Roedd o'n cymryd diddordeb mewn pobol,' meddwn i.

Ac o bob dim, dyma giaridým, na wyddai mo'r gwahaniaeth rhwng seiat a chyfarfod bingo, yn dweud, 'Ac mi edliwiodd i ryw flaenor yn y seiat fod hwnnw yn caru efo gwraig dyn arall ar y slei.' 'Mi 'roedd hynny'n wir hefyd,' meddwn i.

Ac i goroni'r cwbl, dyma ryw fwystfil o ddyn oedd wedi bod o flaen ei well am guro'i wraig yn dweud, 'Hen ddiawl cas ydi o.'

Mi dewais a dwad adre heb ddim un llwnc, a synnu ataf i fy hun fy mod i wedi medru ateb y giwed yn ôl. Fe fu adeg pan na fedrwn wneud hynny. Yr oeddwn wedi dysgu rhywbeth wrth rwbio efo'r Doctor.

Rhoddais fy mhen ar y bwrdd a chrïo, wrth feddwl efallai na chlywaf mohono'n piwsio neb byth eto. Ond mae gobaith.

Nid ydyw geiriau cas y dynion yn y dafarn wedi mennu dim arnaf. Pleser i mi fydd cofio byth, p'run bynnag a fendia'r Doctor ai peidio, fod eu piwsio wedi cyplysu'r Doctor a minnau efo'n gilydd.

Y TRYSOR

Am y pedwerydd tro yn ei bywyd yr oedd Jane Rhisiart yn ceisio rhoi digwyddiadau'r bywyd hwnnw yn eu safle briodol. A hithau'n ddeuddeg a thrigain oed, yr oedd mwy ohono i'w osod yn ei le erbyn hyn, mwy o ddigwyddiadau a phersonau i'w symud a'u gwahanu a'u dosbarthu.

Y tro cyntaf y safodd i fyfyrio uwchben ei bywyd oedd pan oedd hi'n bymtheg-ar-hugain oed, y diwrnod ar ôl i Rolant, ei gŵr, ei gadael, digwyddiad a roes ysgytiad i ardal gyfan, ond nid iddi hi. Pan ddiflannodd Rolant efo'i gyflog un nos Wener tâl, nid oedd yn syndod mawr iddi. Dynes â llygaid i weled oedd hi eithr â gwefusau i gau yn dynn rhag i'w thafod siarad wrth bawb yn ddiwahaniaeth. Oherwydd ei natur ramantus, mae'n wir y cymerai amser i weled, ond pan welai, fe welai'n gliriach nag unrhyw realydd. Dyna pam y rhoes diflaniad ei gŵr fwy o sgytwad i'r ardal nag iddi hi. Dyna pam hefyd na wnaeth hi ddim i geisio dyfod o hyd iddo, na cheisio cael dim at ei chadw. Yr oedd yn well ganddi weithio ddengwaith caletach na chynt, hyd yn oed, na dioddef y creulondeb distaw, pryfoclyd a ddioddefasai gan Rolant ers blynyddoedd. Fe wyddai rhai o'i gyd-chwarelwyr am beth o'r creulondeb hwn; yr oedd yn amhosibl i'w bartneriaid, a thrwyddynt hwy, eu gwragedd, beidio â dyfod i wybod fod Rolant yn clecio'n afresymol o'i gyflog.

Yn yr argyfwng hwnnw, a oedd yn bell iawn erbyn hyn, cafodd hi gydymdeimlad ardal, ond nid oedd arni ddim o'i eisiau. Penderfynodd gadw ymlaen â'r tyddyn heb ofyn help plwy nac arall i fagu ei thri phlentyn. Ni bu hynny'n hawdd, nid oherwydd y frwydr yn erbyn tlodi bob amser—fe gaiff dyn dawelwch meddwl mewn tlodi yn aml—ond oherwydd Ann, y plentyn hynaf, a oedd yn ddigon hen yn ddeuddeg oed i sylweddoli ei cholled ar ôl diflaniad ei thad, am ei bod yn ffefryn ganddo, ac wedi ei defnyddio ganddo lawer gwaith yn erfyn yn erbyn ei wraig. Y bachgen, Wiliam, oedd ei ffefryn hi, a oedd yn ddeg oed ar y pryd, ac nid oedd Alis, chwech oed, yn ddigon hen i sylweddoli pethau.

Yr ail dro yr eisteddodd i synfyfyrio uwchben ei bywyd yr oedd ugain mlynedd yn hŷn, a'i phlant i gyd wedi priodi, a hithau'n gorfod sylweddoli fod pob un ohonynt wedi ei siomi hi drwy eu hunanoldeb. Ni wnaethai'r un ohonynt erioed osgo at roi unrhyw help ariannol iddi, yr hyn a allent yn hawdd. Ond nid hynny a roesai siom iddi, eithr eu hagwedd anniolchgar o gymryd a derbyn pob dim fel pe bai arni hi arian iddynt hwy ac nid fel arall. Ni ddangosodd yr un ohonynt, na Wiliam, hyd yn oed, yr un edrychiad o ddiolch nac o werthfawrogiad. Yn anffortunus, yr oedd y tri yn byw o fewn agosrwydd ymweld â hi bob dydd a manteisiasant ar hynny i'w phluo. Cymryd ei menyn a'i hwyau a thalu amdanynt weithiau, ac anghofio talu o bwrpas yn amlach. Hithau, oblegid hynny, wedi gorfod gofyn i'w chwsmeriaid chwilio am fenyn yn rhywle arall. Medrasai weddro'n well pan oeddynt yn fychain, na phan briodasant a chael cartref iddynt eu hunain. Ni chynigiai'r un ohonyn na'r yng-nghyfraith help llaw iddi ychwaith, ond pan fyddai arnynt hwy angen cymorth, ati hi y doent, ac am flynyddoedd bu hithau'n ddigon dall i'w roi.

Ond yr oedd ganddi gorff cryf ac iach, cymorth mawr i fagu annibyniaeth ysbryd.

Y trydydd tro y cymerodd ddarlun o'i bywyd oedd bum mlynedd yn ddiweddarach, newydd iddi symud o'r tyddyn i fwthyn bychan yn y pentref, ymhen ychydig fisoedd wedi iddi fynd yn ffrindiau â Martha Huws; a hithau'n drigain oed y pryd hynny. Dadrithiasid hi'n llwyr ynghylch ei phlant erbyn hynny; gwelodd nad oedd diben dal at y tyddyn er mwyn eu bwydo hwy a'u plant hwythau, a dioddef eu ffraeo a'u cenfigennu wrth ei gilydd. Gwelai y byddai'n llawn cystal arni ar chweugain yr wythnos mewn tŷ moel, ac yr oedd yn ddigon cryf i fynd allan i weithio os byddai raid. Mor llwyr y dadrithiasid hi, fel na chymerodd ei thwyllo gan Wiliam a geisiodd ei darbwyllo i fuddsoddi arian y gwartheg a'r stoc mewn rhywbeth y medrai ef ei gymeradwyo. Cadwodd ei chwnsel iddi hi ei hun, a rhoes yr arian yn y banc, wedi defnyddio digon ohonynt i wneud ei bwthyn yn glyd.

A dyma hi heddiw, yn ddeuddeg a thrigain, am y pedwerydd tro yn ceisio gosod digwyddiadau ei bywyd yn eu lle ac yn eu golau priodol, a hynny gyda chalon drom a hiraethus; nid mewn chwerwedd fel y troeon cynt. Gwnâi hynny mewn lle rhyfedd iawn, ar lan y môr, ddiwrnod trip yr Ysgol Sul. Bythefnos yn ôl buasai farw Martha Huws, ei ffrind ers deuddeng mlynedd; a'r tro hwn mor fawr ei galar fel na wyddai sut i ail-gydio yn ei bywyd ac ail-gychwyn. Yn wir, dyma alar dwfn cyntaf ei hoes hir. Aethai'n gyfeillgar â Martha Huws ychydig fisoedd cyn gadael y tyddyn, y dymuniad o fod yn nes i'w ffrind a wnaeth iddi benderfynu'n derfynol ymadael â'r tyddyn. Adwaenai hi er erioed, gwyddai iddi gael ei siomi yn ei chariad, stori ardal oedd honno, ac iddi fyned i Loegr i weini, a dychwelyd pan oedd hi tua phymtheg a deugain, i fyw i dŷ bychan ar ei henillion a'r pensiwn bychan a gawsai gan y teulu olaf y bu'n gwasanaethu. Ond nid oedd yn ddim ond cydnabod i Jane Rhisiart hyd onid aeth yr olaf i edrych am Martha Huws pan oedd yn wael. Ac o'r awr honno fe dyfodd y cyfeillgarwch. Canfu Jane Rhisiart y diwrnod hwnnw ddynes hollol wahanol i'r hyn y tybiasai ei bod; dynes a chanddi wyneb agored, deallus, llygaid gleision, hardd, pell oddi wrth ei gilydd a gwallt gwyn trwchus. Ni sylwasai ar hynny pan welsai hi ar gip yn y bws neu yn y siop. Medrai sgwrsio â hi'n rhwydd, gwaith nid hawdd i Jane Rhisiart, a phan ddywedodd y wraig glaf, 'Dowch yma i edrach amdana'i eto,' gyda'r fath daeriineb cynnes, penderfynodd fynd. Sgwrsio'n rhwyddach yr eiltro na'r cyntaf. Erbyn i Jane Rhisiart fudo o'r tyddyn yr oedd sylfeini'r cyfeillgarwch i lawr a'r ddwy'n myned i mewn ac allan i dŷ y naill a'r llall. Oherwydd ei siomi gymaint o weithiau yn y rhai y rhoesai ei holl serch iddynt, ni ruthrodd Jane i arllwys ei chalon i'w ffrind, er mai un felly oedd hi'n naturiol. Ond gwyddai erbyn hyn beth oedd y dioddef a gan-lynai hynny, pan ganfyddai na roddai'r derbynnydd ddim o'r serch yn ôl. Felly y bu am hir amser yn ymbalfalu ei ffordd yn dendar i galon Martha Huws, fel petai hi'n cerdded mewn twnel, ond taflodd personoliaeth Martha ddigon o oleuni o'r pen arall yn y man iddi fedru cerdded yn hy. Nid oedd y cyfeillgarwch heb ei anawsterau ar y cychwyn, ond rhai o'r tu allan oeddynt. Âi'r ddwy i dŷ'r naill a'r llall yn aml, ac ymhen y flwyddyn, yn anfwriadol ac yn ddifeddwl, fe'u caent eu hunain yn gweld ei gilydd ryw ben i bob diwrnod. O gyfeiriad plant Jane Rhisiart y deuai'r anawsterau. Yr oeddynt hwy a'u plant i mewn ac allan beunydd yn ei thŷ. Ni allai eu rhwystro. A phan ddigwyddai Martha fod yno, dalient i aros ac i siarad er gwaethaf crïo'r plant ac er gwaethaf tawedogrwydd y ddwy wraig. Yn wir, yr oedd Ann ac Alis a gwraig Wiliam fel petaent yn anelu at ddyfod ar y pnawniau pan ymwelai Martha â Jane. Ond byddai'n rhaid iddynt fynd adref i wneud swper chwarel i'w gwŷr. Os gyda'r nos y deuai Martha, byddai Wiliam neu wŷr Ann ac Alis yn siŵr o ddyfod yno. Deuid tros yr anhawster hwnnw drwy i Jane fyned yn amlach i dŷ Martha. Ni ddeuent yno, ond unwaith fe lwyddodd Wiliam ar gynllun i fynd i nôl ei fam yno, ar esgus fod arno eisiau ei gweld ar fater pwysig. Ni lwyddodd i'w chael allan oddi yno yr eiltro. Wedyn aeth Wiliam mor bell â cheisio diddyfnu ei fam oddi wrth Martha drwy awgrymu pethau gwael am yr olaf, megis nad oedd wybod beth fuasai ei bywyd pan oedd yn Lloegr. Wedi'r cwbl, pam y gadawsai ei meistr arian iddi yn ei ewyllys a phensiwn. Medrodd Jane wneud iddo edrych yn bur wirion pan ddywedodd mai dynes ac nid dyn oedd ei chyflogydd. Ond, petasai fel arall, ni wnaethai ddim gwahaniaeth iddi erbyn hyn. Yr oedd yn rhy hoff o Martha i adael i unrhyw ddigwyddiad yn y gorffennol fennu arni. Y cwbl y medrai'r merched ei edliw iddi oedd 'nad oedd waeth iddynt hwy heb â dyfod i edrych amdani rŵan, gan fod y Martha Huws yna yno bob tro.'

'Dydi hi ddim yma bob dydd na thrwy'r dydd,' oedd ateb eu mam. Caent ddrws clo yn aml pan âi'r ddwy ffrind am dro neu pan âi Jane i ymweld â Martha, a thynnai hynny hwynt oddi ar eu hechel. Aeth Wiliam cyn belled unwaith ag edliw i'w fam ei bod yn gwario'r arian a oedd ganddi wrth gefn i grwydro efo dynes na wyddai ddim beth oedd ei hanes. Atebodd hithau fel bwled, y byddai'n ddigon buan iddo edliw hynny iddi pan ddeuai hi ar ei ofyn ef am rywbeth at ei chadw, a'i bod yn gobeithio medru eu gwario i gyd cyn marw rhag iddynt achosi mwy o wenwyn nag oedd yn bod yn barod rhwng y tri. Yr oedd diddordeb Wiliam yn y swm bychan yma o arian yn y banc yn fawr. Awgrymasai lawer gwaith i'w fam y buasai'n cychwyn rhyw fusnes bach neu fagu ieir petai'r arian ganddo i gychwyn, a'i fod wedi laru ar y chwarel. 'Ia wir,' fyddai ei hateb hithau, 'biti na baset ti wedi medru hel pan oedd arian i'w gael hyd lawr.' Ei hasgwrn cefn i'r atebion hyn oedd ei chyfeillgarwch â Martha. Ac wrth eistedd i lawr a dadelfennu'r cyfeillgarwch hwnnw o bryd i'w gilydd gwawriai arni mai ei sylfaen ydoedd siarad a dweud. Ni chawsai hi neb erioed o'r blaen a fedrai ymateb yn ddeallus i'r hyn a ddywedai wrthynt. Dywedai rywbeth wrth gymdoges. Ni chymerai honno unrhyw ddiddordeb neu fe ddywedai rywbeth dwl, diddim. Ond o'r cychwyn gyda Martha câi ateb yn ôl a ddangosai ddeall a diddordeb. A dyna ddechrau sgwrs, a dechrau deall ei gilydd, a dechrau cyfeillgarwch. Er hynny, aeth cryn dair blynedd heibio cyn i Jane fedru torri'r garw a medru siarad am Rolant. Nid ef oedd y peth uchaf ar ei meddwl ar y pryd. Aethai ei ddiflaniad yn beth oer ac amherthnasol, ac ni fedrai sôn amdano gydag unrhyw deimlad yn y byd, na thristwch, na chwerwedd na hoffter. Yn wir, ymddangosai peth o'r hanes yn ddigrif erbyn hyn, megis ei bod hi'n gwybod yr hyn na wyddai'r chwarelwyr, sef bod Rolant wedi defnyddio'i gelc i chwyddo arian ei gasgliad mis yn y capel, a'i wneud ei hun yn destun hwyl i lawer am fod ei gyfraniad bron cyn uched ag eiddo'r siopwyr a'r stiward-iaid. Medrodd Martha sôn am ei charwriaeth hithau, ond nid gyda'r un manylrwydd, oblegid yr oedd elfen o dristwch yn yr hyn na chyrhaeddodd ei gyflawniad. Cael gweledigaeth sydyn, rhywbeth tebyg i broffwydoliaeth, na fedrai fyw gyda'i chariad a wnaeth Martha, gweld yn araf ac yn drwyadl a wnaeth Jane. Ond yr hyn a hoffai Jane ym Martha ydoedd ei bod yn dweud nad oedd arni eisiau sôn amdano. A'r hyn a hoffai Martha yn Jane oedd ei bod yn deall hynny.

Aent am dro i'r mynydd yn aml, yr hyn a osododd stamp odrwydd arnynt i'w cymdogion. Nid oedd y mynydd yn ddim iddynt hwy ond rhywbeth a groesai eu gwŷr i'r chwarel a rhywbeth a oedd yn arwydd glaw pan ddôi niwl i lapio'i gorun. Ond ni flinai Jane a Martha ei ddringo, a'r peth mawr oedd cael stelc yn y grug, a sgwrs, 'paned o de o fflasg a theisen

o bapur. Y sgwrs oedd y peth mwyaf. Pan aent am dro i Lan-
dudno neu Fae Colwyn, cerdded strydoedd a llygadrythu yn
ffenestri'r siopau, deuai uchafbwynt y diwrnod pan aent i dŷ
bwyta a chael pryd iawn o fwyd cyn cychwyn adref, a siarad.
Ni fedrasai'r un o'r ddwy wneud hyn â neb arall o'r blaen.
Synient erbyn hyn mai dyma'r unig ffordd y gellid goddef bywyd
bellach, siarad am eu profiadau, nid profiadau'r gorffennol, nid
oedd bywyd yn y rheini, ond eu barn a'u teimlad tuag at
ddigwyddiadau'r dydd, yn eu pentref ac yn eu gwlad, ac ar yr
hyn a ddarllenent. Nid cystwyo ieuenctid heddiw â phastwn
ymddygiad da eu hieuenctid hwy a wnaent, ond llawenhau
iddynt hwy gael byw mewn oes brafiach. I ieuenctid yr ardal
yr oeddynt yn destun chwerthin efo'u dulliau hen ffasiwn o
fynd am dro, o wisgo mor blaen, o fyw mor urddasol, ond fe
synasai'r bobl ieuainc hyn gryn dipyn pe gwybuasent fod y
ddwy yn partïo'r bywyd modern mewn un peth. Pan aent i
ffwrdd am y diwrnod, byddai gan y ddwy ychydig bowdr yn
eu bagiau i dynnu'r sglein oddi ar eu trwynau ar ôl yfed te
rhy dda.

Ond yr oedd hynyna i gyd drosodd erbyn hyn, a Jane ar
ei phen ei hun yn y trip Ysgol Sul. Bythefnos cyn hynny, yn
hollol sydyn gadawsai Martha'r byd a fuasai mor llawn iddi
am ddeuddeng mlynedd. Yr oedd Jane efo hi y noson gynt, a
thystiai ei bod yn edrych yn llwyd a blinedig a chynigiodd
aros yno efo hi. Ond nis mynnai ei ffrind. Bore trannoeth fe'i
cafwyd yn farw yn ei gwely. Dymchwelodd y byd i Jane am
ddyddiau. Heddiw, ar lan y môr, medrai edrych yn dawelach
ar ddigwyddiadau'r pythefnos diwethaf, er ei bod hi'n cofio o
hyd fod ei ffrind gyda hi ar y trip y llynedd. Gweai ei hatgofion
yn gymysg â lliwiau dillad y plant a chwaraeai ar y traeth ac
â'r miliynau perlau a ddawnsiai ar y môr ac a ddisgleiriai ar y

tywod. Fe gawsai drysor yng nghyfeillgarwch Martha, trysor dilychwin, yr unig beth dilychwin yn ei bywyd, ac ni fedrai neb ei ddwyn oddi arni. Fe dorrwyd y llinyn cyn iddo gyrraedd i'r pen. Ond pwy oedd i ddweud ym mha le y gallasai'r pen fod? Efallai (ond ni fedrai feddwl am y peth), y gallasai rhyw-beth ddigwydd a allai wneud y trysor hwn yn llai dilychwin.

Daeth y gweinidog ati ac eistedd ar y cerrig. Siaradodd ar draws ac ar hyd, ac yn y diwedd dywedodd yn reit ddihitio, fel petai newydd feddwl am hynny, 'Mi fydd yn reit chwith i chwi ar ôl Martha Huws, yn bydd?' Ni fedrai ef na neb arall ddeall mai dyma alar dyfnaf ei bywyd. Yr oedd ar fin dweud wrtho, dweud maint ei hiraeth a maint ei gorhoffedd yn y ffrind da a gawsai am ddeuddeng mlynedd. Yr oedd arni eisiau bwrw hynny wrth rywun, er mwyn cael dweud. Ond cofiodd am y sbonc a roesai ei chalon yn y Seiat y noson gynt pan ddywedasai rhyw blentyn yr adnod 'A'i fam Ef a gadwodd yr holl eiriau hyn yn ei chalon,' adnod na roesai funud o sylw iddi erioed. Na, ni fedrai fynegi ei hangerdd wrth y gweinidog am yr hyn a gollasai. Wrth Martha'n unig y gallasai hi ddweud am y golled a gawsai drwy ymadawiad ei ffrind.

Y MUL

'I ble mae mulod yn mynd yn y gaea', nhad?'

Gollyngodd y Parch. Lias Elias y *Goleuad* i lawr yn sydyn ar ganol darllen hanes y Gymdeithasfa.

'Wyddwn i ddim eu bod nhw'n mynd i nunlle yn y gaea'.'

'Wel ydyn', 'dydyn nhw ddim ar lan y môr yn y gaea'. I ble maen' nhw'n mynd?'

'I'r capel ac i'r Senedd am wn i.'

A chwarddodd y tad yn uchel. Yr oedd Jonathan wrth ei fodd. Dyna'r tro cyntaf iddo weld ei dad yn chwerthin yn uchel fel hyn ers tro byd. Yr oedd wedi bod â'i ben yn ei blu ers talwm. Yr oedd hi'n nos Wener heno, ac nid oedd ganddo gyhoeddiad at y Sul nesaf. Aeth Jonathan ymlaen.

'Beth mae mulod yn ei wneud yn y Senedd a'r capel?'

'Siarad.'

'Hew, fedar mul ddim siarad.'

'Mi fedar nadu.'

''Doedd fy mul bach i ddim yn nadu ar lan y môr yn yr ha'.'

'Na, mi'r oedd o'n rhy gall ac yn dallt pethau'n well.'

'Oedd, mi'r oedd o'n gwybod yn iawn ym mhle i stopio.'

'Ym mhle?'

'Wrth y stondin hufen rhew, a wnâi o ddim symud nes câi o gorned.'

'A chditha yn rhoi un iddo fo.'

'Ia, mi fyddwn i wrth fy modd yn ei weld o yn codi'i weflau wrth ei fyta fo.'

28

'A chditha yn rhoi un arall iddo fo.'

'Naci, mi'r oedd o'n barod i ail-gychwyn wedyn, a mi fyddai'n aros amdana'i bob dydd, yn fy nabod i'n iawn.'

'Ella, ond mae o'n nadu ar rywun weithiau.'

'O, dydach chi ddim yn nabod yr un mul â fi. Mi faswn i'n licio cael mul bach go iawn at y Nadolig.'

'Ym mhle basan ni yn ei gadw fo?'

'Yn y cwt rhawiau yng ngwaelod yr ardd.'

'Ym mhle'r rhown ni'r rhawiau?'

'Yn y cwt glo.'

'Fasai dy fam ddim yn licio hynny.'

'Sbïwch, nhad, fasai raid i chi ddim torri'r lawnt, mi fasai'r mul yn i phori hi i chi.'

Mi *fasai* hynny'n help. Ond mi fasai yn gwehyru ac yn nadu yn y nos.'

'Mi fedren i ddysgu o i beidio.'

'Fedri di byth gau ceg mul.'

Ar hynny canodd cloch drws y ffrynt, a daeth blaenor o Gapel Bryn Llaith i mewn. Cododd calon Lias Elias. Cyhoeddiad? Ie. Yr oedd y blaenor yn dipyn o gyfaill iddo, cyfeillgarwch blaenor a gweinidog o eglwysi cyfagos. Dechreuodd y blaenor dipyn yn grynedig.

'Mi ddweda i wrthoch chi be sy gen i. 'Rydan ni heb bregethwr at y Sul, ac mi glywais ych bod chi heb gyhoeddiad a meddwl ella y buasech chi'n dwad acw i lenwi'r bwlch.'

Ni frysiodd Lias i ateb.

'Ydw, mi'r ydw i heb gyhoeddiad, ond' — a stopiodd.

'O cymerwch o, nhad,' meddai Jonathan wrtho'i hun, 'i mi gael siawns i gael mul.'

'Ond,' aeth y tad ymlaen, ' 'rydw i wedi mynd yn hynod ddigalon.'

'*Mae* hi'n ddigalon,' ebe'r blaenor, 'mae cynulleidfaoedd

29

wedi mynd yn fychain ond mi gewch gynulliad go dda ym Mryn Llaith yn enwedig yn y nos.'

'O, 'dydi hynny ddim yn fy mhoeni fi. Fasai ddim ods gen i tasai yno ddim ond chwech, petawn i'n cael dweud beth fynnwn i, a'u bod yn fy nghredu fi.'

'Meddwl yr ydach chi am yr hyn fu yn Nhrosafon?'

'Sut y clywsoch chi?'

'O, mi'r oedd y stori yn dew ac yn denau ar y pryd. 'Roedd sôn bod un o'r blaenoriaid wedi bygwth ych hitio chi.'

Chwarddodd Elias. 'Na, 'doedd hi ddim cyn waethed â hynny. Ond 'cha'i byth fynd yno eto.'

'Sôn am Hitleriaid. Maen' nhw yma ym mhobman.'

'Ydyn. Ond nid ar ddyn ei hun maen' nhw'n effeithio. Maen' nhw'n achosi poen i wraig a phlant.'

'O penderfynwch,' meddai Jonathan wrtho'i hun eto. Wel, mi ddo'i.'

Rhedodd Jonathan i'r gegin i ddweud wrth ei fam. Wedi i'r blaenor fynd, bu yno gryn dipyn o siarad yn y gell — y wraig yn ceisio darbwyllo'i gŵr i beidio â chodi gwrychyn y gynulleidfa drwy sôn am Gymdeithas yr Iaith, a'r gŵr yn dal allan fod yn rhaid iddo bregethu'r gwir. Hithau yn ei atgoffa fod dweud y gwir yn digio llawer.

' 'Dydi neb yn ennill dim wrth gadw'r ddysgl yn wastad,' meddai yntau, 'ond mae dyn yn ennill lot wrth ddweud y gwir.'

'Ella, ac yn colli lot. Colli lot o lonyddwch meddwl.'

'Ydi. Ond mae eisio goleuo pobol. Goleuni ydi'r peth mwya sydd arnyn nhw'i eisio.'

Cydwelai'r wraig.

'Mae o'n beth anodd iawn i'w ddysgu.'

Yr hyn oedd wedi digwydd yng Nghapel Trosafon ychydig

fisoedd yn ôl oedd fod Elias wedi canmol dewrder Cymdeithas yr Iaith Gymraeg wrth sôn am ddifaterwch pobl yn gyffredinol. Gwelodd wrth wynebau rhai o'i gynulleidfa ei fod wedi eu cythruddo; fe arhosodd rhai ar ôl a dyfod i'r sêt fawr ar ddiwedd y bregeth, a'i gyhuddo o bregethu gwleidyddiaeth.

'Naddo,' meddai yntau.

'Beth ydi Cymdeithas yr Iaith ond politics?' meddai un blaenor.

'Ddim o gwbl. Diwylliant ydi iaith.'

'Peth yn perthyn i blaid ydi o,' meddai un arall.

'Naci, peth yn perthyn i fyd addysg ydi o. Yn yr ysgolion mae dysgu iaith, nid yn y Senedd. Peth arall, petai o'n perthyn i'ch plaid chi fasech chi'n dweud dim. 'Rydach chi'n hollol anwybodus.'

Cofiodd y gweinidog am ei ffrind Dafis, ysgolhaig mawr, yn dweud rywdro mai anwybodaeth oedd pechod mwyaf y byd heddiw. A dyma enghraifft deg ohono.

Beth bynnag, ni chafodd gyhoeddiad ganddynt at y flwyddyn wedyn. Teimlai'n anhapus hollol y noson honno. Bob nos Sul wedi pregethu deirgwaith a theimlo'n flinedig byddai'n dyfod adref yn hapus gan edrych ymlaen at ei swper a chael ymlacio wrth y tân a sgwrsio efo Hannah a Jonathan, heb feddwl fawr am ddim. Holai ef ei hun y noson honno, a oedd yn werth dweud y gwir ac aberthu noson o gysur.

Yr oedd yn hynod falch ei fod wedi cael cyhoeddiad yng Nghapel Bryn Llaith, er mai cyhoeddiad i lenwi bwlch ydoedd. Eto ni allai weld Hannah a Jonathan yn byw heb ryw bethau bach a rôi lawenydd iddynt tua'r Nadolig. A oedd yn bosibl dweud y gwir i gyd yn y bywyd hwn a phob amser?

Yr oedd am bregethu'r un bregeth eto y tro hwn, ond ni wyddai eto a soniai am Gymdeithas yr Iaith. Câi weld beth fyddai naws y gynulleidfa. Yr oedd hi'n gynulleidfa dda, yn

31

ymddangos fel petai'n gwrando yn ddeallus. Pan ddaeth at y sôn am bobl ifainc, cyfarfu ei lygad â llygad y blaenor a ddaethai ato i ofyn iddo fynd, ac fe welodd rywbeth tebyg i *Peidiwch* ynddo. Ac yn hollol sydyn dyma fo'n dweud:

'Rhaid inni edmygu'r bobol ifainc yn y colegau sy'n protestio ac yn helpu'r hen bobol yn eu tai a chyda'u gwaith.'

Bu agos iddo stopio a'i longyfarch ei hun am gyfaddawdu. Gwelodd wên ar wyneb y blaenor.

Cyn mynd allan y noson honno daeth llawer ato i ddiolch am ei bregeth. Teimlai yntau ei fod wedi cael hwyl. Dywedodd un hen wraig:

'Diolch i chi am ganmol y bobol ifainc sy'n *sistio* ac yn helpu hen bobol.' (Gobeithiai fod rhai eraill wedi gwneud yr un camgymeriad efo'r *protestio.*)

Diolchodd y blaenoriaid yn gynnes iddo — y bregeth orau a gawsant ers talwm. Yr oedd yntau mor falch iddo fedru cyfaddawdu mor ddeheuig, er ei fod yn teimlo yn llwfr. Aeth adref yn llawen, mewn llonyddwch meddwl, chwedl Hannah. Mwynhaodd ei swper o gig oer a betys a phwdin reis. Yr oedd y tân hyd yn oed yn fwy siriol, a pheth braf oedd eistedd yn ei sliperi o'i flaen.

'Sut hwyl, nhad?'

'Reit dda.'

'Ddaru i chi eu digio nhw?'

'Naddo.'

'Ddaru i chi ddeud am Gymdeithas yr Iaith?'

'Do a naddo. Wnes i mo'u henwi nhw.'

Chwarddodd Jonathan a'i fam.

'Mi'r ydach chi'n un ciwt.'

'Mi fuom heno.'

Yr oedd Jonathan wrth ei fodd yn gweld ei dad yn chwerthin.

'Mam, mi faswn i'n licio cael mul byw at y Nadolig.'

'Be' wnei di â pheth felly?'

' 'Roeddwn i'n licio'r mul bach hwnnw ar lan y môr yn yr ha'. Mi fasa'n pori'r lawnt ac yn sbario gwaith i nhad.'

'Ac mi fasa'i bedolau o yn tyrchu'r lawnt. A pheth arall, mi fasa'n rhaid cael cae iddo fo bori. Rhaid iddo gael bwyd.'

'Ond mi gâi beth yn ei gwt.'

'Twt, rhaid iddo fo gael mwy na bwyd mewn cwt. Rhaid iddo fo gael rhyddid. Fedar o ddim byw yn y cwt yna ddydd a nos, yn gwehyru.'

'Ac yli di, Jon,' meddai'r tad, 'mi fasai yn rhoi lot o waith iti i fwydo fo a phethau felly. Mi fuasai'n well iti gael ci o lawer.'

'Ga'i un byw?'

'Cei. Mae yna gi bach eisio cartre efo'r plismyn rŵan.'

Siriolodd Jonathan drwyddo.

'Mi ddweda i beth wnawn ni efo'r mul. Mi gei di a fi wneud pasiant at yr ha', a'i alw fo'n 'Y mul trwy'r oesoedd.' Mi gawn ni ddigon o ddeunydd o'r Beibl. Yr asyn a gariodd Joseff i'r Aifft, heb anghofio'r asyn a gariodd Iesu Grist i Gaersalem. A dwad yn nes adre, yr oedd y mul yn cario pynnau o flawd o'r siop i'r tyddynwyr drigain mlynedd yn ôl, a chan mlynedd a hanner yn ôl yn cario llechi o'r chwareli i'r porthladdoedd i'w rhoi ar y llongau i fynd â nhw dros y môr. 'Roedd dynion hefyd yn gweithio'n galed y pryd hynny, a fasen' nhw byth yn ymosod ar y pregethwr. 'Roedd ganddyn' nhw asgwrn cefn.'

'Yn lle rhown ni o, Y Pasiant?'

'Mi fyddan wrth eu bodd ei gael o yn y pentre yma. Mae eisio arian at rywbeth o hyd.'

'Gawn ni ddechrau yfory, nhad?'

'Aros nes bydd y Nadolig drosodd.'

'Ond mi ga' i'r ci bach 'fory, yn caf?'

'Cei. Meddylia beth fydd rhoi cartre da i gi bach digartre. Nadolig llawen iddo fo.'

Wrth fynd i gysgu meddyliodd y Parch. Lias Elias: Gwyn dy fyd di, blentyn diniwed, yn medru siarad am fulod mor gariadus.

GWACTER

Brysio golchi llestri cinio a John yn fy helpu. Edrych allan drwy'r ffenest, gweld awyr las glir a chael syniad. Meddwl yr hoffwn fynd allan i eistedd i'r ardd cyn newid. Mae arnaf eisiau rhoi gorffwys i'r meddwl, ac mae'r dyhead wedi fy meddiannu. Ar dân eisiau gweld John yn cychwyn i'r ysgol er mwyn imi gael mynd.

Mae fy meddyliau ormod ar du blaen fy nhalcen, ac mae arnaf eisiau eu gyrru'n ôl fel na byddaf yn meddwl am ddim. Eistedd yn llygad yr haul â'm pen yn ôl a mwynhau munud diddim. Ond nid am hir. Nia yn dwad allan efo'i gwaith gwnïo; mae hi'n paratoi i fynd i'r coleg am y tro cyntaf, ac yr wyf wedi diflasu ar y gêr gwnïo o gwmpas y gegin orau, yr 'oglau cotwm a'r defnyddiau newydd. Ni chaf lonydd.

'Am beth ydach chi'n meddwl, mam?'

'Trio peidio â meddwl yr ydw i.'

'Amhosib.'

'Am beth wyt ti'n meddwl?'

'Meddwl mor braf fydd hi yn y Coleg.'

Euthum yn ddistaw. Gwelodd hithau ei chamgymeriad.

'Wrth reswm, mi fydd arna'i hiraeth ar ych ôl chi i gyd.'

Ar hyn dyna sŵn traed ar y llwybr. Margiad fy ffrind oedd yno. Ta, ta am lonyddwch.

'Dyma ryfeddod' oedd ei geiriau cyntaf.

'Rhyfeddod beth?'

'Dy weld ti yn gorweddian yn yr ardd heb newid.'

'Eisio llonydd oedd arna'i.'

'A dyma finnau'n torri arno fo.'

'Mi gafodd Nia y blaen arnat ti.'

'Mae'n ddrwg genni, mam.'

'Dwn i ddim beth sydd arna i y dyddiau yma. Mae rhyw gryndod yn fy mrest, a theimlaf fy mod yn cael fy rhwystro ymhob dim, methu cael yr hyn sydd arnaf ei eisiau.

'Tyrd i fyny i'r dre,' meddai Margiad.

' 'Does genni fawr o flas.'

'Tyrd, ella y cawn ni fargen wrth y stondin lestri.'

' 'Does arna i ddim eisio bargen.'

'Beth sy'n bod arnat ti, a chdithau mor sgut am fargen.'

Beth pe taswn i'n deud wrthi fod rhyw deimladau rhyfedd yn dwad imi y dyddiau yma, byth ers mis yn ôl pan gefais fy mhenblwydd yn hanner cant. Ni fedraf ddweud wrth John hyd yn oed. Yn y llofft medrwn grïo. Gorweddais ar y gwely am eiliad a gwrthwynebu mynd i'r dre efo Margiad.

Ni welsom ddim bargeinion ar y stondin lestri, ond fe gefais lemonau yn rhad. Mynd i'r siop bysgod a phrynu pysgod i de. Difaru cyn gynted ag y gwneuthum, gweld gwaith ffrïo. Yn y siop, gwraig y tu ôl imi yn dweud, 'Wedi imi brynu pob dim, fydd genni'r un ddimai i brynu sigarets.' Nid yr un peth sy'n poeni pawb.

Erbyn mynd adre, Mai, ffrind Nia, wedi galw a mwy o lanast gwnïo yn y gegin orau. Rhwystr eto, a phoen. Bydd yn rhaid imi ofyn i hon aros i de, a gorfod rhoi llai o bysgod i bawb. Dweud wrth Nia am glirio'r lanast a'm helpu i hwylio te. Hi yn oedi ac yn dal i siarad a chwerthin efo'i ffrind. Finnau'n plygu'r gwaith gwnïo a mynd â fo i'r parlwr mewn tymer.

'Bedi'r brys?'

'Rhaid i'r te fod yn barod erbyn y daw dy dad i'r tŷ.'

Mai yn hwylio i gychwyn a Nia yn dweud wrthi am aros i de. Gallwn ei hitio am fod mor ddifeddwl. John yn dwad i'r gegin bach a rhoi ei fraich dros fy ysgwydd. Minnau'n rhoi winc arno.

'Nia sydd wedi gofyn, nid y fi.'

'Hen dro, llai o bysgod i bawb. Cofia di am dy siâr.'

Rhoes John y platiau gwydr yn y popty i gynhesu a dechrau torri brechdan. Mae o'n haeddu te da. Cawsom deisen 'falau gynta'r tymor ar ôl y pysgod. Pawb yn canmol. Mai yn mynd cynta y cafodd hi de.

' 'Doeddwn i ddim yn gwybod fod gynnoch chi bysgod ne faswn i ddim wedi gofyn i Mai aros,' ebe Nia.

'Dy fam gafodd y siâr leia fel arfer.'

Nia yn mynd allan. John a finnau yn eistedd wrth y tân ar ôl golchi llestri.

' 'Rwyt wedi cynhyrfu am rywbeth.' meddai John.

'Gweld Nia yn ddifeddwl.'

'Mae hi'n waeth na difeddwl. Mae hi'n hunanol.'

' 'Does dim yn iawn rywsut y dyddiau yma.'

'Hitia befo, mi gawn y tŷ i ni'n hunain ymhen sbel.'

MEDI 9:

Gair oddi wrth Gwyn y mab efo'r post heddiw, yn dweud ei fod yn priodi y Pasg. Eleni y dechreuodd o ar ei waith fel athro. Ni chafodd y newydd ddim effaith arnaf. John o'i go', yn gweld Gwyn yn priodi cyn dechrau ennill bron. Nia'n dweud mai mewn rhyw ddawns yn Llandudno y gwelodd o hi gynta, pan oedd o yn y Coleg. 'Mae hi'n dawnsio'n fendigedig,' meddai hi. John yn chwerthin dros bob man.

'Fedar hi ferwi ŵy?' gofynnodd.

Y fi yn penderfynu na phoena i ddim. Y fo dewisodd hi, nid fi, ac ni fydd yntau yn poeni dim os na fedr hi olchi'i grys o.

MEDI 15:

Y ddarpar wraig, Ethel, yn dwad yma i de. Modrwy ag un garreg am ei bys. Mi'r oedd gan Gwyn gelc felly. Yr oedd hi'n gwisgo trywsus lliw gwin a blows gwyn digon blêr. Sandalau am ei thraed a choesau noeth.

'Sut ydach chi bawb?' meddai hi pan gyrhaeddodd, fel petasai hi'n ein nabod er erioed.

'Mae'n ddrwg genni ddwyn Gwyn oddi arnoch chi. Ond ran hynny, mi fasa'n rhaid i rywun i ddwyn o, wedyn 'waeth y fi mwy na rhywun arall. Mae Gwyn yn hen foi iawn — dipyn yn swil, ond mi ddaw dros hynny ar ôl inni briodi.'

Gwyn yn cochi, a'r gweddill ohonom ni fel 'tasem ni'n methu gwybod beth i'w wneud. Yr oedd un peth yn dda: nid oedd raid i neb chwilota beth i'w ddweud nesa.

'Mae gynnoch chi fwyd da. Rhaid i minnau fynd ati hi i ddysgu rŵan; mae yna ddosbarthiadau nos reit dda yn lle'r ydw i yn byw. Ond 'dda genni ddim gwneud gwaith tŷ.'

'Y lolan,' meddwn i wrthyf fy hun. Ond mae hi'n onest os ydi hi'n dweud y gwir. Gwyn yn edrych yn annifyr. John yn ei ddyblau yn chwerthin.

MEDI 16:

Meddwl am ddoe, a dechrau poeni. 'Roedd o'n ddigri ddoe, ond yn boendod heddiw. Margiad yn galw. Dweud yr hanes wrthi.

'Paid â phoeni yn i cylch nhw. Gad iddyn' nhw ferwi'i potes i hunain.'

'Edrach ymlaen i'r dyfodol yr ydw i, a gweld Gwyn yn dwad yma i ofyn am help.'

'Gad iddo fo ddiodde tipyn. Mae gormod o bobol heddiw yn poeni ynghylch i plant, yn lle gadael iddyn' nhw ddiodde' i cosb am i ffolineb i hunain. 'Dwn i ddim beth ydi'r hen ofn yma i'w plant ddiodde. 'Doedd ar neb ofn i ni ddiodde ers talwm. Ella y try hi allan yn well nag wyt ti'n i feddwl.'

Teimlo dipyn gwell wedi i Margiad fod.

MEDI 17:

Penderfynu gyrru Gwyn ac Ethel allan o'm meddwl. John eisiau i mi fynd efo fo i Ffrainc dros yr hanner tymor. Dim eisiau mynd. Cofio am yr ias o bleser a roddai hyn i mi ychydig flynyddoedd yn ôl. Ei weld o'n beth mawr y pryd hynny. Peth bach dibwys erbyn hyn. Edrych ymlaen at fynd i'r dre rhag ofn y caf weld M.C. Ei gweld hi a mynd am goffi. Dweud yr hanes wrthi, hithau'n chwerthin ac yn dweud:

'Mae hi'n swnio'n hen beth joli braf. 'Waeth iti befo os nad ydi hi'n lân. 'Wnaeth tipyn o faw 'rioed ddrwg i neb. Mi ddaw Gwyn i arfer efo fo.'

'Mi elli fynd i'r eitha arall yr un fath â Mrs. Huws, Cadach Llawr, sydd yn sychu ôl troed pawb ddaw i'r tŷ.'

Gweld synnwyr yn y peth. Dechreuodd hithau ladd ar bobl. Byddaf wrth fy modd yn ei chlywed. Y dwytha yw X.Y.

'Yr hen sguthan,' meddai, 'wedi rhoi tri chan punt am fodrwy rŵan, a phobol yn llwgu hyd y byd.'

Byddaf wrth fy modd yn ei chlywed yn dweud 'hen sguthan,' a 'rydw i'n siŵr na ŵyr hi ddim beth mae sguthan yn i feddwl. Teimlo yn ddigalon wedi iddi fynd. Y gryndod yma yn dwad yn ôl i'm brest. Ofn i John fynnu cael mynd i Ffrainc.

MEDI 18:

Penderfynu mynd i weld nhad a mam yr wythnos nesa, heb

39

eu gweld ers tro. Mae'r penderfynu ei hun wedi rhoi gwefr imi. Synnu fod peth mor fychan yn rhoi pleser i mi, mwy o lawer na meddwl am fynd i Ffrainc.

MEDI 19:

Mynd i'r capel. Pregeth gysurlon am dreialon yr Apostol Paul. Gwyddai beth oedd derbyn gwialen ar ei gefn, plygu dan gawod o gerrig. Bu'n wael mewn twymyn ac annwyd. Cafodd ei erlid a'i garcharu. Ond oherwydd ei ymlyniad i Grist, ei ffydd, ei obaith a'i gariad, cafodd fuddugoliaeth yn ei fywyd, a throi pob profiad yn fendith.

Teimlaf yn well.

MEDI 20:

Diwrnod golchi. Wedi rhoi fy nghas ar y peiriant golchi, h.y., ar ei lanhau ar y diwedd. Mynd â'r dillad i'r olchfa gyffredin. Rhyw ddyn yn dangos imi sut i roi'r pres i mewn ag ati. Gwraig ifanc tua 20 oed a llwyth yno a phlentyn tua dyflwydd efo hi. Y fam yn smocio pan oedd y dillad yn mynd trwy'r olchfa. Yn falch fy mod i wedi mynd wrth feddwl na raid imi sychu'r peiriant. Wedi gorffen yn fuan. Gwneud teisen i Nia wedi dwad adre.

MEDI 21:

Nia yn mynd i'r Coleg. Cael pas efo un o'i ffrindiau yn ei char. Teimlo'n chwith wrth ei gweld yn cychwyn, ond y hi wrth ei bodd, yn addo sgwennu cynta y medr. John a minnau wrth y tân heno, y lle yn unig. John yn mynd allan i bwyllgor, minnnau yn cael un o'r pyliau yna a gaf o hyd, tyndra, ofn a chryndod yn fy mrest. Ofni'r daith fy hun i dŷ nhad a mam

40

rŵan. Eisiau mynd ar fy mhen fy hun, felly, gorfod mynd efo trên a bws. Ofn i'r trên fod yn hwyr ac imi golli'r bws ym M—.

MEDI 23:

Dim gair oddi wrth Nia.

MEDI 24:

Dim gair eto heddiw.

MEDI 25:

Dim gair heddiw chwaith.

MEDI 26:

Sul eto. Bedyddio babi bach yn y bore. Yr oedd yn gwenu'n hoffus ar y gweinidog. Minnau'n meddwl beth fyddai ei ddyfodol tybed. Pa dynged fydd iddo?

MEDI 27:

Llythyr o'r diwedd gan Nia. Pedair llinell yn dweud ei bod wedi cyrraedd a'i bod yn brysur. Addo llythyr hir y tro nesa.

MEDI 28:

Mynd i weld nhad a mam. Fy nghalon yn codi. Methu gweld y trên yn cyrraedd ddigon buan. Meddwl y bydd yn siŵr o ddal y bws. Gorwedd yn ôl yn gysurus yn fy sêt, a mwynhau peidio â meddwl am ddim. Cnoi fferins. Tair dynes yn dyfod i mewn. Un mewn tipyn o oed, yn dal ac yn osgeiddig, y ddwy arall yn dew ac yn ganol oed, yn siarad i hochr hi. Yn amlwg yn trin a thrafod rhyw wraig arall. Gwrando yn awchus.

41

Yn amlwg mai newydd ddyfod i fyw i'w pentref neu dref yr oedd y wraig a drafodid, ac yn athrylith ar roi blas enwau ar bobl. Teimlo yr hoffwn ei hadnabod. Dyma un o'r ddwy wraig yn dweud,

'Mae'n siŵr fod gynni hi ryw flas enw arna inna.'

'O na,' meddai'r llall, yr awdurdod ar yr un absennol, 'mi'r ydach chi yn Mrs. Jones *hyd yn hyn.*'

Y wraig dal yn y gongl a minnau'n chwerthin. Cefais fy nal gymaint yn rhwyd y stori, fel yr anghofiais am y bws. Cael a chael ei ddal wneuthum.

Croeso mawr pan gyrhaeddais y tŷ. Nhad a mam ar ben y drws, wedi clywed y bws. Cael fy lapio yn eu gwenau croesawus. Cinio wedi ei osod yn barod. 'Oglau lobscows da dros y tŷ. Nhad yn rhoi ei gadair i mi. Dechreuais grïo dros bob man wrth weld y fath groeso. Y ddau yn edrach ar i gilydd yn syn. Minnau'n difaru gwneud y fath ffŵl ohonof fy hun, a phoen cydwybod yn dwad i mi. Fy ngweld fy hun wedi eu hesgeuluso cyd a chennym ninnau gar. Ond yr unig esgusion oedd gennyf oedd fod y plant yn ei fenthyca drwy fis Awst a chymaint o drafnidiaeth ar y ffyrdd.

'Beth dal dy newydd di?' gofynnodd nhad.

Dyma finnau'n dweud hanes Gwyn.

'Plant yn priodi, bobol,' meddai mam. 'Oes rhywbeth yn i deng ewin hi?'

'Mae arna'i ofn nad oes dim, mae mwy yn i thraed hi.' Dyma mam yn edrych yn boenus fel y bydd hi pan glyw hi ryw newydd fel yna.

'Wyt ti yn poeni? Mae golwg wael arnat ti.'

'Na, 'dydw i ddim yn poeni ynghylch hynna. Ella y byddan nhw reit hapus. Ond mae rhywbeth yn bod arna i.' A dyma fi'n dweud fy hanes.

'Cer i weld y doctor,' ebe nhad.

Y munud hwnnw y daeth y syniad imi a daeth sbonc i mi wrth feddwl. Medrais fwynhau sgwrsio drwy'r p'nawn. Cael hanes yr ardal. Pwy oedd yn sâl. Pwy oedd wedi priodi. Pwy oedd yn caru. Ond y newydd rhyfedda' gefais i oedd bod cyfnither i mi dros ei hanner cant oed yn mynd i briodi efo dyn deg a thrigain, y ddau yn ddibriod. Rhai yn priodi rhy ifanc a'r lleill yn rhy hen.

Llithrodd y prynhawn heibio, a minnau'n fy mwynhau fy hun wrth hel straeon yn nhawelwch y gegin a gweld cymaint oedd fy ymweliad yn ei olygu iddynt. Dim eisiau brysio yma.

'Diolch iti am ddwad. Diolch iti am ddwad, a thŷd yn fuan eto.'

Minnau'n meddwl peth cyn lleied oedd wedi rhoi hapusrwydd iddynt, ac mor ddi-feind y bûm am fisoedd. Nid oeddwn ddim gwell na Nia. Hiraeth mawr yn y trên. Ond caf fynd i weld y meddyg yfory.

DWY FFRIND

Safwn â'm dau benelin ar fwrdd y ffenestr yng nghegin orau fy ffrind Nanw, yn edrych allan i'r wlad. Yr oedd yn ddiwrnod oer yng nghanol gaeaf ond yn ddiwrnod clir, heulog, golau. Yr oedd digon o wahaniaeth rhwng llinell copa'r bryniau a'r awyr uwch eu pennau, a digon o amrywiaeth lliw ar eu hwyn-ebau — golau ar y gwrymiau a chysgodion yn y tolciau. Oddi draw deuai sŵn caled, eglur, hitio pêl. Sŵn genethod yr ysgol yn chwarae hoci ydoedd, a gallwn weled lliwiau gwahanol eu blowsus yn rhedeg groes ymgroes tu ôl i frigau noeth y coed wrth redeg ar ôl y bêl.

Cerddai Nanw yn ôl a blaen rhwng y gegin orau a'r gegin fach yn hwylio te. Ceisiwn gael cip ar ei hwyneb heb iddi hi sylwi ar hynny. Dyna paham y daliwn i edrych drwy'r ffenestr. Nid ymweliad cyffredin â'm ffrind oedd hwn heddiw. Clywswn ychydig amser cyn hyn fod y rhyfel wedi dweud yn arw ar amgylchiadau Nanw, a'i bod hithau o'r herwydd yn dechrau mynd yn od; a dweud y gwir, 'dechrau drysu am ei syn-hwyrau' oedd geiriau'r sawl a ddywedodd wrthyf. Ni ruthrais i edrych amdani. Gadewais i newydd-deb y newydd wisgo tipyn er mwyn i mi fy hun fedru bod yn naturiol yn ei chwmni; oblegid nid peth hawdd yw ymddwyn yn naturiol efo rhywun sy'n dechrau mynd yn od. Penderfynais hefyd gynnig help iddi os medrwn wneud hynny mewn ffordd ddi-dramgwydd. Cymerwn arnaf wylio'r plant yn chwarae, a thrown fy ngolygon at Nanw i ddweud rhywbeth wrthi. Y peth a welwn amlycaf

44

yn ei mynegiant heddiw oedd bodlonrwydd a thawelwch. Gallwn ei weled ar ochr ei hwyneb, wrth iddi ddal y bara ar fforch i'w grasu wrth y tân. Yn ystod yr ugain mlynedd o'm hadnabyddiaeth ohoni, ni welais erioed wyneb a allai newid mor sydyn o dristwch i lawenydd, o ddicter i fwynder, o fwynder i ddicter. Ond yr oedd rhyw dawelwch fel petai wedi dyfod i aros yno erbyn heddiw.

'Mae hi'n braf ar y plant acw,' meddwn i, gan ddal i syllu drwy'r ffenestr.

'Pam?'

'Wel, am eu bod nhw'n blant, am wn i.'

'Lol i gyd. Mae pawb yn meddwl bod pob plentyn yn hapus, dim ond am ei fod o'n blentyn.'

'Mi goelia i *fod* y rhan fwya ohonyn' nhw.'

'Dim o angenrheidrwydd. Amser cas, creulon ydi o, fydda i'n meddwl, yn enwedig i blentyn a chanddo bersonoliaeth. Ac os oes personoliaeth gan y rhieni, dyna iti wrthdarawiad a chlewtan.'

'Mae'n rhaid nad oedd gen i 'run bersonoliaeth felly.'

Aeth ymlaen heb geisio lliniaru ei gosodiad.

'Ond mi ddweda' i un peth iti, Morfudd, 'rydw i'n teimlo'r dyddiau yma, er gwaetha'r holl siarad meddal yma am blentyndod, mai dyna'r unig beth sefydlog yn fy mywyd i.'

'Sut yn hollol?'

' 'Rydw i'n teimlo ar hyn o bryd mai dyna'r unig adeg ar fy mywyd i pan mai fi oeddwn i. Cofia, 'does arna'i ddim hiraeth ar ei ôl.'

' 'Chlywais i 'rioed 'siwn beth.'

' 'Rydw i'n teimlo ers talwm iawn 'rŵan mai rhywun arall ydw i, ac mai'r fi iawn oedd y fi cyn imi ddechrau crwydro'r gwledydd.'

' 'Dwyt ti ddim wedi crwydro llawer.'

45

'Naddo, ond mi eill ceffyl wrth gorddi gerdded reit bell, ac anghofio o b'le y cychwynnodd o.'

Gadawodd y frechdan grasu a daeth at y ffenestr.

'Ond mae gweld y plant acw'n chwarae yn beth reit dlws,' ebr hi, ac ar hynny dechreuodd chwerthin.

'Edrych, Morfudd, edrych, wir, ar y ddwy hen wraig acw.'

'Ym mh'le?'

'Dacw nhw yn mynd ar hyd y llwybr.'

Gwelwn ddwy wraig yn symud yn araf heibio i gae'r ysgol. Ni allwn ddweud pa mor hen oeddynt; eithr, a barnu oddi wrth eu dillad llaes a'u cerdded araf, meddyliwn nad oeddynt yn ifanc.

'O diar,' meddai Nanw, 'dyna iti ddwy hen wraig ddoniol. Mae'r hyna'n siŵr o fod rywle rhwng pedwar ugain a phedwar ugain a deg. A'r 'fenga'n tynnu am ei phedwar ugain. A maen' nhw'n mynd am dro efo'i gilydd fel yna bob dydd.'

'Chwarae teg iddyn' nhw.'

'Ia, mae'n amlwg bod y tro yma'n ddigwyddiad mawr iddyn' nhw, neu mi fuasent wedi diflasu. Mae'r hyna' o'r ddwy yn cerdded â'i phen i lawr fel petai hi'n wynt mawr o hyd ac yn siarad gymaint fyth, ac mae'r lleill yn cerdded yn dalog â'i phen i fyny.'

'Â'i phen yn y gwynt felly?'

'Na, mae hi'n rhy hen i hynny, ond yn gwbl ddihitio; yn sbïo o'i chwmpas, a'r hen wraig yn dweud rhyw stori. Wyddost ti,' meddai Nanw'n sydyn, 'mi fydd arna'i flys ofnadwy stopio i wrando stori'r hen wraig, fel y bydd rhywun mewn trên weithiau yn ysu gan awydd darllen papur ei gyd-deithiwr.'

'Ydi stori'r hen wraig mor ddiddorol â hynny?'

'Mi alla'i ddychmygu ei bod hi. Rhyw dameidiau fel hyn fydda' i'n i glywed: 'Ydach chi'n gweld, 'roedd o wedi anfon arian i mi mewn llythyr, ac mi rois y llythyr dan fatres y

gwely, ac erbyn i mi fynd yno drannoeth, 'doedd o ddim yno.'
'Nag oedd, nag oedd,' meddai'r llall, mor ddihitio â phetai'r
hen wraig yn dweud ei bod wedi colli pin.'

'Ella mai wedi clywed y stori gannoedd o weithiau yr oedd
hi.'

'Wel, 'dwn i ddim. Mi fyddwn yn clywed peth fel hyn dro
arall: 'Y peth fydda i'n ddweud bob amser ydi, y dylai rhywun
gymryd cod-liver oil at annwyd.' 'Dylai, dylai,' meddai'r llall
gan edrych i fyny at awyr-blân. A bob tro y byddwn i'n pasio —
a chofiwch, mi fyddaf yn eu pasio bob dydd — dyna lle byddai'r
hen wraig yn dweud rhywbeth reit ddiddorol, ac ni chlywais
y llall erioed yn dweud dim ond 'Ie, ie' neu 'Nag oes, nag
oes' neu rywbeth fel yna.'

'Am fywyd, yntê?'

'Ie, a mi fyddwn i bron torri ar fy nhraws o eisiau gwybod
stori'r hen wraig. Mi fuasai'n fwyd i mi, fel darllen nofel bron.
'Rydw i wedi mynd i deimlo bod yna fydoedd diddorol iawn
tu ôl i ddrysau cymdogion.'

'Digon gwir, ond busnesa yw i bobl eraill agor y drysau.'

'Wel, mi eill hynny fynd â meddwl rhywun oddi wrth ei
bethau ei hun.'

Codais fy nghlustiau. Daeth gwên ryfedd dros wefusau Nanw.

' 'Rydw i'n siŵr bod yr haul yn taflu patrwm brigau'r coed
ar draws eu cotiau 'rŵan,' meddai, a chan dynnu llenni'r ffenestr
at ei gilydd:

'Beth am de? 'Rydw i'n barod amdano fo.'

'A finnau.'

A dweud y gwir, yr oedd meddwl yn y trên am fynd i dŷ
Nanw yn rhoi pleser mawr i mi, ac efallai, petawn i'n mynd
at waelod achos y pleser hwnnw yn onest, mai'r unig beth a'm
symbylai i ymweled â hi oedd yr amheuthum hwnnw o gael
pryd o fwyd heb orfod ei baratoi fy hun. A meddyliwn cyn i

Nanw olau'r lamp, wrth edrych ar y tân yn taflu'i olau ar goesau'r bwrdd ac ar wyneb y dresel, a gweld y llestri te'n disgleirio, mor braf y buasai pe daethwn i gymowta'n unig.

Wrth fwyta'r frechdan grasu dda, tybiais y byddai'n well imi ddweud fy neges, neu fe ddeuai amser trên.

'Ydi'r rhyfel wedi effeithio'n fawr arnat ti, Nanw?'

'Arna' *i*?'

Gwelais fy nghamgymeriad wrth ofyn y cwestiwn fel yna, a chochais.

'Wel, ar dy amgylchiadau di felly?'

Trodd ei phen at y tân.

'Wel,' meddai hi'n araf, 'mae'n bosibl i boen ynddo'i hun sefrio a di-deimladu teimladau rhywun, fel na theimla ddim rhagor oddi wrtho fo. 'Rydw i'n teimlo fel petawn i'r ochr arall i gwmwl, ac nad ydi'r cwmwl yn effeithio dim arna'i erbyn hyn, er ei fod o yno o hyd. 'Rydw i rywsut wedi ei adael ar fy ôl.'

Sylwais ar ei hwyneb, y tro cyntaf imi gael golwg berffaith glir arno y prynhawn hwnnw. Yr oedd ynddo fwy o dawelwch nag a welais erioed.

'Da iawn,' oedd yr unig beth a adawodd fy syndod imi ei ddweud.

'Wyddost ti,' meddai, 'mi fydda i'n meddwl llawer am fy hen deidiau a'm hen neiniau y dyddiau yma.'

'Diar annwyl, 'dwyt ti 'rioed yn eu cofio *nhw*?'

'Nag ydw. Ond mi glywais ddigon amdanyn' nhw fel y buaswn yn eu 'nabod petaent yn cerdded i'r ystafell yma 'rŵan. Yn wir, mi fydda' i'n treio cael ganddyn' nhw ddweud rhagor o'u hanes wrthyf.'

Bu agos imi dagu. Aeth ymlaen.

' 'Rydw i'n teimlo'u bod nhw'n perthyn yn agosach imi o lawer na pherthnasau nes.'

'O!'

'Ydw. 'Dwn i ddim pam. Ond mi fydda' i'n cofio fel y buon' nhw'n diodde. Gweithio o olau i olau am ychydig bach o arian. Cerdded milltiroedd at eu gwaith. Dim cloc i wybod pryd i gychwyn. Fe aeth rhai ohonyn nhw at eu gwaith erbyn hanner nos yn lle chwech y bore oherwydd hynny. Bwyd gwael, anniddorol. Dillad hyll, digon cynnes efallai. A dim ond swllt neu ddeunaw yr wythnos o'r plwy i'w gweddwon, a hwythau wedi marw'n ifanc wrth weithio'n hir ar fwyd gwael. Mi glywais am wragedd gweddwon yn llwgu ac yn rhynnu ar eu dogn o'r plwy.'

'Wel, ie, ond 'wydden nhw am ddim byd gwell.'

'Gwydden'. Mi wydden' fod yna ffasiwn beth â gorffwys i'w gael i rai pobl. Ond mi aethon i'w beddau heb wybod fawr amdano.'

'Mi gawson' wybod wedyn.'

'Paid â bod mor galed wrth dreio bod yn glyfar.'

'Faint well wyt ti o deimlo fel arall at rywun sydd wedi marw ers can mlynedd?'

'Ond mae eu gwaed nhw yn rhedeg yn ein gwythiennau ni.'

'Wel, ydi, ac mae eu poen nhw wedi peidio â bod.'

'Ydi; ac mi fydd ein poen ninnau wedi peidio â bod i'n disgynyddion ni ymhen can mlynedd eto. Mi fyddan hwythau lawn mor greulon tuag atom ninnau.'

' 'Dydi hynny ddim o'r ods i ni 'rŵan.'

'Nac ydi, am na wyddom ni ddim amdano fo, ond *mi* wyddom am galedi ein cyn-dadau. Ac yr ydym yn greulon wrth anghofio'r gorffennol.'

Daethai rhywfaint o'r hen sŵn gwrthryfelgar i'w llais.

Yn lle taeru tewais, ac fe'm heliais fy hun i gychwyn.

'Diolch yn fawr iti am ddwad i edrych amdanaf,' meddai

wrthyf yn y drws, a'r tawelwch yn ôl ar ei hwyneb erbyn hyn. Ni chynigiodd ddyfod i'm danfon at y trên.

Euthum innau adref â'm cynnig yn fy mhoced ond fy mhen yn llawn o feddyliau rhyfedd.

TEULU

Eisteddai Ela yn y gegin fach a llond bwrdd o fwyd o'i blaen, mwy nag a welsai ers blynyddoedd, platiad o ham, platiad mawr o fara ymenyn, a hwnnw'n fenyn ffarm, a dysgliad o salad a oedd bron yn rhy dlws i dorri iddo. Daeth rhyw hapusrwydd rhyfedd i'w chalon o weled yr haul yn taro ar y cwbl, hithau'n cael gorffwys ar ôl cerdded tair milltir o'r stesion, a chael gorffwys wrth fwyta pethau amheuthum nas cawsai ers blynyddoedd. Mor hapus y teimlai fel y trodd bob tamaid yn hamddenol yn ei cheg, torri'r ham yn fân. Cymerai amser i roddi ei chyllell drwy ei brechdan, a synfyfyriai'n braf wrth ben y cwbl gan anghofio'r hyn a ddaethai a hi yno, gan anghofio sylw awgrymiadol John ei gŵr, a fuasai'n rhincian yn ei meddwl drwy gydol y daith yn y trên. O'r gegin orau, deuai sisial, ambell besychiad isel ac ambell ochenaid, y cwbl yn ddianghenraid fel y gwyddai, a distawrwydd ar eu hôl; o'r cae gerllaw, bref dafad gwynfannus a distawrwydd ar ei hôl hithau. Clywai Lisa Jên, ei chyfnither, yn cerdded i'r lobi ac yn siarad yn ddistaw â rhywun yn y fan honno. Yna, clywai hi'n dyfod yn ôl ac i'r gegin fach, a dyna dorri ar ei myfyrdodau hithau.

'Ydach chi wedi gorffen, Ela? Mae ar Mrs. Jones eisiau clirio'r bwrdd cyn i'r gweinidog gyrraedd,' yn reit chwyrn a stiwardlyd.

Llyncodd Ela y jeli heb ei fwynhau a chododd y gwrid i'w hwyneb. Ie, dyma hi, yr un Lisi Jên, ni fedrai angau na dim

51

arall dynnu'r stiwardio ohoni. Daeth Mrs. Jones, y ddynes helpu, yno i glirio'r bwrdd a rhoi winc ar Ela, ac aeth hithau i eistedd i'r gegin orau gan deimlo fel pe bai'n cerdded i mewn i gyfarfod pregethu chwarter awr yn hwyr. Yno o gwmpas yr ystafell eisteddai ei theulu i gyd, yn fodrybedd, ewythredd, cefndyr, cyfnitherod, brodyr a chwiorydd, neiaint a nithod, yn edrych ar ei gilydd ac arni hithau fel pe na welsant ei gilydd erioed. Yn y gadair freichiau wrth y tân eisteddai Lewis Tomos, gŵr Lisi Jên, â'i ben ar un ochr fel ci. Gyferbyn ag ef eisteddai Dewyth Enoc, yn cnoi baco, â sug yn rhedeg hyd ei farf, a golwg hollol ddihitio arno. Y ddau'n edrych i'r tân. Gorweddai'r gath tu mewn i'r ffender. Dyma'r unig bethau y gellid eu gweled yn eglur. Yr oedd pawb arall mewn hanner tywyllwch. Daliai Lisi Jên i gerdded ôl a blaen i'r gegin fach a syllu ar y cloc wrth fyned heibio. Troes Ela'n reddfol i edrych ar y cloc, ac yr oedd yn chwarter wedi un arno. Tri chwarter awr arall o syllu ar ei theulu! Daeth sylw John yn ôl iddi â mwy o fin. Ceisiasai ei berswadio i ddyfod efo hi i gladdu ei modryb.

'Na, 'ddo'i ddim,' meddai yntau'n bendant. 'Cnebrwng ydi'r lle y mae rhywun yn gweld 'i deulu.'

Nid atebodd hithau, oblegid gwyddai beth fyddai ei hateb:
'Fy nheulu i ydyn' nhw ac nid dy deulu di.'

Gwyddai nad hi a gâi'r gair olaf er y câi'r gair olaf ond un. Felly tawodd. Ffrae fyddai'r diwedd os âi ymlaen, ac yr oedd myned ar daith ar ôl ffrae yn waeth na myned ar daith i wynebu un.

Dechreuodd sylw awdurdodol Lisi Jên am iddi frysio droi yn ei meddwl yn hollol yr un fath ag y troesai sylw John yn y trên, ei ymlid a'i droi'n wir yr un pryd. I beth oedd eisiau iddi frysio dros y bwyd da hwnnw a thri chwarter awr o amser i aros?

'Cadwch lai o sŵn efo'r llestri yna,' Lisi Jên yn snapio eto ar Mrs. Jones. Yr hen gnawes iddi! Yr oedd yn rhaid iddi gael stiwardio ar rywun. Dim rhyfedd fod Lewis Tomos yn gwar-grymu'n barhaol erbyn hyn. Nid oedd waeth iddo heb nag ymsythu. Yr oedd yn llai o drafferth dal y gwar yn barod i dderbyn y warrog. Nid yn unig edrychai fel ci yn y fan honno wrth y tân, ond fel ci wedi cael cweir.

Canai'r tegell yn ddiog ar y pentan a chanai'r gath y grwndi, mor gartrefol â phe bai ei modryb yn fyw ac yn eistedd yn y gadair freichiau. Sisialai rhài o'r teulu a eisteddai ar y soffa, a dywedodd ei Modryb Beca: 'Tewch' reit uchel.

Daeth eisiau chwerthin ar Ela. Beth pe byddai'n rhaid iddi wneud rhag ffrwydro? Cai dafod iawn gan Lisi Jên wedyn reit siŵr. Efallai mai hynny fyddai orau, er mwyn iddi gael bwrw ei bos allan, a gorffen â'r holl dymer ddrwg a grynhoai'r tu mewn iddi er pan wnaeth John y sylw hwnnw am ei theulu. Ond byddai'n beth ofnadwy ffraeo mewn cynhebrwng, er mai dyna'r lle enwog am hynny. I ba beth y daethai i gladdu ei modryb ni wyddai, ac ni wybuasai ei modryb, yr unig un yr hoffasai ei phlesio, ped arosasai gartref. Beth a wna i bobl fyned i gladdu ei gilydd? Parch, dyletswydd, cydymdeimlad? Ni fedrai hi ddweud ynglŷn â'i modryb. Arferiad o fyned i gladdu teulu efallai. Ni theimlai unrhyw alar; yr oedd yn berffaith siŵr o hynny, ond galar o weled yr hen bethau yn myned heibio, a hithau bob tro y deuai i gladdu un o'i theulu yn gweled rhan o'i hieuenctid ei hun yn myned i lawr i'r bedd gyda hwy. Nid oedd waeth iddi heb na phendroni, ni châi ateb, ond yr oedd y pendroni'n help iddi rhag clywed y distawrwydd trwstan, annaturiol a lanwai'r ystafell.

Yr oedd y cloc yn cnocio fel gordd tu ôl iddi, rywle yn asgwrn ei chefn. Cloc Thomas John Cilgerran yn Uffern. Byth! Byth! Felly y parhai'r distawrwydd hwn. Byth! Byth! Daeth ochenaid eto, yr un ag a glywsai o'r gegin fach.

Trodd ei phen i weled pwy ydoedd. Dewyth Lias. Pwy a fuasai'n meddwl? Yr hen greadur! Ond efallai mai ochneidio am weled torri ar y distawrwydd yr oedd yntau ac nid ar ôl Deina ei chwaer.

Cofiodd eiriau ei mam am rywun na faliai ar ôl y marw: 'Rhoth hi ddim ochenaid ar i ôl o.' Nid oedd eisiau ochneidio ar ôl Modryb Deina a hithau wedi cael byw mor hen. Ond nid oedd yno neb i ochneidio ond Lisi Jên, ac mi fyddai hi, yr unig blentyn, yn daclus iawn ar ei hôl. Croeso iddi ar ei harian, meddyliai Ela, gan na newidient le yn y banc. Pa bryd y deuai'r pregethwr i roi taw ar gloc Thomas John?

Daeth gwenyn feirch o rywle ac eistedd ar farf Dewyth Enoc, a'r eiliad nesaf poerodd yntau sug baco yn stremits ar draws y pentan gloyw.

'Pam na drychwch chi i le'r ydach chi'n poeri?' meddai Lisi Jên.

Ond ni chlywodd Dewyth Enoc mohoni, a diolchodd Ela am gymaint â hynny o dorri ar y tawelwch. Yr oedd ar fin dweud rhywbeth, pan deimlodd, yn hytrach na gweled, ddau lygad disglair Nesta, ei nith, a wenai arni oddi ar y soffa. A diolchodd, o waelod ei chalon, am rywbeth a'i rhwystrodd rhag torri allan i weiddi.

Ar hynny, daeth y gweinidog a dechreuwyd y gwasanaeth. Dyn ifanc ydoedd nad adwaenai mo'i modryb ond ar ddiwedd ei hoes. Yr oedd ei lais yn fwyn, ei fynegiant yn glir, a hyfryd i Ela oedd clywed 'Dyddiau dyn sydd fel glaswelltyn,' er na weddent i'w modryb, a oedd ymhell dros ei phedwar ugain. Buasai ei dyddiau hi fel derwen bron, ac wrth feddwl hyn, y meddyliodd gyntaf er pan gyraeddasai am y sawl a oedd yn yr arch yn y llofft.

Yr oedd arni flys cael sefyll yno a chanu moliant yr hen wraig, pan ddiolchai ef i Dduw am ei ffyddlondeb yn y capel.

Nid y capel oedd ei hoffter hi, eithr ei thŷ a'i dillad. Fe hoffai ganu moliant i'w harddwch fel y cofiai hi ddeugain mlynedd cyn hynny. Cofiai ddau beth yn arbennig. Dyfod ar draws ei modryb yn ddiarwybod a hithau'n godro yn y beudy, yn eistedd ar y stôl dan y fuwch, ei sgert yn agor allan fel gwyntyll oddi wrth ei chorff hardd, a hithau â'i phen yn nhynewyn y fuwch, fel pe bai'n gwrando ar y llaeth yn disgyn i'r piser. Meddyliai ar y pryd fel yr hoffai dynnu ei llun yn yr ystum fyfyriol honno, a meddwl tybed a oedd rhywbeth yn ei phoeni pan edrychai felly. Dro arall cofiai gael mynd i eistedd i'w sêt yn y capel, a'i modryb yn gwisgo siwt newydd, las. Het las â phluen wen arni a'r bluen ysgafn yn disgyn dros yr ymyl ac yn mwyneiddio cryfder ei hwyneb. Cofio ei haml gymwynasau a'i charedigrwydd tuag ati hi bob amser. Cofio. Cofio — yr hyn na wyddai'r gweinidog.

Aeth i deimlo'n ddagreuol pan ddarllenai: 'Oherwydd rhaid i'r llygradwy hwn wisgo anllygredigaeth, ac i'r marwol hwn wisgo anfarwoldeb.' Y gair 'llygradwy' a wnâi iddi deimlo felly bob amser. Cofio ei modryb yn ddynes weddol ieuanc. Cofio ei llun fel Nesta yn awr, a chofio amdani hi ei hun yn ieuanc a dyma hi'n awr ar y llithrigfa anniddorol honno rhwng canol oed a henaint. Ond yr oedd heddwch yn y meddyliau hyn. Meddyliau trist oeddynt, yn llifo dros ei hymwybyddiaeth heb rincian.

Wrth fynd allan o'r tŷ gafaelodd ym mraich Nesta, ei nith, ac aeth i'r un cerbyd â hi, er gwaethaf gorchmynion yr ymgymerwr. Nid oedd waeth ganddi am yr anhrefn a achosai. Rhoes ei braich drwy fraich Nesta, a glynodd wrthi hyd at lan y bedd am mai hi a ddaeth â'r mymryn goleuni i'r gegin orau dywyll gynnau.

'Pryd ydach chi'n priodi, Nesta?'

'Ymhen y mis.'

'Gobeithio y byddwch chi'n hapus, wir.'

'Rhaid i chi ddim pryderu, mae Alun yn gariad i gyd.'

'Gobeithio y pery o felly at lan y bedd.'

Yr oedd yn ddrwg ganddi, cyn gynted ag y daeth y gair dros ei gwefus. Pa hawl oedd ganddi hi i awgrymu siom canol oed i eneth ifanc ar drothwy ei nefoedd? Ac un mor hoffus â Nesta, na welid fyth wg ar ei hael na chrychni ar ei thalcen. Ac yr oedd wedi brifo'r un na chymerasai'r byd am ei brifo. Fel yna y digwyddai bob amser — brifo rhai annwyl ganddi.

Yr oeddynt yn ôl o'r fynwent wrth y bwrdd te, a phawb yn siarad, yn union fel pe bai ymadawiad y marw wedi rhoddi trwydded iddynt. Edrychai Dewyth Enoc ar ei blât a bwytâi heb stopio, a'i farf yn codi i fyny fel y cnoai ei geg ddi-ddannedd y bwyd; a phan siaradai, siaradai wrtho ef ei hun, fwy neu lai, gan ei fod yn drwm ei glyw, a neb yn trafferthu ei ateb. Ond dyma dân-belen oddi wrtho:

'Be' ddigwyddodd i gariad cynta Deina, hwnnw y bu hi'n i ganlyn am y fath flynyddoedd cyn priodi Wmffra?'

'Paid â chodi crachod ar ddiwrnod cnebrwng dy chwaer,' oddi wrth Modryb Beca.

Ond ni chlywodd Dewyth Enoc. Aeth yn ei flaen.

'Mi roedd hwnnw yn hogyn smart, da — '

Gwaeddodd Modryb Beca ar uchaf ei llais yn ei glust:

'I be' rwyt ti'n codi crachod ar ddiwrnod cnebrwng dy chwaer?'

'Codi crachod! Nid codi crachod ydi sôn am ffrae cariadon. Codi crachod faswn i'n galw sôn amdanyn' nhw petae' nhw wedi ymadael â'i gilydd ar ôl priodi.'

Gwgodd Modryb Beca, a sisial dan ei hanadl:

'A'r pregethwr yma a chwbl.'

Ond yr oedd y pregethwr yn mwynhau'r cyfan.

Dyma'r tro cyntaf i Ela glywed hanes y cariad nes priododd Modryb Deina.

'Beth ddaeth rhyngddyn' nhw, Dewyth Enoc?' gofynnodd Ela yn uchel.

'Clywch ar honna eto, yn gyrru'r cwch i'r dŵr,' meddai Modryb Beca.

' 'Dŵyr neb beth ddaeth rhyngddyn' nhw. Ond mi glywais i achlust mai wedi dweud celwydd yr oedd y bachgen yna wrthi hi, a'i bod hithau wedi ffeindio, a mynd i feddwl y buasai o'n gwneud rhywbeth gwaeth na dweud celwydd ar ôl priodi.'

'Ac yr oedd hi'n iawn,' meddai Lisi Jên, o deimlad dros ei thad, 'achos mi dwyllodd y ddynes ddaru o briodi dan ei thrwyn, ac mi ymadawsant â'i gilydd.'

'Na, marw wnaeth o,' oddi wrth ei modryb Beca.

Troes Ela i edrych ar Nesta i weled pa effaith a gâi hyn arni, ond yr oedd hi fel yr heulwen o hyd.

Yr oedd Ela ar fin gofyn am ychwaneg, ond ystyriodd mewn pryd y tro hwn y gallai hynny frifo rhywun.

Ochneidiai Dewyth Lias, yr ieuengaf ohonynt.

'Neno'r tad, be' sy ar Lias yn ochneidio o hyd?' meddai Modryb Beca.

Ac am y tro cyntaf fe siaradodd Dewyth Lias:

'Rydw i'n ych gweld chi i gyd wedi anghofio Deina druan, ac wedi anghofio nad oes gan yr un ohonom ni fawr o amser nes byddwn ni yn mynd ar ei hôl hi.'

Ni chlywodd Dewyth Enoc mono, ond daliai i fwyta â'i farf yn esgyn ac yn disgyn.

A daeth distawrwydd ar bawb.

Daeth Nesta i ddanfon ei Modryb Ela beth o'r ffordd at y stesion. Teimlai Ela'n gynnes iawn tuag ati ac yn ddrwg iawn ganddi fod mor llib ei thafod yn y cerbyd ar y ffordd i'r fynwent.

'Mae'n ddrwg iawn gen i, Nesta, i mi eich brifo.'

'Brifo? Pa bryd? Sut?'

'Wel, yn y car, pan ddwedais i mod i'n gobeithio y byddai Alun yn para yn gariad i gyd hyd lan y bedd.'

'Wir, welais i ddim o'i le yn hynny. Beth oedd o'i le ynddo fo?'

'O, wel, dyna fo ynte.'

Cusanodd hi ar y groesffordd, a throes yn ôl i godi ei llaw arni wedyn.

Yn y trên, bu Ela'n myfyrio wedyn ar ddigwyddiadau'r prynhawn, yn enwedig yr hyn a glywodd am gariad cyntaf Modryb Deina. A fu hi'n hapus wedyn gyda Dewyth Wmffra? Ymddangosai felly. Ond dyn diddrwg didda na ffraeai gyda neb oedd ef. Ac ym meddwl Ela, dynes oedd Modryb Deina yr oedd yn rhaid iddi gael rhywun o'i maint hi ei hun i daro yn ei herbyn cyn y byddai'n hapus, ac efallai y byddai'n hapusach gyda'r dyn arall ar ei gelwydd. Ond dyna fo, ni ddigwyddodd felly, ac yr oedd hi a'i gŵr wedi myned tu hwnt i gael eu brifo gan gelwydd na dim arall erbyn hyn. A ffydd fawr Nesta yn ei hapusrwydd. Gobeithio na thwyllid hi beth bynnag yn ei diniweidrwydd gonest. Fel y dynesai at ei chartref, daeth John eto i'w meddwl a'i sylw miniog. Oedd, yr oedd yn iawn. Fe ddywedodd y gwir. Peth fel yna oedd teulu, yn ffraeo yn eu henaint wrth gladdu ei gilydd. Ond yr oedd yn rhincian yn enbyd ar ei meddwl wrth feddwl ei bod wedi anghytuno ag ef pan gychwynnai, a chanfod mai ef oedd yn iawn. Ond penderfynodd na ddywedai mo hynny wedi cyrraedd adref. Fe'i cadwai iddi hi ei hun. Ac os gofynnai gwestiynau, fe gelai oddi wrtho. Wedi'r cyfan, yr oedd Nesta'n hoffus iawn, ac yr oedd hynny'n wir.

TE P'NAWN

Ni wn pryd y bûm mor ddwfn na chyn hired yn y felan ag y bûm yr wythnos hon. Wedi cael gwyliau yn y wlad efo'm chwaer yn fy hen gartref, a dyfod yn ôl i dref bach snobyddol, hanner-Seisnig, ddifater, naturiol i ddyn deimlo'n hiraethus am dipyn o ddyddiau, a gadael i'w feddwl redeg yn ôl: 'Yr adeg yma wythnos i heddiw yr oeddwn i'n rhwymo styciau ŷd efo John.' 'Yr adeg yma bythefnos i heddiw yr oeddwn i'n cael te yn yr ardd, heb eisiau meddwl am fynd i'r seiat nac am bwnc i siarad arno.'

Ond nid rhyw feddyliau trist-foethus fel yna a ddeuai imi y dyddiau diwethaf yma, ond meddyliau na ellid eu galw'n ddim ond iselder ysbryd. Ni chaf wared ohonynt yn y boreau hyd yn oed.

Heddiw, euthum i feddwl na chefais wyliau mor braf wedi'r cwbl. Yr oedd pawb yn garedig wrthyf, yn rhy garedig efallai. Yr oedd plant fy chwaer yn hollol fel y mae plant heddiw, yn bowld a di-feind o bawb arall. Hoffwn, er hynny, eu diffyg parch i'r pregethwr, arwydd o iechyd. John, fy mrawd-yng-nghyfraith, yn hen foi clên, diddan, ac yn gwerthfawrogi pob cymwynas a rown iddo yn y cae gwair. Ond yng nghanol tawelwch y wlad, mi'm cawn fy hun yn dyheu am fwy o dawelwch, a byddwn yn codi am bump y bore er mwyn cael y gegin i mi fy hun, a chael cwpaned o de heb i air na sŵn amharu ar fy mwynhad ohoni. Byddwn wrth fy modd yn clywed y grug yn clecian o dan y tegell, gweld y mwg mor wyryf a glân yn mynd fel cwmwl i fyny'r simnai, a chlywed sŵn y trên yn y pellteroedd wrth y môr. Yr oedd hynny i gyd mor hyfryd yn y distawrwydd ifanc cyn i'r gwlith godi a chyn i ddyn nac anifail symud ei le ar ôl noson o gysgu. Eithr fe glywn sŵn yn y llofft, a deuai John i lawr y grisiau, a theimlwn innau rywbeth yn crensian, fel traed ar farwor, ar y 'fi' hwnnw sydd o'r tu mewn imi, y fi sydd megis ystafell wag lle nad oes croeso i neb groesi ei rhiniog. Dyna'r hud yn darfod, ac ni byddai waeth imi fod yn nwndwr tref mwy nag yn y wlad weddill y diwrnod.

Un peth a roddai bleser imi gynt pan fyddwn ar fy ngwyliau fyddai cyfarfod â'm hen gyfoedion coleg. Ni chefais lawer o flas o'u cwmni eleni. Dyna Huw, sy'n weinidog ar eglwys gyffelyb i minnau mewn tref wledig, Seisnigaidd. Wel, mae o'n anobeithiol. Erbyn hyn, mae ei holl gynulleidfa iddo fo fel cymeriadau mewn nofel. Mae o wedi mynd y tu hwnt i bregethwr, fe aeth yn llenor. Fel hyn yr oedd o'n siarad am ei aelodau:

'Dyna iti Hwn-a-hwn, dyn pwysig, hollol fodlon arno fo'i hun; pan fydda' i'n edrych arno drwy fy sbectol o'r pulpud ar fore Sul, byddaf yn gweld saim ei hunan-fodlonrwydd yn disgleirio ar ei wyneb. A dyna iti Hon-a-hon, sy'n hen ac yn treio edrych yn ifanc, yn ymsythu nes mae hi'n cario'i chorff i gyd ar y tu blaen.'

Ni fedrwn beidio â chwerthin am ben ei ddisgrifiadau, ac am wn i, na byddai o'i le petai o'n gweld dau neu dri fel yna. Ond fel yna yr edrych o ar bawb. Ni fedr, meddai o, weld lori lo yn mynd i fyny'r stryd, a dyn yn eistedd arni a'i draed yn hongian drosodd, heb ei weld fel petai mewn stori neu ddarlun, ac nid mewn amser a llif bywyd. Nid yw awyr bywyd yn awyr naturiol iddo o gwbl, mae'n crynu ac yn cwafrio fel y bydd yr awyr o flaen storm o fellt a tharanau.

Mae fel dyn yn edrych drwy'r pen rong i sbinglas, ac yn gweld pob dim yn fychan ac yn bell. Mae o'n meddwl chwilio am swydd yn y B.B.C. neu'n athro ysgol.

Wedyn dyna Dafydd, hen foi bach annwyl iawn, sy'n weinidog ar eglwys yn y wlad yng nghanol ffermwyr. Nid yw yntau'n ddall i wegni ei weinidogaeth, a'r diffyg effaith ar eu bywydau bychain crintachlyd. Ond deil ef ·i obeithio, ac ni chollodd ei ffydd yn y ddynoliaeth na'i Dduw o achos yr ychydig bach iawn o bobl anhunanol a edwyn. Nid ydyw'n ddall i bydredd ein gwareiddiad, nac i'r perygl i ryfel ddinistrio hynny sydd ar ôl ohono (y pethau sy'n fy mlino innau) ond yn wahanol i mi, mae o fel dyn yn eistedd ar graig uwchben y lli, yn ddiysgog a hyderus, a cyn dweud nad dyma ddiwedd popeth wedyn.

Yr wyf fi'n hoff iawn o Dafydd, ni chefais le erioed i amau ei gywirdeb, a hoffaf ef yn fwy am na chollodd ei synnwyr digrifwch. Eto, weithiau, byddaf yn fy nghael fy hun yn meddwl ei fod wedi cyrraedd y tir yna yn rhy hawdd. Mae o a Huw wedi cyrraedd y ddau dir eithafol yna ymhen deng mlynedd wedi gadael y coleg, a minnau yn yr un amser, heb gyrraedd unman, eithr yn troi a throsi mewn rhyw freuddwydion rhamantaidd heb fod yn bendant ar ddim, ond bod y byd yn mynd â'i ben iddo.

Pe gwyddai Huw fy holl hanes innau fe fyddai wedi fy rhoi yn y galeri ddarluniau sydd ganddo ac yn fy nisgrifio fel hyn: 'Dyna Twm, yr hen greadur meddal, wedi penfeddwi ar ryw wraig weddw bach ifanc, ac wedi ei gosod ar ryw orsedd o berffeithrwydd, yn ceisio ei hennill allan o'i galar ar ôl ei gŵr, fel ffured ar ôl gwningen, a ryw ddiwrnod, wedi iddo ei hennill, mi syrth yr orsedd a hithau, a mi fydd ei lygad o'n hollol glir a golau.' Yn wir, y rhamant a oedd gennyf yma a wnâi imi beidio â siarad yn feddal am fy ngwyliau, ac a wnâi imi edrych ymlaen at ddyfod yn ôl.

Ni wn pa bryd yr ymserchais ym Mair Elis, gweddw ieuanc a ddaethai i fyw at ei rhieni ryw ddwy flynedd yn ôl ar ôl colli ei gŵr. Efallai nad peth sydyn ydoedd, ac mai fy nghael fy hun yn y cyflwr o'i hoffi'n fwy na neb arall a wneuthum. Ei hwyneb hi, a hi yn unig, a welwn i o'r pulpud, a'r un oedd yr wyneb hwnnw o hyd, wyneb trist, mwyn, heb fod byth yn siriol. Cymharwn hi bob amser â'r blodau bach pinc a gwyn hynny a geir yn yr ardd, lliwiau mwyn, ysgafn oedd iddi hi. Yr oedd fel merch o'r ddeunawfed ganrif, a byddai'n hollol naturiol pe deuai i'r capel mewn bonet gotyn a ffrog fyslin, yn cario parasol. Ond yn wir, yr oeddwn yn dechrau blino edrych ar y pen bach cam hwnnw, ac wedi blino ceisio ei thynnu i fyny o ddüwch ei galar. Ac eto, weithiau, gofynnwn i mi fy hun a hoffwn hi fel arall, yn galed a dewr. Onid y mwynder trist hwn ynddi a'm denai ar ei hôl?

Codais yn sydyn o'm cadair brynhawn ddoe a mynd i Ddôl Erw i ail-ddechrau eto. Efallai y gwelwn hi wedi newid llawer ar ôl mis o wyliau. Ni byddaf erbyn hyn yn ceisio twyllo fy ngwraig-lety wrth gychwyn i'r cyfeiriad gwrthgyferbyniol. Meddylied a feddylio.

Yr oedd yn ddiwrnod cynnes a thes ar y gorwel, a rhyw fymryn o naws yr hydref yn yr awyr, diwrnod i godi calon dyn, ond gorweddai'r iselder arnaf fel cwilt yn fy mygu. Ceisiwn beidio â meddwl am Mair, a mynd i Ddôl Erw fel yr arferwn fynd cyn iddi ddychwelyd adref. Dyma'r unig dŷ ymysg tai fy aelodau y medrwn fynd iddo a gwybod y derbynnid fi'n naturiol fel dyn ac nid fel gweinidog. Nid oedd yno byth na ffwdan na chynnwrf: yr oedd yno groeso wyneb-lawen bob amser. Pan gyrhaeddais, yr oedd drws y ffrynt yn agored a goleuni tair ongl o'r gegin orau ar y lobi; pan ganwn y gloch yr oedd godre ffrog olau yn dyfod allan o gysgod y grisiau i oleuni'r lobi, a dyma Enid, nith Mair, yn rhedeg i gyfarfod â mi, ac yn rhoi ei dwylo am fy ngwddw a'm cusanu, a gweiddi yn holl frwdfrydedd ei hieuenctid: 'Mae hi'n ddiwrnod pen-blwydd Nain, ac yr ydw' innau wedi cael ysgoloriaeth i fynd i'r coleg. Mae hi'n de parti yma.'

Ar hyn, daeth Mair o'r gegin orau a'r gwrid wedi codi i'w hwyneb: 'Enid, rhag cwilydd i chi.' Ni chlywswn erioed gymaint o ysbryd yn ei llais. A chlywn Marged Parri yn gweiddi o'r gegin orau: 'Beth mae'r hogan yna yn i wneud rŵan? Mae hi fel gafr ar daranau trwy'r dydd.' 'Wir, cawswn innau dipyn o sgytiad hefyd.

'Rhaid i chi faddau iddi, Mr. Jones,' meddai Mair yn fwyn, 'mae hi'n hapus ofnadwy.'

'Da bod rhywun yn hapus,' meddwn innau.

'Mae hi'n ifanc,' meddai ei nain, wedi imi fyned i'r gegin orau, lle'r oedd bwrdd wedi ei osod yn barod i de, yn llawn o bob math o ddanteithion, a Marged Parri mewn blows wen, yn edrych yn ifanc iawn.

Yr oedd tân siriol yn y grât a rhwng hynny a'r bwrdd hyfryd a'r dodrefn hen ffasiwn yr oedd yn olygfa siriol.

'Mi ddaethoch i'r pwdin teim,' meddai gwraig y tŷ, gan estyn y cadeiriau, a rhoi'r mwgwd ar y tebot. Yr oeddwn fel pe bawn wedi fy nghario gan angel y Bardd Cwsg, a'm gosod wrth fwrdd yng ngwlad hud a lledrith, a'r frenhines ar ei ben yn tywallt te i gwpanau fel plisgyn ŵy, ac yn edrych i lawr i'w dyfnder fel petai hi'n edrych i waelod môr.

'Mwynhewch o, Mr. Jones,' meddai hi, 'fel petai o'n de pen-blwydd i chi, ac nid i mi. 'Dwn i ddim beth oedd ar y plant yma eisiau gwneud stŵr.'

'Nid pawb sy'n cael ei ben-blwydd yn drigain heddiw,' meddai Enid.

'Diar mi, ac mi'r ydach chi'n drigain?' meddwn i.

'O,' meddai, 'dydi trigain ddim yn hen heddiw.'

'Nac ydi, nac ydi,' meddwn innau, ' 'rydach chi'n edrach bron cyn ienged â'ch merch.' (Rhoi fy nhroed ynddi wedyn.)

'Dydi hynny'n dweud dim llawer,' oddi wrth Mair.

'Taw, Mair, rhag cwilydd iti. Mi fasa dyn yn meddwl dy fod ti'n gant, yn ôl fel 'rwyt ti'n siarad.'

Gwenodd Mair.

' 'Rydan' ni i gyd yn edrych yr un faint ag ydan ni,' gan Enid. 'Faint ydi'ch oed chi, Mr. Jones?'

'Deuddeg ar hugain.'

'Pedair blynedd yn hŷn na Modryb Mair.'

Saethau o dân o lygaid ei nain a'i modryb, ond yr oedd Enid yn gwbl ddihitio wrth gymryd tafell fawr arall o'r deisen hufen.

'Wel,' meddai Marged Parri, 'mi ellwch edrach yr un faint â'ch oed neu ddim, 'dydi hynny ddim o'r ods, ond mae o'n ods sut yr ydach chi'n teimlo.'

'Ond mi'r ydach chi'n teimlo'n iawn,' meddwn i, gan genfigennu wrthi.

'Ydw, am wn i, o ran fy iechyd. Ond 'does arna' i ddim eisiau byw llawer eto.'

'Mam!'

Cododd Enid ei phen oddi wrth ei phlât.

'Nac oes, pan ddowch chi i f'oed i, 'does gynnoch chi'r un affliw o ddim i edrach ymlaen ato drannoeth. Dyna chi'n rhoi eich pen ar y gobennydd cyn cysgu, ac yn meddwl beth sydd yna yfory, a 'does yna ddim byd.'

'Mae hynny'n digwydd i rai yn ifanc iawn,' meddai Mair.

'Ydi, am dipyn,' meddai ei mam yn galed, 'ond fel yna y bydda'i rŵan tra bydda' i, yldi, a 'waeth imi fynd odd' 'ma'n fuan mwy nag yn hwyr.'

'Wel, mae gynnoch chi rywbeth i edrych ymlaen ato, Nain, bwydo'r ieir a gwneud bwyd i Taid.'

'Mae dy daid wedi hen flino canmol ei fwyd, a 'dydi bwydo ieir ddim yn rhoi ias o ddisgwyliad i neb.'

'Ydi, pan mae wyau'n brin,' meddai Enid.

Chwarddodd Mair, a rhythais innau.

'Clywch chi ar Enid,' meddai Marged Parri, 'digon hawdd iddi hi siarad, pan mae pob 'fory iddi hi fel cannoedd o lygod bach yn dwad allan o'u tyllau i'r twllwch, yn llawn digwydd-iadau. Ond beth sydd gan neb fel fi i'w ddisgwyl?'

'Wel, mae yna lot o ddiddordeb mewn bywyd o hyd,' meddwn i, 'ond nad ydyn' nhw ddim yn bethau cynhyrfus iawn fel sy gan Enid yma i'w gobeithio, neu Mrs. Elis yma o ran hynny,' gan nodio at Mair.

'Neu chi eich hun,' meddai Marged Parri, 'rhyw dwll du i chi roi eich pen ynddo ddylai'r dyfodol fod, ond 'rydw i wedi rhoi fy mhen trwyddo ers talwm, fel brws y swîp yn dwad allan drwy'r corn.'

Chwarddasom i gyd, a bu agos i Enid dagu.

Yn sydyn hollol fe'm cawn fy hun yn gwneud yr un peth â'm cyfaill Huw, yn edrych o'r tu allan ar y tair, ac ar y te parti. Nid oeddwn i ynddo, ond safwn o'r tu allan. Yn fy myw ni allwn lai na gweld y tair merch fel tri jwg mewn set, y jwg mawr, y jwg canol a'r jwg bach, ac ymddangosai'r peth yn rhyfedd iawn i mi, ein bod yn siarad am bethau mor ddigalon ar ddydd pen-blwydd, ie, ac yn medru chwerthin am ben pethau mor ddigalon. Yr oedd Marged Parri wedi dweud fy nheiml-ladau i yn ei ffordd ddigrif ei hun, yn enwedig pan soniodd am yr 'ias o ddisgwyliad.'

Daeth Ifan Parri adref toc, ac edrychodd yn hurt ac yn gwestiyngar o un i'r llall wrth weld y wledd a'r dillad lliwgar, mae'n debyg. Yr oedd gwên ar wyneb ei briod wrth ddweud:

'Dyma fo, Enid; 'd ydi o ddim wedi cofio dim am benblwydd dy nain.'

'Go drapits las, na 'chofis i ddim,' meddai Ifan Parri, dan chwerthin, 'llawer ohonyn' nhw iti, Margiad.'

' 'Rydan ni newydd fod yn trafod y llawer ohonyn' nhw.' meddwn i, ' 'does ar Mrs. Parri ddim eisiau llawer ohonyn' nhw.'

'Hawdd dweud hynny.' meddai yntau, 'ond tasa'r Main yn taro heibio, mi fasa'n gyrru am y doctor mewn munud.'

Euthum i'r ardd er mwyn i Ifan Parri gael ei de, dan esgus mynd i weld y coed ffrwythau. Daeth Mair ar fy ôl, a rhoddodd hynny ynddo'i hun y fath bleser imi fel yr oedd arnaf ofn siarad â hi rhag ofn imi ei gyrru unwaith eto i'r tywyllwch y daethai allan ohono am ychydig y prynhawn.

'Onid oedd mam yn ddigalon?' meddai hi.

'Oedd, ond yr oedd hi'n dweud pethau mor ddigalon mewn ffordd mor ddigri', fel yr oeddwn i'n meddwl mai smalio'r oedd hi.'

'Dim o gwbwl; mae hi fel yna o hyd, yn sobor o ddigalon, ac yn dweud nad oes yna ddim yfory o hyd.'

' 'Rydw i'n dallt ei digalondid yn iawn, ond 'fedra i ddim dallt y digrifwch yna.'

'Meddwl yr ydw' i ei bod hi wedi cyrraedd ei gwaelod isa,' wedi rhoi ei phen drwy'r simnai, fel y dywedodd, a mai dyna paham y mae hi'n medru bod yn ddigri'. Mae hi'n waeth ar bobl sydd heb gyrraedd y gwaelod, a heb weld trwy bob dim.'

Ond nid oeddwn am ddechrau ar y trywydd yna efo Mair, oblegid gwyddwn yn rhy dda mai gyda'i theimladau hi ei hun y gorffennai. Nid oeddwn am sôn am fy nigalondid fy hun wrthi am yr un rheswm.

'Wyddoch chi,' meddwn i, 'mi fuom i gyd yn greulon iawn wrth Enid y p'nawn yma.'

'Sut felly?' (gyda thipyn o deimlad).

'Yn un peth, ni soniodd neb air am ei hysgoloriaeth.'

' 'D ydi hi ei hun wedi sôn am ddim arall er pan gyrhaeddodd hi'r bore yma efo'r newydd.'

'Chwarae teg iddi, methaf weld na allasem rannu ei llawenydd, am fod un o'r llygod bach wedi dwad allan iddi hi, yn lle gloddesta ar ein sôn ein hunain am ddigalondid. Siarad yr oeddem ni wedi'r cwbwl.'

'O, 'does dim rhaid inni boeni am Enid. Mi fydd hi'n iawn. Yr oedd hi'n mwynhau'r bwyd.'

'A ninnau'n mwynhau'r siarad. Nid fel yna y buasem ni petaem ni'n teimlo o ddifri.'

' 'Rydach chi'n credu nad oedd mam o ddifri?'

Rhag dechrau trafodaeth ar ragrith, dywedais:

'O! nac ydw', ond mae hi llawn mor ddigalon ar Enid ag ar yr un ohonom.'

'Alla' i ddim gweld hynny.'

Ond nid oeddwn yn y dymer i drafod ychwaneg ar bwnc ein te a pheidiais â dweud dim.

Wrth ddychwelyd i'm llety dan leuad glir noson o Fedi, medrwn ddeall tipyn ar fy nghyfaill Huw, a thybiwn y buasai Marged Parri yn ei ddeall yn berffaith, ond na buasai'n medru ei fynegi cystal. Wedi bod yn gwylio bywyd yr oeddwn innau, yn edrych ar ddarn bach ohono'n myned heibio, ac wedi gweld rhywbeth yn yr eilun a addolwn nas gwelswn o'r blaen. Toraswn sgwrs ar ei hanner yn yr ardd rhag imi weled rhagor, a dyfod adref yn ffwrbwt. Efallai y gwnâi hynny fwy o les i Mair na dadlau ac ymresymu. Ac ni allwn beidio â theimlo trueni dros Enid. Ond yr oeddwn yn llai digalon, a'm hedmygedd o Dafydd Bach yn fwy nag erioed.

DICI NED

Eisteddai Dici wrth y bwrdd yn ysgrifennu stori pan ddaeth ei fam i'r tŷ o'i gwaith, a'i dad yn union ar ei hôl.

' 'Dwyt ti ddim wedi cynnau'r tân' oedd geiriau cyntaf y fam.

'Fedrwn i ddim. 'Doedd o ddim wed'i osod.'

'Mi ddylai hogyn naw oed fedru clirio grât a gosod tân yn barod i roi matsen ynddo fo.'

'Fedrwn i ddim. 'Roeddwn i'n rhy wan.'

'Paid â dweud clwyddau.'

'A phaid ag ateb dy fam yn ôl,' meddai'r tad.

Mae gen i hawl i ateb yn ôl pan fydda i'n dweud y gwir.'

Ar hynny rhoes y fam glustan iddo fo, a dechrau ffwdanu gwneud tân heb glirio marwor y diwrnod cynt allan.

'Symud dy bethau oddi ar y bwrdd imi gael hwylio bwyd.'

Rhoes liain carpiog, pyg ar y bwrdd a mynd i nôl tun o ffa pobi o'r gegin bach.

'O Arglwydd,' meddai Dici wrtho'i hun, 'yr un hen dun eto.'

A dechreuodd gyfogi ar lawr.

'Dos allan,' meddai'i dad, 'yn lle rhoi rhagor o waith i dy fam.'

Ac allan yr aeth Dici, i'r stryd. Aeth i fyny o'r gwli gul lle'r oedd yn byw a dechrau cerdded y strydoedd, heibio i dai lle'r oedd golau cynnes, hapus i'w weld yn y ffenestri. Yr oedd llenni'n gorchuddio rhai, a ffurf lamp neu gawell aderyn i'w weld trwyddynt. Yna daeth at dŷ lle na thynesid y llenni, a gallai weld teulu o dad a mam, bachgen a geneth wrth y bwrdd yn bwyta.

'Bwyd,' meddai wrtho'i hun, 'bwyd, bwyd.'

Dywedodd ef lawer gwaith drosodd, gymaint o weithiau fel yr aeth yn air dieithr iddo: nid oedd y fath air yn bod. Penderfynodd fynd i mewn i'r tŷ yma, ac os troid ef allan, ni fyddai ddim gwaeth nag ydoedd cyn hynny. Cerddodd yn araf i fyny llwybr yr ardd; yr oedd ei ben yn troi, a dim ond nerth penderfyniad a'i gyrrodd ymlaen. Cnociodd yn ddistaw ar y drws, a daeth gwraig dal, lyfndew i'w agor.

'Ga'i ddwad i mewn os gwelwch chi'n dda?'

Ond cyn i'r wraig gael ateb, rhoes ei gefn ar y wal, a chael a chael a wnaeth y wraig i'w ddal cyn iddo syrthio. Cariodd ef yn ei breichiau i'r tŷ, a'r teulu wrth y bwrdd yn edrych yn syn arni.

'Y creadur bach, mae o wedi cael gwasgfa.'

Rhedodd ei gŵr i'r gegin bach i nôl dŵr. Ceisiodd Dici ei yfed wedi iddo fedru eistedd.

'Sal ydach chi, machgen i?' gofynnodd y wraig.

'Na eisio bwyd.'

' 'Steddwch chi yn fan'na am funud ac yfwch y dŵr yna i gyd. Mae'r lobscows yma sy gynnon ni yn rhy drwm i chi y munud yma.'

'O, nac ydi. Mae'i oglau o yn ddigon o ryfeddod.'

'Dowch at y bwrdd. Gwyneth, dos i nôl plât arall a chadair. Mi ro' i ddigon 'chydig i chi i gychwyn.'

Yr oeddynt i gyd wedi eu syfrdanu.

'Wedi i chi fyta hwnna, mi gewch bwdin reis, mi fydd hwnnw'n sgafnach i chi.'

'O, mae hwn yn dda.'

'Dyna chi rŵan, bytwch hwn,' ac estyn platiad o bwdin reis hufennog iddo.

Yna cawsant gwpanaid o de. Daeth ei liw yn ôl i wyneb Dici, lliw llwydaidd ddigon er hynny, a dechreuodd yntau grïo.

'O, diolch yn fawr,' meddai.

'Dyna chdi,' meddai'r tad, 'eistedd di'n llonydd wrth y tân rŵan, a mi gei ddweud dy stori wedyn.'

'Mae gen i stori am Jimi.'

'Hidia di befo Jimi rŵan, mi gawn ni dy stori di dy hun gynta.'

'Mae hi reit debyg i stori Jimi.'

Aeth Gwyneth ac Iwan â'r llestri bwyd i'r gegin bach i'w golchi. Yr oedd yr aelwyd yn gysurus, y ci a'r gath yn cysgu efo'i gilydd mewn basged, a'r gath â'i choes flaen dros wddf y ci. Dechreuodd Dici huno cysgu ac meddai'r wraig yn ddistaw wrth ei gŵr :

' 'Ddylsen ni fynd i ddweud wrth y plismon?'

Agorodd Dici ei lygaid a gweiddi :

'O, naci, naci! Mi fuo'r plismon yn tŷ ni am fod nhad a mam yn cwffio ac yn rhegi, ac mi ddaru o fy holi fi am yn hir, hir, yn frwnt, nes oeddwn i'n wag y tu mewn, a mherfedd i wedi dwad allan. A mi fuo y dyn Atal Creulondeb acw am nad oeddwn i'n cael digon o fwyd : mi fuo pethau'n well am ryw fis wedyn, ond maen 'nhw yr un fath eto.'

Aeth y tad a'r fam i'r gegin bach.

'Dos i dŷ Mrs. Elis, Tŷ Pella,' meddai'r wraig wrth ei gŵr, 'mae hi'n helpu'r dyn Atal Creulondeb.'

Yr oedd Bob Williams yn ôl mewn dau funud.

'Ydi, mae o'n dweud y perffaith wir. I lawr yng ngwaelod y dre mae o'n byw, mewn rhyw hen gwli.'

'Y creadur bach !'

Yr oedd pawb yn ôl wrth y tân a dechreuodd Ruth Williams holi.

'Wel, dwedwch rywbeth o'ch hanes rŵan. Bedi'ch enw chi?'

'Richard Edwards ydi fy enw iawn i, ond 'Dici Ned' mae pawb yn fy ngalw fi, a 'rydw i'n byw mewn rhyw hen gwli i lawr yng ngwaelod y dre, hen stablau oedd yno ers talwm.'

'O mi wn i,' meddai Iwan, 'i Ysgol Wernddu ydach chi'n mynd, a ninnau i Ysgol Bron y Coed, dyna sut oedden ni ddim yn ych nabod chi.'

'Ia, a 'dydw i ddim yn chwarae pêl-droed.'

'Felly, 'does gen ti neb yn byw drws nesa iti,' ebe'r tad.

'Nac oes, neu mi fasai'r dyn Atal Creulondeb acw yn amlach o lawer.'

'Ydach chi ddim yn cael cinio yn yr ysgol?' gofynnodd y fam.

'Dim ond weithiau, pan fydd gin mam bres; mae hi a nhad yn mynd i'r dafarn bob nos, wedyn 'does ganddyn' nhw byth bres, er bod y ddau'n gweithio. 'Ches i ddim ond clwff o fara a margarîn i ginio heddiw.'

'Oes gynnoch chi frodyr a chwiorydd?'

'Dwy chwaer. Mae'r ddwy wedi priodi ac yn byw yn bell, rywle yn Lloegr.'

'Fyddwch chi'n clywed oddi wrthyn 'nhw?'

'Bydda' weithiau, ond mae mam yn agor y llythyr, ac mi fydda i'n cael presant gin Nel, crys neu rywbeth felly, ond mae mam yn i werthu o.'

' 'Does gynnoch chi ddim digon amdanoch heno.'

Ni ddywedodd Dici ddim.

'Ella y buasai Wil y Teiliwr yn torri hen dopcot i Iwan i'ch ffitio chi. Dim ond deg ydi Iwan, a mi'r ydach chi mor fychan. Mi gawn ni weld.'

'Roeddech chi'n dweud ych bod chi'n sgwennu storis,' meddai Gwyneth.

'Ydw, ond mi'r ydw i'n gorfod i cuddio nhw.'

'Pam?'

'Am fod mam yn meddwl y dylwn i fynd i werthu papurau newydd hyd y stryd. Fedrwn i ddim rhedeg o ddrws i ddrws. 'Rydw i'n rhy wan.'

'Am be mae'r stori?' gofynnodd Gwyneth.

Yna dechreuodd llygaid Dici loywi.

*   *   *   *

' 'Roedd yna hogyn bach tlawd, tlawd, a'i enw fo oedd 'Jimi,' a'i dad a'i fam o'n gas iawn wrtho fo, a dyma fo'n penderfynu rhedeg i ffwrdd. 'Roedd o'n darllen lot o lyfrau ac wedi dwad i wybod bod yna lot o lefydd crand yn y byd yma, dim ond inni ddwad i wybod amdanyn' nhw. A roedd o wedi breuddwydio ryw noson fod yna blas mawr ar ochr rhyw fynydd heb fod ymhell o'r pentre lle'r oedd o'n byw, plas lle'r oedd yno lestri aur, gwlâu a dillad sidan arnyn' nhw, gerddi mawr a phob dim yn tyfu yno, a bwyd da.

Rhyw noson dyma fo'n cychwyn ar ôl yr ysgol i chwilio am y plas yma. 'Roedd o'n hollol siŵr y basai o'n dwad o hyd iddo fo, achos 'roedd o wedi'i weld o yn i freuddwyd. 'Roedd i ddillad o'n flêr, a darn o'i grys o fel cynffon allan drwy du nôl i drywsus o. 'Roedd o reit hapus am i fod o wedi dechrau gwneud y peth oedd arno fo eisio'i wneud ers talwm, a 'roedd o'n mynd trwy'r dre tan gamu. Ond wedi dwad allan i'r wlad mi stopiodd! 'Roedd arno fo ofn. 'Doedd yna neb yn unman, a mi ddechreuodd deimlo'n wan, achos 'doedd o ddim wedi cael bwyd er ganol dydd yn yr ysgol, a 'roedd o wedi methu byta dim llawer o hwnnw, achos yr oedd o'n sâl o hyd. Ydach chi'n gweld, 'doedd o'n cael dim ond tamaid bach o frecwast, wedyn mi'r oedd cinio'r ysgol yn i wneud o'n sâl. Beth bynnag, mi gerddodd dipyn wedyn, a mi welodd oleuni mewn ffenest, ond 'doedd o ddim yn licio mynd i mewn. Ffarm oedd yno, a mi aeth i ryw hoywal, ac mi'r oedd gwair ar lawr yn honno. 'Roedd o mor wan fel i bod hi'n bleser gorwedd ar y gwair, ac mi gysgodd yn sownd. Mi ddeffrodd yn y nos gan fod yno sŵn gwichian a rhedeg, a mi gesiodd mai llygod mawr oedd yno. 'Doedd ganddo fo ddim matsen i edrach, a dyma fo'n dweud wrth y llygod: 'Cerwch i'ch gwlâu i gysgu.' A wir, mi wrandawodd y llygod. Mi gafodd lonydd i gysgu nes daeth rhyw ddyn yno yn y bore. Y ffarmwr oedd o. Dyma'r ffarmwr yn dweud:

'Be wyt ti yn da yn fanma?'

'Ar fy nhaith yr ydw i,' meddai Jimi.

'Taith, wir, yn yr ysgol mae dy le di.'

'Peidiwch â dweud wrth neb. Chwilio am ryw blas ydw i.' Maen' nhw'n perthyn i mi.'

Dyma'r tro cynta erioed i Jimi ddweud celwydd.

'Plas,' meddai'r ffarmwr, ' a dy grys di allan trwy ben ôl dy drywsus di.'

'Ia, dyna pam yr ydw i'n chwilio am y plas, i edrach ga' i drywsus arall.'

'Oes gen ti fatsus arnat, beth pe tasat ti'n rhoi'r lle yma ar dân?'

' 'Does gen i ddim ceiniog ar fy helw i brynu matsus.'

'Pryd ces di fwyd ddwaetha?'

'Adeg cinio ddoe.'

Aeth â fo i'r tŷ.

'Nel,' meddai wrth ei wraig. 'Gwna damaid o frecwast i'r hogyn yma.'

'O ble yn y byd . . ?' meddai hithau a stopio, wrth weld yr olwg druenus ar Jimi.

' 'Rŵan,' meddai'r ffarmwr, 'byta di reit harti a dos yn 'dôl adre.'

'Ydi'ch tad a'ch mam yn gwybod ych bod chi'n crwydro fel hyn?' gofynnodd y wraig.

' Y nhw sydd wedi fy ngyrru fi.'

A dyna'r ail gelwydd. Cafodd gig moch ac ŵy, bara saim a digon o frechdan. 'Roedd o'n teimlo y medrai o fynd am ddiwrnod cyfa heb ddim bwyd. Dyma fo'n ail gychwyn, a chyfarfod â phlant yn mynd i'r ysgol, ac yn dweud wrtho'i hun: 'Dim cinio ysgol i mi heddiw, na slap, na dril.' 'Roedd yn gas gan Jimi ddril, achos 'roedd o'n rhy wan i neidio, a 'roedd arno fo gwilydd tynnu'i ddillad ucha am fod i ddillad isa fo mor fudr a mor rhacslyd. Mi gerddodd yn hapus trwy'r wlad nes daeth o i olwg mynydd uchel, a 'roedd o'n meddwl i fod o'n gweld tŷ mawr ar i ochr o. Beth bynnag, dyma fo'n troi o'r ffordd bost ac yn dechrau dringo'r mynydd. Ond ddaru o ddim cysidro nad oedd yna ddim tŷ i gael bwyd ar y mynydd, dim ond defaid a gryg a cherrig. A dyma eisio bwyd yn dechrau arno eto. Mi'r oedd yno ffrwd bach o ddŵr glân, ac mi wnaeth gwpan efo'i ddwylo, yfed peth o'r dŵr a theimlo'n well. Mi orweddodd ar y mynydd am dipyn ac edrach i'r awyr, a dweud wrtho fo'i hun: 'Yn fancw mae Duw yn byw. Tybed ydi o'n fy ngweld i rŵan? Os ydi o, mi wneith O fy helpu fi, a dweud wrtha i ble i roi fy nhroed, nes bydda 'i wedi cyrraedd y plas.'

Ail gychwyn wedyn, a'r cerrig yn brifo'i draed o; hen sgidiau sâl oedd gynno fo. Weithiau mi ddôi i ddarn bach lle'r oedd grug, ac mi 'roedd o'n licio clywed i draed yn crensian ar y grug. Ond O! dyma fo'n gweld rhywbeth yn symud ar y gwelltglas, a beth oedd yno ond neidr fawr.

('Ych!' meddai Gwyneth.)

74

A mi ddechreuodd y neidr chwythu a symud, ac 'roedd i chorff hi'n mynd fel tonnau'r môr, a 'doedd waeth faint oedd o yn i redeg, 'roedd y neidr yn gynt na fo. 'O Dduw,' meddai o, 'beth wna i?' Ar hynny dyma lot o bobol bach tua chwe modfedd o daldra yn dwad o gwmpas y neidr ac yn tynnu'i llygad hi oddi ar Jimi.

' 'Wneith hi ddim byd i chi rŵan,' meddai un o'r bobol bach. 'Ewch chi yn ych blaen i'r plas.'

'Yn lle ca'i gysgu heno?' meddai yntau.

'Cysgwch chi ar y ddaear, a mi fyddwn ni o'ch cwmpas chi.'

Ac felly fu. Mi aeth Jimi i gysgu yng nghysgod carreg fawr ar y grug, a'r bobol bach yn dawnsio o'i gwmpas ac yn canu.

'Cysga di, ein plentyn aur,
Daw'r plas i'r golwg 'fory.'

'Doedd neb wedi i alw'n blentyn aur o'r blaen. Erbyn y bore 'roedd y bobol bach wedi mynd, ac 'roedd yna gylch o fwsog gwyrdd golau o'i gwmpas. 'Doedd arno fo ddim eisio bwyd, ond 'roedd o'n poeni nad oedd o ddim yn cael 'molchi. 'Doedd ganddo fo ddim i sychu'i wyneb. Ond meddyliodd y cai o fwy o groeso yn y plas os byddai 'i wyneb yn fudr. Mi fuasent yn siŵr o gredu 'i stori. Cerddodd am hir iawn, a thoc dyma'r plas i'r golwg. Ond 'roedd yno lot fwy o ffordd nag oedd o wedi'i feddwl. Mi aeth gwadnau'i sgidiau o yn dyllau, ac mi benderfynodd y medrai gerdded yn well hebddynt. Ond O! 'roedd i draed o'n fudr a'i sanau'n dyllau i gyd.

Cerddodd trwy giât fawr y plas, giât â lliwiau aur arni hi, ac i fyny at ddrws y ffrynt a chanu'r gloch. Daeth dyn tal i'r drws â dillad gwyrdd amdano wedi'i trimio efo brêd aur.

'Dowch i mewn,' meddai'r dyn, ' 'rydyn ni wedi bod yn disgwyl amdanoch chi ers talwm.'

Mi aeth â fo i rŵm fawr lle'r oedd yna lot o bictiwrs o

75

ferched a dynion, y merched efo gyddfau a brestiau noeth, a'r
dynion efo gwallt hir. 'Roedd y rŵm yn dywyll braidd ond toc
mi welodd Jimi ddynes glws yn dwad ato.

'Fy mhlentyn bach i,' meddai hi a'i gusanu.

'Roedd ganddi hi ffrog neis ac yr oedd oglau da arni.
Canodd gloch a dyma ddyn yn dwad.

'Ewch â fo i gael bath, Richard,' meddai hi, a dyma fynd
â Jimi i'r bathrwm a'i olchi mewn dŵr cynnes braf a lot o
sebon oglau da. 'Doedd Jimi 'rioed wedi cael bath o'r blaen.
Wedyn mi 'roth y dyn yma ddillad neis amdano fo, crys sidan
gwyn, a mynd â fo i rŵm arall a rhoi bwyd iddo fo mewn
llestri â blodau clws arnyn' nhw ac ymyl aur.'

                    *   *   *   *

'Ac mi fuo'n hapus byth wedyn,' meddai Gwyneth.
'Naddo.'
'Naddo?'
'Naddo. Ydach chi'n gweld, 'roedd o'n cael digon o bob
peth, ond 'doedd o ddim yn medru mwynhau dim byd. 'Roedd
ganddo fo ddigon o bres poced, ond 'doedd yno ddim siop i
gwario nhw, ond ambell dro pan fydden' nhw'n mynd â fo yn
y car i lawr i'r dre. Ond 'doedd pres poced yn dda i ddim
iddo fo. 'Roedden' nhw wedi rhoi wats *aur pur* iddo fo, wedi
rhoi pob math o ddillad. Tasa fo'n prynu pêl, 'doedd yno neb
i chwarae pêl efo fo. A 'doedd yno ddim ysgol. Dim ond rhyw
ddyn yn dwad i roi gwers iddo fo bob dydd yn llyfrgell y tŷ.
'Roedd y dyn yn glên ond 'doedd yna ddim hogyn yn eistedd
wrth i ochr o i siarad yn ddistaw efo fo nac i ffraeo na chwffio.
'Doedd yno ddim tîm pêl-droed i chwarae. Ond yn waeth na
dim 'doedd yna ddim clas, na neb i gystadlu efo fo. Felly
'doedd o byth yn cael pleser o fod ar dop y clas. Wrth gwrs,

'doedd o ddim ar i waelod o 'chwaith. Felly, 'doedd yna ddim byd yn rhoi hwb iddo fo ddysgu. A mi'r oedd arno fo hiraeth am y pentre lle'r oedd o wedi'i fagu. Felly mi benderfynodd fynd yn ôl adre.'

'O, hen dro,' meddai Ruth Williams yn siomedig.

'Cyw a fegir yn Uffern . . . ,' meddai ei gŵr.

Edrychodd Dici arno heb ddeall yr ymadrodd.

'Beth ddigwyddodd wedyn?' gofynnodd Iwan.

' 'Dydw i ddim wed'i llawn orffen hi eto, ond fel hyn y bydd hi. 'Roedd y wraig ('doedd ganddi hi ddim gŵr) yn ddigalon iawn pan ddywedodd Jimi i fod yn mynd, ac mi'r oedd Jimi dipyn yn ddigalon, achos 'roedd o wedi dechrau licio'r bobol. Pan ddaeth o adre, mi gafodd dafod iawn gan i fam am ddengid. 'Roedd y plismyn wedi bod yn chwilio amdano fo, ac yn gas iawn wrtho fo am roi cymaint o drafferth iddyn' nhw. Ond 'roedd ganddo fo un cysur, 'roedd pobol y plas wedi dweud wrtho fo, os byddai o mewn unrhyw drwbl, am iddo fo ddwad yn ôl atyn' nhw. 'Roedd yno grïo mawr wrth ffarwelio. Mi wrthododd Jimi adael iddyn' nhw ddwad i'w ddanfon o yn y car, er mwyn iddo fo ddysgu'r ffordd yn iawn, petai arno fo eisiau myned yn ôl.

'A 'rydw i'n meddwl y gwna'i roi i mewn yn y stori fod y car wedi dwad at y tŷ ryw ddiwrnod, a Jimi wedi'i weld o drwy'r ffenest, a mi gafodd ddillad crand ganddyn' nhw, a maen' nhw am ddwad eto cyn y Nadolig. Ond mae Jimi yn poeni dipyn. Mae arno fo ofn iddyn' nhw ddwad yno i'w nôl i fynd yn ôl efo nhw am dipyn am wyliau, a gwneud rhyw dric i gadw fo yno am byth. 'Rydw i'n methu gwybod sut i'w diweddu hi.'

'Mi wn i,' meddai Iwan, 'gwneud i Jimi fynd at y plismyn ymlaen llaw i ddweud wrthyn' nhw am ddwad i'r plas i nôl o, os bydd fwy na hyn-a-hyn o 'cartre.'

'Mae'n gas gen i blismyn, mi ga'i feddwl am y peth eto. 'Rydw i'n meddwl mai gwneud iddo fo wrthod wna i. Beth petasen' nhw yn i ladd o'

'Problem eto,' meddai Gwyneth.

'O mae Jimi yn siŵr o'i setlo hi,' ebe Dic ' 'roedd o'n un da am wneund problemau yn y wers syms yn yr ysgol.'

Wedi dweud hynny, syrthiodd yn ôl yn ei gadair yn llipa flinedig, a brwdfrydedd ei adroddiad o'r stori wedi mynd. Daeth gwrid i'w wyneb a dechreuodd grïo eto.

'Mi wnawn ni paned eto,' meddai Ruth Williams, a phawb o'r teulu yn cytuno. Ond yr oedd asbri Dici wedi mynd.

'Rhaid imi fynd adre,' meddai'n ddigalon. 'Ga' i? Ga' i,' meddai, 'aros yma efo chi am byth?'

Edrychodd pawb ar ei gilydd, a'r tad wedyn yn edrych i'r tân.

'Ylwch chi, Dici,' meddai, 'os dowch chi yma i fyw efo ni, mi fedrai ych tad a'ch mam ddweud ein bod ni wedi'ch dwyn chi, a mi allen' fynd â ni i'r llys, a'n cosbi ni.'

'Na, mi fasen yn falch o gael gwared ohona i.'

'Ella, ond os basen' nhw yn gweld siawns i wneud arian, mi fasen' yn mynd â'r achos i'r llys. Ond dwedwch petasai arnom ni ych eisio chi yma am byth, mi fasai'n rhaid inni fynd at y twrna a seinio papurau i ddweud ein bod ni am ych cymryd chi am byth, rhag i'ch tad a'ch mam fynd â chi oddi yma. A wyddoch chi, ella na fuasech chi ddim yn hapus yma, ac y basai arnoch chi ych hun eisio mynd oddi yma.'

'Dydw i'n dallt dim am bethau fel 'na, ond 'rydw i'n gwybod y baswn i wrth fy modd yma.'

Dyma Ruth Williams yn clepian ei dwyo.

'Mae gen i gynllun,' meddai hi, 'mi geith Dici ddwad yma bob nos yr adeg yma i gael pryd iawn o fwyd efo ni, ac aros yma wedyn i wneud i dasgau efo Gwyneth ac Iwan.'

'Ac i sgwennu storis,' ebe Dici â sêr ei lygaid yn edrych ar y tebot.

'A mi dreiwn ni rywsut dalu am ginio'r ysgol i chi ambell ddiwrnod, beth bynnag.'

'Mi fedr Iwan a minnau roi tipyn o'n pres poced at y cinio,' meddai Gwyneth.

'Mi a'i i lawr at y prifathro i weld fedar Dici gael help at hynny,' meddai Bob Williams.

'P'run oedd y broblem fwya,' ebe Iwan, 'problem Dici a'i problem Jimi?'

Chwarddodd Dici wrth ben ei baned te.

'A dowch yma bob Sul i ginio a the,' meddai Ruth Williams.

' 'Does gen i ddim dillad,' meddai Dici.

'Hitiwch chi befo'r dillad, ella y bydd yma rai ar ôl Iwan.'

A mi molcha i yn lân, ond 'cha' i ddim bath fel Jimi.'

Chwarddodd pawb.

'A dowch yma ddydd Nadolig,' meddai Bob Williams.

'O ia,' meddai Gwyneth.

'A stori newydd efo chi,' meddai Iwan.

'O diolch yn fawr, a diolch am heno. 'Wna i byth anghofio.'

'Na ninnau, cariad,' meddai'r fam.

Gwrthododd Dici i neb ei ddanfon adre. Yr oedd y lle mor fler. Ond nid oedd arno ofn nos na'i dad a'i fam heno.

GOBAITH

Petai rhywun yn cynnig canpunt y munud hwnnw i Sal Huws
am ei meddyliau, ni allai ddweud yn syth beth oeddynt, gan
eu bod yn rhedeg groes ymgroes ar draws ei gilydd yn ei myfyrdodau, ac ar ddau wastad, gwastad ei pherthynas â Huw ei
gŵr, a gwastad ei pherthynas ag Iolo ei bachgen pedair oed, a
oedd yn ddau wastad gwahanol iawn. Gwastad o fân ffraeo
draenogaidd, didor-derfyn oedd y gwastad lle'r oedd Huw, a
gwastad o dangnefedd addoli oedd y gwastad lle'r oedd Iolo.

Yr oedd yr olygfa lle y meddyliai y pethau hyn yn un ryfedd.
Y cae bach wrth ochr y tŷ, a hithau'n eistedd yno ar fainc, yn
gafael yn y rhwymyn lledr oedd am ganol Iolo, Sam y gath
wrth ei hochr, Pero'r ci wrth ei hymyl ar lawr, ac yn gorwedd
ar ganol y cae, y mochyn, ei gefn yn fudr a'i fol yn wyn.

Yr oedd haul haearnaidd Gorffennaf yn disgyn arnynt. Buasai
yn y pentre efo Iolo onibai am y gwres caled yma. Pwnc ei
myfyrdodau oedd ei bywyd hi ei hun ers pum mlynedd a rhagor.
Rhyfedd cyn lleied o amser a gymerai iddi redeg dros y cyfnod
yn ei meddwl, a rhyfedd cymaint o bethau mawr oedd wedi
digwydd yn yr amser. Wedi cael plentyn ar ôl disgwyl amdano
am ddeuddeng mlynedd ar ôl priodi, ac wedi ei gael darganfod
nad oedd yn iawn, fod ei feddwl yn wan. Yr oedd ei chof o
gael y newydd gan y meddyg mor glir â'r noson y cafodd ef;
y llinellau yn sefyll allan fel patrwm edafedd gwawn. Rhoes y
meddyg y newydd yn blwmp ond nid yn blaen, ac ychwanegu
y gallai'r plentyn ymhen amser ddyfod yn gryfach, gorff a

meddwl. Diflannodd fel cysgod o'r tŷ wedi dweud, a Sal yn clywed y gwaed yn mynd i lawr oddi wrth fôn ei gwallt dros ei hwyneb, hithau'n disgyn ar lawr. Huw yn rhedeg i'w chodi a nôl cwpanaid o ddŵr iddi. Yna digwyddodd peth rhyfedd. I'w hysbryd fe ddaeth rhyw deimlad fel dŵr codi ar ffordd sech. Yr oedd y babi yno ac yn fyw. Yr oedd wedi ei anwylo er dydd ei eni, ond yn awr gwelai ef yn drysor i'w anwylo fwy, i'w foli fel duw bach, i'w ddandlwn a'i ymgeleddu. Cododd ef o'i grud a'i wasgu yn ei chesail, a'i gusanu, a'i gŵr yn edrych yn hurt arni.

'A dyma beth gawson ni ar ôl aros am ddeuddeng mlynedd, plentyn heb fod yn gall,' meddai Huw.

'Taw,' meddai hithau, 'â siarad mor amrwd. Paid â sôn am blentyn heb fod yn gall. Glywaist ti beth ddwedodd y doctor — y bydd o'n cryfhau ymhob ffordd fesul tipyn. Mwya'n y byd o ofal sydd ar y peth bach i eisio.'

'Mi fasa'n well tasa fo wedi cael marw wrth i eni.'

'Na fasa,' (yn boeth) 'na fasa. Sbïa gymaint o bleser mae o wedi i roi inni'n barod. Yn trysor ni ydi o.'

'I chdi, ella, ond nid i mi. 'Dydi o'n gwneud dim ond crïo pan afaela i yn'o fo.'

'Clywed dy freichiau di'n wahanol y mae o.'

'Fedra'i mo'i anwylo fo.'

'Mi ddoi fel y cryfheith o.'

' 'Does dim arwydd cryfhau arno fo.'

Yr oedd y misoedd cyn geni'r plentyn wedi bod yn rhai hapus i Sal a Huw. Pan wybuant gyntaf fod gan Sal obaith magu, yr oeddynt fel dau blentyn eu hunain. Nid oedd neb arall erioed wedi disgwyl plentyn ond hwy, gallech dybio. Ef a lanwai eu meddyliau bob munud effro o'u bywyd. Ni fyddai Sal yn stopio gwau. Âi ymlaen gan ddangos ei gorchest fel plentyn, pan ddeuai rhywun yno. Cliriai Huw'r grât yn y bore cyn cychwyn am ei waith, a'i osod yn barod i'w gynnau, ac âi â phaned o de i Sal i'w gwely. Aent am dro ym min tywyllnos gyda'i gilydd fel dau gariad, a siaradent am y babi fel petai eisoes wedi cyrraedd. Os bachgen fyddai, Iolo fyddai ei enw. Os geneth, Branwen. Credai Huw y byddai'n blentyn clyfar, gan eu bod ill dau yn weddol hen, yr un fath â Joni Jones a gafodd dri dosbarth cyntaf yn ei radd; ond tybiai hi mai coel gwrach oedd hyn, er ei bod yn gobeithio fod y goel yn wir. Yr oedd hi am ei ddilladu cyn grandied ag y caniatâi modd. 'Cyn grandied ag y medrwn,' meddai yntau, 'petai'n rhaid inni wneud heb bethau ein hunain.' Âi'r ddau i'r tŷ i freuddwydio breuddwydion.

Yr oedd eu llawenydd yn berwi trosodd pan gafwyd geni gweddol hawdd a bachgen nobl. Galwyd ef yn Iolo; yr oedd Sal wedi penderfynu cael enw nad oedd yn bod yn yr ardal o gwbl. Ond ymhen rhyw ddeufis sylwodd hi nad oedd y babi yn ymateb rhyw lawer i'w amgylchfyd. Yr oedd ei lygaid yn fychain, a heb fod yn cymryd sylw o fawr ddim, ddim o'r lamp drydan hyd yn oed. Byddai'n wyllt ar byliau a methid ei dawelu, a dyma'r pryd y dechreuodd grïo pan gymerai ei dad ef yn ei freichiau. Byddai'n rheibus iawn am ei botel hefyd.

Yna fe ddaeth y siom fawr ymhen ychydig fisoedd wedyn pan ddywedodd y meddyg wrthynt. Newidiodd Huw yn hollol, ac aeth i'w wely y noson honno fel dyn wedi pwdu. Ac wedi pwdu yr oedd, wrth beth na phwy yr oedd yn anodd dweud. Penderfynodd Sal gysgu ar y soffa wrth ymyl Iolo yn ei grud. Ni chysgodd. Cododd Huw fore trannoeth, ond ni ddywedodd air wrth fwyta'i frecwast.

'Yli, Huw, rhaid inni gymryd ein tynged.'

'Tynged greulon iawn, rhaid bod un ohonon ni wedi pechu.'

' 'Waeth inni heb na sôn am bethau fel'na, ac oglau gwrachod arnyn' nhw. Mi ŵyr y doctoriaid mai rhyw anghaffael ar y corff yn rhywle ydi o.'

' 'Rwyt ti'n iawn, a 'rydw i'n gwybod mai treio gafael mewn brwynen i ffeindio rheswm yr ydw i wrth sôn am y coelion gwrachod yma. Ond pam 'roedd yn rhaid i bethau fel hyn ddigwydd i ni?'

'Fedrwn ni byth ddweud, rhaid inni i dderbyn o. 'Rydw i'n siŵr yr eith y peth bach mor annwyl yn ein golwg ni fel y bydd o fel unrhyw fachgen iawn.'

' 'Dwn i ddim. 'Roeddwn i wedi rhoi mryd ar hogyn clyfar.'

' 'Dydi plant clyfar ddim haws i'w magu nac yn fwy annwyl.'

Ond newidiodd Huw yn hollol. Aeth conglau ei geg i droi at i lawr a'i fwstas hefyd. Edrychai fel Tsinead ac mor sur â phot llaeth cadw. Ond am Sal, troes ei dywediad yn gywir; aeth Iolo mor annwyl ag unrhyw blentyn iawn yn ei golwg, yn fwy felly, oblegid fod ei wendid ef yn barod i dderbyn cryfder ei chariad hi. Amheuai'r cariad weithiau, mwy o dosturi efallai, oblegid fe'i câi ei hun o hyd ac o hyd yn mynd yn erbyn ffawd galed, ac yn meddwl beth petai fel plentyn arall, mor ddilychwin y byddai ei chariad tuag ato. Ond fesul tipyn, aeth ei thosturi mor gryf fel na allai ei alw'n ddim ond cariad.

Ar y cychwyn, poenai beth a ddywedai ei chymdogion. Byddai'n fêl ar fysedd rhai, yn achos cydymdeimlad i'r lleill. Ond penderfynodd nad oedd am sylwi ar ymateb pobl. Yn ôl ei breuddwyd cyn geni Iolo penderfynodd gael y pethau gorau iddo. Gwelodd hysbyseb mewn papur am goets bach ail-law, gan rywun y gwyddai amdani, dynes gefnog. Yr oedd cystal â newydd, nid hen ledr caled oddi mewn iddi, ond lledr mor ystwyth â maneg cid. Prynodd hi a phrynodd gantel sidan, liw hufen i'w rhoi drosti yn yr haf. Pan âi i lawr i'r pentref, troai pobl i edrych arni, ond ni wyddai pa un ai at y goets yr edrychent ai disgwyl cael cip ar y babi. 'Piti na fuasai wedi cael marw,' meddai un. 'Mi gewch weld y daw o'n well.' meddai un arall. 'Mae o'n beth bach annwyl iawn, ac yn gysur,' meddai un arall. Dim gwahaniaeth os oeddynt yn rhagrithio.

Fel y prifiai'r babi, ceisiai Huw ymddiddori ynddo, ond yr oedd ef yn dioddef o hyd oddi wrth yr ysgytiad cyntaf. Edrychai arno bob gyda'r nos wedi dyfod o'i waith. Ceisiai ei ddenu trwy wneud sŵn anifeiliaid, ond ni thyciai dim. Troai Huw i ffwrdd oddi wrtho fel cath yn synhwyro'i bwyd ac yn ei adael. Nid bod y babi yn cymryd llawer o sylw ohoni hithau ychwaith, ond yr oedd hi yn ei garu fel yr oedd, a heb fod yn disgwyl ymateb. Yr oedd o'n blentyn iddi hi, ac yr oedd hynny'n ddigon iddi. Aeth Huw yn fwy cuchiog a checrus a gwelai fai yn rhywle o hyd; a'r babi a gâi'r bai yn y pen draw. Un prynhawn, aethai Sal am dro i'r mynydd efo'r goets bach. 'Roedd hi wedi cael rhyw syniad y buasai awyr iach yn gwneud Iolo yn debycach i blant eraill. Eisteddodd ar garreg a Iolo yn dawel yn ei goets yn yfed yr awyr iach, debygai hi. Yr oedd mor braf wrth gael edrych ar blu'r gweunydd yn ysgwyd. Disgwyliai y byddai Iolo yn sylwi arnynt. Arhosodd ac arhosodd, ac erbyn iddi gyrraedd adref, yr oedd Huw yno o'i blaen. 'Mi es i ag Iolo am dro i'r mynydd (siaradai amdano erbyn hyn, ac yntau'n ddwyflwydd oed, fel petai'n fachgen mawr yn ei lawn dwf ac yn bartner iddi); dyma'r tro cyntaf i hyn ddigwydd.'

'Nid dyma'r tro diwaetha, tra byddi di'n moli'r hogyn yma.'

Brysiodd wneud y bwyd. Gwyddai ei bod ar fai yn esgeuluso Huw, ond yr oedd bod yng nghwmni Iolo wedi mynd yn drech na hi, rhwng disgwyl iddo wella a'i chariad tuag ato.

'Mae'n ddrwg gen i, Sal.'

'Am beth?'

'Am imi gwyno ynghylch y bwyd.'

'Twt, anghofia fo.'

84

Dechreuodd ef wneud sŵn crïo.

'Mi fasa'n dda gen i fedru i garu o fel 'rwyt ti, ond fedra'i ddim.'

'Biti. Mi fasa'n bywyd ni'n mynd yn ôl i'r fel yr oedd o, pan oedden ni yn i ddisgwyl o. Amser braf oedd hwnnw.'

'Ia, 'roedd peidio â gwybod yn obaith y pryd hwnnw.'

'Mae o'n obaith o hyd.'

'Wela i ddim arwydd o hynny.'

Ond yn wir, ymhen ychydig, wrth gael ei olchi dangosodd Iolo ei fod yn medru sefyll ar ei draed, a cherddodd at ei dad a rhoi ei bwysau ar ei lin. Edrychodd Huw arno a gwenu.

'Piti na fuasai'n siarad eto,' meddai'r tad.

'Mi ddaw hynny hefyd.'

'Os daw o, mi awn ni at brifathro'r ysgol newydd yna i ofyn gaiff o fynd yno.'

'Mi fydd yn llawn digon buan ymhen dwy flynedd. Dim ond tair oed ydi o.'

Rhoes hi ei ddillad nos amdano a'i gerdded i fyny i'r llofft, ei chalon yn ysgafnach nag y buasai o gwbl. Ni siaradai Huw yn frwdfrydig iawn wedi iddi ddyfod i'r gegin; ni cheid fawr ddim ganddo ond y dymuniad i Iolo fedru siarad. Hynny fuasai yn dangos fod ganddo ddeall, yn ei dyb ef.

Aeth Sal ato a'i gusanu.

'Huw, treia weld gwelliant eto yn'o fo.'

'Mi fydda'i ar ben fy nigon pan ddwedith o rywbeth.'

Yr oedd blwyddyn er hynny, ac âi hithau dros y pethau hyn i gyd yn y gwres yn y cae bach y prynhawn yma. Yr oedd pob man yn ddistaw, ac eithrio bod y mochyn yn rhoi ambell rochiad, a bod yr eithin yn clecian. Yr oedd ei meddwl yn anniddig iawn. Poenai ei bod hi a Huw wedi mynd mor bell oddi wrth ei gilydd, ac eto, ofnai i Huw ddyfod i ennill serch

Iolo i gyd ac iddi hithau ei golli. Ofnai i Iolo farw. Beth a wnâi hi wedyn heb ei gariad. Meddwl beth petai hi ei hun yn marw, ac y buasai'n rhaid i Iolo fynd i ryw gartref lle na châi dosturi na chariad. Poenai hefyd fod Iolo mor grïog, mewn tymer ddrwg mor aml, ac yna mor serchus. Poenai ei fod mor hir yn dysgu rheoli gweithgareddau ei gorff, er bod hynny'n dyfod yn araf. Yr oedd yn rheibus hefyd. Ond ceisiai ei chysuro ei hun y buasai'n medru ei reoli ei hun gyda'r pethau hyn ymhen tipyn, yr un fath ag y dysgodd gerdded. Yr oedd ei phen yn un pwll tro o feddyliau pryderus. Cusanodd Iolo, achos hyn i gyd. Yng nghanol hyn edrychodd ddeugain mlynedd i'r dyfodol, a gallai glywed rhywrai'n pasio'r tŷ ac yn dweud:

'Ydach chi'n cofio Sal Huws yn byw yn fan'ma? 'Roedd gynni hi hogyn bach heb fod yn iawn. Beth ddaeth ohono fo tybed?'

Yn ei ddweud yn ddilachar, fel ffaith mewn papur newydd, a hithau heddiw yn gyforiog o bryder a phoen, na wyddent hwy ddim amdanynt; ei meddwl fel og ar gae tail. Ni wyddent am ei llawenydd ychwaith. Yna cymerodd ei meddwl drywydd arall. Yr oedd hi wedi cael blynyddoedd hir o fywyd hapus ar ôl priodi, ond hapusrwydd diofal mis mêl ydoedd. Cariad yn cynnwys gofal oedd ei chariad at Iolo, cariad â'i thu mewn yn brifo. Gallai weiddi fel Jeremeia, 'Fy mol, fy mol.'

Yna dechreuodd Iolo stwyrain. Tybiodd am eiliad ei fod ar fin cael pwl o dymer ddrwg. Gwnaeth sŵn yn ei wddf a phwyntio i gyfeiriad y mochyn.

'Ny—,' meddai, ac edrych ar ei fam. Pwyntiodd wedyn ar y mochyn.

'Nioch,' meddai'n groyw, a 'Nioch' wedyn a wedyn. Crïodd Sal o lawenydd; yr oedd wedi dweud rhywbeth o'r diwedd. Byddai Huw wrth ei fodd. Ar hyn, daeth gwraig y tŷ nesaf allan, a chamera yn ei llaw.

'Yr oeddwn i yn ych gweld chi mor hapus,' meddai, 'a meddyliais y baswn i'n licio tynnu'ch llun chi.'

Yn rhyfedd iawn, nid oedd Sal erioed wedi meddwl am dynnu llun Iolo. Tybiai, wedi i Iolo dyfu'n fawr na buasai'n hoffi ei weld ei hun, fel yr oedd yn awr.

'Pam yr ydach chi'n crïo, Sali?'

Eglurodd hithau. Cododd y gymdoges ei breichiau mewn llawenydd.

'O, mae'n dda gen i. Rhaid inni gael y llun yma i ddathlu'r amgylchiad.'

Yr oedd Iolo yn dal i bwyntio at y mochyn, a meddyliodd Sal y byddai'n cadw'r mochyn i farw o farwolaeth naturiol. Nid oedd mochyn a enynnodd y fath ebychiad yn haeddu cyllell y cigydd. Tybiai rŵan y byddai'r surni a'r ffrygydu rhyngddi hi a Huw drosodd, efallai, oni fyddai ei wenwyn at Iolo yn esgor ar ryw esgus arall dros beidio â'i garu. P'run bynnag, byddai'n rhaid iddi wynebu hyn a gobeithio. Yr oedd y bywyd mis mêl drosodd, a hyd yn oed os dangosai Huw ei wenwyn, yr oedd ganddi ofal; rhywbeth a roddai amcan i'w bywyd, yn lle rhyw wastadedd undonog o hapusrwydd.

DYCHWELYD

Cerddai'n ysgafn-galon i fyny'r lôn a âi oddi wrth ei thŷ gan ysgwyd ei basged negesi. Yr oedd yn hapus am ei bod wedi gorffen ei gwaith, ac edrychai ymlaen at gael noson o ddarllen wrth y tân. Daeth criw mawr o fechgyn ysgol i lawr y lôn; aeth hithau heibio iddynt heb gymryd sylw ohonynt. Wedi iddynt ei phasio dyma rai ohonynt yn ei dynwared fel y byddai yn eu rhwystro rhag mynd ar gefn eu beiciau ar lôn breifat. Dywedodd hithau y byddai yn anfon at eu prifathro i gwyno ynghylch eu hymddygiad. Ar hynny, dechreuasant weiddi'r iaith futraf a glywsai erioed, iaith ry fudr i'w hailadrodd. Aeth yn ei blaen dan blygu ei phen, ei chrib wedi ei dorri. Yn y dref yr oedd pobl ieuainc y siopau yn hynaws, ond ni allodd hynny leddfu dim ar ei dolur. Pan ddaeth adref eisteddodd ar gadair i synfyfyrio. Sylweddolodd nad oedd hi yn da i ddim erbyn hyn, dim ond rhyw hen greadur oedd yn destun gwawd i labystiaid o hogiau ysgol. Yn ei dyddiau hi yr oedd ysgol yn sefyll dros foneddigeiddrwydd. Erbyn heddiw nid oedd ddim gwell na chartref ciaridymod a'i hiaith yn iaith gwlad yn mynd i'r trueni. Yn lle darllen, aeth i dosturio wrthi hi ei hunan.

*   *   *   *

Cerddodd i fyny at y mynydd a gwelai'r tŷ â'r un ffenestr yn ei dalcen fel dyn unllygeidiog yn edrych ar y rhostir maith. Ysgydwai plu'r gweunydd yn yr awel, a hedai'r cornchwiglod o dwll i dwll. Cerddodd hithau i lecyn gwyrdd wrth ymyl y tŷ a cher twmpath o rug lle y buasai defaid yn pori, a gorwedd yno. Clywai Leusa Parri yn cerdded ôl a blaen o flaen ei thŷ yn ei chlocsiau dan ysgwyd pwcedi. Â chil ei llygad gwelai gorn carw'n tyfu'n gyd-wastad â'r ddaear trwy'r grug. Dechreuodd ei dynnu'n araf, dim ond er mwyn ymyrraeth, i weld a lwyddai i'w dynnu'n un darn cyfa. Nid oedd arni ddim o'i eisiau; tynnu er mwyn tynnu. Llwyddodd i gael darn hir a rhoes ef am ei gwddw. Cododd ar ei heistedd i chwilio am ruglus ond ni welodd yr un. Cystal hynny oblegid nid oedd ganddi lestr i'w dal. Cerddodd at odre tomen y chwarel i chwilio am redyn mynydd neu redyn chwarel. Yr oedd yno dipyn yn tyfu rhwng y crawiau dulas ac yn edrych yn ddigon digalon. Dywedasai ei mam wrthi am beidio â'i dynnu i geisio ei dyfu yn yr ardd wrth ymyl y botwm gŵr ifanc. Marw a wnâi yno am nad oedd yn hoffi ei le, meddai hi. Lle unig oedd o'n ei hoffi, a'i wreiddiau rhwng y crawiau. Cerddodd at y gamfa a mynd drosti i gael golwg ar y cwm lle'r oedd yr afon yn un llinyn llwyd difywyd fel petai wedi stopio rhedeg. Yr oedd yn filan wrth y cwm hwn pan ddarganfu ef gyntaf. Yr oedd hi wedi meddwl nad oedd dim yn y byd ond ei mynydd hi, y pentref a'r môr o'i flaen cyn belled ag y gallai weled. Siom iddi oedd gweld bod llefydd eraill yn bod. Eisteddodd wedyn, tynnu ei hesgidiau a'i sanau a rhoi ei thraed ar fwsog gwlyb.

Yr oedd y falwen yn yr ardd, un dew a bol gwyn ganddi. Dyma hi'n adrodd uwch ei phen:

'Malwen, malwen, estyn dy bedwar corn allan

Ne mi tafla'i di i'r Môr Coch at y gwartheg cochion.'

Dyma'i phedwar corn yn neidio allan fel pigau pennor. Rhaid ei bod yn hoffi'r pennill achos yr oedd hi'n edrych mor dalog. A hi, Annie, oedd wedi gwneud iddi ufuddhau.

Deuai o'r beudy i'r tŷ yn cario cath bach yn ei brat, y gath fawr yn ei dilyn. Rhoes y gath bach ar y bwrdd, a dyma hi'n cerddded yn wysg ei hochr at y lle'r oedd ei mam yn gwneud teisen does ar lechen las. Cyn y gellid ei rhwystro yr oedd hi'n sefyll ar y deisen. Wrth iddi hi a'i mam weiddi neidiodd y gath fawr ar y bwrdd. Dyma hi a'i mam yn dechrau chwerthin. Dywedodd ei mam y câi gadw'r gath bach gan nad oedd dim ond un y tro hwn, os gwnâi edrych ar ei hôl a gofalu mynd â hi i'r beudy i'w gwely bob nos.

Deuai hi a'i brodyr adref o'r ysgol drwy storm fawr o wynt a glaw. Yr oedd y glàw fel cynfas fawr lwyd resog o'u blaenau, a cherddent â'u pennau i lawr. Disgynnai'r dafnau glaw ar eu hwynebau, caeënt eu llygaid, ni allent dynnu ei hancetsi poced allan i'w sychu. Disgynnai'r dafnau oddi ar odre eu cotiau i mewn i'w hesgidiau. Pan ddeuai pwff o wynt yr oedd yn rhaid iddynt stopio a gafael yn ei gilydd. Yr oedd y filltir yn hir. Daeth y fam i gyfarfod â hwy tua hanner y ffordd efo cotiau, ond nid oedd ddiben eu rhoi drostynt. 'Rŵan, at y tân yna, a gollyngwch bob cerryn ar lawr.' Yr oedd mor anodd tynnu'r sanau gan eu bod wedi glynyd yn y croen efo'r glaw. Cymerodd eu mam liain a'u sychu o flaen y tân coch; yr ager yn mynd i fyny oddi wrth eu cyrff. Mor braf oedd y gwres ar ôl y gwlybaniaeth creulon ar eu crwyn. Estynnodd y fam ddillad isaf glân cynnes o'r popty bach, a rhoi eu siwtiau gorau amdanynt. Yna y powleidiau potes poeth wrth y bwrdd.

*   *   *   *

Yr oedd yn mynd eto at y mynydd. Yr oedd wedi penderfynu gwneud hyn cyn mynd i weld ei thad a'i mam. Mor braf fyddai eu gweld eto, cael sgwrs wrth y tân, a chael dweud wrthynt am yr hen hogiau rheglyd hynny. Gallai deimlo'n dalog efo'i rhieni, ac nid yn 'swp bach sbyblyd.' Chwiliodd am y llwybr ond ni allodd ei ganfod. Nid oedd dim i'w wneud ond cerdded drwy'r grug. Nid oedd defaid ar y mynydd ychwaith, felly nid rhyfedd nad oedd yno lwybr dafad. Yr oedd y tŷ yno o hyd efo dau lygad erbyn hyn. Yr oedd wedi anghofio dyfod ag anrheg i'w rhieni. Fe âi i'r tŷ i ofyn i Leusa Parri am furum gwlyb i wneud bara haidd. Erbyn iddi fynd yno, rhywun arall oedd yn byw yno, Saesnes, ni wyddai beth oedd burum gwlyb. Troes ei chefn a rhoi clep ar y llidiart. Aeth at y gamfa gan ddyheu am weld y cwm arall. Yr oedd y rhan fwyaf o'r tai wedi mynd a ffatri fawr yn sefyll yng nghanol y cwm. Brysiodd oddi ar y gamfa a rhedodd at y domen chwarel. Nid oedd sŵn llwyth yn disgyn oddi ar ben y domen. Edrychai'r crawiau'n hen, fel petaent wedi eu taflu yno ers blynyddoedd, yn glynu yn ei gilydd. Yr oedd yno ychydig blanhigion o redyn mynydd yn edrych yn fwy unig nag erioed. Yr oedd y môr o'i blaen fel erioed heb newid dim. Cofiodd fel y byddai'r athro yn yr ysgol yn dweud hanes Math a Gwydion a oedd yn byw wrth lan y môr, fel y byddent yn newid pethau efo'u hudlath. Gresyn. na fyddent yno rŵan i newid y mynydd i'r fel yr oedd ers talwm. Penderfynodd fynd i weld y ffrwd yr ochr isaf i'r ffordd. Yno yn ymddolennu trwy'r dŵr yr oedd un brithyll unig, yn troi'r dŵr yn donnau bychain wrth ben y graean gwyn. Syllodd arno'n hir; yna torrodd allan i ganu dros bob man:

'Ti, frithyll bach, sy'n chwarae'n llon
Yn nyfroedd oer yr afon.'

Yna fe'i cafodd ei hun yn beichio crïo wrth edrych ar y brithyll. Wrth ddyfod i fyny oddi wrth y ffrwd, baglodd a syrthiodd. Yr oedd ei phen glin yn gwaedu ac yn boenus. Meddyliodd am eiliad na allai byth gerdded i'w hen gartref. Ffeindiodd y gallai gyda herc. Wedi mynd i'r ffordd gwelodd griw o labystiaid o hogiau efo gwalltiau hir budr yn dyfod, yr un fath â'r hogiau ysgol a'i rhegodd. Cerddodd cyn nesed ag y medrai i'r clawdd, eithr daethant hwythau yn nes i'r clawdd, a meddai un ohonynt:

'Gwthiwch hi i'r wal i'r diawl, 'does dim eisio i beth hen fel hyn gael byw.'

'Wnewch chi ddim ffasiwn beth,' meddai llais rhyw ddyn y tu ôl iddynt, 'ewch adra i'ch gwlad ych hun. Rŵan, 'y ngenath i, cerddwch yn ych blaen, ac mi gerdda' inna y tu nôl i chi.'

Yr oedd wrth ei bodd fod rhywun wedi ei galw'n 'eneth' a hithau'n hen.

'Dyna chi,' meddai'r dyn, pan ddaethant i'r pentref, 'mi fyddwch yn iawn rŵan.'

Yr oedd tai, tai ymhobman. O'r diwedd, canfu ei hen gartref yn ymguddio rhwng dau dŷ.

Curodd yn ysgafn ar ddrws y portico, a rhoi ei phen i mewn yn y gegin cyn eu gau. Ciliodd y boen o'i phen glin yn sydyn. Yr oedd y gegin fel petai caenen o niwl drosti, ei thad a'i mam fel cysgodion yn ei ganol. Yr oedd eu hwynebau o liw pwti llwyd-wyrdd, eu bochau yn bantiau ac yn bonciau, eu gên a'u trwynau crwbi bron yn cyrraedd ei gilydd. Edrychent fel cartwnau ohonynt eu hunain. Eto medrai eu hadnabod. Yr oedd y tân yn isel yn y grât.

'Dyma hi wedi dwad o'r diwedd,' ebe'r tad.

'Mae hi wedi bod yn hir iawn,' ebe'r fam, 'a finna wedi dweud wrthi am frysio.'

'Mi ddois cynta y medrwn i. 'Roedd yna hen grymffastiau o hogiau ar y ffordd.'

Ni chymerodd yr un o'r ddau sylw o hynny.

'Mae'r bwyd yn dy ddisgwyl di ers blynyddoedd,' meddai'r fam; 'mi fytwn ni rŵan.'

Yr oedd yno gig oer, brechdan a the, ond nid oedd blas dim ar yr un ohonynt. Fesul tipyn cliriai'r niwl, ac fel y deuai'r gegin yn oleuach, deuai wynebau'r ddau yn fwy naturiol: codai'r pantiau. Daeth gwrid i fochau'r tad; aeth wyneb y fam yn llwyd naturiol. Daeth eu trwynau'n ôl i'w ffurf gynt. Aeth y tai o gwmpas y tŷ o'r golwg. Daeth y cae yn amlwg efo'r goeden a'r iâr a'r cywion. Daeth tân siriol i'r grât a goleuodd y gegin i gyd. Gwenai'r tad yn hapus; daeth tiriondeb glas i lygaid y fam.

'Gadwch i'r hen gig yna,' meddai hi, 'mae gen i deisen does.'

Tynnodd blatiad o'r popty bach, yn nofio mewn menyn.

Curodd y ferch ei dwylo.

'Fel ers talwm. Oes gynnoch chi siwgwr coch?'

'Dyna fo ar y bwrdd.'

'O, mae hi'n dda. Ydach chi'n cofio fy nghath bach i yn cerdded i'ch teisen does chi?'

'Ydw,' a chwarddodd y fam. 'Dim ond cofio sydd rŵan.'

'Ia.'

Yr oedd ar fin sôn am yr hen hogiau hynny a'u hiaith fudr, ond yr oedd mor hapus fel y penderfynodd beidio â sôn rhag tarfu ar y sgwrs.

'Ydach chi'n cofio, nhad, y moch yn dengid o'u cwt ganol nos ar wynt mawr gefn gaea', a chithau yn rhedeg ar eu holau hyd y weirglodd yn ych trôns?'

Chwarddodd y tri yn aflywodraethus.

Ydach chi'n cofio? Ydach chi'n cofio? a hithau ar fin gofyn Lle mae . . .? Lle mae . . .? Lle mae'r lleill?

Ond i beth y tarfai ar yr hwyl yma?

'Lle mae'ch pibell chi, nhad?'

' 'Dydw i ddim wedi cael smôc ers blynyddoedd. 'Does gen i ddim baco.'

Yr oedd ganddi sigarennau yn ei bag, ond beth a ddywedai ei mam pe tynnai hwy allan? Câi dafod iawn. Ond yr oedd rhoi pleser i'w thad yn fwy pwysig na chael drwg am bechod cudd.

'Hwdiwch,' meddai, 'rhowch ddwy o'r rheina yn ych pibell.'

Gwenodd y fam.

'Mi gymera' innau un,' meddai, 'rydw i'n cofio fel y byddai fy modryb yn dwad acw ac yn smocio pibell.'

'Beth nesa?' meddai Annie wrthi hi ei hun, mewn syndod agos i fraw; cymerodd hithau un.

A dyna lle'r oedd y tri yn smocio, mor hapus, mor hapus. Lle'r oedd y lleill? Lle'r oedd y lleill? Na, nid oedd am ofyn. Cyrliai mwg glas ysgafn i fyny i'r awyr. Aeth yr haul o'r golwg. Dechreuodd nosi. Dechreuodd eu hamrannau ddisgyn dros eu llygaid fel mewn cerflun. Aeth y tri i gysgu.

TORRI TRWY'R CEFNDIR

F'annwyl Margiad,

Mae'n debyg y synnwch gael llythyr gennyf mor fuan ar ôl imi eich gweld. Yr oedd yn garedig ynoch ddyfod i'm danfon yma ddoe i dŷ fy chwaer, ond yn hollol nodweddiadol o'ch caredigrwydd tuag ataf drwy'r pymtheng mlynedd y bûm yn byw yn Aberdwynant. Yn ystod yr amser yna dylwn fod wedi dweud wrthych am yr hyn a ddigwyddodd i mi cyn imi ddyfod i'ch tref i fyw. Bûm ar fin dweud wrthych lawer gwaith, ond gwyddwn y buaswn yn baglu ac yn hic-hacio wrth fynd ymlaen â'm stori, ac y buaswn yn rhoi'r argraff mai stori wneud oedd hi er mwyn cael cydymdeimlad. Fe aeth yr amser ymlaen, a minnau heb ei dweud, nes o'r diwedd teimlwn nad oedd werth ei dweud. Trennydd byddaf yn mynd i'r ysbyty i gael triniaeth fawr, ac ni wn beth a ddigwydd. Petawn yn marw, ac i chwithau glywed yr hanes wedyn, byddech wedi eich siomi ynof, ac yn methu deall pam na fuaswn wedi dweud yr hanes wrthych. Rhyw ofn swil oedd y rheswm. Digon posibl eich bod yn gwybod rhywfaint o'r stori, ond buoch yn ddigon call i beidio â holi, rhag ofn fy mrifo reit siŵr. Trwy ysgrifennu fel hyn, medraf beidio â hic-hacio, a gwneud fy meddwl yn gliriach, a thrwy hynny fod yn decach tuag at bawb.

Gwyddoch, wrth reswm, mai yn Abertraeth mewn ysgol yr oeddwn i cyn dwad i Aberdwynant, ac yno fe syrthiais mewn cariad â bachgen o'r un oed â mi, tua phump ar hugain. I bob golwg yr oedd yntau mewn cariad efo minnau. Os bu dau wedi gwirioni am ein gilydd erioed, y ni oedd y ddau. Fel y rhan fwyaf o gariadon teimlem nad oedd neb wedi bod mewn cariad o'r blaen ond y ni. Yr oeddwn mor hapus fel y gweithiwn yn galed drwy'r dydd er mwyn gweld y diwrnod yn gorffen ac y cawn fynd allan efo Tom. Yr oedd yn fachgen eitha golygus, canolig o ran taldra, gyda gwallt gwinau tonnog a llygaid glas. Wyneb hynaws yn llawn gwên yn wastadol. Dyna a'm denodd: ni ddeuai'r wên fyth i ffwrdd oddi ar ei wyneb. Yr oeddwn ormod mewn cariad i sylwi ar nodweddion ei gymeriad nac i geisio gweld beth oedd ymateb yr athrawon eraill iddo, a oedd yn hoff ganddynt neu ddim, ac ar y pryd ni buaswn yn malio pa'r un: y fi oedd piau o, ac ni buasai barn anffafriol yn cael dim effaith arnaf, oblegid pe baem yn priodi, y fi fuasai raid byw efo fo. Nid oeddwn ond pumb ar hugain ced, yr oed hwnnw pan mae popeth yn y radd eithaf, o ddaioni gan fwyaf, pawb yn neis, heb ddigon o brofiad o fywyd, i weld tyllau mewn cymeriadau, nac i weld tyllau mewn bywyd ei hun. Byddwn yn dyheu am weld diwrnod yn dirwyn i ben er mwyn cael mynd allan efo Tom, a'r ffordd orau a welais i weld dydd yn darfod oedd rhoi fy holl egni ar waith, ac nid breuddwydio.

Nid oeddwn yn hoffi cael fy mhryfocio gan fy mod yn meddwl nad testun pryfocio oedd caru. Gwyddwn fy mod yn hen ffasiwn yn hynny o beth. Wrth edrych yn ôl rŵan, mae'n debyg fy mod mor feddiannol o Tom fel na fedrwn rannu hwyl ar ei gorn. Byddwn yn teimlo hefyd mai gwastraff amser oedd mynd i barti lle byddai o yno, y byddai'n well inni fod allan ar ein pennau ein hunain. Ni byddai ganddo lawer i'w ddweud mewn cwmni. I mi, 'roedd hynny'n arwydd y buasai yntau'n hoffi bod allan efo mi. 'Rwyf yn barnu'n wahanol erbyn hyn. Treuliem y Sadyrnau yn cerdded y wlad a'r bryniau, a gorffen mewn rhyw dŷ bwyta bach clyd, lle y byddem yn sgwrsio nes dechreuai dywyllu, a cherdded adref, fy mynwes i, beth bynnag, yn ddigon hapus i ganu dros y wlad.

Ambell dro byddem yn ymweld â hen fodryb i Tom oedd yn byw ar ei phen ei hun mewn bwthyn ar lethr bryn, a chaem de a chroeso mawr ganddi. Teimlwn eisoes fy mod yn un o deulu Tom, er mai'r fodryb yma oedd yr unig un o'i deulu yr oeddwn wedi cyfarfod â hi. Yr oedd hi'n hynod glên, ac yn methu gwneud digon i mi. Y tro dwaethaf y buom yno meddyliwn nad oedd Tom mor gysurus ag arfer. 'Roedd mewn brys am gael mynd oddi yno. Fel yna y treuliem yr amser. Buom efo'n gilydd yn nhŷ fy chwaer Lil hefyd (lle yr wyf rŵan) yng Nghaer Afon. Braidd yn oeraidd oedd hi, ond mae hi yn cymryd tipyn o amser i fod yn hy efo pobl ddiarth, ac ni feddyliais fwy am y peth.

Un dydd Sadwrn yr oedd gan Tom bwyllgor athrawon yn Llan y Gaer a threfnasom i beidio â mynd i grwydro. Codais innau'n hwyr a chael brecwast yn fy ngwely. Daeth fy ngwraig lety â'r llythyrau i fyny, a synnais weld un oddi wrth Tom. Agorais ef yn frysiog, ac wedi ei ddarllen, deliais ef yn fy llaw gan geisio amgyffred ei gynnwys. Dweud yr oedd fod yn rhaid i'n carwriaeth ddwad i ben, ei fod wedi syrthio mewn cariad efo un arall o'r ysgol, Miss Griffith yr athrawes hanes. Wedi ei ddarllen, teimlwn fy mod yn berson arall yn perthyn i fyd arall. Pan ddaeth Mrs. Williams i fyny i nôl yr hambwrdd sylwodd nad oeddwn wedi bwyta dim. Dywedais nad oeddwn yn teimlo'n rhy dda. Nid oeddwn am iddi hi gael gwybod rhag ofn nad oedd y newydd yn wir, oblegid ni fedrwn gredu ei fod yn wir. Nid oeddem wedi cael ffrae nac unrhyw anghydfod. Ond yr oedd y llythyr yno o'm blaen yn mynegi'r ffaith. Gwisgais amdanaf tan grynu ac euthum i dŷ'r prifathro. Dywedais fy neges wrtho'n syml, yr hoffwn gael fy rhyddhau o'r ysgol ar unwaith. Dywedodd fod yn ddrwg iawn ganddo, ond na fedrai fy rhyddhau heb roi rhyw gymaint o rybudd er mwyn iddo gael rhywun arall. Dywedodd y byddai'n ddrwg iawn ganddo fy ngholli, ond ei fod yn gweld y byddai'r sefyllfa yn un gas gan fod y tri ohonom yn yr ysgol. Gelwais yn llety un o'm ffrindiau o blith yr athrawon ar fy ffordd yn ôl. Wedi iddi glywed y newydd, rhedodd i'r gegin, a chyn pen dim yr oedd yn ôl efo cwpanaid o goffi a brechdan blaen.

'Hwdiwch,' meddai, 'yfwch hwnna, 'rydach chi fel corff.'

'Rŵan,' aeth ymlaen, 'mae'n anodd iawn gwybod beth i'w ddweud. Mae'n ddrwg iawn gen i drosoch chi, ond os gwela i fai ar Tom Davies, mi fyddaf yn siŵr o'ch brifo chi, achos yr oeddech chi yn caru eich gilydd : y peth gorau ydi i mi beidio â dweuld dim. Mi awn ni am dro i Lan y Gaer y pnawn yma, dim iws i chi fod yn y tŷ yn synfyfyrio.'

Bu Miss Norton a minnau yn cerdded y strydoedd yn Llan y Gaer ac edrych ar ffenestri siopau. Aethom i dŷ bwyta bychan tywyll i gael te, ac fel y troem y gornel tuag ato, pwy a welem yn mynd yn y pellter ond Tom a Dela Griffith. Felly dyma lle'r oedd pwyllgor Tom. O drugaredd ni throesant i mewn i'r tŷ bwyta.

Wrth droi oddi wrth Miss Norton y noson honno, meddai hi : 'Gwn yn iawn y bydd yn gas arnoch ddydd Llun orfod wynebu pobl, ond wynebwch nhw heb falio. Mi fydd y peth yn hen newydd erbyn dydd Mercher; mi fydd wedi bod ac wedi mynd heibio. Os liciwch chi, mi ddweda i'r newydd wrth y lleill, er mwyn ysgafnu pethau i chi.'

Cytunais.

Sylw fy ngwraig lety wedi imi fynd i'r tŷ ydoedd : 'Twt, peidiwch â phoeni, mae mwy o bysgod yn y môr nag a ddaliwyd.' Sylw gwerinol dynes heb wybod fod caru yn garu ac yn beth o ddifrif i rai, nid yn rhyw foddion i gael gŵr.

Euthum i'r capel ddydd Sul, a'm meddwl ar yr un peth.

Meddwl amdano fel ffaith, ac nid ceisio chwilio am resymau dros iddo ddigwydd. Gweddïwn ynof fy hun am gael help i'w anghofio'n fuan, er fy mod yn gweld mai peth afresymol oedd dwad â pheth fel hyn i fyd crefydd, achos serch gwyllt, poeth oedd o, ac nid cariad byd crefydd.

Fe wynebais bobl ddydd Llun gyda mwy o hyder ar ôl i Mr. Ellis, yr athro hynaf, afael ynof yn dadol a dweud:

'Mae'n ddrwg iawn gen i drosoch chi, ond mi gewch chi weld, Ela, ymhen amser mai dyma'r peth gorau allai ddigwydd.'

Agorais fy llygaid, ond ni ddaeth esboniad.

'Peidiwch â bod mor ddigalon, cerddwch o gwmpas yr ysgol fel tasech chi'n malio dim, hynny fyddwch chi yma. Mae'n ddrwg gen i ych colli chi. Mi'r ydach chi'n werth deg o Dela Griffith: iâr bach yr ha' ydi hi, yn ddigon digri, yn arwynebol ddigri, ond 'does yna ddim gwaelod yn fanna.'

Ond yr oedd hi'n hardd; slasen o ddynes dal, bryd golau, gwallt cyrliog liw mêl, llygaid yr un lliw, a chorff fel helygen hydwyth yn cerdded y coridoriau fel brenhines, yn ddigri, a'i ha-ha yn atseinio yn y corneli. Cymerais gyngor Mr. Ellis, a cherdded o gwmpas heb gymryd arna' weld T.D. na D.G. Bu agos imi fwynhau'r wythnosau hynny. Ond bob nos yn y tŷ deuai fy meddwl i'r un fan — fy ngholled.

Cefais le yn Aberdwynant, heb fod yn rhy bell oddi wrth Lil, fy chwaer, ac yn ddigon pell oddi wrth Abertraeth rhag imi glywed dim oddi yno. Yr oedd Lil yn gysur i mi am yr ychydig amser y bûm yno. Dywedai hi nad oedd yn hoffi Tom, ac os oedd o wedi medru gwneud peth fel yna, y medrai wneud unrhyw beth pe baem yn priodi.

Pan ddeuthum i Aberdwynant gyntaf, teimlwn fel dynes wedi colli rhywbeth gwerthfawr ac yn chwilio amdano. Gwelais yn fuan y byddwn yn eitha hapus yn yr ysgol ac yn fy llety, ond yr oeddwn yn unig, hyd nes y gofynasoch chi imi ddyfod i swper y nos Sul hwnnw. Profais gysur cynnes eich tŷ a'ch croeso, ac yr wyf wedi dal i'w brofi am bymtheng mlynedd. Ni allaf ddweud fel yr wyf wedi gwerthfawrogi eich cyfeillgarwch a'ch caredigrwydd cyson; cael dyfod i'ch tŷ bryd y mynnwn heb ofni fy mod ar y ffordd. Eto, efallai pan fyddem ar ganol sgwrs ddifyr, fe redai fy meddwl yn ôl at Tom a'n sgyrsiau ni wrth ben y te yn y tai bwyta bach tu allan i Abertraeth. Dyna oedd cefndir fy mywyd yr holl amser, a pheth marw yw cefndir, ond yn ddigon byw i fod yn nam ar bob pleser a gawn.

Priododd Tom a Dela Griffith. Gwelwn mai peth da oedd fy mod wedi gadael Abertraeth. Buasai bod yno a'u gweld yn ŵr a gwraig yn fy lladd o genfigen. Ymhen peth amser cawsant blentyn. Gweld yr hanes yn y papur y byddwn. Am wythnosau wedyn byddwn yn dychmygu mai fi oedd mam y babi, a byddwn yn gweld Tom yn hoffus fel y byddai gynt, ond yn casáu ei wraig. Breuddwydiwn sut y buaswn yn trin y babi, yn ei ddandlwn, yn ei foli a'i gusanu. Yna deuai fy nghastell o freuddwydion yn deilchion i'r llawr. Ymhen ysbaid wedyn byddwn yn ei gasáu yntau, ac o'i gasáu ef, byddwn yn cyffredinoli ac yn dweud mai pethau fel hyn oedd dynion i gyd. Eithr deuwn ar draws dynion a hoffwn yn fawr a gwelwn beth mor ffôl oedd cyffredinoli. Nid yw teimladau rhywun yr un fath am ddau funud yn olynol. Mae posibiliadau pob sefyllfa yn annherfynol. Eto ni welwn feiau yn Tom, dim ond ei gasáu yn un cyfanswm am iddo fy lluchio.

Yna daeth syniad imi yr hoffwn gael cartref i mi fy hun. Fe wyddoch chi hanes prynu'r tŷ a'i wneud yn gartref, ond ni wyddoch y teimladau tu ôl i hynny. Yr oeddwn yn benderfynol o gael cartref del. Prynais ddodrefn hardd, ac wedi ymgartrefu, addolwn y tŷ. Yna gwadd fy ffrindiau yma. Byddwn yn syllu arno, a'i weld mewn goleuni arall, fel pe bawn yn gweld pob ystafell yn groes mewn drych, a thu cefn imi yn y cefndir byddai Tom yma efo mi. Yna dechreuais brynu dillad costus, mynd i'r lle drutaf i gael trin fy ngwallt, dim ond er mwyn anghofio. Ond nid oeddwn yn anghofio. Yr oedd yr holl bethau materol yno fel trysorau mewn drôr er mwyn cael edrych arnynt weithiau.

Gweithiwn gyda'r capel a chyda'r Urdd. Bûm yn ysgrifennydd i'r peth yma a'r peth arall, ond nid oedd fy nghalon mewn dim a wnawn.

Pan oeddwn yn aros gyda Lil ar fy ngwyliau ryw Basg, ymhen tua saith mlynedd, cyfarfûm ag un o athrawon ysgol Abertraeth, a dywedodd wrthyf nad oedd pethau'n rhy dda rhwng Tom a'i wraig, a bod sôn yn yr ardal eu bod am gael ysgariad. Methu cyd-dynnu y maent meddai. 'Dydi o ddim wedi gweld neb arall i'w charu'n well,' meddai, fel petai'n cofio am ei garwriaeth gyntaf. Dyma ddygyfor a chynnwrf y tu mewn imi eto, wedi imi gyrraedd rhyw wastadedd digynnwrf. Tybed a oedd o wedi 'difaru priodi o gwbl? Tybed a oedd o'n 'difaru fy ngadael i fel y gwnaeth? A oedd wedi ei siomi yn Dela? Fe groesodd fy meddwl i y gallai ofyn i mi ei briodi pe cai ysgariad. Ond dim ond am eiliad. Cwestiwn ofer. Wedi saith mlynedd o anialwch poenus, ofer oedd ail gydio wedyn. 'Roedd y saith mlynedd hynny wedi gwneud fy mlwyddyn i o garu yn ddim ond atgof, ac nid yw atgof yn ddim ond cnoi cil. Tamaid newydd yw'r tamaid cyntaf. Celwydd yw dweud, 'Hawdd cynnau tân ar hen aelwyd.' Chwilfrydedd personol oedd fy niddordeb yn y newydd.

Ymhen ychydig fisoedd, darllenais yn y papur eu bod wedi cael ysgariad, oherwydd ei greulondeb meddwl ef — y hi i gael y bachgen. Rhyfedd cyn lleied a deimlais. Mynd yn ôl yr oeddwn i ac nid edrych at y dyfodol, ac eto yr oedd y gorffennol wedi ei dorri i ffwrdd.

Ymhen ychydig fisoedd synnwyd fi'n fawr ryw brynhawn Sadwrn wrth weld Dela wrth y drws acw yn gofyn a gâi fy ngweld. Gwahoddais hi i'r tŷ a gwneuthum de iddi. Yr oedd wedi heneiddio. Rhychau wrth ei cheg a'i llygaid, ei gwallt wedi dechrau gwynnu a'i wneud yn felynach nag o'r blaen.

'Mae'n debyg ych bod chi wedi darllen bod Tom a finnau wedi cael ysgariad.'

'Do,' a rhyw gryndod yn mynd drosof wrth glywed y gair 'Tom' ganddi hi.

Yr oedd yn cloffi wrth fynd ymlaen.

'Mi ddar'u imi weld ymhen rhyw ddwy flynedd nad oedd gynno fo fawr o ddidordeb yn'o i. 'Roedd o yn fy ngwrth-wynebu am bob dim.'

'Rhaid i chi gofio,' meddwn i, 'nad ydi pob dau ddim yn gweud pâr.'

'Mi ddalia i, na fasa Tom ddim yn gwneud pâr efo neb,' ebe hi.

'Fedar neb ddweud hynny.'

'Dyn eisio tegan am dipyn ydi Tom, a'i daflu i ffwrdd wedyn,' ebe hithau, 'beth bynnag ddywedwn i, byddai'n tynnu'n groes, ac yn ddiweddar byddai'n tynnu'n groes cyn i mi gael gorffen dweud rhywbeth, nes o'r diwedd byddwn yn peidio â dweud fy marn am ddim. Wedyn byddai yn fy nghyhuddo o fod yn duo ac yn digio. Ac felly o hyd, nes gwelais mai'r peth gorau oedd ymwahanu, yn enwedig er mwyn yr hogyn, oedd yn ddigon hen i ddallt pethau ac i boeni.'

'Pam y daethoch chi yma i ddweud y pethau yma wrtha i?'

'Er mwyn i chi ei wrthod petai o'n dwad yma i ofyn i chi 'i briodi. 'Roedd o'n edliw i mi o hyd na fasech *chi* ddim yn gwneud y peth yma a'r peth arall.'

' 'Dydi o ddim yn debyg o ddwad.'

'Dwn i ddim. Ond 'rydw i wedi'ch rhybuddio chi.'

'Dydw i ddim yn licio cawl eildwym.'

Wedi iddi fynd, teimlwn yn dosturiol tuag ati, ac yn ddigalon. Yna synfyfyriais am wir amcan ei hymweliad. Ai rhybuddio oedd ei hamcan, ai cenfigen, rhag ofn iddo ddwad? Buasai'n well gennyf i petai'r ddau wedi bod yn hapus. Yr oedd y peth yn rhy hen erbyn hyn i mi deimlo balchder oherwydd methiant eu priodas. Yr oedd yn dda gennyf na ddaeth â'r bachgen efo hi. Yr oedd hi yn ddigon call i beidio â chodi'r llen oddi ar orffennol ei dad, a buasai wedi rhoi rhyw gynnwrf yn fy nghalon innau. Pe deuai Tom i ofyn imi ei briodi, ni roesai bleser imi o gwbl wedi'r hyn a ddigwyddodd. Yr oedd y gnoc yn y cefndir o hyd, ac ni buasai priodi yn ei diddymu. Trwy drugaredd ni ddaeth. Clywais iddo briodi rhywun arall ymhen dwy flynedd, a Dela ymhen sbel wedyn.

Euthum innau yn fy mlaen yn addoli fy nhŷ, yn darllen, yn cael eich gweld chi, yn gweithio, mynd ar wyliau i'r Cyfandir. Gwelais ddynion a hoffais yn fawr, ond ni'm gwelais fy hun yn priodi.

Rŵan, dyma fi wedi cael cnoc wahanol. Dychryn mawr i mi oedd clywed y meddyg yn dweud fod yn rhaid torri fy mron, hyn yn dangos fod gennyf rywfaint o flas at fywyd er gwaethaf pob dim. Bu'r gnoc gyntaf yn gefndir i'm bywyd am bymtheg mlynedd, yn gefndir, yn lle bod yn llwyfan golau i chwarae arno. Ni threiddiais trwy'r cefndir i'r tywyllwch tu cefn ychwaith. 'Rwyf wedi byw yn arwynebol yr holl amser yma yn lle treiddio i mewn i wir bleser bywyd yn ei olau a'i dywyllwch. Wedi dwad i ystafell aros marwolaeth y gwelaf mor wirion y bûm. Yn wir, bu fy mywyd mor arwynebol fel na allaf ei weld i gyd yn ddim ond ystafell aros i farw.

A oes rhywun wedi medru diffinio a dadansoddi poen a dioddefaint?

Fy nghofion byth atoch eich dau, gan obeithio y caf eich gweled eto.   ELA

103

Fr.

David and Little Emily

STORIES
FROM DICKENS

BY

J. WALKER McSPADDEN

AUTHOR OF
'STORIES OF ROBIN HOOD" "STORIES FROM WAGNER"
ETC.

*" The Genius of Charles Dickens . . . how
brilliant, kindly, beneficent . . . dwelling
by a fountain of laughter imperishable;
though there is something of an alien salt
in the neighbouring fountain of tears."*
ANDREW LANG

GEORGE G. HARRAP & CO. LTD.
LONDON   BOMBAY   SYDNEY

First published June 1906
by GEORGE G. HARRAP & CO.
39-41 *Parker Street, Kingsway, London, W.C.*2

Reprinted: November 1906; *October* 1908;
December 1909; *August* 1911; *July* 1912;
August 1913; *July* 1914; *April* 1916;
May 1917; *January* 1918; *January* 1920;
December 1920; *February* 1923; *January*
1925; *July* 1925; *January* 1927; *July* 1927

Printed in Great Britain by The Riverside Press Limited
Edinburgh

Preface

THE title of this book rings in the ear with a pleasant sound. "Stories from Dickens"! "Stories" alone usually suggests such delightful rambles in the land of dreams! And when it is coupled with the name of a king of story-tellers by divine right, the charm is increased a hundredfold.

These stories are—as the title indicates—taken directly from Dickens, very largely in his own language, and always faithful to his spirit. They are the stories of his most famous boys and girls, merely separated from the big books and crowded scenes where they first appeared. In stage language, the "lime-light" has been turned upon them alone. Their early joys and sorrows are shown, but always with more of the smiles than the tears. There is sadness enough in real life without emphasising it in books for young people, and so only two of the numerous deathbed scenes found in Dickens are given place here.

The book is not intended as a substitute, however small, for the complete texts; but is offered in the reverent hope that it will serve as both introduction and incentive to the bulky volumes which so often alarm young people by their very size. The compiler has in mind one child of the "long ago" who looked with awe upon a stately row of fat books, kept like mummies in a high glass case, and labelled "Dickens." This child never suspected that the books were intended for reading—at any rate, not by children; so he contented himself for the time with trashy little books with highly coloured pictures "intended for children." What a world of delight would have been opened to him if some one had placed in his hands the story of Oliver Twist; or the first part of Nicholas Nickleby relating to Dotheboy's Hall; or the early history of David Copperfield (he might have demanded *all* of *that* story!); or some of the inimitable Christmas tales! Afterwards he would have read on and on for himself.

To other such children this book comes as a friendly guide to Dickens-land—a country which, when once in, may they never leave till every path has been explored.

J. W. M.

CONTENTS

Contents

ILLUSTRATIONS

The Personal History of David Copperfield

I

MY EARLIEST RECOLLECTIONS

THE first things that I seem to remember are the figure of my mother with her pretty hair and youthful face, and Peggotty, our faithful servant, large of figure, black of eye, and with cheeks and arms so hard and red that I wondered the birds didn't peck them in preference to apples. I believe I can remember these two at a little distance apart, dwarfed to my sight by stooping down or kneeling on the floor, and I going unsteadily from the one to the other. My father I never saw, for he died before I was born.

What else do I remember? Let me see. There comes to me a vision of our quaint cosy little home, the " Rookery." On the ground floor is Peggotty's kitchen, opening into a back yard; with a pigeon-house on a pole, in the centre, without any pigeons in it; a great dog-kennel in a corner, without any dog; and a quantity of fowls that look terribly tall to me, walking about, in a ferocious manner. There is one cock who gets upon a post to crow, and seems to take particular notice of me as I look at him through the kitchen window, who makes me shiver, he is so fierce. Of the geese outside the gate who come waddling after me with their long necks stretched out when I go that way, I dream fearfully at night.

Here is a long passage leading from Peggotty's kitchen to the front door. A dark storeroom opens out of it, and that is a place to be run past at night; for I don't know what may be among those tubs and jars and old tea-chests, in which there is the smell of soap, pickles, pepper, candles, and coffee, all at one whiff. Then there are the two parlours: the parlour in which we sit of an evening, my mother and I and Peggotty—for Peggotty is quite our companion, when her work is done and we are alone—and the best parlour where we sit on a Sunday; grandly but not so comfortably.

And now I see the outside of our house, with the latticed bedroom windows standing open to let in the sweet-smelling air, and the ragged old rooks'-nests still dangling in the elm trees at the bottom of the front garden. Now I am in the garden at the back, beyond the yard where the empty pigeon-house and dog-kennel are—a very preserve of butterflies, as I remember it, with a high fence, and a gate and padlock; where the fruit clusters on the trees, riper and richer than fruit has ever been since, in any other garden, and where my mother gathers some in a basket, while I stand by, bolting gooseberries slyly, and trying to look unmoved.

A great wind rises, and the summer is gone in a moment. We are playing in the winter twilight, dancing about the parlour. When my mother is out of breath and rests herself in an elbow-chair, I watch her winding her bright curls round her fingers and straightening her waist, and nobody knows better than I do that she likes to look so well, and is proud of being so pretty.

That is among my very earliest impressions,—that, and a sense that we were both a little afraid of Peggotty, and submit ourselves in most things to her direction.

Peggotty and I were sitting one night by the parlour fire, alone. I had been reading to Peggotty about crocodiles. I must not have read very clearly, for I remember she had a cloudy impression that they were a sort of vegetable. I was tired of reading, and sleepy; but having leave, as a high treat, to sit up until my mother came home from spending the evening at a neighbour's, I would rather have died upon my post than have gone to bed.

We had exhausted the crocodiles, and begun with alligators, when the bell rang. We went out to the door; and there was my mother, looking unusually pretty, I thought, and with her a gentleman with beautiful black hair and whiskers, who had walked home with us from church last Sunday.

As my mother stooped down on the threshold to take me in her arms and kiss me, the gentleman said I was a more highly privileged little fellow than a monarch—or something like that.

" What does that mean ? " I asked him, over her shoulder.

He patted me on the head; but somehow, I didn't like him or his deep voice, and I was jealous that his hand should touch my mother's in touching me—which it did. I put it away as well as I could. My mother

gently chid me for being rude ; and, keeping me close
to her shawl, turned to thank the gentleman for bringing her home.

From the moment that I first saw the gentleman
with the black whiskers, I held a deep instinctive dislike to him. And I am sure Peggotty agreed with me,
from some remarks I chanced to hear her utter to my
mother. But Mr. Murdstone—that was his name—
began coming often to the Rookery, and exerted
himself always to be agreeable to me, calling me
a fine boy and patting me on the head ; so I tried
to think myself very ungrateful. But still I could not
make myself like him. The sight of him made me fear
that something was going to happen—I didn't know
what.

Not long after that, when Peggotty and I were sitting
alone, she darning and I reading farther in the crocodile
book,—for my mother was out, as she often was, with
Mr. Murdstone,—she bit off a thread and asked :

" Master Davy, how should you like to go along
with me and spend a fortnight at my brother's at
Yarmouth ? Wouldn't *that* be a treat ? "

" Is your brother an agreeable man, Peggotty ? "
I inquired doubtfully.

" Oh, what an agreeable man he is ! " cried Peggotty, holding up her hands. " Then there's the sea ;
and the boats and ships ; and the fishermen ; and
the beach ; and 'Am to play with——"

Peggotty meant her nephew Ham, but she spoke of
him as a morsel of English Grammar.

I was flushed by her summary of delights, and
replied that it would indeed be a treat, but what would
my mother say ?

"Why, then, I'll as good as bet a guinea," said Peggotty, intent upon my face, "that she'll let us go. I'll ask her, if you like, as soon as ever she comes home. There now!"

"But what's she to do while we're away?" said I, putting my small elbows on the table to argue the point. "She can't live by herself."

If Peggotty were looking for a hole, all of a sudden, in the heel of that stocking, it must have been a very little one indeed, and not worth darning.

"I say! Peggotty! She can't live by herself, you know."

"Oh, bless you!" said Peggotty, looking at me again at last. "Don't you know? She's going to stay for a fortnight with Mrs. Grayper. Mrs. Grayper's going to have a lot of company."

Oh! If that was it, I was quite ready to go. I waited, in the utmost impatience, until my mother came home from Mrs. Grayper's (for it was that identical neighbour), to ascertain if we could get leave to carry out this great idea. Without being nearly so much surprised as I had expected, my mother entered into it readily; and it was all arranged that night, and my board and lodging during the visit were to be paid for.

The day soon came for our going. It was such an early day that it came soon, even to me, who was in a fever of expectation, and half afraid that an earthquake or a fiery mountain, or some other accident might stop the expedition. We were to go in a carrier's cart, which departed in the morning after breakfast. I would have given any money to have been allowed to wrap myself up over-night, and sleep in my hat and boots.

It touches me nearly now, although I tell it lightly, to recollect how eager I was to leave my happy home; to think how little I suspected what I did leave for ever. I am glad to recollect that when the carrier began to move, my mother ran out at the gate, and called to him to stop, that she might kiss me once more. I am glad to dwell upon the earnestness and love with which she lifted up her face to mine.

As we left her standing in the road, Mr. Murdstone came up to where she was, and chided her for being so moved. I was looking back round the awning of the cart, and wondered what business it was of his. Peggotty, who was also looking back on the other side, seemed anything but satisfied, as the face she brought back into the cart denoted.

The carrier's horse was the laziest horse in the world, I thought, as he shuffled along with his head down. But Peggotty had brought along a basket of refreshments which would have lasted us handsomely for a journey three times as long. And at last we drove up to the Yarmouth tavern, where we found Ham awaiting us. He was a huge, strong fellow, about six feet high, with a simple, good-natured face.

He put me upon his shoulder, and my box under his arm, and trudged away easily down a lane littered with shipbuilders' odds and ends, past forges, yards and gas works, till we came out upon an open waste of sand, with the sea pounding upon it and eating away at it. Then Ham said:

"Yon's our house, Mas'r Davy!"

I looked in all directions, as far as I could, and away at the sea, but no house could I make out. There was a black barge, or some other kind of boat, not far off, high and dry on the ground, with an iron funnel sticking out of it for a chimney and smoking very cosily ; but nothing else in the way of a house that was visible to *me*.

" That's not it ? " said I. " That ship-looking thing ? "

" That's it, Mas'r Davy," returned Ham.

If it had been Aladdin's palace, roc's egg and all, I suppose I could not have been more charmed with the idea of living in it. There was a delightful door cut in the side, and it was roofed in, and there were little windows in it ; but the charm of it was that it was a *real boat* which had no doubt been upon the water hundreds of times, and which had never been intended to be lived in on dry land.

It was beautifully clean inside, and as tidy as possible. There was a table, and a Dutch clock, and a chest of drawers, and a tea-tray with a painting on it. The tray was kept from tumbling down by a Bible ; and the tray, if it had tumbled down, would have smashed a quantity of cups and saucers and a tea-pot around the book. On the walls there were some coloured pictures, framed and glazed, of scripture subjects. There were some hooks in the beams of the ceiling whose use I did not know ; and some lockers and boxes scattered around, which served for seats.

One thing I particularly noticed in this delightful house was the smell of fish, which was so searching that when I took out my pocket handkerchief to wipe my nose, I found it smelt exactly as if it had wrapped up a lobster. On my whispering this to Peggotty, she informed me that her brother dealt in lobsters, crabs, and crawfish ; and I afterwards found that a heap of these creatures, in a state of wonderful confusion with

B

one another, and never leaving off pinching whatever
they laid hold of, were usually to be found in a little
wooden lean-to where the pots and kettles were kept.

We were welcomed by a very civil woman in a white
apron, whom I had seen curtseying at the door when
I was on Ham's back, about a quarter of a mile off;
likewise by a most beautiful little girl with a necklace
of blue beads, who wouldn't let me kiss her when I
offered to, but ran away and hid herself.

By-and-bye, when we had dined in a sumptuous
manner off boiled fish, melted butter, and potatoes,
with a chop for me, a hairy man with a very good-
natured face came home. As he called Peggotty
" Lass," and gave her a hearty smack on the cheek,
I had no doubt that he was her brother; and so he
turned out—being presently introduced to me as
Mr. Peggotty, the master of the house.

"Glad to see you, sir," said Mr. Peggotty. " You'll
find us rough, sir, but you'll find us ready."

I thanked him and replied that I was sure I should
be happy in such a delightful place.

The civil woman with the white apron was Mrs.
Gummidge, an old widowed lady who kept the boat-
house in fine order. The little girl was Emily, a niece
of Mr. Peggotty's. She had never seen her father,
just as I had never seen mine—which was our first bond
of sympathy. She had lost her mother, too; and as
we played together happily in the sand, I told her all
about *my* mother and how we had only each other and
I was going to grow up right away to take care of her.

Of course I was quite in love with little Emily. I am
sure I loved her quite as truly as one could possibly
love. And I made her confess that she loved me. So

when the golden days flew by and the time of parting
drew near, our agony of mind was intense. The fare-
wells were very tearful; and if ever in my life I had a
void in my heart, I had one that day.

I am ashamed to confess that the delightful fortnight by the sea had driven out all thoughts of home.
But no sooner were we on the return journey, than
the home longing came crowding in upon me tenfold.
I grew so excited to see my mother, that it seemed
as if I couldn't wait for that blundering old cart. But
Peggotty, instead of sharing in these transports, tried
to check them, though very kindly, and looked confused and out of sorts.

The Rookery would come, however, in spite of her,
when the carrier's horse pleased—and did. How well
I recollect it, on a cold, grey afternoon, with a dull sky
threatening rain!

The door opened, and I sprang in, half laughing
and half crying as I looked for my mother. It was
not she who met me, but a strange servant.

"Why, Peggotty!" I said, ruefully, "isn't she
come home?"

"Yes, yes, Master Davy," said Peggotty. "She's
come home. Wait a bit, Master Davy, and I'll—
I'll tell you something."

"Peggotty!" said I, quite frightened. "What's the
matter?"

"Nothing's the matter, bless you, Master Davy,
dear!" she answered, with an air of cheerfulness.

"Something's the matter, I'm sure. Where's mamma?"

"Master Davy," said Peggotty, untying her bonnet
with a shaking hand, and speaking in a breathless sort
of way; "what do you think? You have got a Pa!"

I trembled, and turned white. Something—I don't know what, or how—connected with my father's grave in the churchyard, and the raising of the dead, seemed to strike me like an unwholesome wind.

"A new one," said Peggotty.

"A new one?" I repeated.

Peggotty gave a gasp, as if she were swallowing something that was very hard, and, putting out her hand, said:

"Come and see him."

"I don't want to see him."

"And your mamma," said Peggotty.

I ceased to draw back, and we went straight to the best parlour, where she left me. On one side of the fire sat my mother; on the other, Mr. Murdstone. My mother dropped her work, and arose hurriedly but timidly, I thought.

"Now, Clara, my dear," said Mr. Murdstone, "recollect! control yourself. Davy boy, how do you do?"

I gave him my hand. Then I went and kissed my mother; she kissed me, patted me gently on the shoulder, and sat down again to her work. I could not look at her, I could not look at him. I knew quite well that he was looking at us both; and I turned to the window and looked out there, at some shrubs that were drooping their heads in the cold.

As soon as I could, I crept upstairs. My old dear bedroom was changed, and I was to lie a long way off. I rambled downstairs to find anything that was like itself, so altered it all seemed; and roamed into the yard. I very soon started back from there, for the empty dog-kennel was filled up with a great dog—deep-mouthed and black-haired like Him—and he was very angry at the sight of me, and sprang out to get at me.

II

I FALL INTO DISGRACE

THAT first lonely evening when I crept off alone, feeling that no one wanted me, was the most miserable of my life. I rolled up in a corner of my bed and cried myself to sleep.

Presently I was awakened by somebody saying, "Here he is!" and uncovering my hot head. My mother and Peggotty had come to look for me, and it was one of them who had done it.

"Davy," said my mother, "what's the matter?"

I thought it very strange that she should ask me, and answered, "Nothing." I turned over on my face, I recollect, to hide my trembling lip, which answered her with greater truth.

"Davy," said my mother. "Davy, my child!"

I dare say, no words she could have uttered would have affected me so much, then, as her calling me her child. I hid my tears in the bedclothes, and pressed her from me with my hand, when she would have raised me up.

Then I felt the touch of a hand that I knew was neither hers nor Peggotty's, and slipped to my feet at the bedside. It was Mr. Murdstone's hand, and he kept it on my arm as he said:

"What's this? Clara, my love, have you forgotten? Firmness, my dear!"

"I am very sorry, Edward," said my mother. "I meant to be very good."

" Go below, my dear," he answered. " David and I will come down together."

When we two were left alone, he shut the door, and sitting on a chair, and holding me standing before him, looked steadily into my eyes.

" David," he said, making his lips thin, by pressing them together, " if I have an obstinate horse or dog to deal with, what do you think I do ? "

" I don't know."

" I beat him. I make him wince and smart. I say to myself, ' I'll conquer that fellow '; and if it were to cost him all the blood he had, I should do it. What is that upon your face ? "

" Dirt," I said.

He knew it was the mark of tears as well as I. But if he had asked the question twenty times, each time with twenty blows, I believe my baby heart would have burst before I would have told him so.

" You have a good deal of intelligence for a little fellow," he said, with a grave smile that belonged to him, " and you understood me very well, I see. Wash that face, sir, and come down with me."

" Clara, my dear," he said, when I had done his bidding, and he walked me into the parlour, with his hand still on my arm ; " you will not be made uncomfortable any more, I hope. We shall soon improve our youthful humours."

What a little thing will change the current of our lives ! I might have been made another creature perhaps by a kind word just then. A word of welcome home, of assurance that it *was* home, might have made me respect my new father instead of hate him. But the word was not spoken, and the time for it was gone.

From that time my life was a lonely one. My mother petted me in secret, but plainly stood in awe of Mr. Murdstone; and even the dauntless Peggotty must needs keep her peace. His word alone was law.

After a time his sister, Miss Murdstone, came to live with us. And from the second day of her arrival she took charge of the household keys, and managed things with a firmness second only to her brother himself.

There had been some talk of my going to boarding-school. Mr. and Miss Murdstone had originated it, and my mother had of course agreed with them. Nothing, however, was concluded on the subject yet, and in the meantime I learned my lessons at home.

Shall I ever forget those lessons! They were presided over nominally by my mother, but really by Mr. Murdstone and his sister, who were always present, and found them a favourable occasion for giving my mother lessons in that miscalled firmness which was the bane of both our lives. I believe I was kept at home for that purpose. I had been apt enough to learn, and willing enough, when my mother and I had lived alone together. I can faintly remember learning the alphabet at her knee. To this day, when I look upon the fat black letters in the primer, the puzzling novelty of their shapes and the easy good-nature of O and Q and S seem to present themselves again before me as they used to do. But they recall no feeling of disgust or reluctance. On the contrary, I seem to have walked along a path of flowers as far as the crocodile book, and to have been cheered by the gentleness of my mother's voice and manner all the way.

But these solemn lessons which succeeded I remember as the death-blow to my peace, and a grievous daily drudgery and misery. They were very long, very numerous, very hard,—and I was generally as much bewildered by them as I believe my poor mother was herself.

Let me remember how it used to be, and bring one morning back again.

I come into the second-best parlour after breakfast with my books and an exercise-book and a slate. My mother is ready for me at her writing-desk, but not half so ready as Mr. Murdstone in his easy-chair by the window, though he pretends to be reading a book, or as Miss Murdstone, sitting near my mother, stringing steel beads. The very sight of these two has such an influence over me that I begin to feel the words I have been at infinite pains to get into my head all sliding away and going I don't know where. I wonder where they *do* go, by-the-bye?

I hand the first book to my mother. Perhaps it is a grammar, perhaps a history or geography. I take a last drowning look at the page as I give it into her hand, and start off aloud at a racing pace while I have got it fresh. I trip over a word. Mr. Murdstone looks up. I trip over another word. Miss Murdstone looks up. I redden, tumble over half-a-dozen words, and stop. I think my mother would show me the book if she dared, but she does not dare, and she says softly:

"Oh, Davy! Davy!"

"Now, Clara," says Mr. Murdstone, "be firm with the boy. Don't say, 'Oh, Davy! Davy!' That's childish. He knows his lesson, or he does not know it."

"He does *not* know it," Miss Murdstone interposes, awfully.

"I am really afraid he does not," says my mother.

"Then you see, Clara," returns Miss Murdstone, "you should just give him the book back and make him know it."

"Yes, certainly," says my mother; "that is what I intend to do, my dear Jane. Now, Davy, try once more, and don't be stupid."

The natural result of this treatment was to make me sullen, dull, and dogged; and my temper was not improved by the sense that I was daily shut out from my mother.

One morning, after about six months of these lessons, when I went into the parlour with my books, I found my mother looking anxious, Miss Murdstone looking firm, and Mr. Murdstone binding something round the bottom of a cane—a lithe and limber cane, which he left off binding when I came in, and poised and switched in the air.

"Now, David," he said, "you must be far more careful to-day than usual." He gave the cane another poise and another switch, and laid it down beside him with an expressive look and took up his book.

This was a good freshener to my presence of mind, as a beginning. I felt the words of my lessons slipping off, not one by one, or line by line, but by the entire page. I tried to lay hold of them; but they seemed, if I may so express it, to have put skates on and to skim away from me with a smoothness there was no checking.

We began badly, and went on worse. I had come in, with an idea that I was very well prepared, but it turned out to be quite a mistake. Book after book

was added to the heap of failures, Miss Murdstone
being firmly watchful of us all the time. And when
we came to the last, my mother burst out crying.

"Clara!" said Miss Murdstone, in her warning voice.

Mr. Murdstone laid down his book and stood up,
cane in hand.

"David, you and I will go upstairs," he said.

He walked me up to my room slowly and gravely,
and when we got there, suddenly twisted my head
under his arm.

"Mr. Murdstone! Sir!" I cried to him. "Don't!
Pray don't beat me! I have tried to learn, sir, but
I can't learn while you and Miss Murdstone are by.
I can't indeed!"

"Can't you, indeed, David?" he said. "We'll
try that."

He had my head as in a vice, but I twined round
him somehow, and stopped him for a moment, entreat-
ing him not to beat me. It was only for a moment
that I stopped him, for he cut me heavily an instant
afterwards, and in the same instant I caught his hand
in my mouth, and bit it through. It sets my teeth
on edge to think of it!

He beat me then, as if he would have beaten me to
death. Above all the noise we made, I heard them
running up the stairs, and crying out—I heard my
mother crying out—and Peggotty. Then he was gone;
and the door was locked outside; and I was lying,
torn and sore and raging, upon the floor.

How well I recollect, when I became quiet, what an
unnatural stillness seemed to reign through the whole
house! How well I remember, when my smart and
passion began to cool, how wicked I began to feel!

I sat listening for a long while, but there was not a sound. I crawled up from the floor, and saw my face in the glass, so swollen, red, and ugly that it almost frightened me. My stripes were sore and stiff, and made me cry afresh, when I moved; but they were nothing to the guilt I felt. It lay like lead upon my breast.

For five days I was imprisoned thus within my room, seeing no one except Miss Murdstone, who came to bring me food. They live like years in my remembrance. On the fifth night I heard my name softly whispered through the keyhole.

I groped my way to the door, and putting my own lips to the keyhole, whispered:

" Is that you, Peggotty, dear ? "

" Yes, my own precious Davy," she replied. " Be as soft as a mouse, or the Cat'll hear us."

I understood this to mean Miss Murdstone, her room being close by.

" How's mamma, dear Peggotty ? Is she very angry with me ? "

I could hear Peggotty crying softly on her side of the keyhole, as I was doing on mine, before she answered, " No. Not very."

" What is going to be done with me, Peggotty, dear ? Do you know ? "

" School. Near London."

" When, Peggotty ? "

" To-morrow."

" Shan't I see mamma ? "

" Yes," said Peggotty. " Morning."

Then she stole away, fearful of surprises.

In the morning Miss Murdstone appeared as usual,

and told me I was going to school, which was not altogether such news to me as she supposed. She also informed me that when I was dressed, I was to come downstairs into the parlour, and have my breakfast. There I found my mother, very pale and with red eyes, into whose arms I ran, and begged her pardon from my suffering soul.

"Oh, Davy!" she said. "That you could hurt any one I love! Try to be better, pray to be better! I forgive you; but I am so grieved, Davy, that you should have such bad passions in your heart."

They had persuaded her that I was a wicked fellow, and she was more sorry for that than for my going away. I felt it sorely. I tried to eat my parting breakfast, but my tears dropped upon my bread and butter, and trickled into my tea. I saw my mother look at me sometimes, and then glance at the watchful Miss Murdstone, and then look down, or look away.

"Master Copperfield's box there?" said Miss Murdstone, when wheels were heard at the gate.

I looked for Peggotty, but it was not she; neither she nor Mr. Murdstone appeared. My former acquaintance, the carrier, was at the door; the box was taken out to his cart and lifted in.

"Clara!" said Miss Murdstone, in her warning note.

"Yes, my dear Jane," returned my mother. "Goodbye, Davy. You are going for your own good. Goodbye, my child. You will come home in the holidays, and be a better boy. God bless you!"

Miss Murdstone was good enough to take me out to the cart, and to say on the way that she hoped I would

repent, before I came to a bad end; and then I got
into the cart, and the lazy horse walked off with it.

We had not gone half a mile when I was astonished
to see Peggotty burst from a hedge and climb into the
cart. Not a word did she say, but she squeezed me tight,
crammed a bag of cakes into my pockets, and put a
purse into my hand. After a final squeeze she got down
from the cart and ran away as quickly as she had come.

My pocket-handkerchief was now so wet that the
carrier proposed spreading it out upon the horse's back
to dry. We did so, and I then had leisure to look at
the purse. It had three bright shillings in it from
Peggotty, and—more precious still—two half-crowns
folded together in a bit of paper, on which was written,
in my mother's hand, "For Davy. With my love."

I was so overcome by this that I asked the carrier
to reach me my handkerchief again, but he said I had
better let it dry first. I thought so too, and wiped
my eyes on my sleeves this time.

Then the cakes came in for consideration. I offered
the carrier one, which he ate at a gulp, without the
slightest change of expression.

"Did *she* make 'em?" asked the carrier, whose
name, by the way, was Barkis.

"Peggotty, you mean, sir?"

"Ah!" said Mr. Barkis. "Her."

"Yes, she makes all our pastry, and does all our
cooking."

Mr. Barkis said nothing for some moments. Then—

"Perhaps you might be writin' to her, later on?"

"Yes, indeed," I said.

"Then you just say to her that Barkis is willin'.
Would you?"

"Yes, sir," I replied, considerably puzzled by the message. And I did deliver it the very first time I wrote to Peggotty. I did not then know that the carrier meant, by being "willing," he wanted to marry my good Peggotty and was too shy to say so for himself.

III

THE DINNER AT THE INN

AT length we drove into the inn-yard at Yarmouth, and as I alighted from the coach a lady looked out of a bow-window where some fowls and joints of meat were hanging up, and said:
"Is that the little gentleman from Blunderstone?"
"Yes, ma'am," I said.
"What name?" inquired the lady.
"Copperfield, ma'am," I said.
"That won't do," returned the lady. "Nobody's dinner is paid for here, in that name."
"Is it Murdstone, ma'am?" I said.
"If you're Master Murdstone," said the lady, "why do you go and give another name, first?"
I explained to the lady how it was, who then rang a bell, and called out, "William! show the coffee-room!" upon which a waiter came running out of a kitchen on the opposite side of the yard to show it, and seemed a good deal surprised when he was only to show it to me.
It was a long room with some large maps in it. I doubt if I could have felt much stranger if the maps had been real foreign countries, and I cast away in the middle of them. I felt it was taking a liberty to

sit down, with my cap in my hand, on the corner of the chair nearest the door; and when the waiter laid a cloth on purpose for me, and put a set of casters on it, I think I must have turned red all over with modesty.

He brought me some chops, and vegetables, and took the covers off in such a bouncing manner that I was afraid I must have given him some offence. But he greatly relieved my mind by putting a chair for me at the table, and saying very affably, " Now, six-foot! come on! "

I thanked him, and took my seat at the board; but found it extremely difficult to handle my knife and fork with anything like dexterity, or to avoid splashing myself with the gravy, while he was standing opposite, staring so hard, and making me blush in the most dreadful manner every time I caught his eye. After watching me into the second chop, he said :

" There's half a pint of ale for you. Will you have it now ? "

I thanked him and said " Yes." Upon which he poured it out of a jug into a large tumbler, and held it up against the light, and made it look beautiful.

" My eye! " he said. " It seems a good deal, don't it ? "

" It does seem a good deal," I answered with a smile. For it was quite delightful to me to find him so pleasant. He was a twinkling-eyed, pimple-faced man, with his hair standing upright all over his head; and as he stood with one arm a-kimbo, holding up the glass to the light with the other hand, he looked quite friendly.

" There was a gentleman here yesterday," he said

—" a stout gentleman, by the name of Topsawyer—
perhaps you know him ? "

" No," I said, " I don't think——"

" In breeches and gaiters, broad-brimmed hat, grey
coat, speckled choker," said the waiter.

" No," I said bashfully, " I haven't the pleasure."

" He came in here," said the waiter, looking at the
light through the tumbler, " ordered a glass of this
ale—would order it—I told him not—drank it, and
fell dead. It was too old for him. It oughtn't to be
drawn ; that's the fact."

I was very much shocked to hear of this melancholy
accident, and said I thought I'd better have some
water.

" Why, you see," said the waiter, still looking at
the light through the tumbler, with one of his eyes
shut up, " our people don't like things being ordered
and left. It offends 'em. But I'll drink it, if you
like. I'm used to it, and use is everything. I don't
think it'll hurt me, if I throw my head back, and take
it off quick. Shall I ? "

I replied that he would much oblige me by drinking
it, if he thought he could do it safely, but by no means
otherwise. When he did throw his head back, and
take it off quick, I had a horrible fear, I confess, of
seeing him meet the fate of the lamented Mr. Topsawyer, and fall lifeless on the carpet. But it didn't
hurt him. On the contrary, I thought he seemed the
fresher for it.

" What have we got here ? " he said, putting a fork
into my dish. " Not chops ? "

" Chops," I said.

" Lord bless my soul ! " he exclaimed, " I didn't

"Let's see who'll get most"

know they were chops. Why, a chop's the very thing to take off the bad effects of that beer! Ain't it lucky?"

So he took a chop by the bone in one hand, and a potato in the other, and ate away with a very good appetite, to my extreme satisfaction. He afterwards took another chop, and another potato; and after that another chop and another potato. When he had done, he brought me a pudding, and having set it before me, seemed to ruminate, and to become absent in his mind for some moments.

"How's the pie?" he said, rousing himself.

"It's a pudding," I made answer.

"Pudding!" he exclaimed. "Why, bless me, so it is! What!" looking at it nearer. "You don't mean to say it's a batter-pudding?"

"Yes, it is indeed."

"Why, a batter-pudding," he said, taking up a table-spoon, "is my favourite pudding! Ain't that lucky? Come on, little 'un, and let's see who'll get most."

The waiter certainly got most. He entreated me more than once to come in and win, but what with his table-spoon to my tea-spoon, his dispatch to my dispatch, and his appetite to my appetite, I was left far behind at the first mouthful, and had no chance with him. I never saw anyone enjoy a pudding so much, I think; and he laughed, when it was all gone, as if his enjoyment of it lasted still.

Finding him so very friendly and companionable, I asked for the pen and ink and paper, to write to Peggotty. He not only brought it immediately, but was good enough to look over me while I wrote the letter. When I had finished it, he asked me where I was going to school.

I said, "N ar London," which was all I knew.

"Oh! my eye!" he said, looking very low-spirited, "I am sorry for that."

"Why?" I asked him.

"Oh, Lord!" he said, shaking his head, "that's the school where they broke the boy's ribs—two ribs —a little boy he was. I should say he was—let me see—how old are you, about?"

I told him between eight and nine.

"That's just his age," he said. "He was eight years and six months old when they broke his first rib; eight years and eight months old when they broke his second, and did for him."

I could not disguise from myself, or from the waiter, that this was an uncomfortable coincidence, and inquired how it was done. His answer was not cheering to my spirits, for it consisted of two dismal words, "With whopping."

The blowing of the coach-horn in the yard was a seasonable diversion, which made me get up and hesitatingly inquire, in the mingled pride and diffidence of having a purse (which I took out of my pocket) if there were anything to pay.

"There's a sheet of letter-paper," he returned. "Did you ever buy a sheet of letter-paper?"

I could not remember that I ever had.

"It's dear," he said, "on account of the duty. Threepence. That's the way we're taxed in this country. There's nothing else except the waiter. Never mind the ink. I lose by that."

"What should you—what should I—how much ought I to—what would it be right to pay the waiter, if you please?" I stammered, blushing.

" If I hadn't a family, and that family hadn't the cowpock," said the waiter, " I wouldn't take a six-pence. If I didn't support a aged pairint, and a lovely sister,"—here the waiter was greatly agitated—" I wouldn't take a farthing. If I had a good place, and was treated well here, I should beg acceptance of a trifle, instead of taking it. But I live on broken wittles— and I sleep on the coals "—here the waiter burst into tears.

I was very much concerned for his misfortunes, and felt that any recognition short of ninepence would be mere brutality and hardness of heart. Therefore I gave him one of my three bright shillings, which he received with much humility and veneration, and spun up with his thumb, directly afterwards, to try the goodness of.

It was a little disconcerting to me, to find, when I was being helped up behind the coach, that I was supposed to have eaten all the dinner without any assistance. I discovered this, from overhearing the lady in the bow-window say to the guard, " Take care of that child, George, or he'll burst ! " and from observing that the women-servants who were about the place came out to look and giggle at me. My un-fortunate friend the waiter, who had quite recovered his spirits, did not appear to be disturbed by this, but joined in the general admiration without being at all confused. If I had any doubt of him, I suppose this half awakened it ; but I am inclined to believe that with the simple confidence of a child, and the natural reliance of a child upon superior years, I had no serious mistrust of him on the whole, even then.

Throughout the rest of the journey I was made

the subject of continual jokes between the coachman
and the guard, but everything has an end, and so eventu-
ally I arrived at my new distination, and a fresh leaf
of my life was begun.

IV

SCHOOL, STEERFORTH AND TRADDLES

SALEM HOUSE was a square brick building
with wings. The schoolroom was very long,
with three rows of desks running the length
of it and bristling all round with pegs for hats and
slates. Scraps of copybooks and exercises littered
the floor. The other students had not yet returned
from their holidays when I took my first peep into
this room, in company with Mr. Mell, one of the tutors.

Presently I chanced to see a pasteboard sign lying
upon a desk and bearing these words :

"TAKE CARE OF HIM.
HE BITES."

I hurriedly climbed upon the desk, fearful of a dog
underneath ; but saw none.

"What are you doing there ? " asked Mr. Mell.

"I beg your pardon, sir," I replied. "If you please,
I'm looking for the dog."

"Dog ? What dog ? "

I pointed to the sign.

"No, Copperfield," he said gravely. "That's not a
dog ; that's a boy. My instructions are to put this sign
on your back. I'm sorry to do so, but must do it."

With that, he took me down, and tied the placard which was neatly constructed for the purpose, on my shoulders like a knapsack; and wherever I went, afterwards, I had the consolation of carrying it.

What I suffered nobody can imagine. Whether it was possible for people to see me or not I always fancied that somebody was reading it. It was no relief to turn round and find nobody; for wherever my back was, there I imagined somebody always to be, until at last I positively began to have a dread of myself as the boy who *did* bite.

Mr. Creakle, the master of the school, was a short, thick-set man, and bald on the top of his head. He had a little nose and large chin. He had lost his voice and spoke almost in a whisper, which surprised me greatly, for his face always looked angry, and the exertion of talking made his thick veins stick out so that he looked angrier still.

When the boys began to come back I found my ordeal, on account of the sign on my back, not quite so great as I had feared; and it was chiefly on account of the first fellow to arrive, Tommy Traddles. Dear Tommy Traddles! You made a friend of a poor, lonesome, frightened boy that day, who will always be loyal to you so long as he lives.

Traddles was a jolly looking boy who laughed heartily when he first saw the card, as at a great joke; and he saved me from any further shyness by introducing me to every boy and saying gaily, " Look here! Here's a game!" Happily, too, most of the boys came back low-spirited, and were not very boisterous at my expense. Some of them certainly did dance about me like wild Indians and could not resist patting me, lest

I should bite, and saying, "Lie down, sir!" and calling me Towzer. But on the whole I got through rather easily.

I was not considered as being formally received into the school, however, until J. Steerforth arrived. Before this boy, who was reputed to be a great scholar, and was very good-looking, and at least half-a-dozen years my senior, I was carried as before a magistrate. He inquired, under a shed in the playground, into the particulars of my punishment, and was pleased to express his opinion that it was "a jolly shame"; for which I became bound to him ever afterwards.

Then Steerforth asked how much money I had; and when I told him, he suggested that it was the proper thing for a new boy to stand treat to the others. I agreed, but felt helpless; whereupon he kindly volunteered to get the things for me and smuggle them into my room. I was a little uneasy about spending my mother's half-crowns, but didn't dare say so. I handed them over to him and he procured the feast and laid it out on my bed, saying:

"There you are, young Copperfield, and a royal spread you've got!"

I couldn't think of doing the honours of the feast, at my time of life, while he was by; my hand shook at the very thought of it. I begged him to do me the favour of presiding; and my request being seconded by the other boys he acceded to it, and sat upon my pillow, handing round the viands with perfect fairness, I must say. As to me, I sat on his left hand, and the rest were grouped about us, on the nearest beds and on the floor.

How well I recollect our sitting there, talking in

whispers, or their talking, and my respectfully listening, I ought rather to say; the moonlight falling a
little way into the room, through the window, painting a pale window on the floor, and the greater part
of us in shadow, except when Steerforth struck a match,
when he wanted to look for anything on the board,
and shed a blue glare over us that was gone directly.

I heard all kinds of things about the school. I heard
that Mr. Creakle was a tartar and thrashed the boys
unmercifully—all except Steerforth, upon whom he
didn't dare lay his hand. I heard that Mr. Creakle
was very ignorant, and that Mr. Mell, who was not a
bad sort of fellow, was poorly paid. All this and much
more I heard in the whispers of that moonlit room,
before we finally betook ourselves to bed.

From that time on, big handsome Steerforth took
me under his protection, and, for my part, I was his
willing slave. I would tell him tales which I had imbibed from my early reading, while he would help me
do my sums and keep the other boys from tormenting
me. Why he, the fine head-boy, should have taken
notice of me at all, I don't know. But I remember
I all but worshipped him with his easy swagger and
lordly air.

The other boy to whom I always owed allegiance
was Traddles. Poor jolly Traddles! In a tight,
sky-blue suit that made his arms and legs look like
German sausages, he was at once the merriest and
most miserable of all boys. He was always being
caned by that fierce Mr. Creakle, who made all our
backs tingle, except Steerforth's. After Traddles
had got his daily caning he would cheer up somehow
and get comfort by drawing skeletons all over his slate.

He was always drawing these skeletons, just as he was always getting caned. And they did comfort him somehow, for presently he would begin to laugh again before his tears were dry.

He was very honourable, Traddles was, and held it as a solemn duty in the boys to stand by one another. He suffered for this on several occasions ; and particularly once, when Steerforth laughed in church, and the Beadle thought it was Traddles, and took him out. I see him now, going away in custody, despised by the congregation. He never said who was the real offender, though he smarted for it next day, and was imprisoned so many hours that he came forth with a whole church-yard full of skeletons swarming all over his Latin Dictionary. But he had his reward. Steerforth said there was nothing of the sneak in Traddles, and we all felt that to be the highest praise. For my part, I could have gone through a good deal to have won such a reward.

Although Mr. Creakle's school was not noted for scholarship, I can confess without vanity that I did make good progress. I was naturally fond of books and a great reader ; and now I had the first fair chance at learning things. In this I found Mr. Mell, the quiet, gentle tutor, a constant friend to me. I shall always remember him with gratitude.

But Steerforth, I am sorry to say, did not like the tutor, and took no pains to hide his poor opinion. Since many of the other boys followed Steerforth's lead, poor Mr. Mell was not popular. Still, nothing especial came of it until one memorable day when Mr. Creakle was absent. The boys seized the chance to be uproarious, and Mr. Mell could not control them.

Finally even his patience was exhausted, and he sprang to his feet and pounded his desk with a book.

"Silence!" he cried. "This noise must cease! It's maddening! How can you treat me this way, boys?"

It was my book that he struck his desk with; and as I stood beside him, following his eye as it glanced round the room, I saw the boys all stop, some suddenly surprised, some half afraid, and some sorry, perhaps.

Steerforth's place was at the bottom of the school, at the opposite end of the long room. He was lounging with his back against the wall, and his hands in his pockets, and looked at Mr. Mell with his mouth shut up as if he were whistling, when Mr. Mell looked at him.

"Silence, Mr. Steerforth!" said Mr. Mell.

"Silence yourself," said Steerforth, turning red. "Whom are you talking to?"

"Sit down," said Mr. Mell.

"Sit down yourself!" said Steerforth, "and mind your business."

There was a titter, and some applause, but Mr. Mell was so white that there was silence.

"If you think, Steerforth," said Mr. Mell, "that you can make use of your position of favouritism here to disobey rules and insult a gentleman——"

"A what?—where is he?" said Steerforth.

Here somebody cried out, "Shame, J. Steerforth! Too bad!" It was Traddles, whom Mr. Mell instantly routed by bidding him hold his tongue.

—"To insult one who is not fortunate in life, sir, and who never gave you the least offence," continued Mr. Mell, his lip trembling, "you commit a mean and base action. You can sit down or stand up as you please, sir. Copperfield, go on."

"Young Copperfield," said Steerforth, coming forward, "stop a bit. I tell you what, Mr. Mell, once for all. When you take the liberty of calling men mean and base, or anything of that sort, you are an impudent beggar. You are always a beggar, you know; but when you do that, you are an impudent beggar."

I am not clear whether he was going to strike Mr. Mell, or Mr. Mell was going to strike him, or there was any such intention on either side. I saw a rigidity come upon the whole school as if they had been turned into stone, and found Mr. Creakle in the midst of us. Mr. Mell, with his elbows on his desk and his face in his hands, sat for some moments quite still.

"Mr. Mell," said Mr. Creakle, shaking him by the arm; and his whisper was very audible now; "you have not forgotten yourself, I hope?"

"No, sir," said Mr. Mell.

Mr. Creakle looked hard at him and then turned to Steerforth.

"Now, sir, will you tell me what this is about?"

Steerforth evaded the question for a little while; looking in scorn and anger on his opponent, and remaining silent. I could not help thinking what a fine-looking fellow he was, and how homely and plain Mr. Mell looked opposed to him.

"What did he mean by talking about favourites, then?" said Steerforth at length.

"Favourites?" repeated Mr. Creakle, with the veins in his forehead swelling quickly. "Who talked about favourites?"

"He did," said Steerforth.

"And pray, what did you mean by that, sir?" demanded Mr. Creakle, turning angrily on his assistant.

"I meant, Mr. Creakle," he returned, in a low voice, "as I said; that no pupil had a right to avail himself of his position of favouritism to degrade me."

"To degrade *you*?" said Mr. Creakle. "My stars! But give me leave to ask you, Mr. What's your name, whether, when you talk about favourites, you showed proper respect to me? To *me*, sir," said Mr. Creakle, darting his head at him suddenly and drawing it back again, "the principal of this establishment and your employer."

"It was not judicious, sir, I am willing to admit," said Mr. Mell. "I should not have done so if I had been cool."

Here Steerforth struck in.

"Then he said I was mean, and then he said I was base, and then I called him a beggar. If *I* had been cool, perhaps I shouldn't have called him a beggar. But I did, and I am ready to take the consequences of it."

Without considering, perhaps, whether there were any consequences to be taken, I felt quite in a glow at this gallant speech. It made an impression on the boys, too, for there was a low stir among them, though no one spoke a word.

"I am surprised, Steerforth,—although your candour does you honour," said Mr. Creakle, "does you honour, certainly,—I am surprised, Steerforth, I must say, that you should attach such an epithet to any person employed and paid in Salem House, sir."

Steerforth gave a short laugh.

"That's not an answer, sir," said Mr. Creakle, "to my remark. I expect more than that from you, Steerforth."

If Mr. Mell looked homely in my eyes before the handsome boy, it would be quite impossible to say how homely Mr. Creakle looked.

"Let him deny it," said Steerforth.

"Deny that he is a beggar, Steerforth?" cried Mr. Creakle. "Why, where does he go a-begging?"

"If he is not a beggar himself, his near relation's one," said Steerforth. "It's all the same."

"What do you mean?"

"Since you expect me, Mr. Creakle, to justify myself," said Steerforth, "and to say what I mean,—what I have to say is, that his mother lives on charity in an almshouse."

Mr. Creakle turned to his assistant with a severe frown and laboured politeness.

"Now you hear what this gentleman says, Mr. Mell. Have the goodness, if you please, to set him right before the assembled school."

"He is right, sir, without correction," returned Mr. Mell, in the midst of a dead silence; "what he has said is true."

"Be so good then as to declare publicly, will you," said Mr. Creakle, putting his head on one side and rolling his eyes round the school, "whether it ever came to my knowledge until this moment?"

"I believe not directly," he returned.

"Why, you *know* not," said Mr. Creakle. "Don't you, man?"

"Sir, I think you knew my circumstances when I came here, and that a bare living wage——"

"I think, if you come to that," said Mr. Creakle, with his veins swelling again bigger than ever, "that you've been in a wrong position altogether, and mistook this for a charity school. Mr. Mell, we'll part if you please. The sooner the better."

"There is no time," answered Mr. Mell, rising, "like the present."

"Sir, to you!" said Mr. Creakle.

"I take my leave of you, Mr. Creakle, and of all of you," said Mr. Mell, glancing round the room and patting me gently on the shoulder. "James Steerforth, the best wish I can leave you is that you may come to be ashamed of what you have done to-day. At present I would prefer to see you anything rather than a friend to me or to anyone in whom I feel an interest."

Then Mr. Mell walked out with his property under his arm.

Mr. Creakle made a speech, in which he thanked Steerforth for asserting (though perhaps too warmly) the independence and respectability of Salem House; and which he wound up by shaking hands with Steerforth, while we gave three cheers, I did not quite know what for, but I suppose for Steerforth, and so joined in them ardently, though I felt miserable. Mr. Creakle then caned Tommy Traddles for being discovered in tears instead of cheers on account of Mr. Mell's departure: and went back to his sofa or wherever he had come from.

When he had gone there was an awkward silence. Somehow we all felt uncomfortable or ashamed. As for Steerforth, he said he was angry with Traddles and glad he had caught it.

Poor Traddles, who was relieving himself as usual with a burst of skeletons, said he didn't care. Mr. Mell was ill-used.

"Who has ill-used him, you girl?" said Steerforth.

"Why, *you* have," returned Traddles.

"What have I done?" said Steerforth.

"What have you done?" retorted Traddles. "Hurt his feelings and lost him his situation."

"His feelings!" repeated Steerforth, disdainfully. "His feelings will soon get the better of it, I'll be bound. His feelings are not like yours, Miss Traddles. As to his situation,—which was a precious one, wasn't it?—do you suppose I am not going to write home and take care that he gets some money, Polly?"

We thought this intention very noble in Steerforth, whose mother was a widow, and rich, and would do almost anything, it was said, that he asked her. We were all extremely glad to see Traddles so put down, and exalted Steerforth to the skies. But as I look back at it now, I should rather have been Traddles that day than any other boy in the room. And I think the other boys will say so too.

I pass over all that happened at school, until the anniversary of my birthday came round in March. Except that Steerforth was more to be admired than ever, I remember nothing. He was going away at the end of the half-year, if not sooner, and was more spirited and independent than ever; but beyond this I remember nothing. The great event by which that time is marked in my mind, seems to have swallowed up all lesser recollections, and to exist alone.

It was after breakfast, and we had been summoned in from the playground, when Mr. Creakle entered and said:

"David Copperfield is to go into the parlour."

I expected a hamper from Peggotty, and brightened

at the order. Some of the boys about me put in their claim not to be forgotten in the distribution of the goods things, as I got out of my seat with great alacrity. But when I reached the parlour I saw no one except Mrs. Creakle, who held an open letter in her hand and looked at me gravely.

"You are too young to know how the world changes every day," said Mrs. Creakle, "and how the people in it pass away. But we all have to learn it, David; some of us when we are young, some of us when we are old, some of us at all times of our lives."

I looked at her earnestly.

"When you came away from home," said Mrs. Creakle, after a pause, "were they all well?" After another pause, "Was your mamma well?"

I trembled without distinctly knowing why, and still looked at her earnestly, making no attempt to answer.

"Because," said she, "I grieve to tell you that I hear this morning your mamma is very ill."

A mist arose between Mrs. Creakle and me, and her figure seemed to move in it for an instant. Then I felt the burning tears run down my face, and it was steady again.

"She is very dangerously ill," she added.

I knew all now.

"She is dead."

There was no need to tell me so. I had already broken out into a desolate cry, and felt an orphan in the wide world.

She was very kind to me. She kept me there all day, and left me alone sometimes; and I cried and wore myself to sleep, and awoke and cried again.

The next night I left Salem House, after a tender

adieu to Steerforth, Traddles, and all the rest. I little thought that I left the school never to return.

When I reached home I was in Peggotty's arms before I got to the door, and she took me into the house. Her grief burst out when she first saw me; but she controlled it soon, and spoke in whispers, and walked softly, as if the dead could be disturbed. She had not been in bed, I found, for a long time. She sat up at night still, and watched. As long as her poor dear pretty was above the ground, she said, she would never desert her.

Mr. Murdstone took no heed of me when I went into the parlour where he was, but sat by the fireside, weeping silently, and pondering in his elbow-chair. Miss Murdstone, who was busy at her writing-desk, which was covered with letters and papers, gave me her cold finger-nails, and asked me, in an iron whisper, if I had been measured for my mourning.

I will not dwell upon the dull, sorrowful days before and after my dear mother's funeral. The house had been cold and quiet enough before, but was now almost terrifying. And had it not been for Peggotty I do not know how I should have stood it.

But soon even she was denied me. Miss Murdstone had never liked her, and now lost no time in dismissing her from our service. The single ray of light in this gloomy time is a little visit I was allowed to make with her to Yarmouth, to our old friends, Mr. Peggotty, Ham, and Emily. The latter was much grown now, but prettier than ever, and shyer about letting me kiss her.

And Barkis, the honest carrier, after having been " willing " all this time, was hugely gratified to gain a favourable answer from Peggotty. They were married while I was there, and I was glad to leave my faithful old nurse so well provided for.

Then I returned home—no, I cannot say that word —to Mr. and Miss Murdstone.

V

I BEGIN LIFE ON MY OWN ACCOUNT

AND now I fell into a state of neglect, which I cannot look back upon without sorrow. I was as one alone—apart from all friendly notice, apart from the society of all other boys of my own age,—apart from all companionship but my own spiritless thoughts, which seem to cast a gloom upon this paper as I write.

What would I have given to have been sent to the hardest school that ever was kept—to have been taught something, anyhow, anywhere ? No such hope dawned upon me. They disliked me ; and they steadily overlooked me. I think Mr. Murdstone's means were straitened at about this time ; but it is little to the purpose. He could not bear me ; and in putting me from him he tried, as I believe, to put away the notion that I had any claim upon him— and succeeded.

I was not actively ill-used. I was not beaten, or starved ; but day by day I was made to feel that I was in the way, and an altogether useless member of society. Finally Mr. Murdstone called me to him one day, and told me that he could not afford to send

D

me to school, but that I must go to work for myself. He had a partner in the wine trade in London, and I was to be given a position there.

Accordingly, Miss Murdstone packed me off without loss of time ; and I went to work—at ten years old—washing bottles in a vile-smelling warehouse down by the water-side.

There were three or four of us boys, counting me ; and I was shown how to work by an older lad whose name was Mick Walker, and who wore a ragged apron and paper cap. He introduced me to another boy by the queer name of Mealy Potatoes. I discovered, later, that this youth had started out with another name, but had been given this one on account of a pale, mealy complexion.

No words can express the secret agony of my soul as I sank into this companionship ; compared these associates with those of my happier childhood—not to say with Steerforth, Traddles, and the rest of those boys ; and felt my hopes of growing up to be a learned and distinguished man crushed in my bosom. The feeling of being utterly without hope ; of the shame I felt in my position ; of the misery it was to believe that what I had learned would pass away from me, little by little, never to be brought back any more ; cannot be written. As often as Mick Walker went away in the course of that forenoon, I mingled my tears with the water in which I was washing the bottles. But I was careful never to let the others see me in tears.

I was given the splendid salary of seven shillings a week for my services, and out of that I had to feed and clothe myself. My lodgings were provided for at the home of a Mr. Micawber, a portly, dignified man with a large, shiny bald head and rusty, genteel clothes. Mr. Micawber was perpetually dodging creditors while he waited for "something to turn up," as he expressed it. But in his way he was kind to me.

Still I had no one upon earth to go to for friendship or advice. I must needs skimp and save to be sure of having enough bread and cheese to eat; and no one lifted a finger to help me, a frightened little stranger in a large, terrifying city. I look back upon it now as a horrible dream. I know that I worked from morning till night with common men and boys, a shabby child. I know that I lounged about the streets poorly clothed and half starved. I know that but for the mercy of God, I might easily have been— for any other care that was taken of me—a little thief or vagabond.

But in these darkest days a bright idea came to me —I don't know when or how, but come it did, and refused to depart. I remembered having heard of an aunt, Miss Betsey Trotwood, my dear father's sister. I had heard both my mother and Peggotty speak of her, with some awe, it is true, as being a rather eccentric woman, who did not like boys, but still I resolved to find her. So I wrote to Peggotty and asked the address, and also for the loan of half a guinea. I had resolved to run away and appeal to my aunt for protection.

Peggotty's answer soon came with much love and the half guinea. She told me that Miss Betsey lived near Dover, but she couldn't say exactly where. This was vague enough, but didn't deter me in the slightest. I worked my week out at the warehouse, and, bidding

Mick Walker and Mealy Potatoes good-bye, ran away forthwith.

I may have had the notion of running all the way to Dover when I started. I had a small box of clothes and the half guinea, but a carter robbed me of both of them the first day. So, reduced to a few odd pence, I made but slow progress on foot, and sleeping out in the open by night.

For six days I trudged my weary way, pawning my coat for food, and not daring to ask aid from any one, for fear of being seized and sent back to London. But at last I limped in upon the bare white downs near Dover, sunburnt and in rags.

By dint of inquiries I was directed to Miss Betsey Trotwood's house, and I lost no time in going there —a sorry enough figure, as you may imagine. It was a neat little cottage looking out from some cliffs upon the sea.

As I stood at the gate peeping in and wondering how I had best proceed, a tall, slim lady came out of the house. She had a handkerchief tied over her cap, a pair of gardener's gloves on her hands, and carried a pruning-knife.

"Go away!" said Miss Betsey (for it was none other), shaking her head when she saw me, and making a distant chop in the air with her knife. "Go along! No boys here!"

I watched her, with my heart at my lips, as she marched to a corner of her garden, and stooped to dig a root. Then, without a scrap of courage, but with a great deal of desperation, I went softly in and stood beside her, touching her with my finger.

"If you please, ma'am," I began.

She started and looked up.

" If you please, aunt."

" Ен ? " exclaimed Miss Betsey, in a tone of amazement I have never heard approached.

" If you please, aunt, I am your nephew."

" Oh, Lord ! " said my aunt, and sat flat down in the garden-path.

" I am David Copperfield, of the Rookery. I used to hear my dear mamma speak of you before she died. I have been neglected and ill-treated, and so I ran away and came to you. I was robbed at first setting out, and have walked all the way, and have never slept in a bed since I began the journey."

Here my self-support gave way all at once ; and with a movement of my hands, intended to show her my ragged state, and call it to witness that I had suffered something, I broke into a passion of crying, which I suppose had been pent up within me all the week.

My aunt, with every sort of expression, sat on the gravel, staring at me, until I began to cry ; when she got up in a great hurry, collared me, and took me into the parlour. Her first proceeding there was to unlock a tall press, bring out several bottles, and pour some of the contents of each into my mouth. I think they must have been taken out at random, for I am sure I tasted aniseed water, anchovy sauce, and salad dressing. Then she rang the bell.

" Janet," she said, when her servant came in, " go upstairs, give my compliments to Mr. Dick, and say I wish to speak to him."

Mr. Dick proved to be a pleasant-faced man of whimsical ways, but upon whose advice my aunt greatly relied. As he proposed now that I be given a bath and put to bed, my aunt lost no time in following these ideas.

Janet had gone away to get the bath ready, when my aunt, to my great alarm, became in one moment rigid with wrath, and had hardly voice to cry out, " Janet ! Donkeys ! "

Upon which, Janet came running up the stairs as if the house were in flames, darted out on a little piece of green in front, and warned off two donkeys that had presumed to set hoof upon it ; while my aunt, rushing out of the house, seized the bridle of a third animal, led him forth from those sacred precincts, and boxed the ears of the unlucky urchin in attendance.

To this hour I don't know whether my aunt had any lawful right of way over that patch of green ; but she had settled it in her own mind that she had, and it was all the same to her. The one great outrage of her life, demanding to be constantly avenged, was the passage of a donkey over that spot. No matter what she was doing or saying, a donkey turned the current of her ideas in a moment, and she was upon him straight. Jugs of water and watering pots were kept in secret places ready to be discharged on the offending boys ; sticks were laid in ambush behind the door, sallies were made at all hours ; and incessant war prevailed.

Perhaps this was an agreeable excitement to the donkey-boys ; or perhaps the more sagacious of the donkeys, understanding how the case stood, stubbornly delighted in coming that way. I only know that there were three alarms before the bath was ready ; and that on the occasion of the last and most desperate of all, I saw my aunt engage, single-handed, with a sandy-headed lad of fifteen, and bump his sandy head against her own gate, before he realised what was the matter. These interruptions were the more ridiculous to me, because she was giving me broth out of a tablespoon at the time (having firmly persuaded herself that I was actually starving, and must receive food at first in very small quantities), and, while my mouth was yet open to receive the spoon, she would put it back into the basin, cry " Janet ! Donkeys ! " and go out to the assault.

The bath was a great comfort. For I began to be sensible of acute pains in my limbs from lying out in the fields, and was now so tired and low that I could hardly keep myself awake for five minutes together. When I had bathed they enrobed me in a shirt and a pair of trousers belonging to Mr. Dick, and tied me up in two or three great shawls. What sort of bundle I looked like, I don't know, but I felt a very hot one. Feeling also very faint and drowsy, I soon fell asleep.

The next morning at breakfast my aunt said, with a determined shake of her head, " Well, I've written to him."

" To whom ? " I ventured.

" To Mr. Murdstone."

" Does he know where I am, aunt ? " I inquired, alarmed.

" I have told him," said my aunt, with a nod.

" Shall I—be—given up to him ? " I faltered.

" I don't know," said my aunt. " We shall see."

" Oh ! I can't think what I shall do," I exclaimed, " if I have to go back to Mr. Murdstone ! "

" I don't know anything about it," said my aunt,

shaking her head. "I can't say, I am sure. We shall see."

My spirits sank under these words, and I became very downcast and heavy of heart.

For the next few days I felt like a criminal condemned to die; although my aunt and Mr. Dick both were very kind to me. Finally the day of the expected visit from Mr. Murdstone arrived, but without bringing him till late in the afternoon. Our dinner had been postponed; but it was growing so late that my aunt had ordered it to be got ready, when she gave a sudden alarm of donkeys, and to my consternation, I beheld Miss Murdstone, on a side-saddle, ride deliberately over the sacred piece of green, and stop in front of the house, looking about her.

"Go along with you!" cried my aunt, shaking her head and her fist out of the window. "You have no business there. How dare you trespass? Go along! Oh, you bold-faced thing!"

My aunt was so exasperated by the coolness with which Miss Murdstone looked about her, that I really believe she did not know what to do. I hastened to tell her who it was, and that Mr. Murdstone was following behind, but it made no difference. She glared at them as they entered the room in a most terrible way.

"Oh!" said my aunt, "I was not aware at first to whom I had the pleasure of objecting. But I don't allow anybody to ride over that turf. I make no exceptions. I don't allow anybody to do it."

"Your regulation is rather awkward to strangers," said Miss Murdstone.

"*Is* it!" said my aunt.

Mr. Murdstone here cleared his throat and began, " Miss Trotwood——"

" I beg your pardon," observed my aunt, with a keen look. " You are the Mr. Murdstone."

" I am," said Mr. Murdstone.

" You'll excuse my saying, sir," returned my aunt, " that I think it would have been a much better and happier thing if you had left that poor child alone."

Mr. Murdstone coloured, and Miss Murdstone looked as though she could bite nails.

" I received your letter," said Mr. Murdstone, " and thought it best to see you personally about this unhappy boy who has run away from his friends and his position. I need not tell you that he has always given us great trouble and uneasiness. He is sullen and stubborn and has a violent temper. I thought it best that you should know this."

" It can hardly be necessary for me to confirm anything stated by my brother," said Miss Murdstone ; " but I beg to observe, that, of all the boys in the world, I believe this is the worst boy."

" Strong ! " said my aunt, shortly.

" But not at all too strong for the facts," returned Miss Murdstone.

" Ha ! " said my aunt. " Well, sir ? "

" Upon the death of his mother," continued Mr. Murdstone, scowling, " I obtained a respectable place for him——"

" Was it the sort of place you would have put a boy of your own in ? " asked my aunt.

" If he had been my brother's own boy," returned Miss Murdstone, striking in, " his character, I trust, would have been altogether different."

"Or if the poor child, his mother, had been alive, he would still have gone into the respectable business, would he?" said my aunt.

"I believe," said Mr. Murdstone, with a nod of his head, "that Clara would have disputed nothing which myself and my sister were agreed was for the best."

"Humph!" said my aunt. "Well, sir, what next?"

"Merely this, Miss Trotwood," he returned. "I am here to take David back—to take him back unconditionally, and to deal with him as I think right. I am not here to make any promise to anybody. You may possibly have some idea, Miss Trotwood, of abetting him in his running away. Your manner induces me to think it possible. Now I must caution you that if you abet him once, you abet him for good and all. I cannot trifle, or be trifled with. I am here, for the first and last time, to take him away. Is he ready to go? If he is not, my doors are shut against him henceforth, and yours, I take it for granted, are opened to him."

To this address my aunt had listened with the closest attention, sitting perfectly upright, with her hands folded on one knee, and looking grimly on the speaker. When he had finished, she turned her eyes so as to command Miss Murdstone, and said:

"Well, ma'am, have *you* got anything to remark?"

"Indeed, Miss Trotwood," said Miss Murdstone, "all that I could say has been so well said by my brother, that I have nothing to add except my thanks for your politeness."

This ironical remark, however, was wholly lost.

"And what does the boy say?" said my aunt. "Are you ready to go, David?"

I answered no, and entreated her not to let me go.

I said that neither Mr. nor Miss Murdstone had ever liked me, or had ever been kind to me. That they had made my mamma, who always loved me dearly, unhappy about me, and that I knew it well, and that Peggotty knew it. And I begged and prayed my aunt —I forget in what terms now, but I remember that they affected me very much then—to befriend and protect me, for my father's sake.

"Mr. Dick," said my aunt, "what shall I do with this child?"

"Have him measured for a suit of clothes, directly," said Mr. Dick, in his usual sudden way.

"Mr. Dick," said my aunt, triumphantly, "give me your hand, for your common sense is invaluable."

Having shaken it with great cordiality, she pulled me towards her, and said to Mr. Murdstone:

"You can go when you like; I'll take my chance with the boy. If he's all you say he is, at least I can do as much for him then as you have done. But I don't believe a word of it."

"Miss Trotwood," rejoined Mr. Murdstone, shrugging his shoulders, as he rose, "if you were a gentleman——"

"Bah! stuff and nonsense!" said my aunt. "Don't talk to me!"

"How exquisitely polite!" exclaimed Miss Murdstone, rising. "Overpowering, really!"

"Do you think I don't know," said my aunt, turning a deaf ear to the sister, and continuing to address the brother, and to shake her head at him, "what kind of life you must have led that poor, little woman you cajoled into marrying you? Do you think I don't know what a woeful day it was for her and her boy when *you* first came in her way?"

And thereupon she read him such a lecture as I warrant he had never listened to before in his life, nor ever would again. He bit his lip in silence while she lectured, and all the colour left his face. Miss Murdstone tried to interrupt the flow of words repeatedly, with no success at all. When she had ended—

"Good-day, sir," said my aunt, "and good-bye! Good-day to you, too, ma'am," turning suddenly upon his sister. "Let me see you ride a donkey over *my* green again, and as sure as you have a head upon your shoulders, I'll knock your bonnet off, and tread upon it!"

It would require a painter, and no common painter too, to depict my aunt's face as she delivered herself of this very unexpected sentiment, and Miss Murdstone's face as she heard it. But the manner of the speech, no less than the matter, was so fiery, that Miss Murdstone, without a word in answer, discreetly put her arm through her brother's, and walked haughtily out of the cottage; my aunt remaining in the window looking after them, prepared, I have no doubt, to carry her threat into instant execution.

No attempt at defiance being made, however, her face gradually relaxed, and became so pleasant that I was emboldened to kiss and thank her; which I did with great heartiness, and with both my arms clasped round her neck. I then shook hands with Mr. Dick, who shook hands with me a great many times, and hailed this happy close of the proceedings with repeated bursts of laughter.

"You'll consider yourself guardian, jointly with me, of this child, Mr. Dick," said my aunt.

"I shall be delighted," said Mr. Dick, "to be the guardian of David's son."

"Very good," returned my aunt, "*that's* settled. I have been thinking, do you know, Mr. Dick, that I might call him Trotwood?"

"Yes, to be sure. Trotwood Copperfield," said Mr. Dick.

My aunt took so kindly to the notion, that some ready-made clothes, which were purchased for me the next day, were marked "Trotwood Copperfield," in her own handwriting, and in indelible marking-ink, before I put them on.

Thus I began my new life, in a new name, and with everything new about me. Now that the state of doubt was over, I felt, for many days, like one in a dream. I never thought that I had a curious couple of guardians in my aunt and Mr. Dick. I never thought of anything about myself, distinctly. While a remoteness had come upon the old life—which seemed to lie in the haze of an immeasurable distance.

In my new life I was to realise some of my youthful ambitions. I was to struggle, perhaps, but I was to succeed. And I was to find that my aunt—for all her gruff exterior—had a heart of gold.

But whatever there was of happiness or of sorrow, of success or of failure, in my new life, does not belong to these pages. The identity of the child, and of the boy, David Copperfield, is now for ever merged in the personality of Trotwood Copperfield, Esquire, the Prospective Man.

The Story of Oliver Twist

I

OLIVER BEGINS LIFE IN A HARD WAY

SOME years ago when the poorhouses of Eng
land were in a bad state and the poor people
housed within them were often ill-treated,
a little waif began his life under the roof of one of
the worst of them. His mother had wandered there,
weak, wretched and without friends, it seemed, for
she gave no clue to her identity; and after her little
boy was born she had only strength enough to kiss
him once before she breathed her last. As no one
knew anything about her, the child became a charge
upon the parish. He was sent with other orphans
and homeless little ones to be cared for by an elderly
woman named Mrs. Mann, who received from the
parish officers but a scant allowance for the needs of
the children, to whom she gave, in the shape of food
and attention, a still shorter return.

And so the first years of this child's life were devoted
mainly to the struggle to keep body and soul together.
He won the fight by the narrowest of margins, and
his ninth birthday found him a pale, thin lad, somewhat short in stature and decidedly small in girth. But

nature had placed a good sturdy spirit in his breast. It had plenty of room to expand, thanks to the spare diet, else he might not have had any ninth birthday at all.

On this momentous day he received a visitor, in the person of Mr. Bumble, the fat and pompous beadle of the workhouse, who came to see Mrs. Mann in all the glory of his cocked hat and brass buttons.

"Good-morning, ma'am," said the beadle, taking out a leathern pocket-book. "The child that was half baptised Oliver Twist is nine year old to-day."

"Bless him!" interposed Mrs. Mann, inflaming her left eye with the corner of her apron.

"And notwithstanding a offered reward of ten pound, which was afterwards increased to twenty pound; notwithstanding the most superlative, and, I may say, supernat'ral exertions on the part of this parish," said Bumble, "we have never been able to discover who is his father, or what was his mother's settlement, name, or condition."

Mrs. Mann raised her hands in astonishment; but added, after a moment's reflection, "How comes he to have any name at all, then?"

The beadle drew himself up with great pride, and said, "I inwented it."

"You, Mr. Bumble!"

"I, Mrs. Mann. We name our fondlings in alphabetical order. The last was a S,—Swubble I named him. This was a T,—Twist I named *him*. The next one as comes will be Unwin, and the next Vilkins. I have got names ready made to the end of the alphabet, and all the way through it again, when we come to Z."

"Why, you're quite a literary character, sir!" said Mrs. Mann.

"Well, well," said the beadle, evidently gratified with the compliment; "perhaps I may be. But the boy Oliver being now too old to remain here, the Board have determined to have him back into the house. I have come out myself to take him there. So let me see him at once."

"I'll fetch him directly," said Mrs. Mann, leaving the room for that purpose. And so Oliver, having had as much of the outer coat of dirt which encrusted his face and hands removed as could be scrubbed off in one washing, was presently led into the room.

"Make a bow to the gentleman, Oliver," said Mrs. Mann.

Oliver made a bow, which was divided between the beadle on the chair and the cocked hat on the table.

"Will you go along with me, Oliver?" said Mr. Bumble, in a majestic voice.

Oliver was about to say that he would go along with anybody with great readiness, when, glancing upwards, he caught sight of Mrs. Mann, who had got behind the beadle's chair, and was shaking her fist at him with a furious countenance. He took the hint at once, for the fist had been too often impressed upon his body not to be deeply impressed upon his memory.

"Will *she* go with me?" he inquired.

"No, she can't," replied Mr. Bumble, "but she'll come and see you sometimes."

This was no very great consolation to the child. Young as he was, however, he had sense enough to pretend great regret at going away. It was no very difficult matter for the boy to call the tears into his eyes. Hunger and recent ill-usage are great assistants if you want to cry; and Oliver cried very naturally indeed.

Mrs. Mann gave him a thousand embraces, and, what Oliver wanted a great deal more, a piece of bread and butter, lest he should seem too hungry when he got to the workhouse. With the slice of bread in his hand, and the little brown-cloth parish cap on his head, the boy was then led away by Mr. Bumble from the wretched home where one kind word or look had never lighted the gloom of his infant years.

Mr. Bumble walked on with long strides, and little Oliver, firmly grasping his gold-laced cuff, trotted beside him, inquiring at the end of every quarter of a mile whether they were " nearly there." To these interrogations Mr. Bumble returned very brief and snappish replies; for was he not a beadle? But at last they were there, and the boy was looking at his new home with interest not unmixed with dread.

Oliver had not been within the walls of the workhouse a quarter of an hour, and had scarcely completed the slice of bread, when Mr. Bumble, who had handed him over to the care of an old woman, returned, and, telling him it was a board night, took him before that august body forthwith.

" Bow to the Board," said Bumble. Oliver brushed away two or three tears that were lingering in his eyes, and seeing no board but the table, fortunately bowed to that.

" What's your name, boy ? " said a gentleman in a high chair.

Oliver was frightened at the sight of so many fat, red-faced gentlemen, and the beadle gave him another tap behind, which made him cry. These two causes made him answer in a very low and hesitating voice; whereupon a gentleman in a white waistcoat said he

E

was a fool, which was a capital way of raising his spirits and putting him quite at his ease.

"Boy," said the gentleman in the high chair, "listen to me. You know you're an orphan, I suppose?"

"What's that, sir?" inquired poor Oliver.

"The boy *is* a fool—I thought he was," said the gentleman in the white waistcoat.

"Hush!" said the gentleman who had spoken first. "You know you've got no father or mother, and that you were brought up by the parish, don't you?"

"Yes, sir," replied Oliver, weeping bitterly.

"What are you crying for?" inquired the gentleman in the white waistcoat. And, to be sure, it was very extraordinary. What *could* the boy be crying for?

"I hope you say your prayers every night," said another gentleman, in a gruff voice, "and pray for the people who feed you, and take care of you—like a Christian."

"Yes, sir," stammered the boy. The gentleman who spoke last was unconsciously right. It would have been *very* like a Christian, and a marvellously good Christian too, if Oliver had prayed for the people who fed and took care of *him*. But he hadn't, because nobody had taught him.

"Well! You have come here to be educated, and taught a useful trade," said the red-faced gentleman in the high chair.

"So you'll begin to pick oakum to-morrow morning at six o'clock," added the surly one in the white waistcoat.

For the combination of both these blessings in the one simple process of picking oakum, Oliver bowed low, by the direction of the beadle, and was hurried away to a large ward, where, on a rough hard bed, he sobbed himself to sleep.

Poor Oliver! He little knew, as he fell asleep, that the Board had just reached a sage decision in his and other cases. But they had, and this was it. The members of this Board were very wise men, and when they came to turn their attention to the work-house, they found out at once, what ordinary folks would never have discovered—that the poor people liked it!

"Oho!" said the Board, "We'll stop all this high living in no time!" So they brought the diet down to the edge of starvation. They contracted with the waterworks to lay on an unlimited supply of water, and with a mill to supply small quantities of oatmeal; and issued three meals of thin gruel a day, and half a roll on Sundays.

For the first six months after Oliver Twist was removed, the system was in full operation. It was rather expensive at first, in consequence of the increase in the undertaker's bill, and the necessity of taking in the clothes of all the paupers, which fluttered loosely on their wasted shrunken forms, after a week or two's gruel. But the number of workhouse inmates got thin as well as the paupers, and the Board were delighted.

The room in which the boys were fed was a large stone hall, with a copper kettle at one end, out of which the master, dressed in an apron for the purpose, and assisted by one or two women, ladled the gruel at meal times. Of this festive composition each boy had one porringer, and no more—except on occasions of great public rejoicing, when he had two ounces and a quarter

of bread besides. The bowls never wanted washing.
The boys polished them with their spoons till they
shone again; and when they had performed this operation (which never took very long, the spoons being
nearly as large as the bowls), they would sit staring
at the kettle, with eager eyes, as if they could have
devoured the very bricks of which it was composed;
employing themselves, meanwhile, in sucking their
fingers, with the view of catching up any stray splashes
of gruel that might have been cast thereon.

Boys have generally excellent appetites. Oliver
Twist and his companions suffered the tortures of slow
starvation for three months, until at last they got so
voracious and wild with hunger that one boy, who was
tall for his age and hadn't been used to that sort of
thing (for his father had kept a small cook's shop),
hinted darkly to his companions that unless he had
another basin of gruel, he was afraid he might eat the
boy who slept next him, who happened to be a weakly
youth of tender age. He had a wild hungry eye, and
they implicitly believed him. A council was held,
and lots were cast to decide who should walk up to
the master after supper that evening and ask for more;
and it fell to Oliver Twist.

The evening arrived, and the boys took their places.
The master, in his cook's uniform, stationed himself
at the kettle; his pauper assistants ranged themselves behind him; the gruel was served out, and a
long grace was said over the short rations. The gruel
disappeared; the boys whispered to each other, and
winked at Oliver, while his next neighbours nudged
him. Child as he was, he was desperate with hunger
and reckless with misery. He rose from the table and

Oliver in the Workhouse   58

advancing to the master, basin and spoon in hand, said, somewhat alarmed at his own temerity:

"Please, sir, I want some more."

The master was a fat, healthy man, but he turned very pale. He gazed in stupefied astonishment on the small rebel for some seconds, and then clung for support to the copper. The assistants were paralysed with wonder; the boys with fear.

"What!" said the master at length, in a faint voice.

"Please, sir," replied Oliver, "I want some more."

The master aimed a blow at Oliver's head with the ladle, pinioned him in his arms, and shrieked aloud for the beadle.

The Board were sitting in solemn conclave, when Mr. Bumble rushed into the room in great excitement, and, addressing the gentleman in the high chair, said:

"Mr. Limbkins, I beg your pardon, sir! Oliver Twist has asked for more!"

There was a general start. Horror was depicted on every countenance.

"For *more*!" said Mr. Limbkins. "Compose yourself, Bumble, and answer me distinctly. Do I understand that he asked for more, after he had eaten the supper allotted by the dietary?"

"He did, sir," replied Bumble.

"That boy will be hung," said the gentleman in the white waistcoat. "I know that boy will be hung."

Nobody disputed this opinion. An animated discussion took place. Oliver was ordered into instant confinement; and a bill was posted on the outside of the gate, offering a reward of five pounds to anybody who would take Oliver Twist off the hands of the parish. In other words, five pounds and Oliver Twist were offered to any man or woman who wanted an apprentice to any trade, business, or calling.

Oliver had a very narrow escape a few days later, as the result of this bill, from a villainous-looking man who wanted a chimney-sweep. But finally he became the apprentice of an undertaker named Sowerberry. His life here was some improvement over the workhouse, but still hard enough. Nevertheless he did get enough to eat, in the shape of broken victuals, and he slept among the coffins in the shop.

Unfortunately there was another apprentice, a great overgrown fellow named Noah Claypole, who delighted to bully Oliver in every way possible. Oliver stood it as long as he could, but Noah mistook his attitude for cowardice and added insults to rough usage. But, one day, Noah spoke ill of the boy's dead mother.

"What did you say?" asked Oliver quickly.

"A regular right-down bad 'un, she was, Work'us," repeated Noah coolly.

Crimson with fury, Oliver started up, overthrew the chair and table, seized Noah by the throat, shook him, in the violence of his rage, till his teeth chattered in his head, and, collecting his whole force into one heavy blow, felled him to the ground.

A minute ago, the boy had looked the quiet, mild dejected creature that harsh treatment had made him. But his spirit was roused at last; the cruel insult had set his blood on fire. His breast heaved, and he defied his tormentor with an energy he had never known before.

"He'll murder me!" blubbered Noah. "Charlotte: missis! Here's the new boy a-murdering of me! Help! help! Oliver's gone mad! Char–lotte!"

His cries brought the fat maid-servant running to the scene.

"Oh, you little wretch!" screamed Charlotte, seizing Oliver with her utmost force, which was about equal to that of a strong man in good training. "Oh, you little un-grate-ful, murder-ous, hor-rid villain!" And between every syllable Charlotte gave Oliver a blow with all her might, accompanying it with a scream, for the benefit of society.

Charlotte's fist was by no means a light one; but, lest it should not be effectual in calming Oliver's wrath, Mrs. Sowerberry plunged into the kitchen, and assisted to hold him with one hand while she scratched his face with the other. In this favourable position of affairs Noah rose from the ground and pommelled him behind.

This was rather too violent exercise to last long. When they were all three wearied out and could tear and beat no longer, they dragged Oliver, struggling and shouting but nothing daunted, into the dust-cellar, and there locked him up. This being done, Mrs. Sowerberry sank into a chair and burst into tears.

"Oh, Charlotte!" she cried; "what a mercy we have not all been murdered in our beds, with such a little villain in the house!"

And when Mr. Sowerberry presently came home, he gave Oliver a whipping on his own account for good measure.

It was not until he was left alone in the silence and stillness of the cellar that Oliver gave way to the feelings which the day's treatment had awakened. He had listened to their taunts with a look of contempt;

he had borne the lash without a cry, for he felt that pride swelling in his heart which would have kept down a shriek to the last, though they had roasted him alive. But now, when there was none to see or hear him, he fell upon his knees on the floor, and, hiding his face in his hands, wept bitter tears.

For a long time Oliver remained motionless in this attitude. The candle was burning low in the socket when he rose to his feet. Having gazed cautiously round him and listened intently, he gently undid the fastenings of the door and looked abroad.

It was a cold, dark night. The stars seemed, to the boy's eyes, farther from the earth than he had ever seen them before. There was no wind, and the sombre shadows thrown by the trees upon the ground looked sepulchral and deathlike, from being so still. He softly re-closed the door. He resolved to run away in the early morning—to go to that great city of London.

With the first ray of light that struggled through the crevices in the shutters, Oliver arose, and again unbarred the door. One timid look around,—one moment's pause of hesitation,—he had closed it behind him, and was in the open street.

He looked to the right and to the left, uncertain whither to fly. He remembered to have seen the wagons, as they went out, toiling up the hill. He took the same route, and arriving at a footpath across the fields, which he knew led out again into the road, struck into it and walked quickly on.

He was then only ten years old.

II

OLIVER FALLS FROM BAD TO WORSE

IT was seventy miles to London, and the poor boy made his way thither only with great difficulty. Begging was not allowed in many of the villages, and nearly everybody viewed him with doubt, or else shut the door in his face.

Early on the seventh morning of his flight Oliver limped slowly into the little town of Barnet, near the outskirts of London. The window-shutters were closed, the street was empty, and the boy sank down with bleeding feet and covered with dust upon a door-step.

By degrees the shutters were opened, the window-blinds were drawn up, and people began passing to and fro. Some few stopped to gaze at Oliver for a moment or two, or turned round to stare at him as they hurried by; but none relieved him, or troubled themselves to inquire how he came there. He had no heart to beg, and there he sat.

He had been crouching on the step for some time when he was roused by observing that a boy, who had passed him carelessly some minutes before, had returned, and was now surveying him most earnestly from the opposite side of the way. He took little heed of this at first; but the boy remained in the same attitude of close observation so long that Oliver raised his head and returned his steady look. Upon this the boy crossed over, and, walking close up to Oliver, said:

" Hullo ! my covey, what's the row ? "

The boy who addressed this inquiry was about his own age, but one of the queerest-looking fellows Oliver had ever seen. He was a snub-nosed, flat-browed, common-faced boy enough, and as dirty as one would wish to see ; but he had about him all the airs and manners of a man. He was short for his age, with rather bow legs, and little, sharp, ugly eyes. He wore a man's coat, which reached nearly to his heels. He had turned the cuffs back, half-way up his arm, to get his hands out of the sleeves, apparently with the ultimate view of thrusting them into the pockets of his corduroy trousers, for there he kept them. He was altogether as swaggering a young gentleman as ever stood four feet six, or something less, in his shoes.

" Hullo ! my covey, what's the row ? " said this strange young gentleman to Oliver.

" I am very hungry and tired," replied Oliver, the tears standing in his eyes as he spoke. " I have walked a long way. I have been walking these seven days."

The boy looked at him narrowly, and asked him some questions. He took Oliver for a vagrant or worse, but led him into a small tavern, and gave him a feast of ham and bread ; and Oliver, falling to at his new friend's bidding, made a long and hearty meal, during the progress of which the strange boy eyed him from time to time with great attention.

" Going to London ? " said the strange boy, when Oliver had at length concluded.

" Yes."

" Got any lodgings ? "

" No."

" Money ? "

" No."

The strange boy whistled, and put his arms into his pockets as far as the big coat-sleeves would let them go.

" Do you live in London ? " asked Oliver.

" Yes, I do when I'm at home," replied the strange boy. " Want to go along with me ? I know an old gen'elman as lives there wot'll give you lodgings for nothink."

The unexpected offer was too tempting to be resisted, especially when Oliver was told that the old gentleman would doubtless get him a good place without loss of time. This led to a more friendly and confidential chat, in which Oliver learned that his new friend's name was Jack Dawkins, commonly called " The Artful Dodger."

As Dawkins objected to entering London before nightfall, it was nearly eleven o'clock before he piloted Oliver down some of the worst streets of the city's worst section. Finally they entered a tumbledown building, and groped their way up a rickety stairway. Then Dawkins threw open the door of a back room and drew Oliver in after him.

The walls and ceiling of the room were perfectly black with age and dirt. There was a deal table before the fire, upon which were a candle stuck in a bottle, some pewter pots, bread and butter. Several rough beds were huddled side by side upon the floor. Seated around the table were four or five boys, none older than the Dodger, smoking long clay pipes and drinking spirits with the air of middle-aged men. But the chief figure was an old shrivelled Jew, whose villainous face was offset by a mass of matted red hair. He was dressed in a greasy flannel gown, and was busily at work frying sausages over a fire.

The boys crowded around Dawkins as he whispered a few words in the ear of the Jew. Then they all turned, as did the Jew, and grinned at Oliver.

"This is him, Fagin," said Jack Dawkins; "my friend Oliver Twist."

The Jew made a low bow to Oliver, took him by the hand, and hoped he should have the honour of his intimate acquaintance. Upon this, the young gentlemen with the pipes came round him, and shook both his hands very hard—especially the one in which he held his little bundle. One young gentleman was very anxious to hang up his cap for him; and another was so obliging as to put his hands in Oliver's pockets, in order that, as he was very tired, he might not have the trouble of emptying them himself when he went to bed.

"We are very glad to see you, Oliver—very," said the Jew. "Dodger, take off the sausages, and draw a tub near the fire for Oliver."

Oliver ate his share, and the Jew then mixed him a glass of hot gin and water, telling him he must drink it off directly, because another gentleman wanted the tumbler. Oliver did as he was desired. Immediately afterwards, he felt himself gently lifted on to one of the sacks, and then he sank into a deep sleep.

The next morning, Oliver watched the Jew, Dawkins, and Charley Bates, another of the boys, play a curious game. The old man would place a purse and other valuables in his pockets, whereupon the boys would try to slip them out without his knowledge.

The Dodger steals a Handkerchief 66

Oliver didn't understand in the least what it was all about, even when Fagin gave him some lessons in the same game. But he was to learn with a shock, a few days later, when Bates and Dawkins took him with them for a walk about town.

They were just emerging from a narrow court not far from the open square in Clerkenwell, when the Dodger made a sudden stop, and laying his finger on his lip, drew his companions back again with the greatest caution.

"What's the matter?" demanded Oliver.

"Hush!" replied the Dodger. "Do you see that old cove at the bookstall?"

"The gentleman over the way?" said Oliver. "Yes. I see him."

"He'll do," said the Dodger.

"A prime plant," observed Master Charley Bates.

Oliver looked from one to the other with surprise, but he was not permitted to make any inquiries; for the two boys walked stealthily across the road, and slunk close behind the old gentleman. Oliver walked a few paces after them, and, not knowing whether to advance or retire, stood looking on in silent amazement.

The gentleman was a very respectable looking person who had taken up a book from the stall and was reading away as hard as if he were in his own study.

What was Oliver's horror and alarm as he stood a few paces off, looking on with his eyelids as wide open as they would possibly go, to see the Dodger plunge his hand into the gentleman's pocket, and draw from thence a handkerchief; to see him hand the same to Charley Bates; and finally to behold them both running away round the corner at full speed!

Oliver saw in a flash that they were pick-pockets, and that he would be classed among them! He turned to run—the worst possible thing to do—for just then the gentleman missed his handkerchief and glanced around in time to see Oliver scudding away for dear life; and shouting "Stop thief!" made off after him, book in hand.

He was not alone in the cry, for Bates and Dawkins, willing to divert attention from themselves, also shouted "Stop thief!" and joined in the pursuit like good citizens.

"Stop thief! Stop thief!" There is a magic in the sound. The tradesman leaves his counter, and the carman his wagon; the butcher throws down his tray; the baker his basket; the milkman his pail; the errand boy his parcels; the school-boy his marbles. Away they run, pell-mell, helter-skelter, slap-dash, tearing, yelling, screaming and knocking down the passengers as they turn the corners.

"Stop thief! Stop thief!" The cry is taken up by a hundred voices, and the crowd accumulates at every turning. Away they fly, splashing through the mud and rattling along the pavements. Up go the windows, out run the people, and lend fresh vigour to the cry, "Stop thief! Stop thief!"

Stopped at last! A well-aimed blow laid Oliver upon the pavement. Then a policeman seized him by the collar and he was hustled off for trial before a magistrate.

The magistrate was a surly boor who was in the habit of committing prisoners to gaol with the merest pretence of a trial. It did not take him long to decide that Oliver was a hardened criminal, in spite of the protests of the kindly old gentleman whose pocket had been picked; and the boy was, in fact, being carried away in a fainting condition, when the bookseller whose shop had been the scene of action and who had witnessed the whole thing, rushed in and declared Oliver's innocence.

The poor child was thereupon released; and the old gentleman—Mr. Brownlow by name—was so sorry for him, and so taken by his frank face, that he took him to his own home and nursed him through a severe illness, the result of all his early privations and recent trouble. Mr. Brownlow even thought of adopting him, and, as soon as he was well enough, let him have books to read out of his own well-stocked library, greatly to the eager Oliver's delight.

It did indeed seem as though the sky had cleared for the boy, but instead still darker days were threatening. Fagin the Jew heard of Oliver's escape with fear and anger. He knew that it would never do for the boy to tell what he knew about the thieves' den. Their one chance of safety lay in seizing him again and making him a thief like themselves, so that his mouth would be closed.

So Fagin called to his aid a burglar, a big, brutal fellow named Bill Sikes, who always went around with a knotted stick and a surly dog. Nancy, a poor girl of the streets, was also put upon the search, and soon their united efforts were successful.

One day after Oliver had begun to grow strong, he was sent by Mr. Brownlow on an errand to a book-shop. He was well dressed in a new suit, and had some books and a five-pound note of Mr. Brownlow's. It was not far, but he accidentally turned down a

by-street that was not exactly in his way. He started
to turn back, when he heard a girl's voice screaming,
"Oh, my dear brother!" And he had hardly looked
up to see what the matter was, when he was stopped
by having a pair of arms thrown tight around his
neck.

"Don't!" cried Oliver, struggling. "Let go of
me! Who is it? What are you stopping me
for?"

The only reply to this was a great number of loud
lamentations from the young woman who had em-
braced him, and who had a little basket and a large
key in her hand.

"Oh, my gracious!" said the young woman, "I've
found him! Oh, Oliver! Oliver! Oh, you naughty
boy, to make me suffer sich distress on your account!
Come home, dear, come! Oh, I've found him! Thank
gracious goodness heavins, I've found him!" With
these exclamations the young woman burst into another
fit of crying.

"What's the matter, ma'am?" inquired a woman.

"Oh, ma'am," replied the girl, "he ran away, near
a month ago, from his parents, who are hard-working
and respectable people, and went and joined a set of
thieves and bad characters, and almost broke his
mother's heart."

"Young wretch!" said the woman.

"I'm not," replied Oliver, greatly alarmed. "I
don't know her. I haven't any sister, or father and
mother either. I'm an orphan; I live at Pentonville."

"Oh, only hear him, how he braves it out!" cried
the young woman.

"Why, it's Nancy!" exclaimed Oliver, who had

known her at the Jew's, and now saw her face for the first time.

"You see he knows me!" cried Nancy, appealing to the bystanders. "He can't help himself. Make him come home, there's good people, or he'll kill his dear mother and father, and break my heart!"

"What the devil's this?" said a man, bursting out of a beer shop, with a white dog at his heels; "young Oliver! Come home to your poor mother, you young dog! Come home, directly."

"I don't belong to them. I don't know them. Help! help!" cried Oliver, struggling in the man's powerful grasp.

"Help!" repeated the man. "Yes; I'll help you, you young rascal! What books are these? You've been a stealing 'em, have you? Give 'em here." With these words, the man tore the volumes from his grasp and struck him on the head.

"That's right!" cried a looker-on from a garret window, "That's the only way of bringing him to his senses!"

"To be sure!" cried a sleepy-faced carpenter, casting an approving look at the garret window.

"It'll do him good!" said the woman.

"And he shall have it, too!" rejoined the man, administering another blow, and seizing Oliver by the collar. "Come on, you young villain! Here, Bull's-eye, mind him, boy! Mind him!"

Weak from his recent illness and with no one in the idle crowd to befriend him, poor Oliver could only suffer himself to be led away sobbing. Bill Sikes saw his advantage, and pushed him rapidly down the street. Then he commanded him to take hold of Nancy's hand.

F

"Do you hear?" growled Sikes, as Oliver hesitated, and looked round.

They were in a dark corner, quite out of the track of passengers. Oliver saw, but too plainly, that resistance would be of no avail. He held out his hand, which Nancy clasped tight in hers.

"Give me the other," said Sikes. "Here, Bull's-eye!"

The dog looked up and growled.

"See here, boy!" said Sikes, putting his other hand to Oliver's throat; "if he speaks ever so soft a word, hold him! D'ye mind?"

The dog growled again, and, licking his lips, eyed Oliver as if he were anxious to attach himself to his windpipe without delay.

And in this fashion Oliver saw with unspeakable horror that he was being taken back to the Jew. What would the trusting Mr. Brownlow think of him? What, indeed! The hot tears blinded Oliver's eyes at the bare thought.

Presently they arrived before the house, but found it perfectly dark.

"Let's have a glim," said Sikes, "or we shall go breaking our necks, or treading on the dogs. Look after your legs if you do! That's all."

"Stand still a moment, and I'll get you one," replied a voice. The footsteps of the speaker were heard, and in another minute the form of Mr. John Dawkins, otherwise the Artful Dodger, appeared. He bore in his right hand a tallow candle stuck in the end of a cleft stick.

The young gentleman did not stop to bestow any other mark of recognition upon Oliver than a humorous grin; but, turning away, beckoned the visitors to follow him. As they entered the low, dingy room, they were received with a shout of laughter.

"Oh, my wig, my wig!" cried Charley Bates; "here he is! oh, cry, here he is! Oh, Fagin, look at him; Fagin, do look at him! I can't bear it; it is such a jolly game, I can't bear it! Hold me, somebody, while I laugh it out."

With this, Master Bates laid himself flat on the floor, and kicked convulsively for five minutes, in an ecstasy of joy. Then jumping to his feet, he snatched the cleft stick from the Dodger, and, advancing to Oliver, viewed him round and round, while the Jew, taking off his nightcap, made a great number of low bows to the bewildered boy. The Artful, meantime, who seldom gave way to merriment when it interfered with business, rifled Oliver's pockets thoroughly.

"Look at his togs, Fagin!" said Charley, putting the light so close to his new jacket as nearly to set him on fire. "Look at his togs—superfine cloth, and the heavy-swell cut! Oh, my eye, what a game! And his books, too; nothing but a gentleman, Fagin!"

"Delighted to see you looking so well, my dear," said the Jew, bowing with mock humility. "The Artful shall give you another suit, my dear, for fear you should spoil that Sunday one. Why didn't you write, my dear, and say you were coming? We'd have got something warm for supper."

At this Master Bates roared again so loud that Fagin himself relaxed, and even the Dodger smiled; but as the Artful drew forth the five-pound note at that instant, it is doubtful whether the sally or the discovery awakened his merriment.

"Hallo! what's that?" inquired Sikes, stepping forward as the Jew seized the note. "That's mine, Fagin."

"No, no, my dear," said the Jew. "Mine, Bill, mine. You shall have the books."

"They belong to Mr. Brownlow!" cried Oliver, wringing his hands. "Oh, pray send them back! He'll think I stole them!"

"The boy's right," replied Fagin, with a sly wink. "He *will* think you've stole them!"

Oliver saw by his look that all chance of rescue was gone, and shrieking wildly he made a dash for the door. But the dog arrested him with a fierce growl, while a blow laid him upon the floor.

For several days Fagin kept him hid close, for fear of searching parties. Then, resolving to have the boy led deeply into crime as soon as possible, he forced him to accompany Bill Sikes upon a house-breaking expedition.

Accordingly, one raw evening they set forth—Oliver, Sikes, and another burglar, Toby Crackit—the ruffians threatening to shoot the boy if he so much as uttered one word. On account of his small size he was chosen to creep through a little window of the house which was to be robbed. The opening was about five feet from the ground, and so small that the inmates did not think it worth while to defend it securely. But it was large enough to admit a boy of Oliver's size, nevertheless.

"Now listen, you young limb," whispered Sikes, drawing a dark lantern from his pocket and throwing the glare full in Oliver's face: "I'm going to put you through there. Take this light; go softly up the steps straight afore you, and along the little hall, to the street door ; unfasten it and let us in."

So saying, the burglar hoisted Oliver up and put him through the window.

"You see the stairs afore you ? "

Oliver, more dead than alive, gasped out "Yes." Sikes pointed a pistol at him, and advised him to take notice that he was within shot all the way. Nevertheless, the boy had firmly resolved that, whether he died in the attempt or not, he would make one effort to dart upstairs from the hall and alarm the family. Filled with this idea, he advanced at once, but stealthily.

"Come back ! " suddenly cried Sikes aloud. "Back ! back ! "

Scared by the sudden breaking of the dead stillness of the place, and by a loud cry which followed it, Oliver let his lantern fall, and knew not whether to advance or fly.

The cry was repeated—a light appeared—a vision of two terrified half-dressed men at the top of the stairs swam before his eyes—a flash—a loud noise—a smoke —a crash somewhere, but where he knew not—and he staggered back.

Sikes had disappeared for an instant ; but he was up again, and had him by the collar before the smoke had cleared away.

He fired his own pistol after the men, who were already retreating, and dragged the boy up.

"Clasp your arm tighter," said Sikes, as he drew him through the window. "Give me a shawl here. They've hit him. Quick ! How the boy bleeds ! "

Then came the loud ringing of a bell, mingled with the noise of firearms, and the shouts of men, and the sensation of being carried over uneven ground at a rapid pace. And then, the noises grew confused in the distance. A cold deadly feeling crept over the boy's heart, and he saw or heard no more.

III

OLIVER MAKES HIS WAY INTO GOOD SOCIETY

BILL SIKES and Toby Crackit were so hard pressed that they were soon forced to leave Oliver lying in a ditch. The hue and cry passed him to one side, leaving him alone and unconscious through the long cold night. Morning drew on apace. The rain came down thick and fast, but Oliver felt it not as it beat against him.

At length a low cry of pain broke the stillness; and uttering it, the boy awoke. His left arm, rudely bandaged in a shawl, hung heavy and useless at his side; and the bandage was saturated with blood. He was so weak that he could scarcely raise himself into a sitting posture. When he had at last done so, he looked feebly round for help, and groaned with agony. Trembling in every joint from cold and exhaustion, he made an effort to stand upright; but, shuddering from head to foot, fell prostrate on the ground.

After a short return of the stupor in which he had been so long plunged, Oliver got upon his feet, and essayed to walk. His head was dizzy, and he staggered to and fro like a drunken man. But he kept up, nevertheless, and, with his head drooping languidly on his breast, went stumbling onward, he knew not whither.

The rain was falling heavily now, but the cold drops roused him like whiplashes. He pressed forward with the last ounce of his strength, feeling that if he stopped he must surely die, and by chance reached the same house of the attempted burglary. He knew the place at once, but his strength was at an end, and he sank exhausted under the little portico by the door.

The servants who presently opened the door were immensely surprised to find the wounded boy; and two of them were certain he was the same who had broken into the house. But in his pitiful condition they put him to bed and sent for a surgeon.

A very kind-hearted lady, Mrs. Maylie, and her adopted niece Rose, lived here. They cared for Oliver tenderly; for, like his lost friend, Mr. Brownlow, they were greatly taken by his open face, and believed in him, despite the strange story which he presently found strength to tell. With the aid of their friend the surgeon, they convinced the servants that a mistake had been made, and so Oliver was not taken to gaol. Instead, he was received into this kindly home, and it really seemed that now his dark days were over at last.

Oliver resumed the study of his beloved books, which he had begun with Mr. Brownlow. But he also spent much time in the open fields, and soon grew sturdy and strong, with the brown look of health in his face. Between him and Rose Maylie a tender affection sprang up. He was, in fact, her devoted knight.

One beautiful evening, when the first shades of twilight were beginning to settle upon the earth, Oliver sat at his window, intent upon his books. He had been poring over them for some time; and, as the day had been uncommonly sultry, and he had exerted himself a great deal, by slow degrees he fell asleep.

There is a kind of sleep that steals upon us sometimes, which, while it holds the body prisoner, does not free the mind from a sense of things about it, or enable it to ramble at its pleasure.

Oliver knew, perfectly well, that he was in his own little room; that his books were lying on the table before him; that the sweet air was stirring among the creeping plants outside. And yet he was asleep. Suddenly, the scene changed; the air became close and confined; and he thought, with a glow of terror, that he was in the Jew's house again. There sat the hideous old man, in his accustomed corner, pointing at him, and whispering to another man, with his face averted, who sat beside him.

"Hush, my dear!" he thought he heard the Jew say; "it is he, sure enough. Come away."

"He!" the other man seemed to answer; "could I mistake him, think you? If a crowd of ghosts were to put themselves into his exact shape, and he stood among them, there is something that would tell me how to point him out!"

The man seemed to say this with such dreadful hatred, that Oliver awoke with the fear and started up.

Good Heaven! what was that which sent the blood tingling to his heart, and deprived him of his voice and of power to move! There—there—at the window —close before him—so close that he could have almost touched him before he started back—with his eyes peering into the room, and meeting his—there stood the Jew! And beside him were the scowling features of a dark man whom Oliver had seen only once, but had instinctively learned to fear.

It was but an instant, a glance, a flash, before his eyes, and they were gone. But they had recognised him, and he them. He knew they were once again lying in wait to seize him, and that his days of peace and happiness were numbered.

Voice and motion came back to him with the fear; and leaping from the window he called loudly for help.

Nevertheless, no trace of Fagin or the stranger could be found, though the search was pursued with haste; and Oliver's friends were forced to believe that it had been only a feverish dream.

But Oliver had not been mistaken. The two figures at the window were really Fagin and a man named Monks, who for some mysterious reason had been the boy's most vindictive enemy. It was he who had found Oliver again and reported the fact to Fagin; and together they laid cunning plans to get him once more into their clutches.

At this critical moment in Oliver's welfare, an unexpected friend to him appeared in the person of Nancy, the street girl. She had bitterly repented her share in kidnapping him from Mr. Brownlow, and now longed for a chance to do him some service. The chance offered, when she happened to overhear the interview between Monks and the Jew. She could not understand all she heard, but she realised that the boy was in great danger unless she acted at once.

Hastening to the home of Rose Maylie, Nancy contrived to see her alone and repeated word for word the conversation she had overheard. From the dark threats of this man Monks, it seemed that Oliver's very life was in danger, because of some secret connected with his birth. Nancy knew that it meant her own death also if her visit to Miss Maylie became known, but she could not remain silent.

Miss Maylie listened to her story with horror and amazement. She realised that something must be done quickly, but did not know to whom to turn. In her perplexity Oliver made a discovery of great value to both of them. On the very day of Nancy's hurried visit and no less hurried departure he came running in, his eyes all aglow with excitement.

"I have seen him!" he exclaimed excitedly; "I knew that if I kept on looking, I should find him again one day! I mean the gentleman who was so good to me—Mr. Brownlow!"

"Where?" asked Rose.

"Getting out of a coach," replied Oliver. "I didn't have the chance to speak to him, but I took the number of the house he went into. Here it is." And he flourished a scrap of paper delightedly. "Oh, let us go there at once!"

Rose read the address eagerly, and decided to put the discovery to account. Not alone would Oliver be gratified, but Mr. Brownlow might be the very friend they needed at this momentous time.

"Quick!" she said; "tell them to fetch a hackney-coach, and be ready to go with me. I will take you there directly, without a minute's loss of time. I will only tell my aunt that we are going out for an hour, and be ready as soon as you are."

Oliver needed no prompting to hasten, and in little more than five minutes they were on their way. When they arrived at the address noted, Rose left Oliver

in the coach, under pretence of preparing his friend
to receive him; and sending up her card by the servant, requested to see Mr. Brownlow on very pressing
business. The servant soon returned, to beg that
she would walk upstairs; and following him into an
upper room, Miss Maylie was presented to an elderly
gentleman of benevolent appearance, in a bottle-green
coat.

"Dear me," said the gentleman, hastily rising, with
great politeness, "I beg your pardon, young lady
—I imagined it was some importunate person who—
I beg you will excuse me. Be seated, pray."

"Mr. Brownlow, I believe, sir?" said Rose.

"That is my name."

"I shall surprise you very much, I have no doubt,"
said Rose, naturally embarrassed, "but you once
showed great kindness to a very dear young friend
of mine, and I am sure you will take an interest in
hearing of him again."

"Indeed!" said Mr. Brownlow.

"Oliver Twist, as you know him," said Rose.

Mr. Brownlow was naturally surprised, but said
nothing for a few moments. Then looking straight
into her eyes, he remarked quietly but earnestly, "Believe me, my dear young lady, if you can tell me good
news of that child, or lift the shadow which rests upon
his name, you will be doing me the greatest service."

Rose at once related in a few words all that had
befallen Oliver since leaving Mr. Brownlow's house;
how he had searched for him but had only seen him
that very day; and finally of the new danger which
threatened the boy.

You may believe that Mr. Brownlow sat very straight,

upon the extreme edge of his chair, during the latter part of this recital.

"The poor lad!" he exclaimed; "but why have you not brought him with you?"

"I wished to talk with you alone about this plot. He does not know of it. But "—smilingly—" I believe he is now waiting in the coach at the door."

"At this door?" cried Mr. Brownlow. And without another word he rushed from the room.

In less than a minute he was back again, lugging Oliver in bodily and both laughing—yes, and shedding tears—at the same time.

Then after the jolliest of visits, Rose and Oliver took their leave for the present; but not before Mr. Brownlow had told Rose privately that he would turn his whole attention to the new conspiracy.

Nancy had promised to meet Rose on London Bridge, a few nights later, and Mr. Brownlow determined to be there also. In the meantime he made other plans for capturing the rogues.

IV

THE END OF EVIL DAYS

NOW, unbeknown to Nancy, Fagin the Jew had become suspicious of her, and had set a spy upon her heels. This spy was none other than Noah Claypole, the undertaker's apprentice, whom Oliver had so soundly thrashed. Noah had lately come to London to try his fortune in any underhand way that might arise. The Jew was always on the look-out for just such fellows as he. So they soon struck a bargain.

On the night when Nancy set forth to keep her appointment on the Bridge, Noah was kept busy darting from pillar to post, but all the time keeping her in sight. When she met Rose and Mr. Brownlow, the spy quickly slunk behind an abutment where he could hear every word of what she said. And you may be sure he lost no time in taking his story back to the Jew.

Bill Sikes had just returned, in the early morning, from a house-breaking jaunt, and was as usual in an ugly mood. A word from the Jew about Nancy's defection set his brain on fire with hatred against the girl. He hastened to her room, and, disregarding all her appeals for mercy, struck her lifeless to the floor.

This murder proved the beginning of the end for all the gang. Mr. Brownlow had already set the police to work, and now offered a large personal reward for Sikes's arrest. The murderer was tracked in and about the city for several days, until he finally hung himself in endeavouring to escape from the roof of a house.

Fagin the Jew was captured at last, and for his share in this crime, and his other wickednesses, was condemned to death. A great popular clamour had been aroused against him, and he was to be hung without delay.

In the hope that the Jew would throw some light upon Monks and some secret papers which Mr. Brownlow had traced, that gentleman took Oliver with him to the prison to see Fagin on his last night upon earth.

" Is the young gentleman to come, too, sir ? " said the man whose duty it was to conduct them. " It's not a sight for children, sir."

" It is not indeed, my friend," rejoined Mr. Brownlow;

" but my business with this man is intimately connected with him ; and as this child has seen him in the full career of his success and villany, I think it well—even at the cost of some pain and fear—that he should see him now."

These few words had been said apart, so as to be inaudible to Oliver. The man touched his hat ; and glancing at Oliver with some curiosity, opened another gate, opposite to that by which they had entered, and led them on, through dark and winding ways, to the cell.

The condemned criminal was seated on his bed, rocking himself from side to side, with a countenance more like that of a snared beast than the face of a man. His mind was evidently wandering to his old life, for he continued to mutter, without appearing conscious of their presence otherwise than as a part of his vision.

" Good boy, Charley—well done ! "—he mumbled. " Oliver too, ha ! ha ! ha ! Oliver too—quite the gentleman now—quite the—take that boy away to bed ! "

The gaoler took the disengaged hand of Oliver, and, whispering to him not to be alarmed, looked on without speaking.

" Take him away to bed ! " cried the Jew. " Do you hear me, some of you ?   He has been the—the—somehow the cause of all this ! "

" Fagin," said the gaoler.

" That's me ! " cried the Jew, falling, instantly, into the attitude of listening he had assumed upon his trial. " An old man, my Lord ; a very old, old man ! "

" Here," said the turnkey, laying his hand upon his breast to keep him down. " Here's somebody wants to see you, to ask you some questions, I suppose. Fagin, Fagin ! Are you a man ? "

"I shan't be one long," replied the Jew, looking up with a face retaining no human expression but rage and terror. "Strike them all dead! What right have they to butcher me?"

As he spoke he caught sight of Oliver and Mr. Brownlow. Shrinking to the farthest corner of the seat, he demanded to know what they wanted there.

"Steady," said the turnkey, still holding him down, "Now, sir, tell him what you want—quick, if you please, for he grows worse as the time gets on."

"You have some papers," said Mr. Brownlow, advancing, "which were placed in your hands, for better security, by a man called Monks."

"It's all a lie together," replied the Jew. "I haven't one—not one."

"For the love of God," said Mr. Brownlow, solemnly, "do not tell a lie now, upon the very verge of death; but tell me where they are. You know that Sikes is dead; and that there is no hope of any farther gain. Where are those papers?"

"Oliver," cried the Jew, beckoning to him. "Here, here! Let me whisper to you."

"I am not afraid," said Oliver, in a firm voice, as he relinquished Mr. Brownlow's hand.

"The papers," said the Jew, drawing him towards him, "are in a canvas bag, in a hole a little way up the chimney in the top front room. I want to talk to you, my dear. I want to talk to you."

"Yes, yes," returned Oliver. "Let me say a prayer. Do! Let me say one prayer. Say only one, upon your knees, with me, and we will talk till morning."

"Outside, outside," replied the Jew, pushing the boy before him towards the door, and looking vacantly over his head. "Say I've gone to sleep—they'll believe *you*. You can get me out, if you take me so. Now then, now then!"

"Oh! God forgive this wretched man!" cried the boy, with a burst of tears.

"That's right, that's right," said the Jew. "That'll help us on. This door first. If I shake and tremble as we pass the gallows, don't you mind, but hurry on. Now, now, now!"

"Have you nothing else to ask him, sir?" inquired the turnkey.

"No other question," replied Mr. Brownlow. "If I hoped we could recall him to a sense of his position——"

"Nothing will do that, sir," replied the man, shaking his head. "You had better leave him."

The door of the cell opened and the attendants returned.

"Press on, press on," cried the Jew. "Softly, but not so slow. Faster, faster!"

The men laid hands upon him, and disengaging Oliver from his grasp, held him back. He struggled with the power of desperation for an instant, and then sent up cry upon cry that penetrated even those massive walls and rang in their ears until they reached the open yard.

And this, thought Oliver, shudderingly—was the last of the Jew—the man from whose clutches he had so narrowly escaped!

Noah Claypole turned King's evidence at this time, and thus escaped the law. Dawkins, the Artful Dodger, had been caught picking pockets and was transported from the country. Charley Bates was so unnerved by the fate of Nancy, and the swift punishment of his companions, that he reformed and became an honest, hard-working young man.

And, finally, what of Monks? He was shadowed and seized by Mr. Brownlow's agents, and proved to be none other than the half-brother of Oliver Twist! Their father was dead, but he had left a will providing for the boy also. And it was on this account that Monks had wished to get him out of the way, and had employed Fagin in trying to ruin the lad.

The papers were found, as the Jew had indicated, and they not only cleared up Oliver's past history, but proved his right to a share in a considerable family estate. Mr. Brownlow had known Monks's father in their early days, and now used this knowledge to wring a full confession from the villain.

Another strange secret came to light also, at this time. Rose Maylie was found to be a younger sister of Oliver's dead mother, and therefore the boy's own aunt.

"Not aunt!" cried Oliver, when he heard this amazing but delightful news; "I'll never call her aunt! Sister, my own dear sister, that something taught my heart to love so dearly from the first! Rose, dear darling Rose!"

And the two orphans, no longer alone but united and surrounded by loving friends, were clasped in each other's arms.

G

The Story of Smike and His Teacher

I

HOW NICHOLAS NICKLEBY CAME TO DOTHEBOYS HALL

"EDUCATION. — At Mr. Wackford Squeers's Academy, Dotheboys Hall, at the delightful village of Dotheboys, near Greta Bridge in Yorkshire, Youth are boarded, clothed, booked, furnished with pocket-money, provided with all necessaries, instructed in all languages living and dead, mathematics, orthography, geometry, astronomy, trigonometry, the use of the globes, algebra, single stick (if required), writing, arithmetic, fortification, and every other branch of classical literature. Terms, twenty guineas per annum. No extras, no vacations, and diet unparalleled. Mr. Squeers is in town, and attends daily, from one till four, at the Saracen's Head, Snow Hill. N.B.—An able assistant wanted. Annual salary £5. A Master of Arts would be preferred."

To Nicholas Nickleby, a young man of nineteen, who had come to London seeking his fortune, this advertisement in a daily paper seemed a godsend—that is, provided he could secure the position referred to in the last two lines. It is true the salary was not large; but he reflected that his board and living would be included, and that a young man of his education and ability would be bound to rise. He even fancied himself, in a rosy-coloured future, at the head of this model school, Dotheboys Hall, in the delightful village of Dotheboys, near Greta Bridge, in Yorkshire.

But it would not do to sit dreaming. Someone else might snap up this golden opportunity. Nicholas brushed his clothes carefully and lost no time in calling upon Mr. Squeers, at the tavern called the Saracen's Head.

Mr. Squeers's appearance was not prepossessing. He had but one eye which, while it was unquestionably useful, was decidedly not ornamental, being of a greenish gray and in shape resembling the fan-light of a street-door. The blank side of his face was much wrinkled and puckered up, which gave him a very sinister appearance, especially when he smiled, at which times his expression bordered closely on the villainous. He was about two or three and fifty, and a trifle below the middle size; and he wore a white neckerchief with long ends, and a suit of scholastic black.

Mr. Squeers was standing in a box by one of the coffee-room fireplaces, fitted with one such table as is usually seen in coffee-rooms. In a corner of the seat was a very small deal trunk, tied round with a scanty piece of cord; and on the trunk was perched—his lace-up half-boots and corduroy trousers dangling in the air—a diminutive boy, with his shoulders drawn up to his ears, and his hands planted on his knees, who glanced timidly at the schoolmaster, from time to time, with evident dread. Presently the boy chanced to give a violent sneeze.

"Hallo, sir!" growled the schoolmaster, turning round. "What's that, sir?"

"Nothing, please, sir," replied the little boy.

"Nothing, sir!" exclaimed Mr. Squeers.

"Please, sir, I sneezed," rejoined the boy, trembling till the little trunk shook under him.

"Oh! sneezed, did you?" retorted Mr. Squeers. "Then what did you say 'nothing' for, sir?"

In default of a better answer to this question, the little boy screwed a couple of knuckles into each of his eyes and began to cry; wherefore Mr. Squeers knocked him off the trunk with a blow on one side of his face, and knocked him on again with a blow on the other.

"Wait till I get you down to Yorkshire, my young gentleman," said Mr. Squeers, "and then I'll give you the rest. Will you hold that noise, sir?"

"Ye–ye–yes," sobbed the little boy, rubbing his face very hard.

"Then do so at once, sir," said Squeers. "Do you hear?"

The little boy rubbed his face harder, as if to keep the tears back; and, beyond alternately sniffing and choking, gave no farther vent to his emotions.

"Mr. Squeers," said the waiter, looking in at this juncture, "here's a gentleman asking for you at the bar."

"Show the gentleman in, Richard," replied Mr. Squeers, in a soft voice. "Put your handkerchief in your pocket, you little scoundrel!"

The schoolmaster had scarcely uttered these words in a fierce whisper, when the stranger entered. Affecting not to see him, Mr. Squeers feigned to be intent upon mending a pen, and offering benevolent advice to his youthful pupil.

"My dear child," said Mr. Squeers, "all people have their trials. This early trial of yours that is fit to make your little heart burst and your very eyes come out of

your head with crying, what is it ? Nothing ; less than
nothing. You are leaving your friends, but you will
have a father in me, my dear, and a mother in Mrs.
Squeers. At the delightful village of Dotheboys, near
Greta Bridge in Yorkshire, where youths are boarded,
clothed, booked, washed, furnished with pocket-money,
provided with all necessaries—— "

" Mr. Squeers, I believe," said Nicholas Nickleby, as
that worthy man stopped to cough.

" The same, sir. What can I do for you ? "

" I came in answer to an advertisement in this morning's
paper," said Nicholas. " I believe you desire an assistant."

" I do, sir," rejoined Mr. Squeers, coolly ; " but if
you are applying for the place, don't you think you're
too young ? "

" I hope not, sir, and I have a fair education. I
could——"

" Could what ? " interrupted the schoolmaster. " Could
you lick the boys if they needed it ? "

" I do not usually believe in that sort of punishment—"
hesitated Nicholas.

" Could you do it ? " urged Mr. Squeers.

" I think—if they needed it—I could lick anybody
in your school," smiled Nicholas.

" Well, why didn't you say so ? I guess I had better
take you. I've got to leave town at eight o'clock to-
morrow morning, and haven't time to look round. So
be on hand sharp ! "

Nicholas thanked him and promised to be on hand.

The next day he was as good as his word, and reached
the tavern a little in advance of the appointed hour.

He found Mr. Squeers sitting at breakfast, with the
little boy before noticed, and four others who had turned

up by some lucky chance since the interview of the previous day, ranged in a row on the opposite seat. Mr. Squeers had before him a small measure of coffee, a plate of hot toast, and a cold round of beef; but he was at that moment intent on preparing breakfast for the little boys.

"This is twopenn'orth of milk, is it, waiter?" said he, looking down into a large blue mug, and slanting it gently, so as to get an accurate view of the quantity of liquid contained in it.

"That's twopenn'orth, sir," replied the waiter.

"What a rare article milk is, to be sure, in London!" said Mr. Squeers, with a sigh. "Just fill that mug up with lukewarm water, William, will you?"

"To the wery top, sir?" inquired the waiter. "Why, the milk will be drownded."

"Never you mind that," replied Mr. Squeers. "Serve it right for being so dear! You ordered that thick bread and butter for three, did you?"

"Coming directly, sir."

"You needn't hurry yourself," said Squeers; "there's plenty of time. Conquer your passions, boys, and don't be eager after vittles." As he uttered this moral precept, Mr. Squeers took a large bite out of the cold beef, and recognised Nicholas.

"Sit down, Mr. Nickleby," said Squeers. "Here we are, a-breakfasting, you see!"

Nicholas did *not* see that anybody was breakfasting except Mr. Squeers; but he bowed with all becoming reverence, and looked as cheerful as he could.

"Oh! that's the milk and water, is it, William?" said Squeers. "Very good; don't forget the bread and butter presently."

At this fresh mention of the bread and butter the five little boys looked very eager, and followed the waiter out with their eyes; meanwhile Mr. Squeers tasted the milk and water.

"Ah!" said that gentleman, smacking his lips, "here's richness! Think of the many beggars and orphans in the streets that would be glad of this, little boys. A shocking thing hunger is, isn't it, Mr. Nickleby?"

"Very shocking, sir," said Nicholas.

"When I say number one," pursued Mr. Squeers, putting the mug before the children, "the boy on the left hand nearest the window may take a drink; and when I say number two, the boy next him will go in, and so till we come to number five, which is the last boy. Are you ready?"

"Yes, sir," cried all the little boys with great eagerness.

"That's right," said Squeers, calmly getting on with his breakfast; "keep ready till I tell you to begin. Subdue your appetites, my dears, and you've conquered human nature. This is the way we inculcate strength of mind, Mr. Nickleby," said the schoolmaster, turning to Nicholas, and speaking with his mouth very full of beef and toast.

Nicholas murmured something—he knew not what—in reply; and the little boys, dividing their gaze between the mug, the bread and butter (which had by this time arrived), and every morsel which Mr. Squeers took into his mouth, remained with strained eyes in torments of expectation.

"Thank God for a good breakfast," said Squeers, when he had finished. "Number one may take a drink."

Number one seized the mug ravenously, and had just drunk enough to make him wish for more, when

Mr. Squeers gave the signal for number two, who gave up at the same interesting moment to number three; and the process was repeated until the milk and water terminated with number five.

" And now," said the schoolmaster, dividing the bread and butter for three into as many portions as there were children, " you had better look sharp with your breakfast, for the horn will blow in a minute or two, and then every boy leaves off."

Permission being thus given to fall to, the boys began to eat voraciously and in desperate haste; while the schoolmaster (who was in high good-humour after his meal) picked his teeth with a fork, and looked smilingly on. In a very short time the horn was heard.

" I thought it wouldn't be long," said Squeers, jumping up and producing a little basket from under the seat; " put what you haven't had time to eat in here, boys. You'll want it on the road! "

Nicholas was considerably startled by these very economical arrangements; but he had no time to reflect upon them, for the little boys had to be got up to the top of the coach, and this task was in his department. But soon they were all stowed away, and the coach started off with a flourish.

The journey proved long and hard, however. They were detained several times by the bad roads and inclement weather, so that it was not until nightfall of the second day that they reached their destination.

" Jump out," said Squeers. " Hallo there! come and put this horse up. Be quick, will you! "

While the schoolmaster was uttering these and other impatient cries, Nicholas had time to observe that the school was a long, cold-looking house, one storey high,

with a few straggling out-buildings behind, and a barn
and stable adjoining. After a lapse of a minute or two,
the noise of somebody unlocking the yard-gate was
heard, and presently a tall, lean boy, with a lantern in
his hand, issued forth.

" Is that you, Smike ? " cried Squeers.

" Yes, sir," replied the boy.

" Then why the devil didn't you come before ? "

" Please, sir, I fell asleep over the fire," answered
Smike, with humility.

" Fire ! what fire ! Where's there a fire ? " demanded
the schoolmaster, sharply.

" Only in the kitchen, sir," replied the boy. " Missus
said, as I was sitting up, I might go in there for a
warm."

" Your missus is a fool," retorted Squeers. " You'd
have been a deuced deal more wakeful in the cold, I'll
engage."

By this time Mr. Squeers had dismounted ; and after
ordering the boy to see to the pony, and to take care
that he hadn't any more corn that night, he told Nicholas
to wait at the front door a minute while he went round
and let him in.

A host of unpleasant misgivings, which had been
crowding upon Nicholas during the whole journey,
thronged into his mind with redoubled force when he
was left alone. And as he looked up at the dreary
house and dark windows, and upon the wild country
round, covered with snow, he felt a depression of heart
and spirit which he had never experienced before.

Presently he was ushered into a cheerless-looking
parlour where stood a large, angular woman about half
a head taller than Mr. Squeers.

" This is the new young man, my dear," said that
gentleman.

" Oh," replied Mrs. Squeers, nodding her head at
Nicholas, and eyeing him coldly from top to toe.

" He'll take a meal with us to-night," said Squeers,
" and go among the boys to-morrow morning. You can
give him a shakedown here to-night, can't you ? "

" We must manage it somehow," replied the lady.
" You don't much mind how you sleep, I suppose, sir ? "

" No, indeed," replied Nicholas, " I am not particular."

" That's lucky," said Mrs. Squeers. And as the lady's
humour was considered to lie chiefly in retort, Mr. Squeers
laughed heartily, and seemed to expect that Nicholas
should do the same.

After some conversation between the master and
mistress relative to the success of Mr. Squeers's trip,
and the people who had paid, and the people who had
made default in payment, a young servant girl brought
in a Yorkshire pie and some cold beef, which being set
upon the table, the boy Smike appeared with a jug of ale.

Mr. Squeers was emptying his great-coat pockets of
letters to different boys, and other small documents,
which he had brought down in them. The boy glanced,
with an anxious and timid expression, at the papers
as if with a sickly hope that one among them might
relate to him. The look was a very painful one, and
went to Nicholas's heart at once, for it told a long and
very sad history.

It induced him to consider the boy more attentively,
and he was surprised to observe the extraordinary mix-
ture of garments which formed his dress. Although
he could not have been less than eighteen or nineteen
years old, and was tall for that age, he wore a skeleton

suit, such as is usually put upon very little boys, and which, though most absurdly short in the arms and legs, was quite wide enough for his thin body. In order that the lower part of his legs might be in perfect keeping with this singular dress, he had a very large pair of boots, originally made for tops, which might have been once worn by some stout farmer, but were now too patched and tattered for a beggar. He was lame; and as he feigned to be busy in arranging the table, he glanced at the letters with a look so keen, and yet so dispirited and hopeless, that Nicholas could hardly bear to watch him.

"What are you bothering about there, Smike?" cried Mrs. Squeers; "let the things alone, can't you?"

"Eh!" said Squeers, looking up. "Oh! it's you, is it?"

"Yes, sir," replied the youth, pressing his hands together, as though to control, by force, the nervous wandering of his fingers. "Is there——"

"Well!" said Squeers.

"Have you—did anybody—has nothing been heard —about me?"

"Devil a bit," replied Squeers, testily.

The lad withdrew his eyes, and, putting his hand to his face, moved towards the door.

"Not a word," resumed Squeers, "and never will be. Now, this is a pretty sort of thing, isn't it, that you should have been left here all these years, and no money paid after the first six—nor no notice taken, nor no clue to be got who you belong to? It's a pretty sort of thing that I should have to feed a great fellow like you, and never hope to get one penny for it, isn't it?"

The boy put his hand to his head as if he were making

an effort to recollect something, and then, looking vacantly at his questioner, gradually broke into a smile, and limped away.

"I'll tell you what, Squeers," remarked his wife, as the door closed, "I think that young chap's turning silly."

"I hope not," said the schoolmaster; "for he's a handy fellow out-of-doors, and worth his meat and drink anyway. I should think he'd have wit enough for us though, if he was."

Supper being over, Mr. Squeers yawned fearfully and was of opinion that it was high time to go to bed. Upon this, Mrs. Squeers and a servant dragged in a small straw mattress and a couple of blankets, and arranged them into a couch for Nicholas.

"We'll put you into a regular bedroom with the boys to-morrow, Nickleby," said Squeers. "Good-night. Seven o'clock in the morning, mind."

The next morning, when Nicholas appeared in the main room, he found Mrs. Squeers very much distressed.

"I can't find the school spoon," she said.

"Never mind it, my dear," observed Squeers, in a soothing manner; "it's of no consequence."

"No consequence! why, how you talk!" retorted Mrs. Squeers, sharply; "isn't it brimstone morning?"

"I forgot, my dear," rejoined Squeers; "yes, it certainly is. We purify the boys' blood now and then, Nickleby."

"Purify fiddlesticks' ends!" said his lady. "Don't think, young man, that we go to the expense of brimstone and molasses, just to purify them; because if you think we carry on the business in that way, you'll find yourself mistaken, and so I tell you plainly."

"My dear," said Squeers, frowning. "Hem!"

"Oh! nonsense," rejoined Mrs. Squeers. "If the young man comes to be a teacher here, let him understand, at once, that we don't want any foolery about the boys. They have the brimstone and treacle, partly because if they hadn't something or other in the way of medicine they'd be always ailing and giving a world of trouble, and partly because it spoils their appetites and comes cheaper than breakfast and dinner. So it does them good and us good at the same time, and that's fair enough, I'm sure."

A vast deal of searching and rummaging ensued, and it proving fruitless, Smike was called in, and pushed by Mrs. Squeers and boxed by Mr. Squeers; which course of treatment brightening his intellects, enabled him to suggest that possibly Mrs. Squeers might have the spoon in her pocket—as indeed turned out to be the case. But as Mrs. Squeers had previously protested that she was quite certain she had not got it, Smike received another box on the ear for presuming to contradict his mistress; so that he gained nothing of advantage by his idea.

"But come," said Squeers, "let's go to the school-room; and lend me a hand with my school-coat, will you?"

Nicholas assisted his master to put on an old shooting jacket; and Squeers, arming himself with his cane, led the way across a yard, to a door in the rear of the house.

"There," said the schoolmaster, as they stepped in together; "this is our shop, Nickleby!"

It was such a crowded scene, and there were so many objects to attract attention, that, at first, Nicholas stared about him, really without seeing anything at all

By degrees, however, the place resolved itself into a bare and dirty room, with a couple of windows, stopped up with old copybooks and paper. There were two rickety desks, cut and notched, and inked in every possible way; two or three forms; a detached desk for Squeers, and another for his assistant. The ceiling was supported, like that of a barn, by crossbeams and rafters, and the walls were so stained and discoloured that it was impossible to tell whether they had ever been touched with paint or whitewash.

But the pupils! How the last faint traces of hope, the remotest glimmering of any good to be derived from his efforts in this den, faded from the mind of Nicholas as he looked in dismay around! Pale and haggard faces, lank and bony figures, children with the countenances of old men, boys of stunted growth, and others whose long, meagre legs would hardly bear their stooping bodies, all crowded on the view together.

And yet this scene, painful as it was, had its grotesque features. Mrs. Squeers stood at one of the desks, presiding over an immense basin of brimstone and treacle, of which delicious compound she administered a large instalment to each boy in succession, using for the purpose a common wooden spoon, which might have been originally manufactured for some gigantic top, and which widened every young gentleman's mouth considerably; they being all obliged, under heavy penalties, to take in the whole of the bowl at a gulp.

"Now," said Squeers, giving the desk a great rap with his cane which made half the little boys nearly jump out of their boots, "is that physicking over?"

"Just over," said Mrs. Squeers, choking the last boy in her hurry, and tapping the crown of his head with the wooden spoon to restore him. "Here, you Smike; take away now. Look sharp!"

Smike shuffled out with the basin, and Mrs. Squeers having called up a little boy with a curly head and wiped her hands upon it, hurried out after him into a species of washhouse, where there was a small fire and a large kettle, together with a number of little wooden bowls which were arranged upon a board. Into these bowls Mrs. Squeers, assisted by the hungry servant, poured a brown composition, which looked like diluted pincushions without the covers, and was called porridge. A minute wedge of brown bread was inserted in each bowl, and when they had eaten their porridge by means of the bread, the boys ate the bread itself, and had finished their breakfast; whereupon Mr. Squeers said, in a solemn voice, "For what we have received, may the Lord make us truly thankful!"—and went away to his own.

Nicholas filled his stomach with a bowl of porridge, for much the same reason which induces some savages to swallow earth—lest they should be hungry when there is nothing to eat. Having disposed of a slice of bread and butter, allotted to him in virtue of his office, he sat himself down to wait for school time.

He could not but observe how silent and sad the boys all seemed to be. There was none of the noise and clamour of a schoolroom; none of its boisterous play or hearty mirth. The children sat crouching and shivering together, and seemed to lack the spirit to move about. The only pupil who seemed at all playful was Master Squeers, son of the master, and as his chief amusement was to tread upon the other boys' toes in his new boots, his flow of spirits was rather disagreeable than otherwise.

After some half-hour's delay Mr. Squeers reappeared, and the boys took their places and their books, of which latter there might be about one to eight learners. A few minutes having elapsed, during which Mr. Squeers looked very profound, as if he had a perfect apprehension of what was inside all the books, and could say every word of their contents by heart if he only chose to take the trouble, that gentleman called up the first class.

Obedient to this summons there ranged themselves in front of the schoolmaster's desk half-a-dozen scarecrows, out at knees and elbows, one of whom placed a torn and filthy book beneath his learned eye.

" This is the first class in English spelling and philosophy, Nickleby," said Squeers, beckoning Nicholas to stand beside him. " We'll get up a Latin one, and hand that over to you. Now, then, where's the first boy ? "

" Please, sir, he's cleaning the back parlour window," said the temporary head of the class.

" So he is, to be sure," rejoined Squeers. " We go upon the practical mode of teaching, Nickleby ; the regular education system. C-l-e-a-n, clean, verb active, to make bright, to scour. When the boy knows this out of the book, he goes and does it. Second boy, what's a horse ? "

" A beast, sir," replied the boy.

" So it is," said Squeers, " and as you're perfect in that, go and look after *my* horse, and rub him down well, or I'll rub you down. The rest of the class go and draw water till somebody tells you to leave off, for it's washing-day to-morrow, and they want the coppers filled."

So saying, he dismissed the first class to their experiments in practical philosophy, and eyed Nicholas with a look, half cunning and half doubtful, as if he were not altogether certain what he might think of him by this time.

"That's the way we do it, Nickleby," he said, after a pause.

Nicholas shrugged his shoulders in a manner that was scarcely perceptible and said he saw it was.

"And a very good way it is, too," said Squeers. "Now just take them fourteen little boys and hear them some reading, because, you know, you must begin to be useful. Idling about here won't do."

Mr. Squeers said this, as if it had suddenly occurred to him, either that he must not say too much to his assistant, or that his assistant did not say enough to him in praise of the establishment. The children were arranged in a semicircle round the new master, and he was soon listening to their dull, drawling recital of those stories of interest which are to be found in the spelling books.

In this exciting occupation the morning lagged heavily on. At one o'clock the boys, having previously had their appetites thoroughly taken away by stir-about and potatoes, sat down in the kitchen to some hard salt beef, of which Nicholas was graciously permitted to take his portion to his own solitary desk, to eat it there in peace. After this, there was another hour of crouching in the schoolroom and shivering with cold; and this was a fair sample of the school day at Dotheboys Hall.

There was a small stove in the corner of the room, and by it Nicholas sat down, when the school was dismissed, so heavy-hearted that it seemed to him as though every bit of joy had gone out of the world. The cruelty

H

and coarseness of Squeers were revolting, and yet Nicholas did not know how to resent it or which way to turn. He had cast his lot here, and here he must abide.

As he was absorbed in these meditations, he all at once encountered the upturned face of Smike, who was on his knees before the stove, picking a few stray cinders from the hearth and planting them on the fire. He had paused to steal a look at Nicholas, and when he saw that he was observed, shrank back, as if expecting a blow.

" You need not fear me," said Nicholas, kindly. " Are you cold ? "

" N–n–o."

" You are shivering."

" I am not cold," replied Smike, quickly. " I am used to it."

There was such an obvious fear of giving offence in his manner, and he was such a timid, broken-spirited creature, that Nicholas could not help exclaiming " Poor fellow ! "

If he had struck the drudge, he would have slunk away without a word. But now he burst into tears.

" Oh, dear, oh, dear ! " he cried, covering his face with his cracked and horny hands. " My heart will break. It will, it will ! "

" Hush ! " said Nicholas, laying his hand upon his shoulder. " Be a man ; you're nearly one by years, God help you."

" By years ! " cried Smike. " Oh, dear, dear, how many of them ! How many of them since I was a little child, younger than any that are here now ! Where are they all ? "

" Whom do you speak of ? " inquired Nicholas, wishing to rouse the poor, half-witted creature to reason. " Tell me."

"My friends," he replied, "myself—my—oh! what sufferings mine have been!"

"There is always hope," said Nicholas; he knew not what to say.

"No," rejoined the other, "no; none for me. Do you remember the boy that died here?"

"I was not here, you know," said Nicholas, gently; "but what of him?"

"Why," replied the youth, drawing closer to his questioner's side, "I was with him at night, and when it was all silent he cried no more for friends he wished to come and sit with him, but began to see faces round his bed that came from home; he said they smiled, and talked to him; and he died at last lifting his head to kiss them. Do you hear?"

"Yes, yes," rejoined Nicholas.

"What faces will smile on me when I die!" cried his companion, shivering. "Who will talk to me in those long nights! They cannot come from home; they would frighten me if they did, for I don't know what it is, and shouldn't know them. Pain and fear, pain and fear for me, alive or dead. No hope, no hope!"

The bell rang to bed, and the boy, subsiding at the sound into his usual listless state, crept away as if anxious to avoid notice. It was with a heavy heart that Nicholas soon afterwards—no, not retired; there was no retirement there—followed to his dirty and crowded dormitory.

II

HOW SMIKE WENT AWAY FROM DOTHEBOYS HALL

NICHOLAS was of a naturally optimistic temper, however, and he lost as little time as possible brooding over his difficulties. Instead he began at once to try to make the school something more than a farce. He arranged a few regular lessons for the boys, and he treated the poor, half-starved pupils with such gentleness and sympathy that they passed from dumb amazement at the first to blind devotion. Indeed, there was not one of them who would not have lain down cheerfully and let him walk over his body; and the most devoted of them all was Smike.

Nicholas was the one ray of sunlight that had ever come into this wretched creature's life. And in return, Smike now followed him to and fro, with an ever restless desire to serve or help him; anticipating such little wants as his humble ability could supply, and content only to be near him. He would sit beside him for hours, looking patiently into his face; and a word would brighten up his careworn visage, and call into it a passing gleam, even of happiness. He was an altered being; he had an object now; and that object was, to show his attachment to the only person—that person a stranger —who had treated him, not to say with kindness, but like a human creature.

, Needless to say, Squeers speedily took a dislike to Nicholas. He knew of the scarcely concealed disdain with which his assistant regarded his methods. Squeers was jealous, also, of the influence which Nicholas had so soon acquired with the boys. Smike's slavish affection was speedily discovered, and the crafty master was mean enough to strike at Nicholas through him.

Upon this poor being all the spleen and ill-humour that could not be vented on Nicholas were unceasingly bestowed. Drudgery would have been nothing—Smike was well used to that. Buffetings inflicted without cause would have been equally a matter of course ; for to them also he had served a long and weary apprenticeship ; but it was no sooner observed that he had become attached to Nicholas, than stripes and blows, stripes and blows, morning, noon, and night, were his only portion. Nicholas saw it, and ground his teeth at every repetition of the savage and cowardly attack. But at present he saw no way to aid the boy, for a protest would mean his own dismissal, and the lot of Smike and the others would become that much harder.

One day, after especially harsh treatment, the boy sat huddled in a dark corner by himself, sobbing as though his heart would break. The room was dark and deserted, when Nicholas entered, but he heard the sound of weeping and went over and laid his hand on the drudge's head.

" Do not, for God's sake ! " said Nicholas, in an agitated voice ; " I cannot bear to see you."

" They are more hard with me than ever," sobbed the boy.

" I know it," rejoined Nicholas. " They are."

" But for you," said the outcast, " I should die. They would kill me, they would ; I know they would."

"You will do better, poor fellow," replied Nicholas, shaking his head mournfully, "when I am gone."

"Gone!" cried the other, looking intently in his face.

"Softly!" rejoined Nicholas. "Yes."

"Are you going?" demanded the boy, in an earnest whisper.

"I cannot say," replied Nicholas. "I was speaking more to my own thoughts than to you."

"Tell me," said the boy, imploringly, "oh, do tell me, *will* you go—*will* you?"

"I shall be driven to that at last!" said Nicholas. "The world is before me, after all."

"Tell me," urged Smike, "is the world as bad and dismal as this place?"

"Heaven forbid," replied Nicholas, pursuing the train of his own thoughts; "its hardest, coarsest toil were happiness to this."

"Should I ever meet you there?" demanded the boy, speaking with unusual wildness.

"Yes," replied Nicholas, willing to soothe him.

"No, no!" said the other, clasping him by the hand. "Should I—should I—tell me that again! Say I should be sure to find you!"

"You would," replied Nicholas, with the same humane intention, "and I would help and aid you, and not bring fresh sorrow on you as I have done here."

The boy caught both the young man's hands passionately in his, and hugging them to his breast, uttered a few broken sounds which were unintelligible. Squeers entered, at the moment, and he shrank back into his old corner.

The next morning—a cold, grey day in January—

Nicholas was awakened by hearing the voice of Squeers roughly demanding, " Where's that Smike ? "

Nicholas looked over in the corner where the boy usually slept, but it was vacant ; so he made no answer.

" Smike ! " shouted Squeers.

" Do you want your head broke in a fresh place, Smike ? " demanded his amiable lady, in the same key.

Still there was no reply, and still Nicholas stared about him, as did the greater part of the boys, who were by this time roused.

" Confound his impudence ! " muttered Squeers, rapping the stair-rail impatiently with his cane. " Nickleby ! "

" Well, sir."

" Send that obstinate scoundrel down ; don't you hear me calling ? "

" He is not here, sir," replied Nicholas.

" Don't tell me a lie," retorted the schoolmaster. " He is."

" He is not," retorted Nicholas, angrily. " Don't tell me one."

" We shall soon see that," said Mr. Squeers, rushing upstairs. " I'll find him, I warrant you."

With which assurance, Mr. Squeers bounced into the dormitory, and, swinging his cane in the air ready for a blow, darted into the corner. The cane descended harmlessly upon the ground. There was nobody there.

" What does this mean ? " said Squeers, turning round. " Where have you hid him ? "

" I have seen nothing of him since last night," replied Nicholas.

" Come," blustered Squeers, " you won't save him this way. Where is he ? "

" At the bottom of the nearest pond, for aught I know,"

rejoined Nicholas, in a low voice, and fixing his eyes full on the master's face.

"Confound you, what do you mean by that?" retorted Squeers. Without waiting for a reply, he inquired of the boys whether anyone among them knew anything of their missing schoolmate.

There was a general hum of anxious denial, in the midst of which one shrill voice was heard to say (as, indeed, everybody thought):

"Please, sir, I think Smike's run away, sir."

"Ha!" cried Squeers, turning sharp round. "Who said that?"

And, pouncing suddenly, he seized a small urchin, who was rewarded for his suggestion so soundly that he howled with pain.

"There," said Squeers. "Now, if any other boy thinks Smike has run away, I shall be glad to have a talk with him."

There was, of course, a profound silence, during which Nicholas showed his disgust as plainly as looks could show it.

"Well, Nickleby," said Squeers, eyeing him maliciously. "*You* think he has run away, I suppose?"

"I think it extremely likely," replied Nicholas, in a quiet manner.

"Oh, you do, do you?" sneered Squeers. "Maybe you know he has."

"I know nothing of the kind."

"He didn't tell you he was going, I suppose, did he?" continued Squeers.

"He did not," replied Nicholas; "I am very glad he did not, for it would then have been my duty to have warned you in time."

Nicholas and Mr. Squeers 110

"Which, no doubt, you would have been devilish sorry to do," said Squeers, in a taunting fashion.

"I should indeed," replied Nicholas.

Meanwhile, Mrs. Squeers, who had been hunting elsewhere for the boy, bustled in with great excitement.

"He is off!" said she. "The cow-house and stable are locked up, so he can't be there; and he's not downstairs anywhere, for the girl has looked. He must have gone York way, and by a public road too."

"Why must he?" inquired Squeers.

"Stupid!" said Mrs. Squeers, angrily. "He hadn't any money, had he?"

"Never had a penny of his own in his whole life, that I know of," replied Squeers.

"To be sure," rejoined Mrs. Squeers, "and he didn't take anything to eat with him; that I'll answer for. So, of course, he must beg his way, and he could do that nowhere but on the public road."

"That's true," exclaimed Squeers, clapping his hands.

"True! Yes; but you would never have thought of it, for all that, if I hadn't said so," replied his wife. "Now, if you take the chaise and go one road, and I borrow Swallow's chaise and go the other; what with keeping our eyes open and asking questions, one or other of us is pretty certain to lay hold of him."

The worthy lady's plan was put into action without delay; while Nicholas remained behind in a tumult of anxiety. He realised the bitter consequences of Smike's rash act. The boy was liable to freeze or starve to death on the roadside—which could not, perhaps, be much worse than to fall again into the clutches of Mr. and Mrs. Squeers.

All that day there was no tidings of the runaway.

But at daybreak the second morning the sound of wheels was heard. Nicholas hardly dared to look out of the window; but he did so, and the very first object that met his eyes was the wretched Smike; so bedabbled with mud and rain, so haggard and worn and wild, that, but for his garments being such as no scarecrow was ever seen to wear, he might have been doubtful, even then, of his identity.

"Lift him out," said Squeers, after he had literally feasted his eyes, in silence, upon the culprit. "Bring him in; bring him in!"

Smike, to all appearance more dead than alive, was brought into the house and securely locked up in a cellar until such time as Mr. Squeers should deem it expedient to operate upon him in presence of the assembled school.

After a hasty breakfast of very thin porridge, the boys were summoned to the schoolroom by resounding whacks on the desk from an ugly-looking whip in the hands of the master.

"Is every boy here?" asked Squeers, in a tremendous voice.

Every boy was there, but every boy was afraid to speak; so Squeers glared along the lines to assure himself; and every eye dropped, and every head cowered down, as he did so.

"Each boy keep his place," said Squeers, administering his favourite blow to the desk, and regarding with gloomy satisfaction the universal start which it never failed to occasion. "Nickleby! to your desk, sir!"

It was remarked by more than one small observer that there was a very curious and unusual expression in the usher's face; but he took his seat without opening his lips in reply. Squeers, casting a triumphant glance at his assistant and a scowl on the boys, left the room, and shortly afterwards returned, dragging Smike by the collar.

In any other place the appearance of the wretched, jaded, spiritless object would have occasioned a murmur of compassion and remonstrance. It had some effect, even there; for the lookers-on moved uneasily in their seats, and a few of the boldest ventured to steal looks at each other, expressive of indignation and pity.

They were lost on Squeers, however, whose gaze was fastened on the luckless Smike, as he inquired, according to custom in such cases, whether he had anything to say for himself.

" Nothing, I suppose ? " said Squeers, with a diabolical grin.

Smike glanced round, and his eye rested, for an instant, on Nicholas, as if he had expected him to intercede; but his look was riveted on his desk.

" Have you anything to say ? " demanded Squeers again, giving his right arm two or three flourishes to try its power and suppleness. " Stand a little out of the way, Mrs. Squeers, my dear ; I've hardly got room enough."

" Spare me, sir ! " cried Smike.

" Oh ! that's all, is it ? " said Squeers. " Yes, I'll flog you within an inch of your life, and spare you that."

" Ha, ha, ha," laughed Mrs. Squeers, " that's a good 'un ! "

" I was driven to do it," said Smike, faintly, and casting another imploring look about him.

" Driven to do it, were you ? " said Squeers. " Oh ! it wasn't your fault ; it was mine, I suppose—eh ? "

Then he caught the boy firmly in his grip. One desperate cut had fallen on his body—he was wincing from the lash and uttering a scream of pain—it was raised again, and again about to fall—when Nicholas Nickleby, suddenly starting up, cried, "*Stop !*" in a voice that made the rafters ring.

"Who cried stop ? " said Squeers, turning savagely round.

"I," said Nicholas, stepping forward. "This must not go on."

"Must not go on ! " cried Squeers, almost in a shriek.

"*No !*" thundered Nicholas.

Aghast at the boldness of this interference, Squeers released his hold of Smike, and, falling back a pace or two, gazed upon Nicholas with looks that were positively frightful.

"I say *must not !*" repeated Nicholas, nothing daunted; "*shall not !* I will prevent it !"

Squeers continued to gaze upon him, with his eyes starting out of his head ; but astonishment had actually, for the moment, bereft him of speech.

"You have disregarded all my quiet interference in the miserable lad's behalf," said Nicholas; "you have returned no answer to the letter in which I begged forgiveness for him, and offered to be responsible that he would remain quietly here. Don't blame me for this public interference. You have brought it upon yourself; not I."

"Sit down, beggar ! " screamed Squeers, almost beside himself with rage, and seizing Smike as he spoke.

"Wretch," rejoined Nicholas, fiercely, "touch him at your peril ! I will not stand by, and see it done. My blood is up, and I have the strength of ten such men as

you. Look to yourself, for by Heaven I will not spare
you, if you drive me on ! ''

" Stand back," cried Squeers, brandishing his weapon.

" I have a long series of insults to avenge," said
Nicholas, flushed with passion ; " and my indignation
is aggravated by the cruelties of this foul den. Have a
care ; for if you rouse me farther, the consequences shall
fall heavily upon your own head ! ''

He had scarcely spoken, when Squeers, in a violent
outbreak of wrath, struck him a blow across the face which
raised up a bar of livid flesh as it was inflicted. Smarting
with the agony of the blow, and concentrating into that
one moment all its feelings of rage and scorn, Nicholas
sprang upon him, wrested the weapon from his hand,
and pinning him by the throat, beat the ruffian till he
roared for mercy.

Then Nicholas left the astounded boys and the crest-
fallen master, and stalked out of the room. He looked
anxiously around for Smike, as he closed the door, but
he was nowhere to be seen.

There was nothing left for him to do. He must face
the world again ; but *anything*—he told himself—
would be better than this. So he packed up a few clothes
in a small valise, and, finding that nobody offered to
oppose him, he marched boldly out by the front door
and struck into the road which led to Greta Bridge.

He did not travel far that day, as there had been a
heavy fall of snow which made the way toilsome and hard
to find. He lay, that night, at a cottage, where beds
were let at a cheap rate to the more humble class of travellers ; and, rising betimes next morning, made his way
before night to Boroughbridge. Passing through that
town in search of some cheap resting-place, he stumbled

upon an empty barn within a couple of hundred yards of the roadside; in a warm corner of which he stretched his weary limbs, and soon fell asleep.

When he awoke next morning, and tried to recollect his dreams, which had been all connected with his recent sojourn at Dotheboys Hall, he sat up, rubbed his eyes, and stared—not with the most composed countenance possible—at some motionless object which seemed to be stationed within a few yards in front of him.

"Strange!" cried Nicholas; "can this be some lingering creation of the visions that have scarcely left me! It cannot be real—and yet I—I am awake! Smike!"

The form moved, rose, advanced, and dropped upon its knees at his feet. It was Smike indeed.

"Why do you kneel to me?" said Nicholas, hastily raising him.

"To go with you—anywhere—everywhere—to the world's end!" replied Smike, clinging to his hand. "Let me, oh, do let me! You are my home—my kind friend—take me with you, pray!"

"I am a friend who can do little for you," said Nicholas, kindly. "How came you here?"

He had followed him, it seemed; had never lost sight of him all the way; had watched while he slept, and when he halted for refreshment; and had feared to appear before, lest he should be sent back. He had not intended to appear now, but Nicholas had awakened more suddenly than he looked for, and he had had no time to conceal himself.

"Poor fellow!" said Nicholas, "your hard fate denies you any friend but one, and he is nearly as poor and helpless as yourself."

"May I—may I go with you?" asked Smike, timidly. "I will be your faithful, hard-working servant, I will, indeed. I want no clothes," added the poor creature, drawing his rags together; "these will do very well. I only want to be near you."

"And you shall," cried Nicholas. "And the world shall deal by you as it does by me, till one or both of us shall quit it for a better. Come!"

With these words he strapped his valise on his shoulders, and, taking his stick in one hand, extended the other to the delighted boy, and so they passed out of the old barn together.

And in the days to come—through thick and thin—Smike and Nicholas fought their battles together—and *won!*

The Story of Little Nell

I

IN THE OLD CURIOSITY SHOP

IT was a queer home for a child—this place where little Nell lived with her grandfather. He was a dealer in all sorts of curious old things: suits of mail which stood like ghosts in armour here and there; fantastic carved tables and chairs; rusty weapons of various kinds; distorted figures in china and wood and iron. And, amid it all, the oldest thing in the shop seemed to be the little old man with the long gray hair.

The only bit of youth was Nell herself; and yet she had a strange intermingling of dignity and responsibility in spite of her small figure and childish ways. Her fourteen years of life had left her undecided between childhood and girlhood. She had not begun to grow up; and yet she was an orphan, accustomed to doing everything for herself.

Her grandfather tried in his way to take care of her, for he loved her dearly. But between the tending of his shop and the mysterious journeys which he made night after night, the child was often sent upon strange errands or left alone in the old house. And at all times it was she who took care of him. But the old man did not see that this lonely life was putting lines of sorrow into her face.   To him she was still the child of yesterday, care-free and happy.

She had been happy once.   She had gone singing through the dim rooms, and moving with gay step among their dusty treasures, making them older by her young life, and sterner and more grim by her cheerful presence. But now the chambers were cold and gloomy, and when she left her own little room to wile away the tedious hours, and sat in one of them, she was still and motionless as their inanimate occupants, and had no heart to startle the echoes—hoarse from their long silence—with her voice.

In one of these rooms was a window looking into the street, where the child sat, many and many a long evening, and often far into the night, alone and thoughtful. None are so anxious as those who watch and wait ; and at these times mournful fancies came flocking on her mind in crowds.

She knew instinctively that her grandfather was hiding something from her.   What it was she could not guess ; but these regular journeys at night, while she watched and waited, left him only the more fretful and careworn.   He seemed to have a constant fever for something ; yet all he would say was that he would some day leave her a fortune.   Meanwhile he had fallen into the clutches of Quilp, a terrible dwarf, who had lent him money from time to time, until the entire contents of the shop were mortgaged.   So it is not strange that Little Nell should have mournful thoughts.

When the night had worn away, the child would close the window and even smile, with the first dawn of light, at her night-time fears.   Then after praying earnestly for her grandfather and the restoring of their former happy days, she would unlatch the door for him and fall into a troubled sleep.

One night the old man said that he would not leave home. The child's face lit up at the news, but became grave again when she saw how worried he looked.

" You took my note safely to Mr. Quilp, you say ? " he asked fretfully. " What did he tell you, Nell ? "

" Exactly what I told you, dear grandfather, indeed."

" True," said the old man faintly. " Yes. But tell me again, Nell. My head fails me. What was it that he told you ? Nothing more than that he would see me to-morrow or next day ? That was in the note."

" Nothing more," said the child. " Shall I go to him again to-morrow, dear grandfather ? Very early ? I will be there and back before breakfast."

The old man shook his head and, sighing mournfully, drew her towards him.

" 'Twould be no use, my dear, no earthly use. But if he deserts me, Nell, at this moment—if he deserts me now, when I should, with his assistance, be recompensed for all the time and money I have lost and all the agony of mind I have undergone, which makes me what you see, I am ruined and worse—far worse than that—I have ruined you, for whom I ventured all. If we are beggars——! "

" What if we are ? " said the child, boldly. " Let us be beggars and be happy."

" Beggars—and happy ! " said the old man. " Poor child ! "

" Dear grandfather," cried the girl with an energy which shone in her flushed face, trembling voice, and impassioned gesture, " I am not a child in that I think, but even if I am, oh, hear me pray that we may beg, or work in open roads or fields, to earn a scanty living, rather than live as we do now."

"Nelly!" said the old man.

"Yes, yes, rather than live as we do now," the child repeated, more earnestly than before. "If you are sorrowful, let me know why and be sorrowful too; if you waste away and are paler and weaker every day, let me be your nurse and try to comfort you. If you are poor, let us be poor together; but let me be with you, do let me be with you; do not let me see such change and not know why, or I shall break my heart."

The child's voice was lost in sobs, as she clasped her arms about the old man's neck; nor did she weep alone.

These were not words for other ears, nor was it a scene for other eyes. And yet other ears and eyes were there and greedily taking in all that passed, and moreover they were the ears and eyes of no less a person than Mr. Daniel Quilp, who, having entered unseen when the child first placed herself at the old man's side, stood looking on with his accustomed grin. Standing, however, being tiresome, and the dwarf being one of that kind of persons who usually make themselves at home, he soon cast his eyes upon a chair, into which he skipped with uncommon agility, and perching himself on the back with his feet upon the seat, was thus enabled to look on and listen with greater comfort to himself, besides gratifying at the same time that taste for doing something fantastic and monkey-like, which on all occasions had strong possession of him. Here, then, he sat, one leg cocked carelessly over the other, his chin resting on the palm of his hand, his head turned a little on one side, and his ugly features twisted into a complacent grimace. And in this position the old man, happening in course of time to look that way, chanced to see him.

The child uttered a suppressed shriek on beholding this figure; in their first surprise both she and the old man, not knowing what to say, and half doubting its reality, looked shrinkingly at it. Not at all disconcerted by this reception, Daniel Quilp preserved the same attitude, merely nodding twice or thrice with great condescension. At length, the old man pronounced his name and inquired how he came there.

"Through the door," said Quilp, pointing over his shoulder with his thumb. "I'm not quite small enough to get through keyholes. I wish I was. I want to have some talk with you, particularly, and in private—with nobody present, neighbour. Good-bye, little Nelly."

Nell looked at the old man, who nodded to her to retire, and kissed her cheek.

The dwarf said never a word, but watched his companion as he paced restlessly up and down the room, and presently returned to his seat. Here he remained, with his head bowed upon his breast for some time, and then suddenly raising it, said:

"Once, and once for all, have you brought me any money?"

"No!" returned Quilp.

"Then," said the old man, clenching his hands desperately and looking upward, "the child and I are lost!"

"Neighbour," said Quilp, glancing sternly at him, and beating his hand twice or thrice upon the table to attract his wandering attention, "let me be plain with you, and play a fairer game than when you held all the cards, and I saw but the backs and nothing more. You have no secret from me, now."

The old man looked up, trembling.

"You are surprised," said Quilp. "Well, perhaps that's natural. You have no secret from me now, I say; no, not one. For now I know that all those sums of money, that all those loans, advances, and supplies that you have had from me, have found their way to—shall I say the word?"

"Aye!" replied the old man, "say it if you will."

"To the gaming-table," rejoined Quilp, "your nightly haunt. This was the precious scheme to make your fortune, was it; this was the secret certain source of wealth in which I was to have sunk my money (if I had been the fool you took me for); this was your inexhaustible mine of gold, your El Dorado, eh?"

"Yes," cried the old man, turning upon him with gleaming eyes, "it was. It is. It will be, till I die."

"That I should have been blinded," said Quilp, looking contemptuously at him, "by a mere shallow gambler!"

"I am no gambler," cried the old man, fiercely. "I call Heaven to witness that I never played for gain of mine, or love of play. It was all for *her*—for my little Nelly! I had sworn to leave her rich!"

"When did you first begin this mad career?" asked Quilp, his taunting inclination subdued, for a moment, by the old man's grief and wildness.

"When did I first begin?" he rejoined, passing his hand across his brow. "When *was* it, that I first began? When should it be, but when I began to think how little I had saved, how long a time it took to save at all, how short a time I might have, at my age, to live, and how she would be left to the rough mercies of the world with barely enough to keep her from the sorrows that wait on poverty; then it was that I began to think about it."

"Humph! the old story," said the dwarf. "You lost what money you had laid by, first, and then came to me. While I thought you were making your fortune (as you said you were) you were making yourself a beggar, eh? Dear me! And so it comes to pass that I hold every security you could scrape together, and a bill of sale upon the—upon the stock and property. But did you never win?"

"Never!" groaned the old man. "Never won back my loss!"

"I thought," sneered the dwarf, "that if a man played long enough he was sure to win at last, or, at the worst, not to come off a loser."

"And so he is!" cried the old man, "so he is; I have felt that from the first, I have always known it, I've seen it, I never felt it half so strongly as I feel it now. Quilp, I have dreamed, three nights, of winning the same large sum. I never could dream that dream before, though I have often tried. Do not desert me, now I have this chance! I have no resource but you—give me some help, let me try this one last hope."

The dwarf shrugged his shoulders and shook his head.

"Nay, Quilp, *good* Quilp!" gasped the old man, extending his hands in entreaty; "let me try just this once more. I tell you it is not for me—it is for *her!* Oh, I cannot die and leave her in poverty!"

"I couldn't do it, really," said Quilp, with unusual politeness. And grinning and making a low bow he passed out of the door.

The dwarf was, for once, as good as his word. He not only refused to lend any more money, but he at once began to make plans for closing the shop. The old man was so broken-hearted that he fell ill of a raging fever, and for days was delirious. Little Nell, his only nurse, gradually learned the truth about her grandfather's evening pursuit—the gaming-table—and it added all the more to her sorrow.

At last, when he was well enough to go about again, the impatient dwarf would not be put off any longer in regard to the sale. An early day was fixed for it, and the old dealer no longer offered any objections. Instead, he sat quietly, dully in his chair, looking at a tiny patch of green through his window.

To one who had been tossing on a restless bed so long, even these few green leaves and this tranquil light, although it languished among chimneys and house-tops, were pleasant things. They suggested quiet places afar off, and rest and peace.

The child thought, more than once, that he was moved and had forborne to speak. But now he shed tears— tears that it lightened her aching heart to see—and making as though he would fall upon his knees, he besought her to forgive him.

"Forgive you—what?" said Nell, interposing to prevent his purpose. "Oh, grandfather, what should *I* forgive?"

"All that is past, all that has come upon you, Nell," returned the old man.

"Do not talk so," said the child. "Pray do not. Let us speak of something else."

"Yes, yes, we will," he rejoined. "And it shall be of what we talked of long ago—many months—months is it, or weeks, or days? Which is it, Nell?"

"I do not understand you," said the child.

"You said, let us be beggars and happy in the open fields," he answered. "Oh, let us go away—anywhere!"

"Yes, let us go," said Nell, earnestly; "there will we find happiness and peace."

And so it was arranged. On the night before the public auction they were to steal forth quietly, out into the wide world.

The old man had slept for some hours soundly in his bed, while she was busily engaged in preparing for their flight. There were a few articles of clothing for herself to carry, and a few for him; old garments, such as became their fallen fortunes, laid out to wear; and a staff to support his feeble steps, put ready for his use. But this was not all her task, for now she must visit the old rooms for the last time.

And how different the parting with them was from any she had expected, and most of all from that which she had oftenest pictured to herself! How could she ever have thought of bidding them farewell in triumph, lonely and sad though her days had been! She sat down at the window where she had spent so many evenings— darker far than this—and every thought of hope or cheerfulness that had occurred to her in that place came vividly upon her mind, and blotted out all its dull and mournful associations in an instant.

Her own little room, too, where she had so often knelt down and prayed at night—prayed for the time which she hoped was dawning now—the little room where she had slept so peacefully, and dreamed such pleasant dreams—it was hard to leave it without one kind look or grateful tear.

But at last she was ready to go, and her grandfather was awakened. Just as the first rays of dawn were seen they stole forth noiselessly, hand in hand. They dared not awaken Quilp, who was sleeping that night in the shop to guard his prospective wealth. Out in the middle of the street they paused.

" Which way ? " said the child.

The old man looked irresolutely and helplessly, first at her, then to the right and left, then at her again, and shook his head. It was plain that she was thenceforth his guide and leader. The child felt it, but had no doubts or misgivings, and putting her hand in his led him gently away.

II

OUT IN THE WIDE WORLD

IT was a bright morning in June when Nell and her grandfather set forth upon their travels. Out of the city they walked briskly, for the desire to leave their old life—to elude pursuit—lay strong upon them. Nell had provided a simple lunch for that day's needs ; and at night they stopped, footsore and weary, at a hospitable farmhouse.

Late in the next day they chanced to pass a country church. Among the tombstones, at one side, they saw two men who were seated upon the grass, so busily at work as not to notice the newcomers.

It was not difficult to guess that they were of a class of travelling showmen who went from town to town show- ing Punch and his antics, for perched upon a tombstone was a figure of that hero himself, his nose and chin as hooked and his face as beaming as usual.

Scattered upon the ground were the other members

of the play, in various stages of repair ; while the two showmen were engaged with glue, hammer, and tacks, in putting their proper parts more strongly together.

The showmen raised their eyes when the old man and his young companion were close upon them, and pausing in their work, returned their looks of curiosity. One of them, the actual exhibitor, no doubt, was a little merry-faced man with a twinkling eye and a red nose, who seemed to have unconsciously imbibed something of his hero's character. The other—that was he who took the money—had rather a careful and cautious look, which was perhaps inseparable from his occupation also.

The merry man was the first to greet the strangers with a nod ; and following the old man's eyes, he observed that perhaps that was the first time he had ever seen a Punch off the stage.

" Why do you come here to do this ? " asked the old man, after answering their greeting.

" Why, you see," rejoined the little man, " we're putting up for to-night at the public-house yonder, and it wouldn't do to let 'em see the present company undergoing repair."

" No ! " cried the old man, making signs to Nell to listen, " why not, eh? Why not ? "

" Because it would destroy all the delusion, and take away all the interest, wouldn't it ? " replied the little man. " Would you care a ha'penny for the Lord Chancellor if you know'd him in private and without his wig ?—certainly not."

" Good ! " said the old man, venturing to touch one of the puppets, and drawing away his hand with a shrill laugh. "Are you going to show em to-night ? Are you ? "

"That is the intention, governor," replied the other. "Look here," he continued, turning to his partner, "here's all this Judy's clothes falling to pieces again. Much good *you* do at sewing things!"

Seeing that they were at a loss, the child said timidly: "I have a needle, sir, in my basket, and thread too. Will you let me try to mend it for you? I think I can do it neater than you could."

The showman had nothing to urge against a proposal so seasonable. Nelly, kneeling down beside the box, was soon busily engaged in her task, and accomplishing it to a miracle.

While she was thus engaged, the merry little man looked at her with an interest which did not appear to be diminished when he glanced at her helpless companion. When she had finished her work he thanked her, and inquired whither they were travelling.

"N—no farther to-night, I think," said the child, looking towards her grandfather.

"If you're wanting a place to stop at," the man remarked, "I should advise you to take up at the same house with us. That's it—the long, low, white house there. It's very cheap. Come along."

The tavern was kept by a fat old landlord and landlady who made no objection to receiving their new guests, but praised Nelly's beauty and were at once prepossessed in her behalf. There was no other company in the kitchen but the two showmen, and the child felt very thankful that they had fallen upon such good quarters. The landlady was very much astonished to learn that they had come all the way from London, and appeared to have no little curiosity touching their farther destination. But Nell could give her no very clear replies.

That evening the wayfarers enjoyed the Punch show, though poor Nell was so tired that she went to sleep early in the performance.

The next morning she met the showmen at breakfast.

"And where are you going to-day?" asked the little man with the red nose.

"Indeed, I hardly know. We have not decided," replied the child.

"We're going to the races," said the little man. "If that's your way and you'd like to have us for company, let us travel together."

"We'll go with you, and gladly," interposed Nell's grandfather, eagerly; for he had been as pleased as a child with the performance of Punch.

Nell was a trifle alarmed over the prospect of a crowded race-course; but this seemed their best chance to press forward, so she accepted the invitation thankfully.

For several days they travelled together, and despite the wearisome way the child found much novelty and interest in the wandering life. But presently she became uneasy in the changed attitude of the two showmen. From being ordinarily kind, they now seemed to watch Nell and her grandfather so closely as not to suffer them out of their sight.

The showmen had, in fact, got it into their heads that the two wayfarers were not common people, but runaways for whom a reward must even now be posted in London. And so they resolved to deliver them over to the proper authorities at the first opportunity and claim the reward.

Now, although Nell and her grandfather had a perfect right to go where they pleased, and there was no reward offered, they were at all times fearful of being pursued by that terrible Quilp. So Nell determined to flee from those two watchful men at the earliest moment.

The chance of escape offered during one of the busy days at the race-course. While the two men were busy showing off Punch to the delighted crowd, she took her grandfather by the hand and hurriedly slipped away.

At first they pressed forward regardless of whither their steps led them, and from time to time casting fearful glances behind them to see if they were being pursued. But as they drew farther away they gained more confidence. Weariness also forced them to slacken their pace. When they had come into the middle of a little woodland they rested a short time ; then they struck a path which led to the opposite side. Taking their way along it for a short distance they came to a lane, so shaded by the trees on either hand that they met together overhead, and arched the narrow way. A broken finger-post announced that this led to a village three miles off ; and thither they resolved to bend their steps.

The miles appeared so long that they sometimes thought they must have missed their road. But at last, to their great joy, it led downward in a steep descent, with overhanging banks over which the footpaths led ; and the clustered houses of the village peeped from the woody hollow below.

It was a very small place. The men and boys were playing at cricket on the green ; and as the other folks were looking on, they wandered up and down, uncertain where to seek a humble lodging. There was but one man in the little garden before his cottage, and him they were timid of approaching, for he was the schoolmaster, and had " School " written up over his window in black letters on a white board. He was a pale, simple-looking man, and sat among his flowers and beehives, smoking his pipe, in the little porch before his door.

"Speak to him, dear," the old man whispered.

"I am almost afraid to disturb him," said the child, timidly. "He does not seem to see us. Perhaps if we wait a little, he may look this way."

But as nobody else appeared and it would soon be dark, Nell at length ventured to draw near, leading her grandfather by the hand. The slight noise they made in raising the latch of the wicket-gate caught his attention. He looked at them kindly, but seemed disappointed too, and slightly shook his head.

Nell dropped a courtesy, and told him they were poor travellers who sought a shelter for the night which they would gladly pay for, so far as their means allowed. The schoolmaster looked earnestly at her as she spoke, laid aside his pipe, and rose up directly.

"If you could direct us anywhere, sir," said the child, "we should take it very kindly."

"You have been walking a long way," said the schoolmaster.

"A long way, sir," the child replied.

"You're a young traveller, my child," he said, laying his hand gently on her head. "Your grandchild, friend?"

"Aye, sir," cried the old man, "and the stay and comfort of my life."

"Come in," said the schoolmaster.

Without farther preface he conducted them into his little schoolroom, which was parlour and kitchen likewise, and told them they were welcome to remain under his roof till morning. Before they had done thanking him, he spread a coarse white cloth upon the table, with knives and platters; and bringing out some bread and cold meat, besought them to eat.

They did so gladly, and the schoolmaster showed them, soon after, to some plain but neat sleeping chambers up close under the thatched roof. Here they slept the sound sleep of the very weary, and awoke refreshed and light-hearted the following day.

But the schoolmaster, while kind and courteous, was sad and quiet. He gave his small school a half-holiday that day, and Nell learned that it was because of the illness of a favourite pupil—a boy about her own age.

"If your journey is not a long one," he added to the travellers, "you're very welcome to pass another night here. I should really be glad if you would do so, as I am very lonely to-day."

They accepted and thanked him with grateful hearts. Nell busied herself tidying up the rooms and trying in many little ways to add to the master's comfort. And that evening, when his pupil died, Nell's grief was almost as deep in its sympathy as the master's own.

She bade him a reluctant farewell the next morning. School had already begun, but he rose from his desk and walked with them to the gate.

It was with a trembling and reluctant hand that the child held out to him the money which a lady had given her at the races for some flowers; faltering in her thanks as she thought how small the sum was, and blushing as she offered it. But he bade her put it up, and stooping to kiss her cheek, turned back into his house.

They had not gone half-a-dozen paces when he was at the door again; the old man retraced his steps to shake hands, and the child did the same.

"Good fortune and happiness go with you!" said

the poor schoolmaster. "I am quite a solitary man now. If you ever pass this way again, you'll not forget the little village school."

"We shall never forget it, sir," rejoined Nell; "nor ever forget to be grateful to you for your kindness to us."

"I have heard such words from the lips of children very often," said the schoolmaster, shaking his head and smiling thoughtfully, "but they were soon forgotten. I had attached one young friend to me, the better friend for being young—but that's over—God bless you!"

They bade him farewell very many times and turned away, walking slowly and often looking back, until they could see him no more. At length they had left the village far behind, and even lost sight of the smoke among the trees. They trudged onward now at a quicker pace, resolving to keep the main road, and go wherever it might lead them.

But main roads stretch a long, long way. With the exception of two or three inconsiderable clusters of cottages which they passed without stopping, and one lonely roadside public-house where they had some bread and cheese, this highway had led them to nothing— late in the afternoon—and still lengthened out, far in the distance, the same dull, tedious, winding course that they had been pursuing all day. As they had no resource, however, but to go forward, they still kept on, though at a much slower pace, being very weary and fatigued.

Finally, just at dusk, they came upon a curious little house upon wheels—a travelling show somewhat more pretentious than the Punch performance they had run away from. This little house was mounted upon a cart,

Mrs. Jarley

with white dimity curtains at the windows and shutters of green set in panels of bright red. Altogether it was a smart little contrivance. Grazing in front of it were two comfortable-looking horses; while at its open door sat a stout lady—evidently the proprietor—sipping tea.

This lady, Mrs. Jarley by name, had seen Nell and her grandfather at the races, so hailed them and asked about the success of the Punch show. She was greatly astonished to learn that they had nothing to do with it, and were wandering about without any object in view.

Her own performance was more "classic," as she expressed it. It was a Waxwork exhibition; and as she looked at Nell's attractive face she was seized with an idea. This bright little girl was just the sort of assistant she had been needing. So she invited them to stop and have some tea with her. They did so; and when Mrs. Jarley presently unfolded her plan—which was to engage Nell to exhibit the wax figures and describe them in a set speech—Nell was delighted to accept the offer, especially since it involved no separation from her grandfather, who could dust the figures and do other light tasks.

It was really not a very hard position for Nell. At the first town where the Waxworks were to be shown, Nell was given a private view and instructed in her new duties. The figures were displayed on a raised platform some two feet from the floor, running round the room and parted from the rude public by a crimson rope breast high. They represented celebrated characters, singly and in groups, clad in glittering dresses of various climes and times, and standing more or less unsteadily upon their legs, with their eyes very wide open, and

K

their nostrils very much inflated, and the muscles of their legs and arms very strongly developed, and all their countenances expressing great surprise. All the gentlemen were very pigeon-breasted and very blue about the beards, and all the ladies were miraculous figures; and all the ladies and all the gentlemen were looking with extraordinary earnestness at nothing at all.

Nell was taught a little speech about each one of them, and so apt was she that one rehearsal rendered her able to take the willow wand, which Mrs. Jarley had formerly wielded, and tell the interesting history of this very select Waxwork show to the audiences which presently began to come.

Mrs. Jarley herself was delighted with her venture. She saw at once that Nell would be a strong drawing card. And in order that the child might remain contented she made her and her grandfather as comfortable as possible, besides paying them a fair salary.

So the wanderers now rode in the van from town to town, and lived almost happily. Nell carefully saved all their money, and watched over her feeble grandfather with the tenderness of a little mother. She had one scare in almost meeting face to face with Quilp, the dwarf, but he had not recognised her.

Quilp, indeed, was a perpetual nightmare to the child, who was constantly haunted by a vision of his ugly face and stunted figure. She slept, for their better security, in the room where the waxwork figures were, and she never retired to this place at night but she tortured herself—she could not help it—with imagining a resemblance, in some one or other of their death-like faces, to the dwarf, and this fancy would sometimes so gain upon her that she would almost believe he had removed the figure and stood within the clothes.

But presently a deeper and more real concern came to her. Her grandfather had never alluded to their former life, nor to his passion for gambling. He did not see the card-tables out in the country; and that was the reason why she had been so eager to wander even without a roof over their heads. But now, as the Waxworks exhibited only in the towns, temptation came again to the poor, weak, old man. He saw some men playing cards in a tavern, and instantly his slumbering passion was aroused. He would play again and win a great fortune—for Nell!

He began to play, and, of course, with the old result. He was but a tool in the hands of the sharpers, and presently he had exhausted all the slender hoard which Nell had so carefully made. She watched his actions with a bursting heart, but was powerless to stop him or keep the money out of his grasp. At last the villains who had led him on—not satisfied with their small winnings from him—urged him to get the money belonging to the Waxwork show, saying that when he won he could pay it all back.

Nell had followed her grandfather upon this visit to the gamblers, and overheard their plot. She knew there was but one thing to do to save her grandfather. They must flee out into the world again at once. That night she roused him from his sleep, and told him they must go away.

" What does this mean ? " he cried.

" I have had dreadful dreams," said the child. " If we stay here another night something awful will happen Come ! "

The old man looked at her as if she were a spirit, and trembled in every joint.

" Must we go to-night ? " he asked.

" Yes, to-night," she replied.   " To-morrow night will be too late.   The dream will have come again.   Nothing but flight can save us.   Up ! "

The old man rose obediently and made ready to follow. She had already packed their scanty belongings.   She gave him his wallet and staff, and secretly, in the night, they fled away.

The wanderings of the next few days seemed like a nightmare to them.   Nell had brought only a few pennies in her pockets and these went for a scant supply of bread and cheese.   Two days and a night they rode on an open canal-boat in company with some rough but not unkind men.   It was easier than walking, but the rain descended in torrents and drenched them to the skin.

Finally the boat drew up to a wharf in an ugly manufacturing town, and the travellers were cast adrift as lonely and helpless as though they had just awakened from a sleep of a thousand years.   They had not one friend, nor the least idea where to turn for shelter.   But a rough stoker at one of the furnaces told them that they might pass the night in front of his fire.   It was nothing but a bed of ashes, yet they were warm and the heat dried out the poor travellers' drenched garments.

The child felt stiff and weak in every joint the next morning, but the furnace-tender told them that it was two days' journey to the open country and sweet, pure fields, and she felt that they must press forward at any cost.   So they started forth, slowly and wearily, for their journey and privations had almost exhausted them, but still with brave hearts.   Through long rows of red brick houses, that looked exactly alike, they wended their way, asking for bread to eat only when obliged to, and meeting little else but scowls from the dirty factory workers.

Finally, to their great joy, the open country began again to appear; and with fresh courage in their hearts they continued to press on.

They were dragging themselves along through the last street, and the child felt that the time was close at hand when her enfeebled powers would bear no more; when there appeared before them, going in the same direction as themselves, a traveller on foot, who, with a portmanteau strapped to his back, leaned upon a stout stick as he walked, and read from a book which he held in his other hand.

It was not an easy matter to come up with him, and beseech his aid, for he walked fast, and was a little distance in advance. At length he stopped to look more attentively at some passage in his book. Animated with a ray of hope, the child shot on before her grandfather, and going close to the stranger without rousing him by the sound of her footsteps, began, in a few faint words, to implore his help.

He turned his head. The child clapped her hands together, uttered a wild shriek, and fell senseless at his feet.

III

AT THE END OF THE JOURNEY

IT was the poor schoolmaster. Scarcely less moved and surprised by the sight of the child than she had been on recognising him, he stood, for a moment, without even the presence of mind to raise her from the ground.

But quickly recovering his self-possession, he threw down his stick and book, and dropping on one knee beside her, endeavoured by such simple means as occurred to him to restore her to herself; while her grandfather, standing idly by, wrung his hands, and implored her with many endearing expressions to speak to him, were it only a word.

"She is quite exhausted," said the schoolmaster, glancing upward into his face. "You have taxed her powers too far, friend."

"She is perishing of want," rejoined the old man. "I never thought how weak and ill she was till now."

Casting a look upon him, half reproachful and half compassionate, the schoolmaster took the child in his arms, and, bidding the old man gather up her little basket and follow him directly, bore her away at his utmost speed.

There was a small inn within sight, to which, it would seem, he had been directing his steps when so unexpectedly overtaken. Towards this place he hurried with his unconscious burden, and rushing into the kitchen deposited it on a chair before the fire.

A doctor was hastily called in and restoratives were applied; after which Nell was given what she most needed, some warm broth and toast, and was put to bed.

The schoolmaster asked anxiously after her health the next morning, and was greatly relieved to find that she was much better, though still so weak that it would require a day's careful nursing before she could proceed upon her journey. That evening he was allowed to see her, and was greatly touched by the sight of her pale, pinched face. But she held out both hands to him.

" It makes me unhappy even in the midst of all this kindness," said the child, " to think that we should be a burden upon you. How can I ever thank you? If I had not met you so far from home, I must have died, and poor grandfather would have no one to take care of him."

" We'll not talk about dying," said the schoolmaster, "and as to burdens, I have made my fortune since you slept at my cottage."

" Indeed! " cried the child, joyfully.

" Oh, yes," returned her friend. " I have been appointed clerk and schoolmaster to a village a long way from here—and a long way from the old one as you may suppose—at five and thirty pounds a year. Five and thirty pounds! "

" I am very glad," said the child—" so very, very glad."

" I am on my way there now," resumed the schoolmaster. " They allowed me the stage-coach hire — outside stage-coach hire all the way. Bless you, they grudge me nothing. But as the time at which I am

expected there left me ample leisure, I determined
to walk instead. How glad I am to think I did
so ! "

" How glad should we be ! "

" Yes, yes," said the schoolmaster, moving restlessly
in his chair, " certainly, that's very true. But you—
where are you going, where are you coming from, what
have you been doing since you left me, what had you
been doing before ? Now, tell me—do tell me. I know
very little of the world, and perhaps you are better fitted
to advise me in its affairs than I am qualified to give
advice to you ; but I am very sincere, and I have a reason
(you have not forgotten it) for loving you. I have felt
since that time as if my love for him who died had been
transferred to you."

Nell was moved in her turn by this allusion to the
favourite pupil who had died, and by the plain, frank
kindness of the good schoolmaster. She told him all—
that they had no friend or relative—that she had fled
with the old man to save him from all the miseries he
dreaded—that she was flying now to save him from
himself—and that she sought an asylum in some quiet
place, where the temptation before which he fell would
never enter, and her late sorrows and distresses could
have no place.

The schoolmaster heard her with astonishment. " This
child ! " he thought ; " she is one of the heroines and
saints of earth ! "

Then he told her of a great idea which had occurred
to him. They were all three to travel together to the
village where his new school was located, and he made
no doubt he could find them some simple and congenial
employment.

The child joyfully accepted this ; and the journey was made very comfortably in a stage which went that way. Stowed among the softer bundles and packages she thought this to be a drowsy, luxurious way of going, indeed.

At last they came upon a quiet, restful-looking hamlet clustered in a valley among some stately trees.

" See—here's the church ! " cried the delighted schoolmaster, in a low voice ; " and that old building close beside it is the schoolhouse, I'll be sworn. Five and thirty pounds a year in this beautiful place ! "

They admired everything—the old grey porch, the green churchyard, the ancient tower, the very weathercock ; the brown thatched roofs of cottage, barn, and homestead, peeping from among the trees ; the stream that rippled by the distant watermill ; the blue Welsh mountains far away. It was for such a spot the child had wearied in the dense, dark, miserable haunts of labour. Upon her bed of ashes, and amidst the squalid horrors through which they had forced their way, visions of such scenes—beautiful indeed, but not more beautiful than this sweet reality—had been always present to her mind. They had seemed to melt into a dim and airy distance, as the prospect of ever beholding them again grew fainter ; but, as they receded, she had loved and panted for them more.

" I must leave you somewhere for a few minutes," said the schoolmaster, at length breaking the silence into which they had fallen in their gladness. " I have a letter to present, and inquiries to make, you know. Where shall I take you ? To the little inn yonder ? "

" Let us wait here," rejoined Nell. " The gate is open. We will sit in the church porch till you come back."

"A good place, too," said the schoolmaster, leading the way towards it. "Be sure that I come back with good news, and am not long gone."

So the happy schoolmaster put on a brand-new pair of gloves which he had carried in a little parcel in his pocket all the way, and hurried off, full of ardour and excitement.

The child watched him from the porch until the intervening foliage hid him from her view, and then stepped softly out into the old churchyard—so solemn and quiet that every rustle of her dress upon the fallen leaves, which strewed the path and made her footsteps noiseless, seemed an invasion of its silence. It was an aged, ghostly place; the church had been built hundreds of years before; yet from this first glimpse the child loved it and felt that in some strange way she was a part of its crumbling walls and grass-grown churchyard.

After a time the schoolmaster reappeared, hurrying towards them and swinging a bunch of keys.

"You see those two houses?" he asked, pointing, quite out of breath. "Well, one of them is mine."

Without saying any more, or giving the child time to reply, the schoolmaster took her hand, and, his honest face quite radiant with exultation, led her to the place of which he spoke.

They stopped before its low, arched door. After trying several of the keys in vain, the schoolmaster found one to fit the huge lock, which turned back, creaking, and admitted them into the house.

It was a very old house, and, like the church, falling into decay, yet still handsome with high vaulted ceilings and queer carvings. It was not quite destitute of furniture. A few strange chairs, whose arms and legs looked as though they had dwindled away with age; a table, the very spectre of its race; a great old chest that had once held records in the church, with other quaintly fashioned domestic necessaries, and store of firewood for the winter, were scattered around, and gave evident tokens of its occupation as a dwelling-place, at no very distant time.

The child looked around her, with that solemn feeling with which we contemplate the work of ages that have become but drops of water in the great ocean of eternity. The old man had followed them, but they were all three hushed for a space, and drew their breath softly, as if they feared to break the silence, even by so slight a sound.

"It is a very beautiful place!" said the child, in a low voice.

"I almost feared you thought otherwise," returned the schoolmaster. "You shivered when we first came in, as if you felt it cold or gloomy."

"It was not that," said Nell, glancing round with a slight shudder. "Indeed, I cannot tell you what it was, but when I saw the outside from the church porch, the same feeling came over me. It is its being so old and grey, perhaps."

"A peaceful place to live in, don't you think so?" said her friend.

"Oh, yes," rejoined the child, clasping her hands earnestly. "A quiet, happy place—a place to live and learn to die in!"

"A place to live, and learn to live, and gather health of mind and body in," said the schoolmaster; "for this old house is yours."

"Ours!" cried the child.

"Aye," returned the schoolmaster, gaily. "For many a merry year to come, I hope. I shall be a close neighbour—only next door—but this house is yours."

Having now disburdened himself of his great surprise, the schoolmaster sat down, and drawing Nell to his side told her how he had learned that the ancient tenement had been occupied for a very long time by an old person, who kept the keys of the church, opened and closed it for the services, and showed it to strangers; how she had died not many weeks ago, and nobody had yet been found to fill the office; how, learning all this in an interview with the sexton, he had hurried to the clergyman and obtained the vacant post for Nell and her grandfather.

"There's a small allowance of money," said the schoolmaster. "It is not much, but still enough to live upon in this retired spot. By clubbing our funds together, we shall do bravely; no fear of that."

"Heaven bless and prosper you!" sobbed the child.

"Amen, my dear," returned her friend, cheerfully; "and all of us, as it will, and has, in leading us through sorrow and trouble to this tranquil life. But we must look at *my* house now. Come!"

They repaired to the other tenement; tried the rusty keys as before; at length found the right one; and opened the worm-eaten door. It led into a chamber, vaulted and old, like that from which they had come, but not so spacious, and having only one other little room attached. It was not difficult to divine that the other house was of right the schoolmaster's, and that he had chosen for himself the least commodious, in his care and regard for them. Like the adjoining habitation, it held such old articles of furniture as were absolutely necessary, and had its stack of firewood.

To make these dwellings as habitable and full of comfort as they could, was now their pleasant care. In a short time, each had its cheerful fire glowing and crackling on the hearth, and reddening the pale old walls with a hale and healthy blush. Nell, busily plying her needle, repaired the tattered window-hangings, drew together the rents that time had worn in the threadbare scraps of carpet, and made them whole and decent. The schoolmaster swept and smoothed the ground before the door, trimmed the long grass, trained the ivy and creeping plants, which hung their drooping heads in melancholy neglect; and gave to the outer walls a cheery air of home. The old man, sometimes by his side and sometimes with the child, lent his aid to both, went here and there on little patient services, and was happy. Neighbours, too, as they came from work, proffered their help; or sent their children with such small presents or loans as the strangers needed most. So it was not many days before they were quite cosy and Nell felt again, in that strange way which had come over her at the church, that she had always been a part of the place.

And how she loved her work from the very first! Hour after hour she would spend in the old church, dusting its pews or casements with reverent fingers, or more often, sitting quietly before some tablet or inscription, looking at it or beyond it, with a dreamy light in her eyes.

Her grandfather noted her attitude anxiously. He saw that she grew more listless and frail, day by day, and he sought constantly—poor old man!—to lighten her few tasks. But it was not these which wearied her; it was merely the burden of all things earthly.

Every person in the village soon grew to love this frail, spiritual-looking child; but from the first she seemed a being apart from them. They were constantly showing her kindness, or pausing at the church gate to speak with her; but as they went their way, a sad smile or shake of the head told only too plainly of their fears. She was like some rare, delicate flower which, they knew, could not endure the frost of winter.

The good schoolmaster gently chided her for spending so much of her time in the church and among the graves, instead of out in the light and sunshine. But she only smiled and said she loved to tend the graves and keep them neat, for she could not bear to think that any lying there should be forgotten, or that she herself might be forgotten some day.

"There is nothing good that is forgotten," he replied, kindly. "There is not an angel added to the host of Heaven but does its blessed work on earth in those that loved it here."

As the cold days of autumn and winter drew on, the child spent more and more time within doors, on a couch before the fire. The slightest task wearied her now, and her grandfather kept watch night and day to save her needless steps. He could scarcely bear her out of his sight; and often would creep to the side of her couch during the night, listening to her breathing or stroking her slender fingers softly. And if by chance she awoke and smiled on him, he would creep back to his own bed comforted.

But one chill morning in midwinter, when the snow lay thickly on the ground, it seemed to him that she slept more quietly than usual. The schoolmaster, coming in, found him crouched over a fire, muttering softly to himself, and wondering why she slumbered so long. The two went softly into her chamber, and then the schoolmaster knew why she was so quiet.

For she was dead. Dear, gentle, patient, noble Nell was dead. No sleep so beautiful and calm, so free from trace of pain, so fair to look upon. She seemed a creature fresh from the hand of God, and waiting the breath of life; not one who had lived and suffered death.

The old man held one languid arm in his, and had the small hand tight folded to his breast for warmth. It was the hand she had stretched out to him with her last smile—the hand that had led him on, through all their wanderings. Ever and anon he pressed it to his lips, then hugged it to his breast again, murmuring that it was warmer now; and, as he said it, he looked in agony to the schoolmaster, as if imploring him to help her.

She was dead, and past all help, or need of it. The ancient rooms she had seemed to fill with life, even while her own was waning fast; the garden she had tended; the eyes she had gladdened; the noiseless haunts of many a thoughtful hour; the paths she had trodden as it were but yesterday—could know her never more.

"It is not," said the schoolmaster, as he bent down to kiss her on the cheek, and gave his tears free vent, "it is not on earth that Heaven's justice ends. Think what earth is, compared with the world to which her young spirit has winged its early flight, and say, if one deliberate wish expressed in solemn terms above this bed could call her back to life, which of us would utter it?"

The whole village, young and old, came to the church-yard when they laid her to rest—save only the old man.

He could not realise that she was dead, and he had gone to pick winter berries to decorate her couch.

When he returned and could not find her, they were obliged to tell him the truth—that her body had been put away in the cold earth—and then his grief and distress were pitiful to see. He seemed at once to lose all power of thought or action, save as they concerned her alone.

Day by day he sought for her about the house or in the garden, calling her name wildly. At other times he sat before the fire staring dully, and did not seem to hear when they spoke to him.

At length, they found, one day, that he had risen early, and, with his knapsack on his back, his staff in hand, her own straw hat, and little basket full of such things as she had been used to carry, was gone. As they were making ready to pursue him far and wide, a frightened schoolboy came who had seen him, but a moment before, sitting in the church—upon her grave, he said.

They hastened there, and going softly to the door, espied him in the attitude of one who waited patiently. They did not disturb him then, but kept a watch upon him all that day. When it grew quite dark, he rose and returned home, and went to bed, murmuring to himself, " She will come to-morrow ! "

Upon the morrow he was there again from sunrise until night ; and still at night he laid him down to rest and murmured, " She will come to-morrow ! "

And thenceforth, every day, and all day long, he waited at her grave for her. How many pictures of new journeys over pleasant country, of resting-places under the free broad sky, of rambles in the fields and woods, and paths not often trodden ; how many tones of that one well-remembered voice ; how many glimpses of the form, the fluttering dress, the hair that waved so gaily in the wind ; how many visions of what had been, and what he hoped was yet to be—rose up before him, in the old, dull, silent church ? He never told them what he thought, or where he went. He would sit with them at night, pondering with a secret satisfaction they could see, upon the flight that he and she would take before night came again ; and still they would hear him whisper in his prayers, " Lord ! Let her come to-morrow ! "

The last time was on a genial day in spring. He did not return at the usual hour, and they went to seek him. He was lying dead upon the stone.

They laid him by the side of her whom he had loved so well ; and, in the church, where they had often prayed and mused and lingered hand in hand, the child and the old man slept together.

The Story of Paul and Florence Dombey

I

THE HOUSE OF DOMBEY AND SON

PAUL DOMBEY was a boy born to achieve great things. His birth was the one historic event of the Dombey household—at least, so his father said. 'Tis true that Paul's sister Florence was six years older than he, but then Florence was only a girl. What Mr. Dombey had long wanted was a son who could grow up to carry on the business of the great expert house, and who from his birth would make possible the imposing title of Dombey and Son.

So Florence, who had remained quietly neglected in her nursery, now came into notice only as the sister of Paul, or as a faithful little nurse who could help amuse him.

As for Mr. Dombey himself, he was a cold, haughty man, very proud of what he had done, and at all times exacting obedience from everyone else. Paul's mother had died soon after he was born, and Mr. Dombey having engaged the best nurses he could find, expected them forthwith to bring the child through all the round of infant ailments—of which the frail little fellow had more

than his full share. Indeed, Mr Dombey loved his son
with all the love he had. If there were a warm place
in his frosty heart, his son occupied it ; though not so
much as an infant or a boy, as a man to be—the " Son "
of the firm. Therefore he was impatient to have him
grow up ; feeling never a doubt but that the boy *must*
become the man around whom all his hopes centred.

Thus Paul grew to be nearly five years old. He
was a pretty little fellow, though there was something
wan and wistful in his small face, that gave occasion
to many significant shakes of his nurse's head. His
temper gave abundant promise of being imperious, like
his father's, in after life. He was childish and sportive
enough at times ; but he had a strange, old-fashioned,
thoughtful way at other times of sitting brooding in his
miniature arm-chair, when he looked and talked like
one of those terrible little beings in the fairy tales, who,
at a hundred and fifty or two hundred years of age,
fantastically represent the children for whom they have
been substituted. He would frequently be stricken
with this mood upstairs in the nursery, and would sometimes lapse into it suddenly, exclaiming that he was
tired, even while playing with Florence, or driving his
nurse in single harness. But at no one time did he fall
into it so surely, as when, his little chair being carried
down into his father's room, he sat there with him after
dinner by the fire. They were the strangest pair at such
a time that ever firelight shone upon. Mr. Dombey,
so erect and solemn, gazing at the blaze ; his little image,
with an old, old face, peering into the red perspective
with the fixed and rapt attention of a sage ; the two so
very much alike, and yet so monstrously contrasted.

On one of these occasions, when they had both been

perfectly quiet for a long time, little Paul broke the silence thus :

" Papa ! what's money ? "

The abrupt question had such immediate reference to the subject of Mr. Dombey's thoughts, that Mr. Dombey was quite disconcerted.

" What is money, Paul ? " he answered. " Money ? "

" Yes," said the child, laying his hands upon the elbows of his little chair, and turning the old face up towards Mr. Dombey's, " what is money ? "

Mr. Dombey was in a difficulty. He would have liked to give him some grown-up explanation ; but looking down at the little chair, and seeing what a long way down it was, he answered : " Gold, and silver, and copper. Guineas, shillings, halfpence. You know what they are ? "

" Oh, yes, I know what they are," said Paul. " I don't mean that, papa. I mean what's money, after all."

" What is money, after all ! " said Mr. Dombey, backing his chair a little, that he might the better gaze at the atom that made such an inquiry.

" I mean, papa, what can it do ? " returned Paul.

Mr. Dombey drew his chair back to its former place, and patted him on the head. " You'll know better, by-and-bye, my man," he said. " Money, Paul, can do anything."

" Anything, papa ? "

" Yes. Anything—almost," said Mr. Dombey.

" Anything means everything, don't it, papa ? " asked his son, not observing, or possibly not understanding the qualification.

" Yes," said Mr. Dombey.

" Why didn't money save me my mamma ? " returned the child. " It isn't cruel, is it ? "

"Cruel!" said Mr. Dombey, settling his neckcloth, and seeming to resent the idea. "No. A good thing can't be cruel."

"If it's a good thing, and can do anything," said the little fellow, thoughtfully, as he looked back at the fire, "I wonder why it didn't save me my mamma."

Mr. Dombey having recovered from his surprise, not to say his alarm (for it was the very first occasion on which the child had ever broached the subject of his mother to him), expounded to him how that money, though a very potent spirit, could not keep people alive whose time was come to die; and how that we must all die, unfortunately, even in the city, though we were never so rich.

Paul listened to all this and much more with grave attention, and then suddenly asked a question which was still more alarming :

"It can't make me strong and quite well, either, papa, can it ? "

"Why, you *are* strong and quite well," returned Mr. Dombey. "Are you not ? "

Oh ! the age of the face that was turned up again, with an expression, half of melancholy, half of slyness on it !

"You are as strong and well as such little people usually are, eh ? " said Mr. Dombey.

"Florence is older than I am, but I'm not as strong and well as Florence, I know," returned the child; "but I believe that when Florence was as little as me, she could play a great deal longer at a time without tiring herself. I am so tired sometimes that I don't know what to do."

"But that's at night," said Mr. Dombey, drawing his own chair closer to his son's, and laying his hand gently on his back; "little people should be tired at night, for then they sleep well."

"Oh, it's not at night, papa," returned the child, "it's in the day; and I lie down in Florence's lap, and she sings to me.   At night I dream about such cu-ri-ous things!"

Mr. Dombey was so astonished, and so perfectly at a loss how to pursue the conversation, that he could only sit looking at his son by the light of the fire.

Here they sat until Florence came timidly into the room to take Paul upstairs to bed; when he raised towards his father, in bidding him good-night, a countenance so much brighter, so much younger, and so much more child-like altogether, that Mr. Dombey, while he felt greatly reassured by the change, was quite amazed at it.

After they had left the room together, he thought he heard a soft voice singing; and remembering that Paul had said his sister sang to him, he had the curiosity to open the door and listen, and look after them.   She was toiling up the great, wide staircase, with him in her arms; his head was lying on her shoulder, one of his arms thrown negligently round her neck.   So they went, toiling up; she singing all the way, and Paul sometimes crooning out a feeble accompaniment.

Mr. Dombey was so alarmed about Paul's remarks as to his health, that he called the family doctor in consultation the very next day.   The doctor admitted that Paul was not as strong as he could hope, and sug-gested that sea air might benefit him.   So the boy was sent to the home of a Mrs. Pipchin at Brighton.   But he refused to go without Florence, much to the secret displeasure of Mr. Dombey, who did not like to see any-one—especially this neglected daughter—gain more influence with Paul than he himself had.

Paul and Mrs. Pipchin   156

Mrs. Pipchin was a cross-grained old lady who gained a livelihood by taking care of delicate children. But she was not unkind to Paul, whose patient little face and strange way of asking questions attracted her, as they did everybody else.

When he had been with her for some time and it was found that he did not gain in strength, a little carriage was hired for him, in which he could lie at his ease with his books and be wheeled down to the seaside.

Consistent in his odd tastes, the child set aside a ruddy-faced lad who was proposed as the drawer of this carriage, and selected, instead, the boy's grandfather—a weazen, old, crab-faced man, in a suit of battered oil-skin. With this attendant to pull him along, and Florence always walking by his side, he went down to the margin of the ocean every day; and there he would sit or lie in his carriage for hours together; never so distressed as by the company of children—Florence alone excepted, always.

Some small voice, near his ear, would ask him how he was, perhaps.

"I am very well, I thank you," he would answer. "But you had better go and play, if you please."

Then he would turn his head, and watch the child away, and say to Florence, "We don't want any others, do we? Kiss me, Floy."

His favourite spot was quite a lonely one, far away from most loungers; and with Florence sitting by his side at work, or reading to him, or talking to him, and the wind blowing on his face, and the water coming up among the wheels of his bed, he wanted nothing more.

"Floy," he said one day, "where's India?"

"Oh, it's a long, long distance off," said Florence, raising her eyes from her work.

"Weeks off?" asked Paul.

"Yes, dear. Many weeks' journey, night and day."

"If you were in India, Floy," said Paul, after being silent for a minute, "I should—what is it that mamma did? I forget."

"Loved me?" answered Florence.

"No, no. Don't I love you now, Floy? What is it? —Died. If you were in India, I should die, Floy."

She hurriedly put her work aside, and laid her head down on his pillow, caressing him. And so would she, she said, if he were there. He would be better soon.

"Oh! I am a great deal better now!" he answered. "I don't mean that. I mean that I should die of being so sorry and so lonely, Floy!"

Another time, in the same place, he fell asleep, and slept quietly for a long time. Awaking suddenly, he started up, and sat listening.

Florence asked him what he thought he heard.

"I want to know what it says," he answered, looking steadily in her face. "The sea, Floy; what is it that it keeps on saying?"

She told him that it was only the noise of the rolling waves.

"Yes, yes," he said. "But I know that they are always saying something. Always the same thing. What place is over there?" He rose up, looking eagerly at the horizon.

She told him that there was another country opposite, but he said he didn't mean that; he meant farther away—farther away.

Very often afterwards, in the midst of their talk, he

would break off to try to understand what it was that the waves were always saying; and would rise up in his couch to look towards that invisible region far away.

But in spite of Paul's brooding fancies, the days in the open air, and with the salt spray blowing about him, began to have good effect. Little by little he grew stronger until he became able to do without his carriage; though he still remained the same old, quiet, dreamy child.

One day after he had been with Mrs. Pipchin about a year, Mr. Dombey came to see her. He informed Mrs. Pipchin that, as Paul was now six years old and so much stronger, it was time his education was being considered; and so the child was to be sent to a certain Dr. Blimber, who lived near by and managed a select school of boys. Meanwhile, Florence could continue to live here, so that Paul need not be entirely separated from his sister.

Accordingly, a few days later, Paul stood upon the doctor's doorsteps, with his small right hand in his father's, and his other locked in that of Florence. How tight the tiny pressure of that one, and how loose and cold the other!

The doctor was sitting in his portentous study, with a globe at each knee, books all round him, Homer over the door, and Minerva on the mantel-shelf.

" And how do you do, sir," he said to Mr. Dombey, when they had been ushered in, " and how is my little friend ? "

Grave as an organ was the doctor's speech; and when he ceased, the great clock in the hall seemed (to Paul at least) to take him up, and to go on saying, " how–is–my–lit–tle–friend–how–is–my–lit–tle–friend," over and over again.

The little friend being something too small to be seen at all from where the doctor sat, over the books on his table, the doctor made several futile attempts to get a view of him round the legs; which Mr. Dombey perceiving, relieved the doctor from his embarrassment by taking Paul up in his arms and sitting him on another little table, over against the doctor, in the middle of the room.

"Ha!" said the doctor, leaning back in his chair with his hand in his breast. "Now I see my little friend. How do you do, my little friend?"

The clock in the hall wouldn't subscribe to this alteration in the form of words, but continued to repeat, "how–is–my–lit–tle–friend–how–is–my–lit–tle–friend!"

"Very well, I thank you, sir," returned Paul, answering the clock quite as much as the doctor.

"Ha!" said Doctor Blimber. "Shall we make a man of him?"

"Do you hear, Paul?" added Mr. Dombey, Paul being silent.

"Shall we make a man of him?" repeated the doctor.

"I had rather be a child," replied Paul.

"Indeed!" said the doctor. "Why?"

The child sat on the table looking at him, with a curious expression of suppressed emotion in his face, and beating one hand proudly on his knee as if he had the rising tears beneath it, and crushed them. But his other hand strayed a little way the while, a little farther —farther from him yet—until it lighted on the neck of Florence. "This is why," it seemed to say, and then the steady look was broken up and gone, the working lip was loosened, and the tears came streaming forth.

"Never mind," said the doctor, blandly nodding his head. "Ne-ver mind; we shall substitute new cares and new impressions, Mr. Dombey, very shortly. You would wish my little friend to acquire——"

"Everything, if you please, doctor," returned Mr. Dombey, firmly.

"Yes," said the doctor, who, with his half-shut eyes, and his usual smile, seemed to survey Paul with the sort of interest that might attach to some choice little animal he was going to stuff. "Yes, exactly. Ha! We shall impart a great variety of information to our little friend, and bring him quickly forward, I dare say. I dare say."

As soon as Mr. Dombey and Florence were gone, Dr. Blimber gave into the charge of his learned daughter, Cornelia, the little new pupil, saying, "Bring him on, Cornelia, bring him on."

Miss Blimber received her young ward from the doctor's hands; and Paul, feeling that the spectacles were surveying him, cast down his eyes.

"How old are you, Dombey?" said Miss Blimber.

"Six," answered Paul, wondering, as he stole a glance at the young lady, why her hair didn't grow long like Florence's, and why she was like a boy.

"How much do you know of your Latin Grammar, Dombey?" said Miss Blimber.

"None of it," answered Paul. Feeling that the answer was a shock to Miss Blimber's sensibility, he looked up and added timidly:

"I haven't been well. I have been a weak child. I couldn't learn a Latin Grammar when I was out, every day, with old Glubb. I wish you'd tell old Glubb to come and see me, if you please."

" What a dreadfully low name ! " said Miss Blimber.
" Unclassical to a degree !   Who is the monster, child ? "

" What monster ? " inquired Paul.

" Glubb."

" He's no more a monster than you are," returned
Paul.

"What ! " cried the doctor, in a terrible voice. "What's
that ? "

Paul was dreadfully frightened ; but still he made a
stand for the absent Glubb, though he did it trembling.

" He's a very nice old man, ma'am," he said. " He
used to pull my carriage for me, down along the beach.
I wish you'd let him come to see me. He knows lots
of things."

" Ha ! " said the doctor, shaking his head ; " this
is bad, but study will do much."

Mrs. Blimber opined, with something like a shiver,
that he was an unaccountable child ; and, allowing for
the difference of visage, looked at him pretty much as
Mrs. Pipchin had been used to do.

As for Miss Blimber, she told him to come down to
her room that evening at tea-time. When he did so
he noticed a little pile of new books, which she was
glancing over.

" These are yours, Dombey," she said.

" All of 'em, ma'am ? " said Paul.

" Yes," returned Miss Blimber ; " and Mr. Feeder
will look you out some more very soon, if you are as
studious as I expect you will be, Dombey."

" Thank you, ma'am," said Paul.

" I am going out for a constitutional," resumed Miss
Blimber ; " and while I am gone, that is to say, in the
interval between this and breakfast, Dombey, I wish

you to read over what I have marked in these books, and to tell me if you quite understand what you have got to learn. Don't lose time, Dombey, for you have none to spare, but take them downstairs, and begin directly."

" Yes, ma'am," answered Paul.

There were so many of them that although Paul put one hand under the bottom book and his other hand and his chin on the top book and hugged them all closely, the middle book slipped out before he reached the door, and then they all tumbled down on the floor. Miss Blimber said, " Oh, Dombey, Dombey, this is really very careless ! " and piled them up afresh for him ; and this time, by dint of balancing them with great nicety, Paul got out of the room.

But if the poor child found them heavy to carry downstairs, how much harder was it to cram their contents into his head. Oh, how tired he grew ! But always there was a never-ending round of lessons waiting for him during these long days and nights that Dr. Blimber and Cornelia tried to make a man of him. And all week long his aching head held but one longing desire —for Saturday to come.

Oh, Saturdays ! Oh, happy Saturdays ! when Florence always came at noon, and never would, in any weather, stay away.

And when Florence found how hard Paul's studies were for him, she quietly bought books just like his and studied them during the week, so that she might keep along with him and help him when they were together.

Not a word of this was breathed to Mrs. Pipchin ; but many a night when she was in bed and the candles were spluttering and burning low, Florence tried so hard

to be a substitute for one small Dombey, that her fortitude
and perseverance might have almost won her a free right
to bear the name herself.

And high was her reward, when, one Saturday evening,
as little Paul was sitting down as usual to " resume his
studies," she sat down by his side, and showed him all
that was so rough made smooth, and all that was so dark
made clear and plain before him. It was nothing but
a startled look in Paul's wan face—a flush—a smile
—and then a close embrace—but God knows how
her heart leaped up at this rich payment for her
trouble.

" Oh, Floy ! " cried her brother, " how I love you !
How I love you, Floy ! "

" And I you, dear ! "

" Oh ! I am sure of that, Floy."

And so little Paul struggled on bravely under his
heavy load, never complaining, but growing more old-
fashioned day by day—and growing frailer, too.

Then came the holidays, and a grand party at the
school, to which Florence came, looking so beautiful
in her simple ball dress that Paul could hardly make
up his mind to let her go again.

" But what is the matter, Floy ? " he asked, almost
sure he saw a tear on her face.

" Nothing, dear. We will go home together, and I'll
nurse you till you are strong again."

" Nurse me ! " echoed Paul.

Paul couldn't understand what that had to do with
it, nor why the other guests looked on so seriously, nor
why Florence turned away her face for a moment, and
then turned it back, lighted up again with smiles.

" Floy," said Paul, holding a ringlet of her dark hair

in his hand. " Tell me, dear. Do *you* think I have
grown old-fashioned ? "

His sister laughed and fondled him, and told him
" No."

" Because I know they say so," returned Paul, " and
I want to know what they mean, Floy."

Florence would have sat by him all night, and would
not have danced at all of her own accord, but Paul made
her, by telling her how much it pleased him. And he
told her the truth too ; for his small heart swelled, and
his face glowed, when he saw how much they all admired
her, and how she was the beautiful little rosebud of the
room.

Then after the party came the leave-takings, for Paul
was going home. And everyone was good to him—
even the pompous doctor, and Cornelia—and bade him
good-bye with many regrets ; for they were afraid, as
they looked upon his pinched, wan face, that he would
not be able to come back and take up that load of heavy
books ever again.

There was a great deal, the next day and afterwards,
which Paul could not quite get clear in his mind. As
why they stopped at Mrs. Pipchin's for a while instead
of going straight home ; why he lay in bed, with Florence
sitting by him ; whether that had been his father in the
room, or only a tall shadow on the wall.

He could not even remember whether he had often
said to Florence, " Oh, Floy, take me home and never
leave me ! " but he thought he had. He fancied sometimes he had heard himself repeating, " Take me home,
Floy ! take me home ! "

But he could remember, when he got home, and was
carried up the well-remembered stairs, that there had

been the rumbling of a coach for many hours together
while he lay upon the seat, with Florence still beside
him, and Mrs. Pipchin sitting opposite. He remembered his old bed too, when they laid him down in it;
but there was something else, and recent, too, that still
perplexed him.

"I want to speak to Florence, if you please," he said.
"To Florence by herself, for a moment!"

She bent down over him, and the others stood away.

"Floy, my pet, wasn't that papa in the hall, when
they brought me from the couch?"

"Yes, dear."

"He didn't cry, and go into his room, Floy, did he,
when he saw me coming in?"

Florence shook her head, and pressed her lips against
his cheek.

"I'm very glad he didn't cry," said little Paul. "I
thought he did. Don't tell him that I asked."

Paul never rose from his little bed. He lay there,
listening to the noises in the street quite tranquilly;
not caring much how time went, but watching everything about him with observing eyes. And when visitors
or servants came softly to the door to inquire how he
was, he always answered for himself, "I am better;
I am a great deal better, thank you! Tell papa so!"

And sometimes when he awoke out of a feverish
dream, in which he thought a river was bearing him
away, he would see a figure seated motionless, with
bowed head, at the foot of his couch. Then he would
stretch out his hands and cry, "Don't be so sorry for
me, dear papa! Indeed, I am quite happy!"

His father coming, and bending down to him—which
he did quickly, and without first pausing by the bed-

side—Paul held him round the neck, and repeated those words to him several times, and very earnestly; and Paul never saw him in his room at any time, whether it were day or night, but he called out "Don't be so sorry for me! Indeed, I am quite happy!" This was the beginning of his always saying in the morning that he was a great deal better, and that they were to tell his father so.

Then one day he asked to see all his friends, and shook hands with each one quietly, and bade them good-bye. His father he clung to as though he felt more deeply for that proud man's sorrow and disappointment, than any unhappiness on his own account. For he was going to his mother—about whom he had often talked with Florence in these closing days.

"Now, lay me down," he said, "and Floy, come close to me, and let me see you!"

Sister and brother wound their arms around each other, and the golden light came streaming in, and fell upon them, locked together.

"How fast the river runs, between its green banks and the rushes, Floy! But it's very near the sea. I hear the waves! They always said so!"

Presently he told her that the motion of the boat upon the stream was lulling him to rest. How green the banks were now, how bright the flowers growing on them, and how tall the rushes! Now the boat was out at sea, but gliding smoothly on. And now there was a shore before him. Who stood on the bank?

He put his hands together, as he had been used to do at his prayers. He did not remove his arms to do it; but they saw him fold them so, behind her neck.

M

"Mamma is like you, Floy. I know her by the face. But tell them that the print upon the stairs at school is not divine enough. The light about the head is shining on me as I go!"

The golden ripple on the wall came back again, and nothing else stirred in the room. The old, old fashion! The fashion that came in with our first garments, and will last unchanged until our race has run its course, and the wide firmament is rolled up like a scroll. The old, old fashion—Death!

Oh, thank God, all who see it, for that older fashion yet, of Immortality! And look upon us, angels of young children, with regards not quite estranged, when the swift river bears us to the ocean!

II

HOW FLORENCE CAME INTO HER OWN

THE death of Paul, far from softening Mr. Dombey's heart toward his daughter, only served to widen the gap between them. He had been secretly hurt by Paul's preference for Florence, and now was more cold and distant with her than ever.

She, poor child, had this deep sorrow to bear in addition to the loss of Paul. Many and many a night when no one in the house was stirring, and the lights were all extinguished, she would softly leave her own room, and with noiseless feet descend the staircase, and approach her father's door. Against it, scarcely breathing, she

would rest her face and head, and press her lips, in the
yearning of her love. She crouched upon the cold stone
floor outside it, every night, to listen even for his breath ;
and in her one absorbing wish to be allowed to show
him some affection, to be a consolation to him, to win
him over to some tenderness for her, his solitary child,
she would have knelt down at his feet, if she had dared,
in humble supplication.

No one knew it. No one thought of it. The door
was ever closed, and he shut up within.

But one night Florence found the door slightly ajar.
She paused a moment tremblingly, and then pushed it
open and entered.

Her father sat at his old table in the middle room.
He had been arranging some papers and destroying
others, and the latter lay in fragile ruins before him.
The rain dripped heavily upon the glass panes in the
outer room, where he had so often watched poor Paul,
a baby ; and the low complainings of the wind were
heard without.

He sat with his eyes fixed on the table, so immersed
in thought that a far heavier tread than the light foot
of his child could make might have failed to rouse him.
His face was turned towards her. By the waning lamp,
and at that haggard hour, it looked worn and dejected ;
and in the utter loneliness surrounding him there was
an appeal to Florence that struck home.

" Papa ! papa ! Speak to me, dear papa ! "
He started at her voice.

" What is the matter ? " he said, sternly. " Why
do you come here ? What has frightened you ? "

If anything had frightened her, it was the face he
turned upon her. The glowing love within the breast

of his young daughter froze before it, and she stood and looked at him as if stricken into stone. There was not one touch of tenderness or pity in it.

Did he see before him the successful rival of his son, in health and life ? Did he look upon his own successful rival in that son's affection ? Did a mad jealousy and withered pride poison sweet remembrances that should have endeared and made her precious to him ? Could it be possible that it was gall to him to look upon her in her beauty and her promise : thinking of his infant boy !

Florence had no such thoughts. But love is quick to know when it is spurned and hopeless ; and hope died out of hers, as she stood looking in her father's face.

" I ask you, Florence, are you frightened ? Is there anything the matter, that you come here ? "

" I came, papa——"

" Against my wishes. Why ? "

She saw he knew why—it was written broadly on his face—and dropped her head upon her hands with one prolonged low cry.

He took her by the arm. His hand was cold and loose, and scarcely closed upon her.

" You are tired, I dare say," he said, taking up the light and leading her towards the door, " and want rest. We all want rest. Go, Florence. You have been dreaming."

The dream she had had was over then, God help her ! and she felt that it could never more come back.

" I will remain here to light you up the stairs. The whole house is yours, above there," said her father, slowly. " You are its mistress now. Good-night ! "

Still covering her face, she sobbed, and answered " Good-night, dear papa," and silently ascended. Once she looked back as if she would have returned to him, but for fear. It was a momentary thought, too hopeless to encourage ; and her father stood there with the light—hard, unresponsive, motionless—until her fluttering dress was lost in the darkness.

Two years passed slowly away, days and weeks and months of neglect, unrelieved by one touch of tenderness from the hard stern parent. The little hope that Florence had ever held for happiness was quite gone now. Even the patient trust that was in her could not survive the daily blight of such an experience.

Florence loved her father still, but by degrees had come to love him rather as some dear one who had been, or who might have been, than as the hard reality before her eyes. Something of the softened sadness with which she loved the memory of little Paul or her mother, seemed to enter now into her thoughts of him, and to make them, as it were, a dear remembrance. Whether it was that he was dead to her, and that partly for this reason, partly for his share in those old objects of her affection, and partly for the long association of him with hopes that were withered and tendernesses he had frozen, she could not have told ; but the father whom she loved began to be a vague and dreamy idea to her ; hardly more substantially connected with her real life than the image she would sometimes conjure up of her dear brother yet alive, and growing to be a man, who would protect and cherish her.

The loving and tender nature, however, had not become entirely proof against injustice. There came a moment when Florence could not resist the dictates of her heart, and in momentary forgetfulness of past rebuffs she yielded again to an impulse of affection.

But on this occasion her father thrust her from him so roughly that she almost fell to the floor.

She did not sink down at his feet ; she did not shut out the sight of him with her trembling hands ; she did not weep nor speak one word of reproach. She only uttered a single low cry of pain and then fled from the house like a hunted animal.

Without a roof over her head—without father or mother, she was indeed an orphan.

*   *   *   *   *   *

The sea had ebbed and flowed through a whole year. Through a whole year the winds and clouds had come and gone ; the ceaseless work of Time had been performed, in storm and sunshine. Through a whole year the famous house of Dombey and Son had fought a fight for life, against doubtful rumours, unsuccessful ventures, and most of all, against the bad judgment of its head, who would not contract its enterprises by a hair's breadth, and would not listen to a word of warning that the ship he strained so hard against the storm was weak, and could not bear it.

For Mr. Dombey had grown strangely indifferent and reckless, and plunged blindly into speculation.

The year was out, and the great House was down.

One summer afternoon there was a buzz and whisper, about the streets of London, of a great failure. A certain cold, proud man, well known there, was not there, nor was he represented there. Next day it was noised abroad that Dombey and Son had stopped, and next night there was a list of bankrupts published, headed by that name.

Nobody's opinion stayed the misfortune, lightened it, or made it heavier. It was understood that the affairs of the House were to be wound up as they best could be ; that Mr. Dombey freely resigned everything he had, and asked no favour from anyone. That any resumption of the business was out of the question, as he would listen to no friendly negotiations having that compromise in view ; that he had relinquished every post of trust or distinction he had held as a man respected among merchants ; and that he was a broken man.

The old home where Paul had died and whence Florence had fled away was now empty and deserted—a wreck of what it had been. All the furniture and hangings had been sold to satisfy Mr. Dombey's creditors ; and he now lived there alone in one cheerless room—a man without friends, without hope.

But at last he began to come to his senses ; to see what a treasure he had cast away in Florence ; to recall his own injustice and cruelty toward her.

In the miserable night he thought of it ; in the dreary day, the wretched dawn, the ghostly, memory-haunted twilight, he remembered. In agony, in sorrow, in re-morse, in despair !

"Papa ! papa ! " He heard the words again, and saw the face. He saw it fall upon the trembling hands, and heard the one prolonged, low cry go upward.

Oh ! He did remember it ! The rain that fell upon the roof, the wind that mourned outside the door, had foreknowledge in their melancholy sound. He knew now what he had done. He knew now that he had called down that upon his head, which bowed it lower than the heaviest stroke of fortune. He knew now what it was to be rejected and deserted ; now, when every loving blossom he had withered in his innocent daughter's heart was snowing down in ashes on him.

He thought of her as she had been in all the home events of the abandoned house. He thought now that of all around him, she alone had never changed. His boy had faded into dust, his flatterer and friend had been transformed into the worst of villains, his riches had melted away, the very walls that sheltered him looked on him as a stranger; she alone had turned the same mild, gentle look upon him always. Yes, to the latest and the last. She had never changed to him— nor had he ever changed to her—and she was lost.

As, one by one, they fell away before his mind—his baby hope, his wife, his friend, his fortune—oh, how the mist through which he had seen her cleared, and showed him her true self! How much better than this that he had loved her as he had his boy, and lost her as he had his boy, and laid them in their early grave together!

As the days dragged by, it seemed to him that he should go mad with remorse and longing. He haunted Paul's room and Florence's room—so empty now—as though they were his only dwelling-place. He had meant to go away, but clung to this tie in the house as the last and only thing left to him. He would go to-morrow. To-morrow came. He could go to-morrow. Every night, within the knowledge of no human creature, he came forth, and wandered through the despoiled house like a ghost. Many a morning when the day broke, with altered face drooping behind the closed blind in his window, he pondered on the loss of his two children. It was one child no more. He reunited them in his thoughts, and they were never asunder.

Then, one day, when strange fancies oppressed him more than usual, he paused at Florence's door and gazed wildly down as though suddenly awakened from a dream.

He heard a cry—a loving, pleading voice—and there at his knees knelt Florence herself.

"Papa! Dearest papa! I have come back to ask forgiveness. I never can be happy more, without it!"

Unchanged still. Of all the world, unchanged. Raising the same face to his as on that miserable night. Asking *his* forgiveness!

"Dear papa, oh, don't look strangely at me! I never meant to leave you. I never thought of it, before or afterwards. I was frightened when I went away and could not think. Papa, dear, I am changed. I am penitent. I know my fault. I know my duty better now. Papa, don't cast me off or I shall die!"

He tottered to his chair. He felt her draw his arms about her neck; he felt her put her own round his; he felt her kisses on his face; he felt her wet cheek laid against his own; he felt—oh, how deeply!—all that he had done.

Upon the breast that he had bruised, against the heart that he had almost broken, she laid his face, now covered with his hands, and said, sobbing:

"I have been far away, dear papa, and could not come back before this. I have been across the seas, and I have a home of my own over there now. Oh, I want you to see it! I want to take you there; for my home is *your* home—always, always! Say you will pardon me, will come to me!"

He would have said it if he could. He would have raised his hands and besought *her* for pardon, but she caught them in her own and put them down hurriedly.

"You will come, I know, dear papa! And I will know by that that you forgive me. And we will never talk about what is past and forgotten; never again!"

As she clung closer to him, in another burst of tears, he kissed her on the lips, and, lifting up his eyes, said, " Oh, my God, forgive me, for I need it very much ! "

With that he dropped his head again, lamenting over and caressing her, and there was not a sound in all the house for a long, long time ; they remaining clasped in one another's arms, in the glorious sunshine that had crept in with Florence.

The Story of Pip

I

HOW PIP HELPED THE CONVICT

MY father's family name being Pirrip, and my Christian name Philip, my infant tongue could make of both names nothing longer than Pip. So I called myself Pip, and came to be called Pip.

I give Pirrip as my father's family name, on the authority of his tombstone and my sister—Mrs. Joe Gargery, who married the blacksmith. As I never saw my father or my mother, my first fancies regarding what they were like were unreasonably derived from their tombstones.

Ours was the marsh country down by the river, within twenty miles of the sea. My most vivid memory of these early days was of a raw evening about dusk. At such a time I found out for certain that this bleak spot where I chanced to be wandering all alone was the churchyard; that the low, leaden line beyond was the river; and that the small bundle of shivers growing afraid of it all and beginning to cry was myself—Pip.

"Hold your noise!" cried a terrible voice, as a man started up from among the g es at the side of the church porch.

He was a fearful-looking man, clad in coarse grey,

covered with mud and brambles, and with a great clank-
ing chain upon his leg.

"Tell us your name!" said the man. "Quick!"

"Pip, sir."

"Show us where you live," said the man. "P'int
out the place!"

I pointed to where our village lay, on the flat in-shore
among the trees a mile or more from the church.

The man, after looking at me for a moment, turned
me upside down and emptied my pockets. There was
nothing in them but a piece of bread. When the church
came to itself—for he was so sudden and strong that
he made it go head-over-heels before me, and I saw the
steeple under my feet—when the church came to itself,
I say, I was seated on a high tombstone, trembling,
while he ate the bread ravenously.

"You young dog," said the man, licking his lips,
"what fat cheeks you ha' got."

I believe they were fat, though I was at that time
undersized for my years, and not strong.

"Darn *me* if I couldn't eat 'em," said the man, with
a threatening shake of his head, "and if I ha'nt half
a mind to't!"

I earnestly expressed my hope that he wouldn't, and held
tighter to the tombstone on which he had put me; partly
to keep myself upon it; partly to keep myself from crying.

"Now lookee here!" said the man. "Where's your
mother?"

"There, sir!" said I.

He started, made a short run, and stopped and looked
over his shoulder.

"There, sir!" I timidly explained, pointing to an
inscription on a stone; "that's my mother."

"Oh!" said he, coming back. "And is that your father alonger your mother?"

"Yes, sir," said I; "him too; 'late of this parish.'"

"Ha!" he muttered then, considering. "Who d'ye live with—supposin' you're kindly let to live, which I ha'nt made up my mind about?"

"My sister, sir—Mrs. Joe Gargery—wife of Joe Gargery, the blacksmith, sir."

"Blacksmith, eh?" said he, and looked down at his leg.

After darkly looking at his leg and at me several times, he came closer to my tombstone, took me by both arms, and tilted me back as far as he could hold me, so that his eyes looked most powerfully down into mine, and mine looked most helplessly up into his.

"Now lookee here," he said, "the question being whether you're to be let to live. You know what a file is?"

"Yes, sir."

"And you know what wittles is?"

"Yes, sir."

After each question he tilted me over a little more, so as to give me a greater sense of helplessness and danger.

"You get me a file." He tilted me again. "And you get me some wittles. If you don't—— !"

He tilted me again and shook me till my teeth chattered.

"In—indeed—I will, sir," said I, "if you will only let me go. I'll run all the way home."

"Well, see that you come back. But to-morrow morning will do—early—before day. I'll wait for you here."

As he released me, I needed no second bidding, but scurried away as fast as I could, and soon reached the blacksmith's shop.

My sister, Mrs. Joe Gargery, was more than twenty years older than I, and had established a great reputation with herself and the neighbours because she had brought me up " by hand." Having at that time to find out for myself what the expression meant, and knowing her to have a hard and heavy hand, and to be much in the habit of laying it upon her husband as well as upon me, I supposed that Joe Gargery and I were both brought up by hand.

She was not a good-looking woman, my sister ; and I had a general impression that she must have made Joe Gargery marry her by hand. Joe was a fair man, with curls of flaxen hair on each side of his smooth face, and with eyes of such a very undecided blue that they seemed to have somehow got mixed with their own whites. He was a mild, good-natured, sweet-tempered, easy-going, foolish, dear fellow—a sort of Hercules in strength, and also in weakness.

My sister, Mrs. Joe, with black hair and eyes, had such a prevailing redness of skin that I sometimes used to wonder whether it was possible she washed herself with a nutmeg-grater instead of soap. She was tall and bony, and almost always wore a coarse apron, fastened behind with two loops, and having a bib in front that was stuck full of pins and needles.

Joe's forge adjoined our house, which was a wooden house, as many of the dwellings in our country were— most of them, at that time. When I ran home from the churchyard the forge was shut up, and Joe was sitting alone in the kitchen. Joe and I being fellow-sufferers, and having confidences as such, Joe imparted a confidence to me the moment I raised the latch of the door and peeped in at him opposite to it, sitting in the chimney corner.

" Mrs. Joe has been out a dozen times looking for you, Pip. And she's out now, making it a baker's dozen."

" Is she ? "

" Yes, Pip," said Joe; " and what's worse, she's got Tickler with her."

At this dismal intelligence, I twisted the only button on my waistcoat round and round, and looked in great depression at the fire. Tickler was a wax-ended piece of cane, worn smooth by collision with my tickled frame.

" She sot down," said Joe, " and she got up, and she made a grab at Tickler, and she rampaged out. That's what she did," said Joe, slowly clearing the fire between the lower bars with the poker, and looking at it ; " she rampaged out, Pip."

" Has she been gone long, Joe ? " I always treated him as no more than my equal.

" Well," said Joe, glancing up at the Dutch clock, " she's been on the rampage, this last spell, about five minutes, Pip. She's a-coming ! Get behind the door, old chap, and have the jack-towel betwixt you."

I took the advice. My sister, Mrs. Joe, throwing the door wide open, and finding an obstruction behind it, immediately divined the cause, and applied Tickler to its farthest investigation.

" Where have you been ? " she demanded, between tickles.

" I have only been to the churchyard," said I, crying and rubbing myself.

" Churchyard ! " repeated my sister. " If it warn't for me you'd been to the churchyard long ago and stayed there ! Who brought you up by hand ? "

My thoughts strayed from that question as I looked disconsolately at the fire. For the fugitive out on the marshes with the ironed leg, the file, the food, and the dreadful pledge I was under to steal from under my sister's very roof, rose before me in the avenging coals.

" Ha ! " said Mrs. Joe, restoring Tickler to his station. " Churchyard, indeed ! You may well say churchyard, you two." (One of us, by-the-by, had not said it at all.) " You'll drive *me* to the churchyard betwixt you, one of these days, and oh, a pr-r-recious pair you'd be without me ! "

As she applied herself to set the tea-things, Joe peeped down at me over his leg, as if he were mentally calculating what kind of pair we should make, under such circumstances. After that, he sat feeling his right-side flaxen curls and whisker, and following Mrs. Joe about with his blue eyes, as his manner always was at squally times.

My sister had a sudden, severe way of cutting and buttering bread, which never varied. Now she sawed me off a section of loaf, bidding me eat and be thankful. Though I was hungry, I dared not eat ; for she was a strict housekeeper who would miss any further slices, and I must not let that dreadful man out in the churchyard go hungry. So I resolved to put my hunk of bread and butter down the leg of my trousers—a plan which I presently found the chance to carry out.

It was Christmas Eve, and I had to stir the pudding for next day with a copper stick. I tried it with the load upon my leg (and that made me think afresh of the man with the load on *his* leg), and found the tendency of exercise to bring the bread and butter out at my ankle quite unmanageable. Happily, I slipped away and deposited that part of my conscience in my garret bedroom.

"Hark!" said I, when I had done my stirring, and was taking a final warm in the chimney corner before being sent up to bed; "was that great guns, Joe?"

"Ah!" said Joe. "There's another convict off."

"What does that mean, Joe?" said I.

Mrs. Joe, who always took explanations upon herself, said snappishly, "Escaped. Escaped."

"There was a convict off last night," added Joe, "after sunset-gun. And they fired warning of him. And now it appears they're firing warning of another."

"Who's firing?" said I.

"Drat that boy," interposed my sister, frowning at me over her work, "what a questioner he is. Ask no questions, and you'll be told no lies."

It was not very polite to herself, I thought, as she always answered. But she never was polite, unless there was company.

Presently Joe said to me in a quiet kind of whisper, "Hulks, Pip; prison ships. They're firing because one of the thieves on the hulks is got away."

Thieves! Prison ships! And here I was planning to rob my sister of the bread and butter, and honest Joe of a file! Truly conscience is a fearful thing, yet there was no turning back for me.

That night the rest of the dreadful deed was done. Just before daybreak I crept out, carrying the file which I had found among Joe's tools, the slice of bread, and a pie which was too convenient in the pantry, and which I took in the hope it was not intended for early use and would not be missed for some time.

I found the man with the iron waiting for me, crouched behind a tombstone.

"Are you alone?" he asked, hoarsely.

N

" Yes, sir."

" No one following you ? "

" No, sir."

" Well," said he, " I believe you. Give me them wittles, quick."

I had often watched a large dog of ours eating his food ; and I now noticed a decided similarity between the dog's way of eating and the man's. The man took strong, sharp, sudden bites, just like the dog. He swallowed, or rather snapped up, every mouthful, too soon and too fast ; and he looked sideways here and there while he ate, as if he thought there was danger in every direction of somebody's coming to take the pie away.

" Now give us hold of the file, boy," he said, when he had finished swallowing.

I did so, and he bent to the iron like a madman, and began filing it away in quick, fierce rasps. I judged this a good time to slip away and he paid no further attention to me. The last I heard of him, the file was still going.

" And where the mischief ha' *you* been ? " was Mrs. Joe's Christmas salutation, when I and my conscience showed ourselves.

I said I had been down to hear the chimes.

" Ah well ! " observed Mrs. Joe. " You might ha' done worse."

Not a doubt of that, I thought.

We were to have a superb dinner—so Joe slyly told me—consisting of a leg of pork and greens, a pair of roast stuffed fowls, and a handsome pie which had been baked the day before.

I started when he spoke about the pie, but his blue eyes beamed upon me kindly.

My sister having so much to do, was going to church vicariously; that is to say, Joe and I were going. In his working clothes, Joe was a well-knit characteristic-looking blacksmith; in his holiday clothes, he was more like a scarecrow in good circumstances, than anything else. Nothing that he wore then fitted him or seemed to belong to him. On the present festive occasion he emerged from his room, when the blithe bells were ringing, the picture of misery, in a full suit of Sunday penitentials. As to me, I think my sister must have had some general idea that I was a young offender who must be punished each holy-day by being put into clothes so tight that I could on no account move my arms and legs without danger of something bursting.

Joe and I going to church, therefore, must have been a moving spectacle for compassionate minds. Yet, what I suffered outside was nothing to what I underwent within. The terrors that had assailed me whenever Mrs. Joe had gone near the pantry, or out of the room, were only to be equalled by the remorse with which my mind dwelt on what my hands had done. Under the weight of my wicked secret, I pondered whether even the Church would be powerful enough to shield me from the wrath to come.

Mr. Wopsle, the clerk at church, was to dine with us; and Mr. Hubble, the wheelwright, and Mrs. Hubble; and Uncle Pumblechook (Joe's uncle, but Mrs. Joe appropriated him), who was a well-to-do cornchandler in the nearest town, and drove his own chaise-cart. The dinner hour was half-past one.

When Joe and I got home, we found the table laid, and Mrs. Joe dressed, and the dinner dressing, and the front door unlocked (it never was at any other time) for the company to enter by, and everything was splendid. And still, not a word of the robbery.

Oh, the agony of that festive dinner! During each helping of my place I ate mechanically, hardly daring to lift my eyes, and clutching frantically at the leg of the table for support. With each mouthful we drew nearer to that pie—and discovery! But as they chattered away, I felt a faint hope that they might perhaps forget the pie.

They did not, for presently my sister said to Joe, " Clean plates—cold."

I got a fresh hold on the table leg. I foresaw I was doomed.

" You must taste," said my sister, addressing the guests with her best grace, " you must finish with a pie, in honour of Uncle Pumblechook."

The company murmured their compliments. Uncle Pumblechook, sensible of having deserved well of his fellow-creatures, said—quite vivaciously, all things considered—" Well, Mrs. Joe, we'll do our best endeavours ; let us have a cut at this same pie."

My sister went out to get it. I heard her steps proceed to the pantry. I saw Mr. Pumblechook balance his knife. I saw reawakening appetite in the Roman nostrils of Mr. Wopsle. I heard Mr. Hubble remark that " a bit of savoury pie would lay atop of anything you could mention, and do no harm," and I heard Joe say, " you shall have some, Pip." I have never been absolutely certain whether I uttered a shrill yell of terror, merely in spirit, or in the bodily hearing of the company. I felt that I could bear no more, and that I must run away. I released the leg of the table and ran for my life.

But I ran no farther than the house door, for there

I ran headforemost into a party of soldiers with their muskets, one of whom held out a pair of handcuffs to me, saying, " Here you are, look sharp, come on ! "

The vision of a file of soldiers caused the dinner party to rise from the table in confusion, and caused Mrs. Joe, re-entering the kitchen empty-handed, to stop short and stare, in her wondering lament of " Gracious goodness, gracious me, what's gone—with the—pie ! "

" Excuse me, ladies and gentlemen," said the sergeant, " but as I have mentioned at the door to this smart young shaver " (which he hadn't), " I am on a chase in the name of the king, and I want the blacksmith."

" And pray, what might you want with *him ?* " retorted my sister, quick to resent his being wanted at all.

" Missis," returned the gallant sergeant, " speaking for myself, I should reply, the honour and pleasure of his fine wife's acquaintance ; speaking for the king, I answer, a little job done."

This was received as rather neat in the sergeant ; insomuch that Mr. Pumblechook cried audibly, " Good again ! "

" You see, blacksmith," said the sergeant, who had by this time picked out Joe with his eye, " we have had an accident with these, and I find the lock of one of 'em goes wrong, and the coupling don't act pretty. As they are wanted for immediate service, will you throw your eye over them ? "

Joe threw his eye over them, and pronounced that the job would necessitate the lighting of his forge fire, and would take nearer two hours than one.

" Will it ? Then will you set about it at once, black-smith," said the off-hand sergeant, " as it's on His Majesty's service. And if my men can bear a hand anywhere, they'll make themselves useful." With that, he called to his men, who came trooping into the kitchen one after another, and piled their arms in a corner.

All these things I saw without then knowing that I saw them, for I was in an agony of apprehension. But, beginning to perceive that the handcuffs were not for me, and that the military had so far got the better of the pie as to put it in the background, I collected a little more my scattered wits.

The soldiers were out hunting for the convicts that had escaped. And as soon as Joe had mended the handcuffs, they fell in line and started again for the marshes. Joe caught an appealing look from me, and timidly asked if he and I might go along with them. The consent was given and away we went.

After a rough journey over bogs and through briars, a loud shout from the soldiers in front announced that one of the fugitives had been caught. We ran hastily up and peered into a ditch. It was my convict.

He was hustled into the handcuffs and hustled up hill where stood a rough hut or sentry-box, and here we halted to rest.

My convict never looked at me, except once. While we were in the hut, he stood before the fire looking thoughtfully at it, or putting up his feet by turns upon the hob. Suddenly he turned to the sergeant and remarked :

" I wish to say something respecting this escape. It may prevent some persons laying under suspicion alonger me."

" You can say what you like," returned the sergeant, standing coolly looking at him with his arms folded, " but you have no call to say it here. You'll have opportunity enough to say about it, and hear about it, before it's done with, you know."

"I know, but this is another p'int, a separate matter. A man can't starve; at least *I* can't. I took some wittles, up at the village over yonder—where the church stands a'most out on the marshes."

"You mean stole," said the sergeant.

"And I'll tell you where from. From the blacksmith's."

"Hallo!" said the sergeant, staring at Joe.

"Hallo, Pip!" said Joe, staring at me.

"It was some broken wittle—that's what it was—and a dram of liquor, and a pie."

"Have you happened to miss such an article as a pie, blacksmith?" asked the sergeant, confidentially.

"My wife did, at the very moment when you came in. Don't you know, Pip?"

"So," said my convict, turning his eyes on Joe in a moody manner, and without the least glance at me; "so you're the blacksmith, are you? Then I'm sorry to say I've eat your pie."

"God knows you're welcome to it—so far as it was ever mine," returned Joe, with a saving remembrance of Mrs. Joe. "We don't know what you have done, but we wouldn't have you starve to death for it, poor miserable fellow-creature. Would us, Pip?"

Something that I had noticed before clicked in the man's throat again, and he turned his back. The boat had returned, and his guard were ready, so we followed him to the landing-place made of rough stakes and stones, and saw him put into the boat, which was rowed by a crew of convicts like himself. No one seemed surprised to see him, but they looked at him stolidly and rowed him back to the hulks as a matter of course.

My state of mind regarding the pie was curious. I do not recall that I felt any tenderness of conscience in reference to Mrs. Joe, when the fear of being found out was lifted off me. But I loved Joe—perhaps for no better reason in those early days than because the dear fellow let me love him—and, as to him, my inner self was not so easily composed. It was much upon my mind (particularly when I first saw him looking about for his file) that I ought to tell Joe the whole truth. Yet I did not, and for the reason that I mistrusted that if I did he would think me worse than I was. The fear of losing Joe's confidence and of thenceforth sitting in the chimney corner at night staring drearily at my for ever lost companion and friend, tied up my tongue. And so the whole truth never came out.

II

PIP AND ESTELLA

AT this time I was only an errand boy around the forge, and my education was limited to spelling out the names on the tombstones. So in the evenings they sent me to school to Mr. Wopsle's aunt, a worthy woman who used to go to sleep regularly from six to seven while her small class was supposed to study.

But I was lucky enough to find a friend in her granddaughter, Biddy. She was about my own age, and, while her shoes were generally untied and her hands sometimes dirty, her heart was in the right place and

she had a good head. So with her help I struggled
through my letters as if they had been a bramble-bush,
getting considerably worried and scratched by each
letter in turn. Then came the dreaded nine figures to
add to my troubles. But at last I learned to read and
cipher.

I do not know which was the prouder, Joe or I, when
I wrote him my first letter (which was hardly needed,
as he sat beside me while I wrote it).

"I say, Pip, old chap!" he cried, opening his eyes
very wide, "what a scholar you are! Ain't you?"

"I should like to be," I answered, looking at the
slate with satisfaction.

Mrs. Joe made occasional trips with Uncle Pumblechook on market-days, to assist him in buying such
household stuffs and goods as required a woman's judgment; Uncle Pumblechook being a bachelor and reposing
no confidences in his domestic servant. On this particular evening she came home from such a trip, bringing
Uncle Pumblechook with her.

"Now," said she, unwrapping herself with haste
and excitement, and throwing her bonnet back on her
shoulders, where it hung by the strings, "if this boy
ain't grateful this night, he never will be!"

I looked as grateful as any boy possibly could, who
was wholly uninformed why he ought to assume that
expression.

"You have heard of Miss Havisham up town, haven't
you?" continued my sister, addressing Joe. "She
wants this boy to go and play there. And of course
he's going. And he had *better* play there," said my
sister, shaking her head at me as an encouragement to be
extremely light and sportive, "or I'll work him!"

I had heard of Miss Havisham up town—everybody
for miles round had heard of Miss Havisham up town—
as an immensely rich and grim lady who lived in a large
and dismal house barricaded against robbers, and who
led a life of seclusion.

" Well to be sure ! " said Joe, astounded.   " I wonder
how she come to know Pip ! "

" Noodle ! " cried my sister.   " Who said she knew
him ?   Couldn't she ask Uncle Pumblechook if he knew
of a boy to go and play there ?   And couldn't Uncle
Pumblechook, being always considerate and thoughtful
of us, mention this boy that I have been a willing slave
to ?   And couldn't Uncle Pumblechook, being sensible
that for anything we can tell, this boy's fortune may
be made by his going to Miss Havisham's, offer to take
him into town to-night in his own chaise-cart, and to
keep him to-night, and to take him with his own hands
to Miss Havisham's to-morrow morning ?   And Lor-
a-mussy me ! " cried my sister, casting off her bonnet
in sudden desperation, " here I stand talking to mere
Mooncalfs, with Uncle Pumblechook waiting, and the mare
catching cold at the door, and the boy grimed with
dirt from the hair of his head to the sole of his foot ! "

With that, she pounced on me, like an eagle on a lamb,
and my face was squeezed into wooden bowls in sinks,
and my head was put under taps of water-butts, and I
was soaped and kneaded, and towelled, and thumped,
and harrowed, and rasped, until I really was quite beside
myself.

When my ablutions were completed, I was put into
clean linen of the stiffest character, like a young penitent into sackcloth, and was trussed up in my tightest
and fearfullest suit.   I was then delivered over to

Mr. Pumblechook, who formally received me as if he were the Sheriff, saying pompously, " Boy, be for ever grateful to all friends, but especially unto them which brought you up by hand ! "

" Good-bye, Joe ! "

" God bless you, Pip, old chap ! "

I had never parted from him before, and what with my feelings and what with soap-suds, I could at first see no stars from the chaise-cart. But they twinkled out one by one, without throwing any light on the questions as to why on earth I was going to play at Miss Havisham's, and what on earth I was expected to play at.

I spent the night at Uncle Pumblechook's, and the next morning after breakfast we proceeded to Miss Havisham's. It was a dismal looking house with a great many iron bars to it. Some of the windows had been walled up, and the others were rustily barred. There was a courtyard in front, which was also barred ; so we had to wait, after ringing the bell, for some one to open it.

Presently a window was raised, and a clear voice demanded, " What name ? "

" Pumblechook," was the reply.

The voice returned, " Quite right," and the window was shut again, and a young lady came across the court-yard, with keys in her hand.

" This," said Mr. Pumblechook, " is Pip."

" This is Pip, is it ? " returned the young lady, who was very pretty and seemed very proud ; " come in, Pip."

Mr. Pumblechook was coming in also, when she stopped him with the gate.

" Oh ! " she said. " Did you wish to see Miss Havisham ? "

" If Miss Havisham wished to see me," returned Mr. Pumblechook, discomfited.

" Ah ! " said the girl ; " but you see she don't."

She said it so finally, and in such an undiscussible way, that Mr. Pumblechook, though in a condition of ruffled dignity, could not protest.

We went into the house by a side door—the great front entrance had two chains across it outside—and the first thing I noticed was that the passages were all dark, and that she had left a candle burning there. She took it up, and we went through more passages and up a staircase, and still it was all dark, and only the candle lighted us.

At last we came to the door of a room, and she said, " Go in."

I answered, more in shyness than politeness, " After you, miss."

To this she returned, " Don't be ridiculous, boy ; I am not going in." And scornfully walked away, and —what was worse—took the candle with her.

This was very uncomfortable, and I was half afraid. However, the only thing to do being to knock at the door, I knocked, and was told from within to enter. I entered, therefore, and found myself in a pretty large room, well lighted with wax candles. No glimpse of daylight was to be seen in it. It was a dressing-room, as I supposed from the furniture, though much of it was of forms and uses then quite unknown to me. But prominent in it was a draped table with a gilded looking-glass, and that I made out at first sight to be a fine lady's dressing-table.

In an arm-chair, with an elbow resting on the table and her head leaning on that hand, sat the strangest lady I have ever seen, or shall ever see.

She was dressed in rich materials—satins and lace and silks—all of white. Her shoes were white. And she had a long white veil dependent from her hair, and she had bridal flowers in her hair, but her hair was white. Some bright jewels sparkled on her neck and on her hands, and some other jewels lay sparkling on the table. Dresses, less splendid than the dress she wore, and half-packed trunks, were scattered about. She had not quite finished dressing, for she had but one shoe on—the other was on the table near her hand—her veil was but half arranged, her watch and chain were not put on, and her handkerchief, gloves, some flowers, and a prayer-book lay confusedly heaped about the looking-glass.

" Who is it ? " said the lady at the table.

" Pip, ma'am."

" Pip ? "

" Mr. Pumblechook's boy, ma'am. Come—to play."

" Look at me," said Miss Havisham. " You are not afraid of a woman who has never seen the sun since you were born ? "

I regret to state that I was not afraid of telling the enormous lie comprehended in the answer " No."

" I am tired," said Miss Havisham. " I want diversion, and I have done with men and women. Play."

I looked foolish and bewildered, not knowing what to do.

" I sometimes have sick fancies," she went on, " and I have a sick fancy that I want to see some play. There, there ! " with an impatient movement of the fingers of her right hand ; " play, play, play ! "

For a moment, with the fear of my sister before my eyes, I had a desperate idea of starting round the room in the assumed character of Mr. Pumble-chook's chaise-cart. But I felt myself so unequal to the performance that I gave it up, and stood looking at Miss Havisham in what I suppose she took for a dogged manner, inasmuch as she said, when we had taken a good look at each other:

"Are you sullen and obstinate?"

"No, ma'am, I am very sorry for you, and very sorry I can't play just now. If you complain of me I shall get into trouble with my sister, so I would do it if I could; but it's so new here, and so strange, and so fine, and melancholy——" I stopped, fearing I might say too much.

"Call Estella," she commanded, looking at me. "You can do that."

To stand in a strange house calling a scornful young lady by her first name was almost as bad as playing to order. But she answered at last.

"My dear," said Miss Havisham, "let me see you play cards with this boy."

"What do you play, boy?" asked Estella, with the greatest disdain.

"Nothing but 'beggar my neighbour,' miss."

"Beggar him," said Miss Havisham to Estella.

So we sat down to cards.

It was then I began to understand that everything in the room had stopped, with the watch and the clock, a long time ago. I noticed that Miss Havisham put down the jewel exactly on the spot from which she had taken it up. As Estella dealt the cards, I glanced at the dressing-table again, and saw that the shoe upon it, once white, now yellow, had never been worn.

" He calls the knaves, Jacks, this boy ! " said Estella, with disdain, before our first game was out. " And what coarse hands he has ! And what thick boots ! "

I had never thought of being ashamed of my hands before ; but now I began to consider them. Her contempt for me was so strong that I caught it.

She won the game, and I dealt. I misdealt, as was only natural, when I knew she was lying in wait for me to do wrong ; and she denounced me for a stupid, clumsy labouring boy.

" You say nothing of her," remarked Miss Havisham to me, as she looked on. " She says many hard things of you, but you say nothing of her. What do you think of her ? "

" I don't like to say," I stammered.

" Tell me in my ear," said Miss Havisham, bending down.

" I think she is very proud," I replied, in a whisper.

" Anything else ? "

" I think she is very pretty."

" Anything else ? "

" I think she is very insulting." (She was looking at me then with a look of supreme aversion.)

" Anything else ? "

" I think I should like to go home."

" You shall go soon," said Miss Havisham aloud; " play the game out."

I played the game to an end with Estella, and she beggared me. She threw the cards down on the table when she had won them all, as if she despised them for having been won of me.

" When shall I have you here again ? " said Miss Havisham. " Let me think. I know nothing of days

of the week, or of weeks of the year. Come again after
six days. You hear ? "

"Yes, ma'am."

"Estella, take him down. Let him have something
to eat, and let him roam and look about him while he
eats. Go, Pip."

I followed the candle down, as I had followed the
candle up, and she stood it in the place where we had
found it. Until she opened the side entrance, I had
fancied, without thinking about it, that it must neces-
sarily be night-time. The rush of the daylight quite
confounded me, and made me feel as if I had been in
the candle-light of the strange room many hours.

When I reached home, my sister was very curious
to know all about Miss Havisham and what I had seen
and done at her house. Uncle Pumblechook, too, came
hurrying over, armed with many questions.

I was naturally a truthful boy—as boys go—but I knew
instinctively that I could not make myself understood
about that strange visit. So I didn't try. When he fired
his first question, as to "What was Miss Havisham
like ?"

"Very tall and dark," I told him.

"Is she, Uncle ? " asked my sister.

Mr. Pumblechook winked assent ; from which I at
once inferred that he had never seen Miss Havisham,
for she was nothing of the kind.

"Good ! " said Mr. Pumblechook, conceitedly. "Now
boy ! What was she a-doing of when you went in
to-day ? " he continued.

"She was sitting," I answered, "in a black velvet
coach."

Mr. Pumblechook and Mrs. Joe stared at one another

—as they well might—and both repeated, " In a black velvet coach ? "

" Yes," said I. " And Miss Estella—that's her niece, I think—handed her in cake and wine at the coach-window, on a gold plate. And we all had cake and wine on gold plates. And I got up behind the coach to eat mine, because she told me to."

" Was anybody else there ? " asked Mr. Pumblechook.

" Four dogs," said I.

" Large or small ? "

" Immense," said I. " And they fought for veal cutlets out of a silver basket."

Mr. Pumblechook and Mrs. Joe stared at one another again in utter amazement. I was perfectly frantic— a reckless witness under the torture—and would have told them anything.

" Where *was* this coach, in the name of gracious ? " asked my sister.

" In Miss Havisham's room." They stared again. " But there weren't any horses to it." I added this saving clause, in the moment of rejecting four richly caparisoned coursers which I had had wild thoughts of harnessing.

" Can this be possible, uncle ? " asked Mrs. Joe. " What can the boy mean ? "

" I'll tell you, Mum," said Mr. Pumblechook. " My opinion is, it's a sedan-chair. She's flighty, you know —very flighty—quite flighty enough to pass her days in a sedan-chair."

" Did you ever see her in it, uncle ? " asked Mrs. Joe.

" How could I ? " he returned, forced to the admission, " when I never see her in my life. Never clapped eyes upon her ! "

o

"Goodness, uncle! And yet you have spoken to her!"

"Just through the door," he replied testily. "Now, boy, what did you play?"

"We played with flags."

"Flags!" echoed my sister.

"Yes," said I. "Estella waved a blue flag, and I waved a red one, and Miss Havisham waved one sprinkled all over with little gold stars, out at the coach-window. And then we all waved our swords and hurrahed."

"Swords!" repeated my sister. "Where did you get swords from?"

"Out of a cupboard," said I. "And I saw pistols in it—and jam—and pills. And there was no daylight in the room, but it was all lighted up with candles."

"That's true, Mum," said Mr. Pumblechook, with a grave nod. "That's the state of the case, for that much I've seen myself." And then they both stared at me, and I at them, and plaited the right leg of my trousers with my right hand.

If they had asked me any more questions I should undoubtedly have betrayed myself, for I was even then on the point of mentioning that there was a balloon in the yard, and should have hazarded the statement but for my invention being divided between that phenomenon and a bear. They were so much occupied, however, in discussing the marvels I had already presented for their consideration, that I escaped. The subject still held them when Joe came in from his work to have a cup of tea. To whom my sister, more for the relief of her own mind than for the gratification of his, related my pretended experiences.

Now, when I saw Joe open his blue eyes and roll them

all round the kitchen in helpless amazement, I was
overtaken by penitence; but only as regarded him—
not in the least as regarded the other two. Towards
Joe, and Joe only, I considered myself a young monster,
while they sat debating what results would come to me
from Miss Havisham's acquaintance and favour. They
had no doubt that Miss Havisham would " do something "
for me; their doubts related to the form that something
would take. My sister stood out for " property." Mr.
Pumblechook was in favour of a handsome premium
for binding me apprentice to some genteel trade—say,
the corn and seed trade, for instance. Joe fell into
the deepest disgrace with both, for offering the bright
suggestion that I might only be presented with one of
the dogs who had fought for the veal cutlets. " If a
fool's head can't express better opinions than that,"
said my sister, " and you have got any work to do, you
had better go and do it." So he went.

After Mr. Pumblechook had driven off, and when
my sister was washing up, I stole into the forge to Joe,
and remained by him until he had done for the night,
when I said, " Before the fire goes out, Joe, I should
like to tell you something."

" Should you, Pip ? " said Joe, drawing his shoeing-
stool near the forge. " Then tell us. What is it, Pip ? "

" Joe," said I, taking hold of his rolled-up shirt sleeve,
and twisting it between my finger and thumb, " you
remember all that about Miss Havisham's ? "

" Remember ? " said Joe. " I believe you! Wonderful!"

" It's a terrible thing, Joe; it ain't true."

" What are you telling of, Pip ? " cried Joe, falling
back in the greatest amazement. " You don't mean
to say it's——"

"Yes, I do; it's lies, Joe."

"But not all of it? Why, sure you don't mean to say, Pip, that there was no black welwet co — ch?" For, I stood shaking my head. "But, at least, there was dogs, Pip? Come, Pip," said Joe, persuasively, "if there warn't no weal cutlets, at least there was dogs?"

"No, Joe."

"A dog?" said Joe. "A puppy? Come?"

"No, Joe, there was nothing at all of the kind."

As I fixed my eyes hopelessly on Joe, Joe contemplated me in dismay. "Pip, old chap! This won't do, old fellow! I say! Where do you expect to go to?"

"It's terrible, Joe; ain't it?"

"Terrible?" cried Joe. "Awful! What possessed you?"

"I don't know what possessed me, Joe," I replied, letting his shirt sleeve go, and sitting down in the ashes at his feet, hanging my head; "but I wish you hadn't taught me to call knaves at cards Jacks; and I wish my boots weren't so thick nor my hands so coarse."

And then I told Joe that I felt very miserable, and that I hadn't been able to explain myself to Mrs. Joe and Pumblechook, and that there had been a beautiful young lady at Miss Havisham's who was dreadfully proud, and that she had said I was common, and much more to that effect.

"There's one thing you may be sure of, Pip," said Joe, after some rumination, "namely, that lies is lies. Howsever they come, they didn't ought to come, and they come from the father of lies, and work round to the same. Don't you tell no more of 'em, Pip. *That* ain't the way to get out of being common, old chap.

And as to being common, I don't make it out at all clear. You are oncommon in some things. You're oncommon small. Likewise, you're a oncommon scholar."

" No, I am ignorant and backward, Joe."

" Why, see what a letter you wrote last night. Wrote in print even ! I've seen letters—Ah ! and from gentle-folks !—that I'll swear weren't wrote in print," said Joe.

" I have learnt next to nothing, Joe. You think much of me. It's only that."

" Well, Pip," said Joe, " be it so or be it son't, you must be a common scholar afore you can be a oncommon one, I should hope ! The king upon his throne, with his crown upon his 'ed, can't sit and write his Acts of Parliament in print, without having begun, when he were an unpromoted prince, with the alphabet—Ah ! " added Joe, with a shake of the head that was full of meaning, " and begun at A too, and worked his way to Z ! "

There was some hope in this piece of wisdom, and it rather encouraged me.

" You're not angry with me, Joe ? "

" No, old chap. But you might bear in mind about them dog fights and weal cutlets when you say your prayers to-night. That's all, old chap, and don't never do it no more."

III

HOW PIP FELL HEIR TO GREAT EXPECTATIONS

THE happy idea occurred to me a morning or two later when I woke, that the best step I could take towards making myself uncommon was to get out of Biddy everything she knew. In pursuance of this idea, I mentioned to Biddy, when I went to Mr. Wopsle's aunt's at night, that I had a particular reason for wishing to get on in life, and that I should feel very much obliged to her if she would impart all her learning to me. Biddy, who was the most obliging of girls, immediately said she would, and indeed began to carry out her promise within five minutes.

The books at the school were few and ragged, but we attacked them all valiantly during the course of the winter, and even refreshed our budding minds with newspaper scraps. And with every new piece of knowledge I could fancy myself saying to Miss Estella, " *Now am I common ?* "

At the appointed time I returned to Miss Havisham's, and my hesitating ring at the gate brought out Estella.

" You are to come this way to-day," she said after admitting me, and took me to quite another part of the house.

We went in at a door, which stood open, and into a gloomy room with a low ceiling on the ground floor at the back. There was some company in the room, and Estella said to me as she joined it, "You are to go and stand there, boy, till you are wanted." "There," being the window, I crossed to it, and stood "there," in a very uncomfortable state of mind, looking out.

Presently she brought a candle and led the way down a dark passage to a staircase. As we went up the stairs we met a man coming down. He was large and bald, with bushy black eyebrows and deep-set eyes which were disagreeably keen. He was nothing to me at the time, and yet I couldn't help observing him.

He stopped and looked at me.

"How do *you* come here?" he asked.

"Miss Havisham sent for me, sir," I explained.

"Well! Behave yourself. I have a pretty large experience of boys, and you're a bad set of fellows. Now mind!" said he, biting the side of his great forefinger as he frowned at me, "you behave yourself!"

With those words he released me—which I was glad of, for his hand smelt of scented soap—and went his way downstairs. I wondered whether he could be a doctor; but no, I thought; he couldn't be a doctor, or he would have a quieter manner. There was not much time to consider the subject, for we were soon in Miss Havisham's room, where she and everything else were just as I had left them. Estella left me standing near the door, and I stood there until Miss Havisham cast her eyes upon me from the dressing-table.

"So!" she said, without being startled or surprised "the days have worn away, have they?"

"Yes, ma'am. To-day is——"

"There, there, there!" with the impatient movement

of her fingers, " I don't want to know. Are you ready
to play ? "

I was obliged to answer in some confusion. " I don't
think I am, ma'am."

" Not at cards again ? " she demanded, with a searching look.

" Yes, ma'am ; I could do that, if I was wanted."

" Since this house strikes you old and grave, boy,"
said Miss Havisham, impatiently, " and you are unwilling to play, are you willing to work ? "

I could answer this inquiry with a better heart than
I had been able to find for the other question, and I said
I was quite willing.

" Then go into that opposite room," said she, pointing
at the door behind me with her withered hand, " and
wait there till I come."

I did so, and after hearing mice scamper about the
faintly lighted room for a few minutes, Miss Havisham
entered and laid a hand upon my shoulder. In her
other hand she had a crutch-headed stick on which she
leaned, and she looked like the Witch of the place.

" This," said she, pointing to the long table with her
stick, " is where I will be laid when I am dead. They
shall come and look at me here."

With some vague misgiving that she might get upon
the table then and there and die at once, the complete
realisation of the ghastly wax-work at the Fair, I shrank
under her touch.

" What do you think that is ? " she asked me, again
pointing with her stick ; " that, where those cobwebs
are ? "

" I can't guess what it is, ma'am."

" It's a great cake. A bride-cake. Mine ! "

She looked all around the room in a glaring manner, and then said, leaning on me while her hand twitched my shoulder, " Come, come, come ! Walk me, walk me ! "

From this I made out that the work I had to do was to walk Miss Havisham round and round the room. So I started at once, she following at a fitful speed, twitching the hand upon my shoulder. After a while she said, " Call Estella," and I did so. Then the company I had noticed before filed in and paid their respects, which Miss Havisham hardly seemed to hear.

While Estella was away lighting them down, Miss Havisham still walked with her hand on my shoulder, but more and more slowly. At last she stopped before the fire, and said, after muttering and looking at it some seconds :

" This is my birthday, Pip."

I was going to wish her many happy returns, when she lifted her stick.

" I don't suffer it to be spoken of. I don't suffer those who were here just now or anyone to speak of it. They come here on the day, but they dare not refer to it."

Of course *I* made no further attempt to refer to it.

" On this day of the year, long before you were born, this heap of decay," stabbing with her crutched stick at the pile of cobwebs on the table but not touching it, " was brought here. It and I have worn away together. The mice have gnawed at it, and sharper teeth than teeth of mice have gnawed at me."

She held the head of her stick against her heart as she stood looking at the table ; she in her once white dress, all yellow and withered ; the once white cloth, all yellow and withered ; everything around, in a state to crumble under a touch.

" When the ruin is complete," said she, with a ghastly look, " and when they lay me dead, in my bride's dress on the bride's table—which shall be done, and which will be the finished curse upon him—so much the better if it is done on this day ! "

She stood looking at the table as if she stood looking at her own figure lying there. I remained quiet. Estella returned, and she too remained quiet. It seemed to me that we continued thus a long time. In the heavy air of the room, and the heavy darkness that brooded in its remoter corners, I even had an alarming fancy that Estella and I might presently crumble to dust.

And thus passed my second visit to Miss Havisham's.

On my next visit, the following week, I saw a garden-chair—a light chair on wheels, that you pushed from behind. I entered, that same day, on a regular occupation of pushing Miss Havisham in this chair (when she was tired of walking with her hand upon my shoulder) round her own room, and across the landing, and round the other room. Over and over and over again, we would make these journeys, and sometimes they would last as long as three hours at a stretch. I insensibly fall into a general mention of these journeys as numerous, because it was at once settled that I should return every alternate day at noon for these purposes, and because I am now going to sum up a period of at least eight or ten months.

As we began to be more used to one another, Miss Havisham talked more to me, and asked me such questions as, what had I learned and what was I going to be ? I told her I was going to be apprenticed to Joe, I believed ; and I enlarged upon my knowing nothing and wanting to know everything, in the hope that she might offer some help towards that desirable end. But she did not ; on the contrary, she seemed to prefer my being ignorant. Neither did she ever give me any money nor anything but my daily dinner.

Estella was always there to let me in and out. Sometimes she would coldly tolerate me ; sometimes she would condescend to me ; sometimes she would be quite familiar with me ; sometimes she would say she hated me. But always my admiration for her grew apace, and I was the more firmly resolved not to be common.

There was a song Joe used to hum fragments of at the forge, of which the burden was Old Clem. This was not a very ceremonious way of rendering homage to a patron saint ; for I believe Old Clem stood in that relation towards smiths. It was a song that imitated the measure of beating upon iron, and was a mere lyrical excuse for the introduction of Old Clem's respected name. Thus, you were to hammer boys round—Old Clem ! With a thump and a sound—Old Clem ! Beat it out, beat it out—Old Clem ! With a clink for the stout—Old Clem ! Blow the fire, blow the fire—Old Clem ! Roaring dryer, soaring higher—Old Clem ! One day soon after the appearance of the chair, Miss Havisham suddenly saying to me, with the impatient movement of her fingers, " There, there, there ! Sing ! " I was surprised into crooning this ditty as I pushed her over the floor. It happened so to catch her fancy that she took it up in a low brooding voice as if she were singing in her sleep. After that, it became customary with us to have it as we moved about, and Estella would often join in ; though the whole strain was so subdued, even when there were three of us, that it made less noise in the grim old house than the lightest breath of wind.

What could I become with these surroundings ?   How could my character fail to be influenced by them ?   Is it to be wondered at if my thoughts were dazed, as my eyes were, when I came out into the natural light from the misty yellow rooms ?

Perhaps I might have talked it all over with Joe, had it not been for those enormous tales about coaches, dogs, and veal cutlets.   But I felt a natural shrinking from having Miss Havisham and Estella discussed, which had come upon me in the beginning, and which grew much more potent as time went on.   I reposed complete confidence in no one but Biddy ; and so I told her everything.   Why it came natural for me to do so, and why Biddy had a deep concern in everything I told her, I did not know then, though I think I know now.

We went on in this way for a long time, and it seemed likely that we should continue to go on in this way for a long time, when, one day, Miss Havisham stopped short as she and I were walking, she leaning on my shoulder ; and said with some displeasure, "You are growing tall, Pip."

She said no more at the time ; but she presently stopped and looked at me again ; and presently again ; and after that, looked frowning and moody.   On the next day of my attendance, when our usual exercise was over, and I had landed her at her dressing-table, she stayed me with a movement of her impatient fingers :

" Tell me the name again of that blacksmith of yours."

" Joe Gargery, ma'am."

" Meaning the master you were to be apprenticed to ? '

" Yes, Miss Havisham."

" You had better be apprenticed at once.   Would Gargery come here with you, and bring your indentures, do you think ? "

I signified that I had no doubt he would take it as
an honour to be asked.

" Then let him come."

" At any particular time, Miss Havisham ? "

" There, there ! I know nothing about times. Let
him come soon, and come alone with you."

So, on my very next visit, I conducted Joe, stiffly
arrayed in his Sunday clothes, into Miss Havisham's
presence. She asked him several questions about himself and my apprenticeship, while the poor fellow twisted
his hat in his hand and persisted in answering *me*. I am
afraid I was the least bit ashamed of him, when I saw
that Estella stood at the back of Miss Havisham's chair,
and that her eyes laughed mischievously.

Miss Havisham glanced at him as if she understood
what he really was, better than I had thought possible,
seeing what an awkward figure he cut ; and took up a
little bag from the table beside her.

" Pip has earned a premium here," she said, " and
here it is. There are five and twenty guineas in this bag.
Give it to your master, Pip."

As if he were absolutely out of his mind with the
wonder awakened in him by her strange figure and the
strange room, Joe, even at this pass, persisted in
addressing me.

" This is very liberal on your part, Pip," said Joe,
" and it is as such received and grateful welcome, though
never looked for, far nor near nor nowheres. And now,
old chap, may we do our duty ! May you and me do
our duty, both on us, by one and another, and by them
which your liberal present—have—conweyed—to be—
for the satisfaction of mind—of—them as never—" here
Joe showed that he felt he had fallen into frightful

difficulties, until he triumphantly rescued himself with the words, "and from myself far be it!" These words had such a round and convincing sound for him that he said them twice.

"Good-bye, Pip!" said Miss Havisham, after my papers were signed. "Let them out, Estella."

"Am I to come again, Miss Havisham?" I asked.

"No. Gargery is your master now. Gargery! One word!"

Thus calling him back as I went out of the door, I heard her say to Joe, in a distinct emphatic voice. "The boy has been a good boy here, and that is his reward. Of course, as an honest man, you will expect no other and no more."

How Joe got out of the room, I have never been able to determine; but I know that when he did get out he was steadily proceeding upstairs instead of coming down, and was deaf to all remonstrances until I went after him and laid hold of him. In another minute we were outside the gate, and it was locked, and Estella was gone. When we stood in the daylight alone again, Joe backed up against a wall, and said to me "Astonishing!" And there he remained so long, saying "Astonishing!" at intervals, so often, that I began to think his senses were never coming back. At length he prolonged his remark into "Pip, I do assure *you* this is as-TON-ishing!" and so, by degrees, became able to walk away.

It is a most miserable thing to feel ashamed of home. There may be black ingratitude in the thing, and the punishment may be retributive and well-deserved; but that it is a miserable thing, I can testify.

Home had never been a pleasant place to me, because of my sister's temper. But, Joe had sanctified it, and

I believed in it. I had believed in the best parlour as a most elegant place ; I had believed in the front door as a mysterious portal of the Temple of State whose solemn opening was attended with a sacrifice of roast fowls ; I had believed in the kitchen as a chaste though not magnificent apartment ; I had believed in the forge as the glowing road to manhood and independence. Within a single year all this was changed. Now, it was all coarse and common, and I would not have had Miss Havisham and Estella see it on any account.

How much of my ungracious condition of mind may have been my own fault, how much Miss Havisham's, how much my sister's, is now of no moment to me or to anyone. The change was made in me ; the thing was done.

Once, it had seemed to me that when I should at last roll up my shirt-sleeves and go into the forge, Joe's apprentice, I should be distinguished and happy. Now that the reality was here, I only felt that I was dusty with the dust of small-coal, and that I had a weight upon my daily remembrance to which the anvil was a feather.

I remember that at a later period of my " time," I used to stand about the churchyard on Sunday evenings, when night was falling, comparing my own perspective with the windy marsh view, and making out some like-ness between them by thinking how flat and low both were, and how on both there came an unknown way and a dark mist and then the sea. I was quite as dejected on the first working-day of my apprenticeship as in that after-time ; but I am glad to know that I never breathed a murmur to Joe while my indentures lasted. It is about the only thing I *am* glad to know of myself in that connection.

For, though it includes what I proceed to add, all the merit was Joe's. It was not because I was faithful, but because Joe was faithful, that I never ran away and went for a soldier or a sailor. It was not because I had a strong sense of the virtue of industry, but because of Joe, that I worked with tolerable zeal against the grain.

As I was getting too big for Mr. Wopsle's aunt's room, my education under that lady ended. Not, however, until Biddy had imparted to me everything she knew, from the little catalogue of prices to a comic song she had once bought for a halfpenny. Although the only coherent part of the latter piece were the opening lines :

> When I went to Lunnon town, sirs,
> Too rul loo rul
> Too rul loo rul
> Wasn't I done very brown, sirs?
> Too rul loo rul
> Too rul loo rul.

—still, in my desire to be wiser, I got this composition by heart with the utmost gravity ; nor do I recollect that I questioned its merit, except that I thought (as I still do) the amount of Too rul somewhat in excess of the poetry.

Thus matters went until I reached the fourth year of my apprenticeship ; and they bade fair to end that way, but for an unusual event.

I had gone with Joe one Saturday night to a neighbouring tavern to join some friends. In the course of the conversation, a strange gentleman, who had been listening to us, stepped between us and the fire, and said : "I understand that one of you is a blacksmith, by name, Joseph Gargery. Which is the man ? "

"Here is the man," said Joe.

"You have an apprentice," pursued the stranger, "commonly known as Pip. Is he here?"

"Here," I answered.

The stranger did not recognise me, but I did recognise him as the man I had once met on the stair at Miss Havisham's.

"I wish to have a private talk with you both," he said. "Perhaps we had better go to your house."

So, in a wondering silence we left the inn and walked home, where Joe, vaguely recognising the occasion to be important, opened the front door and ushered us into the state parlour.

The stranger told us that he was a lawyer in London, and was now acting as confidential agent for some one else. He wished to purchase my apprenticeship papers from Joe, if Joe were willing to release me.

"Lord forbid that I should want anything for not standing in Pip's way," said Joe, staring.

"Lord forbidding is pious, but not to the purpose," returned the lawyer. "The question is, Would you want anything? Do you want anything?"

"The answer is," returned Joe, sternly, "No."

"Then I am instructed to communicate to him," said Mr. Jaggers, throwing his finger at me, sideways, "that he will come into a handsome property. Further, that it is the desire of the present possessor of that property, that he be immediately removed from his present sphere of life and from this place, and be brought up as a gentleman—in a word, as a young fellow of great expectations."

My dream was out; my wild fancy was surpassed by sober reality; Miss Havisham was going to make my fortune on a grand scale!—at least, so I thought at the time.

"Now, Mr. Pip," pursued the lawyer, "I address the rest of what I have to say to you. You are to understand, first, that it is the request of the person from whom I take my instructions, that you always bear the name of Pip. You will have no objection, I dare say, to that easy condition. But if you have any objection, this is the time to mention it."

I gasped, but had no objection.

"The second condition," he resumed, "is that you are not to know the name of your benefactor, for the present. I will act as your guardian and see that you are educated properly. You desire an education, don't you?"

I replied that I had always longed for it.

"Good. Then we will see to getting you a tutor. But first you should have some new clothes to come away in. When will you be ready to leave? Say this day week. You'll want some money. Shall I leave you twenty guineas?"

He produced a long purse, with the greatest coolness, and counted them out on the table and pushed them over to me. This was the first time he had taken his leg from the chair. He sat astride of the chair when he had pushed the money over, and sat swinging his purse and eyeing Joe.

"Well, Joseph Gargery? You look dumb-foundered?"

"I *am I*" said Joe, in a very decided manner.

"It was understood that you wanted nothing for yourself, remember?"

"It were understood," said Joe. "And it *are* understood. And it ever will be similar according."

"But what," said the lawyer, swinging his purse, "what if it was in my instructions to make you a present, as compensation?"

" As compensation what for ? " Joe demanded.
" For the loss of his services."

Joe laid his hand upon my shoulder with the touch
of a woman. I have often thought of him since, like
the steam-hammer, that can crush a man or pat an
egg-shell, in his combination of strength with gentleness.
" Pip is that hearty welcome," said Joe, " to go free
with his services, to honour and fortun', as no words
can tell him. But if you think as Money can make
compensation to me for the loss of the little child—
what come to the forge—and ever the best of friends——"

Oh, dear, good Joe, whom I was so ready to leave
and so unthankful to, I see you again, with your muscular
blacksmith's arm before your eyes, and your broad
chest heaving, and your voice dying away. Oh, dear,
good faithful, tender Joe, I feel the loving tremble of
your hand upon my arm, as solemnly this day as if it
had been the rustle of an angel's wing !

But at the time I was lost in the mazes of my future
fortunes, and could not retrace the by-paths we had
trodden together. I begged Joe to be comforted. Joe
scooped his eyes with his disengaged wrist, as if he were
bent on gouging himself, but said not another word.

After the lawyer had taken his leave, Joe and I went
into the kitchen, where we found Biddy and my sister,
and told them of my good fortune.

They dropped their sewing and looked at me. Joe
held his knees and looked at me. I looked at them,
in turn. After a pause they heartily congratulated
me ; but there was a certain touch of sadness in their
congratulations that I rather resented.

Now that I was actually going away I became quite
gloomy. I did not know why, but I sat in the chimney

corner looking at the fire, my elbow on my knee; and while the others tried to make the conversation cheerful, I grew gloomier than ever.

But the bright sunlight of the next morning dispelled my doubts and fears, and I began to count the days eagerly. I went down to Trabb's, the tailor's, and got measured for a wonderful suit of clothes, much to the consternation of Trabb's boy, who thought himself equal to any blacksmith that ever lived. Then I went to the hatter's and the bootmaker's and the hosier's, and felt rather like Mother Hubbard's dog, whose outfit required the services of so many trades. I also went to the coach-office and took my place for seven o'clock Saturday morning. And everywhere about the village the news of my great expectations preceded me and I was heartily stared at.

Uncle Pumblechook was especially officious at this time. He acted as though he were the sole cause of all this.

"To think," said he, swelling up, "that I should have been the humble instrument of this proud reward."

He thought, like all the rest of us, that Miss Havisham was my unknown benefactor. It was a natural mistake, as she had been kind to me in her way; and I had seen the lawyer at her house. But it was a mistake after all and led to other unhappy blunders ere I learned the truth.

For, many years afterwards, I found that " my convict "—the man I had helped down in the churchyard— was none other than the friend who had left me this fortune. He had escaped again from the hulks and coming into a considerable property, had arranged with the lawyer to use it in making a gentleman out of the little boy he had found crying on the tombstone. But, as I say, none of us knew it or suspected it at first.

And now, those six days which were to have run out so slowly, had run out fast and were gone, and to-morrow looked me in the face more steadily than I could look at it. As the six evenings had dwindled away to five, to four, to three, to two, I had become more and more appreciative of the society of Joe and my sister and Biddy. On this last evening I dressed myself out in my new clothes, for their delight, and sat in my splendour until bedtime. We had a hot supper on the occasion, graced by the inevitable roast fowl, and we had some flip to finish with. We were all very low, and none the higher for pretending to be in spirits.

It was a hurried breakfast, the next morning, with no taste in it. I got up from the meal, saying with a sort of briskness, as if it had only just occurred to me, "Well! I suppose I must be off!" and then I kissed my sister, and kissed Biddy, and threw my arms around Joe's neck. Then I took up my little portmanteau and walked out. The last I saw of them was, when I presently heard a scuffle behind me, and, looking back, saw Joe throwing an old shoe after me and Biddy throwing another old shoe. I stopped then, to wave my hat, and dear old Joe waved his strong right arm above his head, crying huskily " Hooroar ! " and Biddy put her apron to her face.

I walked away at a good pace, thinking it was easier to go than I had supposed it would be, and reflecting that it would never have done to have an old shoe thrown after the coach in sight of all the High Street. I whistled and made nothing of going. But the village was very peaceful and quiet, and the light mists were solemnly rising, as if to show me the world, and I had been so innocent and little there, and all beyond was so unknown and great, that in a moment with a strong heave and sob I broke into tears. It was by the finger-post at the end of the village, and I laid my hand upon it, and said, " Good-bye, oh, my dear, dear friend ! "

So subdued was I by those tears, that when I was on the coach, and it was clear of the town, I deliberated with an aching heart whether I would not get down when we changed horses, and walk back, and have another evening at home, and a better parting. But while I deliberated, we had changed and changed again, and it was now too late and too far to go back, and I went on. And the mists had all solemnly risen now, and the world lay spread before me. My boyhood was over. Henceforth, I was to play a man's part—a man with Great Expectations.¹

The Story of Little Dorrit

I

THE CHILD OF THE MARSHALSEA

SOME years ago when the laws of England were harsher than they are now, there were debtors' prisons, or big, gloomy gaols into which men were put, if they couldn't pay what they owed. This was cruel and unjust, for the prisoner was of course cut off from the chance to earn any more money ; and so he might linger there for years or even his whole life long, if some friend did not come to his relief. But otherwise the prisoner was given many liberties not found in ordinary gaols. His family might live with him, if they chose, and come and go as they pleased.

One of the largest of these debtors' prisons was called the " Marshalsea." One day a gentleman was brought there who had lost his money in business ; but so confident was he of speedily regaining his liberty, that he would not unpack his valise, at first. His name was William Dorrit, an easy-going man who had spent his money freely and paid little attention to his tradesmen's bills. Now that he had fallen upon evil days, he thought that his friends would be glad to help him. But as the days and weeks passed with no prospect of aid, he was persuaded not only to unpack his belongings, but also to have his wife and two children brought to live with him.

The two children, Fanny and Edward—commonly called " Tip "—were so young when they were brought to the Marshalsea, that they soon forgot any earlier life, and played very happily with other children in the prison yard. Not long after, a little sister was added to their family. She was christened Amy, but was so tiny that everybody called her " Little Dorrit."

Being born in the prison, Little Dorrit was petted and made much of. Everyone there seemed to claim her, and visitors were proudly shown " the Child of the Marshalsea."

The turnkey, who was a kind-hearted man, took an especial interest in her.

" By rights," he remarked, when she was first shown to him, " I ought to be her godfather."

Mr. Dorrit looked at the honest fellow for a moment, and thought that he would suit better than some of their false friends.

" Perhaps you wouldn't object to really being her godfather ? " he said.

" Oh, I don't object, if you don't," replied the turnkey.

Thus it came to pass that she was christened one Sunday afternoon, when the turnkey, being relieved, went up to the font of Saint George's church, and promised and vowed on her behalf, as he himself related when he came back, " like a good un."

This invested the turnkey with a new proprietary share in the child, over and above his former official one. When she began to walk and talk, he became fond of her ; bought a little arm-chair and stood it by the high fender of the lodge fireplace ; liked to have her company when he was on the lock ; and used to bribe her with cheap toys to come and talk to him. The child, for her part, soon grew so fond of the turnkey, that she would come climbing up the lodge steps of her own accord at all hours of the day. When she fell asleep in the little arm-chair by the high fender, the turnkey would cover her with his pocket handkerchief; and when she sat in it dressing and undressing a doll—which soon came to be unlike dolls on the other side of the lock—he would contemplate her from the top of his stool, with exceeding gentleness. Witnessing these things, the inmates would express an opinion that the turnkey, who was a bachelor, had been cut out by nature for a family man. But the turnkey thanked them, and said, "No, on the whole it was enough for him to see other people's children there."

At what period of her early life the little creature began to perceive that it was not the habit of all the world to live locked up in narrow yards, surrounded by high walls with spikes at the top, would be a difficult question to settle. But she was a very, very little creature indeed, when she had somehow gained the knowledge, that her clasp of her father's hand was to be always loosened at the door which the great key opened; and that while her own light steps were free to pass beyond it, his feet must never cross that line. A pitiful and plaintive look, with which she had begun to regard him when she was still extremely young, was perhaps a part of this discovery.

Wistful and wondering, she would sit in summer weather by the high fender in the lodge, looking up at the sky through the barred window, until bars of light would arise, when she would turn her eyes away.

"Thinking of the fields," the turnkey said once, after watching her, "ain't you?"

"Where are they?" she inquired.

"Why, they're—over there, my dear," said the turnkey, with a vague flourish of his key. "Just about there."

"Does anybody open them, and shut them? Are they locked?"

The turnkey was at a loss. "Well!" he said, "not in general."

"Are they very pretty, Bob?" She called him Bob, by his own particular request and instruction.

"Lovely. Full of flowers. There's buttercups, and there's daisies, and there's"—the turnkey hesitated, being short of names—"there's dandelions, and all manner of games."

"Is it very pleasant to be there, Bob?"

"Prime," said the turnkey.

"Was father ever there?"

"Hem!" coughed the turnkey. "Oh, yes, he was there, sometimes."

"Is he sorry not to be there now?"

"N—not particular," said the turnkey.

"Nor any of the people?" she asked, glancing at the listless crowd within. "Oh, are you quite sure and certain, Bob?"

At this difficult point of the conversation Bob gave in, and changed the subject; always his last resource when he found his little friend getting him into a political, social, or theological corner. But this was the origin of a series of Sunday excursions that these two curious companions made together. They used to issue from the lodge on alternate Sunday afternoons with great gravity, bound for some meadows or green lanes that had been elaborately appointed by the turnkey in the course of the week ; and there she picked grass and flowers to bring home, while he smoked his pipe. Afterwards they would come back hand in hand, unless she was more than usually tired, and had fallen asleep on his shoulder.

In those early days the turnkey first began profoundly to consider a question which cost him so much mental labour, that it remained undetermined on the day of his death. He decided to will and bequeath his little property of savings to his godchild, and the point arose how could it be so "tied up" that she alone should benefit by it. He asked the knotty question of every lawyer who came through the lodge gate on business.

"Settle it strictly on herself," the gentleman would answer.

"But look here," quoth the turnkey. "Supposing she had, say a brother, say a father, say a husband, who would be likely to make a grab at that property when she came into it—how about that ? "

" It would be settled on herself, and they would have no more legal claim on it than you," would be the professional answer.

"Stop a bit," said the turnkey. "Supposing she was tender-hearted, and they came over her. Where's your law for tying it up then ? "

The deepest character whom the turnkey sounded was unable to produce his law for tying such a knot as that. So, the turnkey thought about it all his life, and died without a will after all.

But that was long afterwards, when his god-daughter was past sixteen. She was only eight when her mother died, and from that time the protection that her won-dering eyes had expressed towards her father became embodied in action, and the Child of the Marshalsea took upon herself a new relation.

At first, such a baby could do little more than sit with him, deserting her livelier place by the high fender, and quietly watching him. But this made her so far necessary to him that he became accustomed to her, and began to be sensible of missing her when she was not there. Through this little gate she passed out of childhood into the care-laden world.

What her pitiful look saw, at that early time, in her father, in her sister, in her brother, in the gaol; how much, or how little of the wretched truth it pleased God to make visible to her, lies hidden with many mysteries. It is enough that she was inspired to be something which was not what the rest were, and for the sake of the rest.

And while the mark of the prison was seen only too clearly in her vain, selfish sister, and weak, wayward brother, Little Dorrit's life was singularly free from taint; her heart was full of service and love.

And so, in spite of her small stature and want of strength, she toiled and planned, and soon became the real head of this poor, fallen house.

At thirteen, she could read and keep accounts—that is, could put down in words and figures how much the bare necessaries that they wanted would cost, and how much less they had to buy them with. She had been, by snatches of a few weeks at a time, to an evening school outside, and got her sister and brother sent to day schools during three or four years. There was no instruction for any of them at home; but she knew well—no one better—that her broken-spirited father could no longer help them.

To these scanty means of improvement, she added another of her own contriving. Once, among the curious crowd of inmates, there appeared a dancing-master. Her sister Fanny had a great desire to learn to dance, and seemed to have a taste that way. At thirteen years old, the Child of the Marshalsea presented herself to the dancing-master, with a little bag in her hand, and said timidly, "If you please, I was born here, sir."

"Oh! You are the young lady, are you?" said the man, surveying the small figure and uplifted face.

"Yes, sir."

"And what can I do for you?"

"Nothing for me, sir, thank you," anxiously undrawing the strings of the little bag; "but if, while you stay here, you could be so kind as to teach my sister cheap——"

"My child, I'll teach her for nothing," said the dancing-master, shutting up the bag.

He was as good-natured a master as ever danced to the Insolvent Court, and he kept his word. Fanny was so apt a pupil, and made such wonderful progress that he continued to teach her after he was released from prison. In time, he obtained a place for her at a small theatre. It was at the same theatre where her uncle—who was also now a poor man—played a clarinet for a living; and Fanny left the Marshalsea and went to live with him.

The success of this beginning gave Little Dorrit courage to try again, this time on her own behalf. She had long wanted to learn how to sew, and watched and waited for a seamstress to come to the prison. At last one came, and Little Dorrit went to call upon her.

"I beg your pardon, ma'am," she said, looking timidly

round the door of the milliner, whom she found in tears and in bed; "but I was born here."

Everybody seemed to hear of her as soon as they arrived; for the milliner sat up in bed, drying her eyes, and said, just as the dancing-master had said:

"Oh! *You* are the child, are you?"

"Yes, ma'am."

"I am sorry I haven't got anything for you," said the milliner, shaking her head.

"It's not that, ma'am. If you please I want to learn needlework."

"Why should you do that," returned the milliner, "with me before you? It has not done me much good."

"Nothing—whatever it is—seems to have done anybody much good who comes here," she returned in all simplicity; "but I want to learn, just the same."

"I am afraid you are so weak, you see," the milliner objected.

"I don't think I am weak, ma'am."

"And you are so very, very little, you see," continued the milliner.

"Yes, I am afraid I am very little indeed," returned the Child of the Marshalsea; and so began to sob over that unfortunate defect of hers, which came so often in her way. The milliner—who was not morose or hard-hearted, only newly insolvent—was touched, took her in hand with good-will, found her the most patient and earnest of pupils, and made her a cunning work-woman in course of time.

And so, presently, Little Dorrit had the immense satisfaction of going out to work by the day, and of supplying her father with many little comforts which otherwise he would not have enjoyed.

But her hardest task was in getting her brother out of prison and into some useful employment. The life there had been anything but good for him; and at eighteen he was idle and shiftless, not caring to lift a finger for himself. In her dilemma, Little Dorrit went to her old friend, the turnkey.

"Dear Bob," said she, "what is to become of poor Tip?"

The turnkey scratched his head. Privately he had a poor opinion of the young man.

"Well, my dear," he answered, "something ought to be done with him. Suppose I try to get him into the law?"

"That would be so good of you, Bob!"

The turnkey was as good as his word, and by dint of buttonholing every lawyer who came through the gate on business, he found Tip a place as clerk, where the pay was not large, but the prospects good.

Tip idled away in the law office for six months, then came back to the prison one evening with his hands in his pockets and told his sister he was not going back again.

"Not going back!" she exclaimed.

"I am so tired of it," said Tip, "that I have cut it."

Tip tired of everything. With intervals of Marshalsea lounging, his small second mother, aided by her trusty friend, got him into a variety of situations. But whatever Tip went into, he came out of tired, announcing that he had cut it.

Nevertheless, the brave little creature did so fix her heart on her brother's rescue, that while he was ringing out these doleful changes, she pinched and scraped enough together to ship him for Canada. When he was tired of nothing to do, and disposed in its turn to cut even that, he graciously consented to go to Canada. And there was grief in her bosom over parting with him, and joy in the hope of his being put in a straight course at last.

"God bless you, dear Tip. Don't be too proud to come and see us, when you have made your fortune."

"All right!" said Tip, and went.

But not all the way to Canada ; in fact, not farther than Liverpool. After making the voyage to that part from London, he found himself so strongly impelled to cut the vessel, that he resolved to walk back again. Carrying out which intention, he presented himself before her at the expiration of a month, in rags, without shoes, and much more tired than ever.

At length he found a situation for himself, and disappeared for months. She never heard from him but once in that time, though it was as well for her peace of mind that she did not. He had been given some sort of a berth by a not too respectable horse dealer.

One evening she was alone at work—standing up at the window, to save the twilight lingering above the wall—when he opened the door and walked in.

She kissed and welcomed him ; but was afraid to ask him any questions. He saw how anxious and timid she was, and appeared sorry.

"I am afraid, Amy, you'll be vexed this time. Upon my life I am ! "

"I am very sorry to hear you say so, Tip. Have you come back ? "

"Why—yes. But that's not the worst of it."

"Not the worst of it ? "

"Don't look so startled, Amy. I've come back in a

Little Dorrit

new way. I'm one of the prisoners now. I owe forty pounds."

For the first time in all those years, she sank under her cares. She cried, with her clasped hands lifted above her head, that it would kill their father if he ever knew it ; and fell down at Tip's graceless feet.

It was easier for Tip to bring her to her senses, than for her to bring *him* to understand what a pitiable thing he had done. But he agreed to help keep it a secret from their father ; and Little Dorrit toiled harder than ever, in the hope of one day getting him out again.

Thus passed the life of the Child of the Marshalsea until she became a young woman.

II

HOW THE PRISON GATES WERE OPENED

AMONG the ladies for whom Little Dorrit sewed by the day was a Mrs. Clennam, a cold, stern person who lived in a cold, stern house. Yet she gave the child plenty of work and paid her fairly well. So Little Dorrit was often to be found in some gloomy corner there, sewing away busily and adding nothing at all to the few far-away sounds of the quiet old rooms.

Mrs. Clennam lived alone, except for a dried-up servant or two, and she herself had lost the use of her limbs. So it is no wonder that the house was gloomy, and that Mrs. Clennam's son Arthur found it so, when he returned from a long visit in India. Arthur Clennam was a young man who had ideas of his own, and who had disappointed

Q

his mother by refusing to continue his father's business. They were not in sympathy—which made the house seem all the colder. But he was kind, open-hearted, and impulsive.

Though timid Little Dorrit kept as much in the dark corners as possible, Arthur soon noticed her, and asked one of the old servants who she was. He could learn nothing except that she was a seamstress who came by the day to sew, and who went away every night, no one knew where. The child interested him, and he resolved to follow her one evening and learn where she lived. He did so, and was amazed to see her enter the gate of a large forbidding building—he did not know what building, as he had been long abroad.

Just then he saw an old man, in a thread-bare coat, once blue, come tottering along, carrying a clarinet in a limp, worn-out case. As this old man was about to enter the same gate, Arthur stopped him with a question.

" Pray, sir," said he, " what is this place ? "

" Ay ! This place ? " returned the old man, staying a pinch of snuff on its road, and pointing at the place without looking at it. " This is the Marshalsea, sir."

" The debtors' prison ? "

" Sir," said the old man, with the air of deeming it not quite necessary to insist upon that name, " the debtors' prison."

He turned himself about, and went on.

" I beg your pardon," said Arthur, stopping him once more, " but will you allow me to ask you another question ? Can anyone go in here ? "

" Anyone can *go in*," replied the old man; " but it is not everyone who can go out."

"Pardon me once more. Are you familiar with the place?"

"Sir," returned the old man, squeezing his little packet of snuff in his hand, and turning upon his interrogator as if such questions hurt him, "I am."

"I beg you to excuse me. I am not impertinently curious, but have a good object. Do you know the name of Dorrit here?"

"My name, sir," replied the old man most unexpectedly, "is Dorrit."

Arthur pulled off his hat to him. "Grant me the favour of half a dozen words. I have recently come home to England after a long absence. I have seen at my mother's—Mrs. Clennam in the city—a young woman working at her needle, whom I have only heard addressed or spoken of as Little Dorrit. I have felt sincerely interested in her, and have had a great desire to know something more about her. I saw her, not a minute before you came up, pass in at that door."

The old man looked at him attentively. "Are you in earnest, sir?"

"I do assure you that I am."

"I know very little of the world, sir," returned the other, who had a weak and quavering voice. "I am merely passing on, like the shadow over the sun-dial. It would be worth no man's while to mislead me; it would really be too easy—too poor a success, to yield any satisfaction. The young woman whom you saw go in here is my brother's child. My brother is William Dorrit; I am Frederick. You say you have seen her at your mother's (I know your mother befriends her), you have felt an interest in her, and you wish to know what she does here. Come and see.'

He went on again, and Arthur accompanied him.

"My brother," said the old man, pausing on the step, and slowly facing round again, "has been here many years; and much that happens even among ourselves, out of doors, is kept from him for reasons that I needn't enter upon now. Be so good as to say nothing of my niece's working at her needle. If you keep within our bounds, you cannot well be wrong. Now! Come and see."

Arthur followed him down a narrow entry, at the end of which a key was turned, and a strong door was opened from within. It admitted them into a lodge, or lobby, across which they passed, and so through another door and a grating into the prison. The old man always plodding on before, turned round, in his slow, stiff, stooping manner, when they came to the turnkey on duty, as if to present his companion. The turnkey nodded; and the companion passed in without being asked whom he wanted.

The night was dark; and the prison lamps in the yard, and the candles in the prison windows faintly shining behind many sorts of wry old curtain and blind, had not the air of making it lighter. A few people loitered about, but the greater part of the population was within doors. The old man taking the right-hand side of the yard, turned in at the third or fourth doorway, and began to ascend the stairs.

"They are rather dark, sir, but you will not find anything in the way," he said.

He paused for a moment before opening the door on the second storey. He had no sooner turned the handle, than the visitor saw Little Dorrit, and understood the reason of her dining alone, as she always preferred to do. She had brought the meat home that she should have eaten herself, and was already warming it on a gridiron over the fire, for her father, who, clad in an old grey gown and a black cap, was awaiting his supper at the table. A clean cloth was spread before him, with knife, fork, and spoon, salt-cellar, pepper-box, glass, and pewter ale-pot. Such zests as his cayenne pepper and pickles in a saucer were not wanting.

She started, coloured deeply, and turned white. The visitor, more with his eyes than by the slight impulsive motion of his hand, entreated her to be reassured and to trust him.

"I found this gentleman," said the uncle—"Mr. Clennam, William, son of Amy's friend—at the outer gate, wishful, as he was going by, of paying his respects, but hesitating whether to come in or not. This is my brother William, sir."

"I hope," said Arthur, very doubtful what to say, "that my respect for your daughter may explain and justify my desire to be presented to you, sir."

"Mr. Clennam," returned the other, rising, taking his cap off in the flat of his hand, and so holding it, ready to put on again, "you do me honour. You are welcome, sir." With a low bow. "Frederick, a chair. Pray sit down, Mr. Clennam."

He put his black cap on again as he had taken it off, and resumed his own seat. There was a wonderful air of benignity and patronage in his manner.

These were the ceremonies with which he received all visitors.

"You are welcome to the Marshalsea, sir. I have welcomed many gentlemen to these walls. Perhaps you are aware—my daughter Amy may have mentioned —that I am the Father of this place."

"I—so I have understood," said Arthur, dashing at the assertion.

"You know, I dare say, that my daughter Amy was born here. A good girl, sir, a dear girl, and long a comfort and support to me. Amy, my dear, put the dish on; Mr. Clennam will excuse the primitive customs to which we are reduced here. Is it a compliment to ask you if you would do me the honour, sir, to——"

"Thank you," returned Arthur. "I have dined."

She filled her father's glass, put all the little matters on the table ready to his hand, and then sat beside him while he ate his supper. She put some bread before herself, and touched his glass with her lips; but Arthur saw she looked troubled and took nothing. Her look at her father, half admiring him and proud of him, half-ashamed for him, all devoted and loving, went to his inmost heart.

He could not say anything to her here, but when he rose to take his leave, Arthur asked her by a look to come with him to the gate. He felt he must make some explanation for thus intruding and learning her secret.

"Pray forgive me," he said, when they paused alone at the gate. "I followed you to-night from my mother's. I should not have done so, but, believe me, it was only in the hope of doing you some service. What I have seen here, in this short time, has increased tenfold my heartfelt wish to be a friend to you."

She seemed to take courage while he spoke to her.

"You are very good, sir. You speak very earnestly to me. But I—but I wish you had not watched me."

She was so agitated, and he was so moved by compassion for her, and by deep interest in her story as it dawned upon him, that he could scarcely tear himself away. But the stoppage of the bell, and the quiet in the prison, were a warning to depart; and with a few hurried words of kindness he left her gliding back to her father.

The next day, Arthur missed Little Dorrit at his home, and wondered if she might be ill. The weather was stormy, but she was not usually hindered by that. So he walked out toward the prison to look for her; and was presently rewarded by seeing her hurrying along in the face of the gale.

She had just reached the iron bridge, some distance from the gates, when his voice caused her to stop short. The wind blew roughly, the wet squalls came rattling past them, skimming the pools on the road and pavement, and raining them down into the river. The clouds raced on furiously in the lead-coloured sky, the smoke and mist raced after them, the dark tide ran fierce and strong in the same direction. Little Dorrit seemed the least, the quietest, and weakest of Heaven's creatures.

"Let me put you in a coach," said Arthur Clennam, very nearly adding, "my poor child."

She hurriedly declined, thanking him, and saying that wet or dry made little difference to her; she was used to go about in all weathers. He knew it to be so, and was touched with more pity, thinking of the slight figure at his side, making its nightly way through the damp, dark, boisterous streets, to such a place of rest.

"But I am glad to have seen you, sir," she added shyly. "I did not want you to think that we were ungrateful for your interest and kindness, last night. And, besides, I had something else to say—— "

She paused as if unable to go on.

" To say to me—— " he prompted.

" That I hope you will not misunderstand my father.
Don't judge him, sir, as you would judge others outside
the gates. He has been there so long ! I never saw
him outside, but I can understand that he must have
grown different in some things since."

" My thoughts will never be unjust or harsh towards
him, believe me."

" Not," she said, with a prouder air, as the misgiving
evidently crept upon her that she might seem to be
abandoning him, " not that he has anything to be ashamed
of for himself, or that I have anything to be ashamed
of for him. He only requires to be understood. I
only ask for him that his life may be fairly remembered.
All that he said was quite true. He is very much respected. Everybody who comes in is glad to know
him. He is more courted than any one else. He is
far more thought of than the Marshal is." If ever
pride were innocent, it was innocent in Little Dorrit when
she grew boastful of her father.

" It is often said that his manners are a true gentleman's, and quite a study. He is not to be blamed for
being in need, poor love. Who could be in prison a
quarter of a century, and be prosperous ! "

What affection in her words, what compassion in her
repressed tears, what a great soul of fidelity within her,
how true the light that shed false brightness round him !

" If I have found it best to conceal where my home is,
it is not because I am ashamed of him. God forbid !
Nor am I so much ashamed of the place itself as might
be supposed. People are not bad because they come
there. I have known many good friends there, and
have spent many happy hours."

She had relieved the faithful fulness of her heart, and modestly said, raising her eyes appealingly to her new friend's, " I did not mean to say so much, nor have I ever but once spoken about this before. But it seems to set it more right than it was last night. I said I wished you had not followed me, sir. I don't wish it so much now, unless you should think—indeed I don't wish it at all, unless I should have spoken so confusedly, that—that you can scarcely understand me, which I am afraid may be the case."

Thereafter, Arthur Clennam, who was a man of some means, devoted a great part of his time to tracing out the Dorrit records. He went from one government office to another—a long, weary round of them—before he could get any light on the matter. He employed an agent whose specialty was to search out lost estates. And at last, after several months, their combined efforts were rewarded.

Mr. Dorrit was found to be heir-at-law to a large estate that had long lain unknown, unclaimed, and growing greater. His right to it was cleared up by his skilful agent ; so that Mr. Dorrit would now be in a position to discharge his debts and to leave the prison a free man.

When Arthur was convinced of this surprising fortune, he hastened first to Little Dorrit, whom he wished to see alone. But before he could say a word, his face told her that something unusual was afoot.

Hastily dropping her sewing, she cried, " Mr. Clennam ! What's the matter ? "

" Nothing, nothing ! That is—nothing bad. I have come to tell you good news."

" Good fortune ? "

" Wonderful fortune ! "

Her lips seemed to repeat the words, but no sound came.

" Dear Little Dorrit," he said, " your father——"

The ice of the pale face broke at the word, and little lights of expression passed all over it. They were all expressions of pain. Her breath was faint and hurried. Her heart beat fast, but he saw that the eyes appealed to him to go on.

" Your father can be free within this week. He does not know it ; we must go to him from here, to tell him of it. Your father will be free within a few days. Remember we must go to him, from here, to tell him of it ! "

That brought her back. Her eyes were closing, but they opened again.

" This is not all the good fortune. This is not all the wonderful good fortune, Little Dorrit. Shall I tell you more ? "

Her lips shaped " Yes."

" He will be a rich man. A great sum of money is waiting to be paid over to him, as his inheritance ; you are all henceforth very wealthy. Bravest and best of children, I thank Heaven that you are rewarded ! "

She turned her head towards his shoulder, and raised her arm towards his neck ; then cried out, " Father ! Father ! Father ! " and swooned away.

The housekeeper came running in at this, and Little Dorrit was soon revived, smiling bravely at her own weakness. But the news had been too much for her. It was the dream of her lifetime—come true !

" Come ! " she exclaimed, " we must not lose a moment, but must hasten to my father ! "

When the turnkey, who was on duty, admitted them

into the lodge, he saw something in their faces which filled him with astonishment. He stood looking after them, when they hurried into the prison, as though he perceived that they had come back accompanied by a ghost apiece. Two or three debtors whom they passed, looked after them too, and presently joining the turnkey, formed a little group on the lodge steps, in the midst of which there originated a whisper that the Father was going to get his discharge. Within a few minutes it was heard in the remotest room in the prison.

Little Dorrit opened the door from without, and they both entered. Her father was sitting in his old grey gown, and his old black cap, in the sunlight by the window, reading his newspaper. His glasses were in his hand, and he had just looked round; surprised at first, no doubt, by her step upon the stairs, not expecting her until night; surprised again, by seeing Arthur Clennam in her company. As they came in, the same unwonted look in both of them, which had already caught attention in the yard below, struck him. He did not rise or speak, but laid down his glasses and his newspaper on the table beside him, and looked at them with his mouth a little open, and his lips trembling. When Arthur put out his hand, he touched it, but not with his usual state; and then he turned to his daughter, who had sat down close beside him with her hands upon his shoulder, and looked attentively in her face.

"Father! I have been made so happy this morning!"

"You have been made so happy, my dear!"

"By Mr. Clennam, father. He brought me such joyful and wonderful intelligence about you!"

Her agitation was great, and the tears rolled down

her face. He put his hand suddenly to his heart, and looked at Clennam.

"Compose yourself, sir," said Clennam, "and take a little time to think. To think of the brightest and most fortunate accidents of life. We have all heard of great surprises of joy. They are not at an end."

"Mr. Clennam? Not at an end? Not at an end for——" He touched himself upon the breast, instead of saying "me."

"No," returned Clennam.

He looked at Clennam, and, so looking at him, seemed to change into a very old haggard man. The sun was bright upon the wall beyond the window, and on the spikes at the top. He slowly stretched out the hand that had been upon his heart, and pointed to the wall.

"It is down," said Clennam. "Gone!"

He remained in the same attitude, looking steadfastly at him.

"And in its place," said Clennam, slowly and distinctly, "are the means to possess and enjoy the utmost that they have so long shut out. Mr. Dorrit, there is not the smallest doubt that within a few days you will be free, and highly prosperous. I congratulate you with all my soul on this change of fortune, and on the happy future into which you are soon to carry the treasure you have been blessed with here—the best of all the riches you can have elsewhere—the treasure in the dear child at your side."

With those words, he pressed Mr. Dorrit's hand and released it; and his daughter, laying her face against his, encircled him in the hour of his prosperity with her arms, as she had in the long years of his adversity encircled him with her love and toil and truth; and poured out her full heart in gratitude, hope, joy, blissful ecstasy, and all for him.

"I shall see him, as I never saw him yet. I shall see my dear father, with the dark cloud cleared away. I shall see him, as my poor mother saw him long ago Oh, my dear, my dear! Oh, father, father! Oh, thank God, thank God!"

Mr. Dorrit came slowly out of the daze into which he had seemed to fall. To divert his mind, Arthur told him how the good fortune had been found through the skill of an agent.

"He shall be rewarded!" he exclaimed, starting up. "Everyone shall be—ha!—handsomely rewarded! No one shall say that he has an unsatisfied claim against me. Oh! can this be true? A free man, and all my debts paid!"

With the air of a man whose pockets are overflowing with gold, he paced rapidly up and down the room. Just then a great cheering arose in the prison yard.

"The news has spread already," said Clennam, looking down from the window. "Will you show yourself to them, Mr. Dorrit? They are very earnest, and evidently wish it."

"I—hum—ha—I confess I could have desired, Amy, my dear," he said, jogging about in a more feverish flutter than before, "to have made some change in my dress first, and to have bought a—hum—a watch and chain. But if it must be done as it is, it—ha—it must be done. Fasten the collar of my shirt, my dear. Mr. Clennam, would you oblige me—hum—with a blue neckcloth you will find in that drawer at your elbow. Button my coat across at the chest, my love. It looks—ha—it looks broader, buttoned."

With his trembling hand he pushed his gray hair up, and then, taking Clennam and his daughter for supporters, appeared at the window leaning on an arm of each. The inmates cheered him very heartily, and he kissed his hand to them with great urbanity and protection. When he withdrew into the room again, he said " Poor creatures ! " in a tone of much pity for their miserable condition.

Presently he said, unexpectedly :

" Mr. Clennam, I beg your pardon. Am I to understand, my dear sir, that I could—ha—could pass through the lodge at this moment, and—hum—take a walk ? "

" I think not, Mr. Dorrit," was the unwilling reply. " There are certain forms to be completed ; and although your detention here is now in itself a form, I fear it has to be observed for a few hours longer."

" A few hours, sir," he returned in a sudden passion. " You talk very easily of hours, sir ! How long do you suppose, sir, that an hour is to a man who is choking for want of air ? "

It was the cry of a man who had been imprisoned for nearly a quarter of a century.

Little Dorrit had been thinking too. After softly putting his gray hair aside, and touching his forehead with her lips, she looked towards Arthur, who came nearer to her, and pursued in a low whisper the subject of her thoughts.

" Mr. Clennam, will he pay all his debts before he leaves here ? "

" No doubt. All."

" All the debts for which he has been imprisoned here, all my life and longer ? "

" No doubt."

There was something of uncertainty and remonstrance in her look ; something that was not all satisfaction.   He wondered to detect it, and said :

"Are you not glad ? "

"It seems to me hard," said Little Dorrit, "that he should have lost so many years and suffered so much, and at last pay all the debts as well.   It seems to me hard that he should pay in life and money both."

"My dear child——" Clennam was beginning.

"Yes, I know I am wrong," she pleaded timidly, "don't think any worse of me ; it has grown up with me here."

The prison which could spoil so many things, had tainted Little Dorrit's mind no more than this.   It was the first speck Clennam had ever seen, it was the last speck Clennam ever saw, of the prison atmosphere upon her.

He thought this, and forbore to say another word. With the thought, her purity and goodness came before him in their brightest light.   The little spot made them the more beautiful.